THE YAWNING GAP

Book One of the Wanderers Cycle

C.V. Vobh

THE YAWNING GAP

Book One of the Wanderers Cycle

by C.V. Vobh

With thanks to A.C. Baizas for his brilliant work on the cover art.

eBook ISBN: 978-1-961425-00-2
Paperback ISBN: 978-1-961425-01-9
Hardback ISBN: 978-1-961425-06-4

Library of Congress Control Number: 2023909737

Published in New York, New York by Thuban Books.

Here, on the Dawn's frontier, the seven Wanderers,
Peers to those Powers careering through the spheres,
Shall sear Dust's progeny. Beaming clear through dole,
Here shall the son of Sun and soul of Sol
Veer from the blue serene to a bleary green.
A teen's control shall keep this broken sphere whole;
By a queen's son shall their holy goal cohere.
Here shall they circumvene Chaos, saith the Seer,
She by Her bloodshed and he by Her tear.
Here, in Grand Cross with three peers, Luna's progeny,
Careening nearer the Gloamy One and dominant,
Shall see, in two hours, thirty Springs and Falls
Before, in tears, she bears forth the foreseen one,
Bidding adieu her Chaos-convening dear one.

-Excerpt from Mercune's Prophecy, transcribed at
Wraithing Research Center, ca. 15 A.P.

PROLOGUE

Wait. What did I just read? No answer came, not in the first few seconds. And, if not now, he'd surely not recall that page next month, much less next year. If not, what use is reading?

Flipping back, smiling faintly, he reread.

To read, one needs to *read*: these above all, these purple grimoires, with peculiar grammar and syntax, page-long sentences and fey script. One failure of focus and he'd miss some metaphor, some meaning lurking in between the lines. And then he'd miss a whole scene's second sense, beauty that'd be destroyed if bared by language. By beauty alone are partial intimations perfected into full truths.

This, he mused, was where one ought to start out when attempting the works of Kalos Omma, who'd recorded the First's last words as He lay dying. *Be with me!*

A slight breeze from the subterranean sea vexed the twin torches blazing by the doorway. He barely observed their volatile glow upon the yellowed leaves. Once, he'd have stilled the wind and stoked the flames. But now, vicissitudes of fickle light were just a fact of life.

He checked the clocks. The wards would need renewing. Next to this work, the warding seemed so trivial: a squatter's claim of the mundane upon the sanctuary of the mind. At midnight, the Warlock would recite those few fey words that kept him from the searching eye of Lenvira. She'd never had his way with wards. Her mind's eye, dim as it was, would not scry past the wards.

Dim, but not blind. Forget the wards just once, and all his forebears' work would be for naught. He'd come to naught. And all would come to naught.

Standing impatient, he spun and strode, white hair aswirl above his cloak of midnight blue, toward spiral stairs, down toward a ritual room fretted with Star fulgence. *Time to be done with it.*

Part I
The Sea of Stars

CHAPTER 1

Sol hovered low aloft the west horizon. Broaching a narrow gap between the Fyrst Rocks, his rays lit glaringly upon Cor's gaze, but left what loomed ahead shrouded in shade. The radiant beaming reached the River Lysa and weakly was reflected by the Boundary—a wall of half-seen crimson to his side, parting his whole world from the world to the east—and shone on past it, spreading cross the greensward. The sunlight brushed against the thirst-paled grass, so little lines of shadow stretched out eastward. Cor squinted but did not avert his gaze.

He'd had high hopes for life. When he'd been young, his mother had spoken sometimes of how *"important you are"* and how, *"when your time comes, I'll say why."* He'd wondered what this meant, and asked and wheedled. But the appointed time had never come.

Not when she'd sickened with his unborn sibling: stomaching less solid food by the week, then water, withering to a bony frame. And not when, in the Winter of 290, the flour had had that fungal hue of grey. Harvested from a barley field that'd sprung up on barren soil, where blight had claimed the crops some five years prior, that flour had given their hamlet hope for a future when Winters weren't hungry.

Well, not for long. They'd bought bread from the baker, ate it together on Noversday morning. And, by the evening, they had fallen to retching, then feverish throes and flushed hallucinations. Cor and his father had come close to the edge. His mother, though, already starved and parched, had never stood a chance. She'd waned away and never woken, while Cor was half-unconscious and tossing in a bed too hot and too cold.

So, seventeen years later, here he was, without a clue still why he was "important." He'd have to find out for himself. *Or why not.* The latter looked more likely by the year.

Idly, he seized a stone, wound up, and whipped it toward River Lysa. Halting halfway there, soundless, it fell and was lost in the foliage. High on the Boundary rippled waves of red, where the rock had hit. His throwing arm was good—the other boys had picked him often as pitcher—but he'd no hope of hurling rocks through a Boundary.

He'd have to head home soon. It'd been already a longer Noversday than normal, starting when Sol was scarcely peeking from the Lion.

Cupping his palm against the glare, he peered toward Warden Knoll, some five miles south of here, a welt upon the Earth's waving hair of green. From there to Beldria's borders was a half mile.

Lost in thought, he began the long trek back. His hometown, Beldria, was the smaller of two towns within the Fragment. Farmers there grew barley. Cowherds grazed cattle. Both retired at Dusk to homes of wattle-and-daub with peat-lit hearths, which formed the unofficial border of Beldria. One house was vacant and had been for ages. Its unplowed fields were overgrown with flax, and what had been its barnyard now was bare dirt. Cor had played baseball there with the other boys, as had his father and his father's father.

Some stone-built houses stood near Beldria's center. Several might be called stately; none majestic, except the Mayor's mansion. Hewn from limestone, his home was like a castle's keep, if smaller. A spire of grey ascended from its center. Tower Belladrengr, Beldrians called that spire.

Their forebears, centuries past, had built the place as a last-ditch bastion when the orks were looting. Back when there'd still been orks. Tower Belladrengr, already old back then, became its core. Deep in the tower ran cables, cords and wires of copper. No one knew what role they'd served.

Cor had been brought up in a big white barn upon the peatlands west of town by Faxlath, his father. *"Never great with kids,"* he'd noted. *"Figured I'd have enough help from my wife, your mother, that I'd make do. Hmph. That's life: you make do."* Upstairs were the beds and washroom. The downstairs was the hamlet's lone distillery, run by his father, like his father's father.

In some respects, Cor liked the stillman's life: malting and mashing barley; waiting as the wort brewed; boiling it through two stout stills, collecting from the stream the middle cut; pouring the whisky into casks; and pushing those rolling oak-staved barrels to the cellar, where they would age as slowly as their makers. The first few barrels he'd distilled in boyhood had not been tapped yet, save a single cask. *"Already oaky?"* his father had frowned on first taste, four years past. *"Well, this stuff's coarse. But Winter's cold this year, and this'll warm you."*

But Cor, like other boys, had been brought up on tales of turning back the orkish raids, not plying useful trades: tales of the times when orks still ranged and raged across the hills outside the hamlet. Back then, Beldrian warriors had wandered through the greensward wielding swords and slaying orks, before their bands could raid too many farms. They'd breached the border once and burnt the town down, save the few stone buildings. The Beldrians had survived behind the walls of Tower Belladrengr, as their warriors battled.

The orks had been on Gurtag Jidh: a week past harvest, every Fall, when the orks had massed and poured upon the farms for pillaging. They'd harried Beldria and Oldstorr, the other hamlet within the Fragment. Seizing well-stocked farms to fat themselves for Winter, lugging loot off, they'd left the fresh-cut fields in conflagration.

Each Fall, the Beldrian men had battled back the orks, before they advanced too far beyond the outmost farms. Two or three barns were burnt on good years; maybe five or six on bad years. The Beldrian men had battled with the tactics and blade techniques they'd honed from boyhood onward, knowing that there'd be none but them to turn back the raids. They'd felled a bevy of orks each Fall; and, most often, lost men too. And this was why the warrior had been held in higher esteem than any other trade in Beldria. Back then.

Now, only one of those warriors was left: the "Master of War." A high and hoary office, it'd once been held by Beldria's leader in battle. Now, it was ceremonial, being bestowed on some strong-armed layabout with a lack of prospects. When wolves were harrying some poor cowherd's cattle, or someone saw a boar sound straying townward, the Master of War might sally forth on horseback, waving his sword and shouting till they spooked and fled, felling a beast or two if need be.

But mostly, he just traipsed the training yard, testing his swords and pikes on practice dummies. Sometimes, as day declined, he'd sketch out diagrams of possible variants on the old Sword Postures, or register his recent feats in the Annals of War, beside the ancient deeds of heroes.

Cor clung a little longer than his fellows to boyhood dreams of being a Beldrian warrior: not merely a slayer of mangy wolves and boars, but a *warrior*, as the older Annals told of. He spent his spare time sparring with Aldartal, the current Master of War. At age fourteen, he'd fought his first bout, and been badly drubbed in seconds. By his later adolescence, he'd won more often than not. That gap had widened, as teen years turned to twenty, then to twenties.

Aldartal lavished liberal praise on Cor, and sighed about how he himself would fight if not for his *"confounded age"*—near fifty. In fact, the Master was in finer form now than in youth's bloom, with a sparring partner so gifted. And he liked like-minded company. Despite their differences of age and station, Cor counted old Aldartal as his best friend.

That was one part of Cor's life, which was waning as the other waxed. He spent his weekdays working beside his father Faxlath at the stills, or flipping barley on the malting floor, or cutting peat bricks from the furrowed fields, or selling bottles at the Sahngday market. His father pressed him more and more to focus upon distillery duties, delegating more by the week to Cor. And all that work of the whisky tradesman left scant time for training. Tedious and vexing; but he didn't fault his father. Just a good man being a father.

Cor was approaching life's close-cropping phase, when hair and hopes are trimmed; when, having breathed in two decades worth of buoyant boyish dreams, those aspirations turn to exhalations. He had pursued his passions, leading nowhere. After his weary days at the distillery, sometimes, he wondered whether he'd regret his bright-eyed boyhood wasted in the yard, practicing pointless violence with his elder, far from the cheerful chatter of his peers.

It seemed just yesterday that on his birthday—his eighteenth, which, as always, he'd spent sparring—Aldartal had surprised him with a sword. A real one, dating to the days of orks and Beldria's warriors. *"Won't be needing two. So, thought I'd give you this one,"* he'd explained. But he'd bestowed on Cor the better sword, as both knew well. *"Heaven knows I'll have no student who's earned it more,"* he'd added, as his pupil paused to accept so fine a birthday present.

Even now, that epoch-biding blade was sheathed beside his waist. On Noversday each week, once he had burnt the first cut with his father unto the day, and broke the darkling fast with what was left, Cor's favorite pastime was to fare afar from Beldria's borders, hying toward the secrets hiding beyond the skyline. He would scour the pathless ways for wolves, or bears, or brigands, or some such fell foes. Just like Beldria's warriors. Thrilling though it'd felt at first, he'd never found any real peril, save a single asp.

Indeed, the problems plaguing Beldria now were more mundane. More crops were killed by blight each season. Former fields were dirt and dust, however much the farmers fertilized them. A full fourth of the dams' broods were deformed: some lacking limbs, some mangled, some misshapen. Some elder women whispered of an increase in stillbirths mid the Beldrian mothers too. The hamlet faced, in fine, some serious evils these days, demanding serious swift solutions.

But these weren't evils that a sword could slay. And after several uneventful Summers patrolling desolate plains each Noversday, his polished sword unbaptized at his waist, he had begun to feel a bit of a fool. He wondered what his mother would've thought, watching her sole son wander with an old sword.

Grimacing, letting loose its graven pommel self-consciously, he seized a quartzite stone and cast it sidearm toward the River Lysa. It spiraled through the air and fleetly flashed with Sol's rays, arcing toward the rushing water and—*plunk*—descending to pellucid depths.

Cor blinked and stared. He took another stone and tossed it, now a little to the left. It hit the zenith of its arc—then, halted, bumping the red-rippling Boundary and dropping.

How . . . ? Reaching down, he grabbed another rock, now aiming faintly right again, and flung it. The stone soared out, then down, plopping in water.

The Boundary ran along the River Lysa, sometimes quite close, but never crossing over. *So, how . . . ?* He headed toward the stream, his palm held forth—and suddenly, it was pressed against a shimmer of limpid red, which rippled at his touch.

The Boundary gave a bit upon being pushed, like balsa more than stone. But you could crash a wagon full of stones athwart that wall, and all that'd break would be the wagon.

Feeling his way along the wall, Cor's fingers slid suddenly around an edge. And in his breast, butterflies fluttered. The Boundaries round Beldria had no gaps; none that anyone had known of, and none that several centuries' histories told of. Yet here one was.

He headed toward the River and dipped his hand, feeling the flow and foam like foreign things. Cupping a bit within his palm, he sipped. It tasted—well, like water.

Squinting Sunward, he mused a moment on its low-lying amber. An hour or so before it struck the skyline; one more till Sol Descendant fled from Dusk. Plenty of time to explore. He'd just jog home if need be. Just in time to drink a dram, or two or three, together with his father.

Feeling giddy, he followed gushing water east at a rapid pace, resting a palm atop his pommel, scanning his surroundings. Familiar prospects from a foreign prospect, with not a wight in sight but fraught with flora. Peering behind him, he beheld what must be Moss Hillock, by its bluish mats. But the side he saw now, past his Fragment's eastern Boundary, no Beldrian man had seen in Beldria's history.

Wandering, he wondered about that word, "Fragment." It seemed to evoke some wider, fractured world, with one shard being the sprawling land he lived in, where Beldria, Oldstorr, barley fields, the Fyrst Rocks, and all his friends and family had their home. But with the Boundaries blocking off the Fragment, no one could *know* what the wider world was; could they? Had all the world been cracked to Fragments? Or was the only "Fragment" Cor's own Fragment: one small chunk fractured from a solid Earth?

A snorting bark behind him caught his ear. Frowning, he held a hand before his eyes and, squinting Sunward, saw four silhouettes, four-legged and shambling toward him. Not as livestock lumbered, long bred to be all bulk and belly, but with loping wolflike strides, leap in their steps; not with the skinny-legged girth of a grazer, but with a hunter's balanced burliness.

Scanning the rushing River Lysa on one side, and then the faint red Boundary on the other, and then the narrow strip of sward between them, he started jogging east, suddenly uneasy. He'd *hoped* to find some conflict, true. But fighting a pack of predators in a slender pass was not the introduction to adventure he'd had in mind.

He glanced back, moments later, and saw the beasts had gained upon him greatly, so now it seemed he could discern some features. And yet he doubted what he saw: some cross of feral boars and ferrets, big as ponies, two abreast, bounding toward him with their tusks bared.

About four furlongs east, the torrent turned and flowed left round a cliff-face. By that crag, boulders were strewn about, man-high and sheer. Doubtful these beasts could climb them; maybe he could.

He took off running. In the town of Beldria, a couple men might be as strong as Cor—the blacksmith Stalbart; likely Aldartal still—but none so fast. If any man could outsprint four-legged creatures, it was fleetfoot Cor.

But moments later, peering fleetly backward, the Beldrian found those ferret-piglike predators had halved the distance to their fugitive prey. He heard the snarls and snorting of the foremost, some thirty yards away. No way he'd beat that first one to the boulders.

Forcing strained legs to speed up further, harking to the footsteps and hissing exhalations to his hind, he played out in his mind the impending moment.

And now, with naked sword outstretched, he spun blindly upon the beast—mere feet from biting upon his heels—while hopping sidelong, slashing downward from left to right in Sol's Rebuke, as it was dubbed in the Annals of War. The first three books were chronicles. But the fourth, titled The Sword

Postures, taught what the warriors of Beldria, through their slow and bitter centuries of striving with the orks, had learnt of swordplay.

Too close to halt, the beast just lowered its head, leveling long tusks upon the attacking Beldrian. Its hot breath brushed him. But the snout behind it slipped by his flank as he sprang to the side. His ancient blade bit deep into the beast's ham, its first taste of the stuff in centuries time.

Squealing, the lamed beast slumped and slid to a stop. Its brethren slowed at the unexpected cry.

Not halting to assess the harm, the Beldrian whirled toward the boulders and bolted with bared blade. Six feet away from one flat-surfaced rock, rising a foot above his head, he flung his sword atop and *jumped*.

His torso slammed the solid stone, blasting his breath out. And, with both hands clawing for a hold atop it, he slipped two inches ere he caught sharp rock and clutched it, scarcely feeling as it cut him.

Canines clamped down upon his leather boot and grated off its steel toe, with a growl nasal and gurgling. Cor kicked back on instinct, striking its snout and eliciting a snort. Before a bite could come, he climbed a foot higher, holding there fast as the fell creature fumed; then, gritting teeth against his palms' sharp protest, he hauled himself upon the man-high rock, scraping his limbs as he scrabbled atop it.

Swiftly, he scanned the barking beasts beneath him. A pair were padding balefully round the boulder—leaping in vain sometimes against the sheer stone, scraping their snouts and snarling as they fell. The one he'd slashed was growling weakly, groundling and bleeding from a ham now hewn in half. The fourth was sniffing at it like a slab of almost-ready steak atop the stove.

Through his relief's delirium, he discerned a cutting hotness in his hands and kneecaps, and scanned them. Four red furrows from the sharp stone, now leaking sanguine down his limbs and digits.

Euphoria faded as he mulled his straits. With fell beasts cornering him between the Boundary and cliff ahead, he literally was caught between a rock and hard place.

He peered down at the pig-and-ferret things, slavering below. What should he do? Jump down, jab one straight off, then swing to a second? *You miss, you're dinner.* Maybe wait them out? They seemed in no rush. And a chill was settling beneath the sullen skies. He still was warm, but try to rest atop this windy rock and, ere long, he'd be shivering chatter-toothed.

He eyed the bluff again, ten yards away. Squinting, he saw a crevice on the cliff-face, lit by a stray beam breaking through the clouds. Maybe he'd fit. Maybe some shelter there.

One problem: how to get there? The open crevice was high upon the cliff. Too high to climb in. These stones were steep enough that he could leap in. But first, he'd have to reach a closer rock, five yards away. And the only way to get there without a fight was jumping. Awfully far, with little room to run or space to land on.

Well, bottoms up. The stillman's son stepped back, praying he wouldn't face-plant on the hard stone; then, sprinted two steps forth and sprang afar.

He lighted right where he had hoped to land, but glimpsed too late the moist moss layered atop it. His feet flew forward from the dewy verdance, his bottom up, and the impact blasted breath out.

Backbound, he shut his eyes and finally sighed. His shoulder blade would soon be solid purple. So would his hip, where he'd fallen on his flask. *Welp, didn't faceplant. Thanks.*

He rose as slowly as Winter Sun, studying the man-wide crevice. Some fifteen feet away, and quite a close squeeze.

Gritting his teeth against his welts and gashes, rallying his spirits, he ran three steps and leapt, swiveling in midair to make himself slimmer. He felt his wind-borne hair brush stone and winced in midair. But he slipped inside unslowed. Throwing his hands out to block his advance, he found not stone but thin air. On he stumbled, catching himself on an outcrop ahead.

A cave. And deep, he now could see. Shade swallowed the tunnel ten yards forth. With each step inward, the air warmed, and the winds of evening waned. Still brisk, though. He'd be warmer deeper down. Maybe enough to sleep, instead of shivering the night away.

Scanning the floor, he found a single branch and a slew of twigs, strewn just inside the entrance; blown in, perhaps, by some forgotten storm. Grabbing the branch and his blade-cleaning cloth, he tied the latter round the former's top, then took his Sun-blazoned flask. *"Always drink cask-strength,"* Cor's father always told him. And his friends. *"And always carry it with you for a cold night."* Wiser words than he'd realized.

Cor dumped whisky atop the cleaning towel till it was doused. Retrieving from his satchel flint and steel, he felt a faint smile form. He'd been both eager and slightly embarrassed when he'd bought the stuff. *"Thought Faxlath had a top-notch flintlock, no? You going camping?"* Kaup had questioned Cor, that day at the general store. Well, here he was.

Angling the flint toward the fabric, he struck the steel. Once, twice, thrice. On the thirtieth try, a large spark leapt out to the spirit-doused towel and, in a blink, burst into bluish flame. He yanked his hand back, singed but not burnt badly.

Time to be moving. His towel-torch already was shrinking black around the burning stick. Holding it forth, glaring against its glare, he sent a prayer to Heaven and went through the Earth.

CHAPTER 2

"You know I'm with you, know I stand with you."

Writing her speech last night, it'd seemed to Celeste this struck the right note. But she hadn't pictured making her speech from the old monarch's balcony, to masses so far off and far below her they'd scarcely hear her. *Heavens, I sound absurd.*

She winced at what the next words were. *Well, too late to write a new speech now.*

"I'm one of you. And it's for all of you that now I ask you all to keep the faith: to keep your firm will, keep our future alive, by giving—yes, by joining me in giving this dream we've dreamt the time to turn to reality! We share that shining dream. The rest will follow, as surely as morning light must follow midnight."

Scattered cheers mingled with chuckles and jeers of some grizzled men, ruddy with scorn and brandy. Some sniffed and drew back from those burly scoffers. But both these sides were small, and the majority silently waited, wan of face, with stares that said, *Whatever we are, it's not with you.*

"The Tyrant caused our suffering, squalor and starving!" *Ours? Ours?* She glanced down at her evening gown. *What was I thinking when I wrote this stuff?* "The Tyrant was the one who helped his nobles amass the massive wealth withheld from *you*. His armed thugs on the hills still harry our forces; and so our People's Commonwealth is forced to squander our wealth on soldiers." *And on gowns*, those stares below the balcony seemed to say.

"Soon, I assure you, soon, from Tyranny's ashes, from royalty's ruins, this People's Commonwealth will rise, ablaze with vigor and vibrancy; with fervent faith that, when we seek equality, and, in our breasts, each rank injustice burns, no foe can face for long our passionate progress. Till then, keep fast the faith that's kept us all till now; and, so doing, naught can douse our future!"

This hot crescendo kindled scattered clapping, which died down like a host of little campfires under the sprinkling of a sullen sky.

"Finally, to prove our goodwill"—poshlost curled her tongue as she continued—"our commitment to *make this work* for you, for whom we do all that we do, our leader and our equal, Lothar, hereby declares today a holiday: the Day of Labor. And to mark this day, the common kitchens will be free of charge."

Now, the cheers came.

She raised an open palm. "Please, save the applause! For this is not my charity; nay, but the magnanimity of one man, Lothar; that very Lothar who deposed the villain at the bottom of our banes; Lothar, who leads us toward our bright tomorrow!"

At this, beside her on the castle balcony emerged the man himself: a man of more than average height, clad in a purple cloak billowed by Boreal winds behind broad shoulders, and velvet pantaloons of ruffled crimson. About his furrowed brow fell jet-black hair, which framed a face with features rather off-kilter, but not too jarringly, amid the general majesty of his vestiture and mien.

Some "hear hears!" at this theatric revelation. But mostly, now, the crowd was mobbing toward the common kitchens. Even now, queues were forming by food halls that'd been empty moments earlier.

"Bravo." Beside her at the balcony's ledge stepped Lothar, waving winningly and smiling.

"The free food won them over," Celeste shrugged. "And that was your suggestion."

Lothar waved. "An obvious win-win. All that blasted barley was going bad. Why not placate the polloi and, at once, rid ourselves of rotting rations?"

She looked at Lothar, and he chuckled lightly. "I jest. The people are rightly irate about the sorry state the Tyrant left them in. They've every right to have the help we give them! And I know none who tells that truth so fairly as you do, Celeste. So, in short: Bravo."

Bravo, Miss I'm-With-You-But-on-a-Balcony. "Well, kind words. Thank you."

"Yes, well said, well said!" Lord Toadson tepidly had stepped beside them atop the balcony moments prior, and now nodded his way into the exchange. "Fine thought. Free food for all!"

The Lord of Shattingway, Toadson, was technically a country noble, but he'd not found much favor with the King. So, unlike others, after Lothar's coup, Lord Toadson promptly had provided troops *"to firm up our defenses, free of charge, and show my most sincere support for Lothar, our lawful leader."*

His expedient gamble had paid off ten times over: every time another treasonous noble's lands were taken, Lord Toadson's tracts became a little larger.

Shifting his weight from foot to foot, knees touching, palms pressed and facing his good fortune's font, he looked like he would overflow with gushing enthusiasm; and then go use the privy. "A fine thought," he repeated. "Food for all!"

"Well. Anyway." The man once called the Merchant, and now the First of Equals, faced his orator. "Come! Let's go try that wine we took last Tievsday. It's stunning, absolutely stunning! Toadson, you're in, yes? Celeste?"

"Well." She searched for words. "I'm—weary. Spent the whole night on my speech . . . "

"Ah, say no more. Even golden geese must sleep!" Lothar grinned lightly. "Well, wordsmith, go rest up!"

Still waving, Lothar cast his cloak behind him and, with a swish of crimson pantaloons, stepped out of sight with Lord Toadson in tow, vanishing like the crimson Sun's reflection in swamp waves stirred up by a small amphibian.

Through time's mist, memories of the many accidents that'd driven her hither drifted through her mind: the fire that'd borne away her family and birthplace;

her wanderings through the wild, three days and nights, an eight year old with no one in the world; how, in the dim delirium of her hunger, hallucinatory whim had borne her wayward behind the waterfall, where she had found an alcove: cozy and hidden, a perfect place to curl up, fall asleep, and face no longer the shadow looming now upon this world's ways.

And it was there, shining in depths unseen at a distance, that she had discovered—*that.* The memory faded here to a misty fulgence; but it had nursed her back to health, she knew. *"Fare toward the Dawn till thou findest thy dwelling."*

Toward Dawn: she'd known what *those* words meant, at least, and memorized them, made them into a mantra, which she'd recited in her inner silence against the nothingness of nightly gloom, through nights and days and over nights and days, through woods and wolds and ways; and, in a daze, through wooden gates, past the wondering guards—who'd held up their hands and hailed her, made as though to halt her; then, stopped at seeing her briar-bedraggled frame and blank stare, neither sure what they should do—and onward on a cobbled way, which cut off before a cottage at an intersection: faint blue, with hearth heat billowing from a chimney atop the thatched roof, and a yellow door. Behind it blazed the last of yellowing Dawn.

Not knowing what to do next, she had knocked, stood for a moment outside, knocked once more, and only then heard footsteps, shuffling faintly inside. The door had creaked open, and she'd seen a middle-aged man, bag-eyed with morning hair, bespectacled and skinny as a signpost, garbed in a mauve gown, with the motley wrinkles of something worn a few times since its last wash.

Rail-thin and ratty-clothed, her blonde hair stained with soot, she'd stared at the unfamiliar man. And now the memory lay before her dreamlike:

"How can I help you?" he asked hesitantly.

"There was a fire. I saw it from far away. I found my house burnt down. I found my parents . . . "

"Oh." The man stood in silence for a moment. *"Oh. Well, you'd best come in."* He started inward, then turned and held a hand out for a handshake. *"My name is Clausiglade."*

"My name is Celeste." She didn't shake the hand, but grasped it as a girl might hold her father's hand while walking. She looked inside, then looked up at the adult.

Blinking once more, he breathed the moment in and out; then, mustered up an unsure smile. "Do you like oatmeal? Should be ready soon."

Rubbing the reds of her eyes with her fingers, she forced herself from times past to the present. She realized she'd been standing in the hallway. *How long?* She peered back—saw two orkish soldiers squinting with heads craned, confusion on faces of warty white and olive green—and faced forward again smooth-faced and stepped away.

Her eyelids drooped low. Dusk had not descended; but its oblivion beckoned her already to sink in sleep beneath a shadowy cover, like Luna, swathed in a recurrent darkness.

CHAPTER 3

Cor delved into the cavern's shadowy depths, wielding his burning brand. Its whisky-covered wiping cloth now was half-burnt, but he pressed on. Still a bit brisk and the floor was uneven. He'd find a better spot ahead, he felt sure.

Halting a few seconds later, he frowned.

The shifting torchlight showed, ten yards ahead, the left side of the tunnel suddenly ended. The path continued as a little ledge, a foot broad; and beside it, an abyss.

End of the road, the Beldrian mused. He grimaced, studying the stone-strewn ground beneath his boots. Then, peering toward the pit, he held his torch forth. On the other side was a wide, smooth sprawl of stone: perfect for sleeping.

Well. "Perfect" was a little strong, perhaps. "Perfect" would be that homey bed and breakfast he'd stayed at once in Oldstorr, with its windows facing the Fyrst Rocks, where the foam-jawed waves bit vainly at the bluff, and seagulls soared.

The ledge that led across the pit looked slender, but not so slim he'd run the risk of slipping. With footholds half this wide, he'd climbed the Fyrst Rocks. And what good's life if one's too afraid to live it?

So, brimming overtop with boyhood's boldness, he shuffled with his back against the wall along the ledge, holding the torch in one hand and pressing the other palm against the rock. He took it slowly, testing every step.

Step. Shift. Step. Shift. His cautious testing caught a few hidden hazards, which he avoided.

Then, he missed one. And abruptly his leg slid pitward, even as his heart heaved halfway up his throat.

But slow strides, and his one hand to the wall, together saved him. Shifting back his weight to solid ground, he stopped and breathed a bit. *Hmph. Harder than I thought.* And on he went. Step. Shift. Step. Shift.

Inhuman shrieking filled his ear, and in his face a monster flapped. *No, not a monster*, somehow he perceived even as he whipped his head back from its batting webbed wings. *A bat.*

His backflung head banged hard on solid stone. His torch hand, thrown up wildly to ward the bat off, hit it—and the wall too.

And, with the burning bat, his torch was tumbling into the pit. He didn't hear it hit ground.

Cor stood still on the ledge, blind as a bat. Closing his eyes, he took a calming breath. He tried to summon up his last sight, wondering how far along the ledge he'd fared. *Three-fourths?* He'd not been keeping track; keeping his balance had been his focus. Should he keep going forward, find some flat ground and make another torch? Or should he turn back?

Am I going to die?

Sighing and shaking the broodings away, he fixed his focus on the path ahead—then, blinked. Beyond the bare expanse, and gleaming weakly within his Sun-gorged gaze, was wan light.

The light of Luna, seeping through the stones? An exit, maybe?

That resolved the matter.

He stepped right, testing twice as warily now. Step. Shift. Step. Shift. He slowly sought the light. Step. Shift. Step. Shift. Letting his mass move right, he slid his back along the wall—and suddenly felt bare space to his back right.

Taking a few more soft steps past the pit, he sighed and let his weight sag; then, stared onward.

The cavern's dark seemed less dark by the second. He now could see the flat stone floor sprawled forward some fifty yards. And, through the shadow-shimmers of quickly adjusting eyes, he saw the light was flickering brighter at the room's far end.

He tiptoed toward the glow. Upon the far wall, he soon could see the vague shape of a tunnel, winding away from the cavern's far end. The strange light's source must lay beyond that bend. Whatever it was—*Dusk? Moonlight? Glowing mushrooms?*—it wasn't ferret-boars and shivering through a night of frigid Fall and Boreal breezes.

He went within the flickering passage, one palm upon his pommel, the other raised as though to react to something. Fifteen yards he walked through swelling fulgence, wondering more with each stride what mundane process might explain this strangeness. Gaze narrowing in the glare, the Beldrian went around the bend.

And now he gaped and halted, hand grasping at his hilt, but merely holding stiffly in place, not moving to attack.

Before Cor, silent at the cavern's center, a Creature—man-like, but of more than man's height—was crumpled, wan and white, and swathed in light.

He had the facial features of a man mature and middle-aged, prominent chin and cheek bones bereft of boyhood's softness, but unmarred by lines. The vast Being brimmed with virile beauty, completely classical rather than romantic; save how His bent frame was fraught with fallen glory, with long hair hanging round His head, all stained with the Sun's hue: white, yet somehow hinting yellow, suggesting bright youth more than blanching years.

Bending back gracefully above His brow were two great horns of ivory, and about Him were folded huge and feathery wings of white. A Being of grace, hunched groundling under pinions that'd broached empyreal Heaven: a broken eagle.

With labored breaths, He leaned to face the Beldrian.

Cor's mouth fell open, but only breath came out.

"Hail, human," said the Creature. "I am named Dievas." His deep voice was weak, but with traces of eminence almost lost, like day's last rays: a dim and sinking radiance, soon going gloomward. "Art thou, belike, dispatched here by My brethren?"

"Your—'brethren'?" said the simple boy from Beldria.

The Creature peered at Cor. "Know'st thou my kind? The Elements? Cailleach, Velnias and Aitvaras? Ausron and Perkunos? The Pandaemonium?" It stared, then sighed. "Nay, nay, I mark thy mien. Yea, one forgets how years flow by for man. His memories fade like seashells on the shore, with each brief generation breaking more till they become mere bits of broken memory: the sand from which he views the Sea of Life."

The Beldrian blinked, uncertain what to say.

"But this is neither here nor there," He sighed. "Fain for some word of my fellows were I. Fond hopes, I fear. I've sensed the Elements fade with the fleeting centuries. Still, somehow, I fancied my senses were mistaken, mere fretful musings."

Still, Cor said nothing, wondering what to say to a Being who spoke about His "fleeting centuries."

"Still have I lain here most of this millennium, sparing my meager vestige of vitality," said Dievas. "Every moment that I muster words from this waning form, another year is lost from life within this breathing world; wherefore, I've neither time nor life to tell our story in its sorry plenitude. I'll share the short of it; much as I might. May 'might' make do for 'must'!" the Creature mused. "Thou know'st the Fragments, nay? The Boundaries, nay?"

"I—know that they exist," the Beldrian managed. "The Boundaries round my Fragment: Beldria; Oldstorr; the Fyrst Rocks; in between, the fields and forests. I know the Boundaries can't be crossed. Well, couldn't."

"Not 'can't,' but 'couldn't?'" Dievas' forehead furrowed.

"I came across a gap in Beldria's Boundary. Today. That's how I came here," Cor recounted. "I'd never known the Boundary had a hole. It might be new."

"A new gap in the Boundary? And 'Beldria,' say'st thou?" Dievas bent his brow. "Words ever ebb with time's flow. Might this 'Beldria' be Belladrengr, where my bulls once wandered?" At Cor's blank face and blink, he cast a hand. "Nay, tarry not on this; no time, no time. A Boundary gap. This bodeth ill, I reckon. Might all my brethren, now, be so depleted, the Boundaries draining us have started dwindling?" pondered the grave Power, peering into gloom. "Yea, shifting Stars have always stirred the Boundaries, so breaches briefly form; but I sense not that sort of chaotic Star configuration."

Not fully following Dievas, Cor kept quiet.

"Have others fared betwixt the Fragments, boy?" asked Dievas finally.

"Nobody I know of," said Cor. "I'd never known why we had called our Fragment, well, a 'Fragment.' All we had was there, between our Boundaries. No one goes out. The hole I found—the gap—that's why I reckon it must be new. Since someone should've found it. Someone before me should've left by now."

The fallen Being's shoulders sagged. "The Boundaries fail, and all my blackest fears are come to be. The Elements die, drained dry. Earth falls to blight as Spirit takes flight. And man must follow, like the shadow stretching from the death of day." He peered into the corner of the cave, where granite crags were overrun with gloom.

"But each wight born to light must bear his weird. So too, it seemeth, must the Lord of Light." From dark, he uplifted sky-blue eyes, a spark of daylight glaring there against his Doom. "Still, ere I go to Mist and shade, mayhap I'll give some little light to lingering life. Hark, Sir." He turned to Cor. "How hightest thou?"

He forced himself to meet the great Being's gaze. "I'm Cor Volucre."

"Cor Volucre. Yes, I sense a heart that soars and longs for light. Born at high noon beneath the Lion, no? Yes. Mayhap 'tis happenstance thou'rt here; mayhap the Fates have fixed for thee a shining future beyond even my ken, Cor Volucre. Be it so or not, it vaileth naught. We work with such tools as 'must' and 'might' together make available."

"So, with what life I've left, this charge I give thee!" Abruptly at this, his wan voice waxed with brightness, as when the clouds clear from the setting Sun.

To His feet He rose, His feathery wings unfurling to fill the cave's crepuscular expanse, giving off glory. Suddenly, shadowed walls were whitewashed. Weakness fell away from features now smooth and stern, as when a longtime slave casts off his load and lours upon his captors with clenched fists, casting off a slow, sad future to face his swift Fate in a burning blaze. "Mark well the words of Dievas, Lord of Light and Master of the Skies! My kind and I are Elements: wardens of this breathing world, dispatched from Mists to make this world like ours, and make its dreamlike beauties real as life. Among the works we've wrought here, man is foremost: he bears our breath in full; our Spirit inspires him."

Narrowing his gaze against the numinous glare, Cor raised a hand halfway to his eyes, then halted, bedazzled into thrall by a Power unbound.

"Hark, Cor Volucre. Hearken unto *us*; for, here, I speak for all my fellow Elements." The voice of Dievas had the waning vibrance of Sol dying westward, spilling ruddy grandeur. "We're dying—a slow death, spanning dismal centuries—drained by the sightless Boundaries that divide this breathing world. And when we wane to nothing, so too should life, like swards bereft of light: blighting and fading, degrading and falling. Ye Children of the Mist would yield your world to the Children of the Dust; who soon would die, being creatures of consumption, not creation. Death, vileness, then eternity devoid of both: this be thy world's weird, absent the Elements."

"I charge thee, Cor Volucre," Dievas ordered, "to save what of the Elements can be saved; to resurrect what can be resurrected; to see, at least, that some of us survive. For, failing that, this fair realm hath no future."

"So, I . . . " began the Beldrian boy, uncertain.

"Nor would I lightly burden thee with this," Dievas went on, with one halting hand raised. "Indeed, in succor of thy sacred quest, I grant what's mine to give. What's mine is thine of power and puissance. Not that potency which, erewhile, moved both Earth and Heaven, yet still such as might move a man to feats heroic: to strive in spite of Fate, and not to yield. This gift, I grant, shouldst thou accept this charge."

As weird and wondrous as this offer sounded, this strange chance to fulfill his farfetched dreams, it wasn't that which won the Beldrian over.

"'Blighting and fading,' you said," quoted Cor, struggling to wrap his head around its speech. "Like, blighted fields, you mean? With literal blight? And 'waning'—what, like sickness? People dying?"

Tilting its brow, the Element nodded back.

"And this would be the only way to stop it?"

Lips parting briefly, the Element nodded back.

A vivid memory sprang up in his mind:

"Bread's from that field, sprang up on Morty's farm. The part the blight took five years back," he heard from Hyrgalt, speaking downstairs with his father, as Cor sat silent at his mother's bedside.

"Some half the hamlet's taken ill. Old Dehrk's dead. Moll's dead. And Morty? Burnt that blighted field and jumped right in. Just couldn't take the guilt." His mother—half-asleep but murmuring something, as Cor clung softly to her bony hand—feebly was stroking the six year old's fingers.

"I accept your charge. I'll strive to satisfy it with all my breath and Spirit." The words rushed out as on a swelling wind of warm assurance.

"Fair-spoken. Thou hast my thanks and blessing, boy." The Lord of Light, with these words, lowered his brow to the simple Beldrian, then faced far off shadows. "Now, fare east, Cor Volucre. Follow sunrise. There shalt thou find thy passage cross this plane: the power to breach the Boundaries. Be thou steadfast—changeless in change as Sol aloft the sky, making the shining Sun thy kin and kind—and thou'lt surround thyself with splendid sige like him, victorious over dark each day."

As Dievas so directed, through the chamber swelled a low hum, like an electric charge gathering and galvanizing the air itself. Around the Element welled a pool of light that seeped into the shade and made it bright, illumining all the rubble about that great Being. "Be guided in thy goings by the inspiration that breathes warm in thy breast. 'Twill be my Spirit, billowing from far beyond, where now I fare. Now would I bid farewell to thee, and all this breathing world; but this were premature, for I'll persist upon this plane in thee. Adieu, instead. May Earth be made like Heaven once more by man, being blessed by Us. Adieu."

The glow now waxed unto a Sunlike white, obliterating all besides the light. The Beldrian flung his arm forth, blocking brightness battering right through his gaze's lidded gates and lighting on the sealed-off sight beyond them. And now his bones were shivering with the stones being shaken by the low hum, swelling still.

A thousand glass bells broke to a thousand shards.

Or so it sounded. When the shattering waned to silence, and his tight-pressed eyes peeped open, the only sign of the Element was an ember.

Slowly, Cor stepped toward it. *No, not an ember.* A Sun-shaped rock, its color argent-or. It didn't look like much. But as he leaned to seize it, at his touch, its surface swirled with shining mists of white-gold, and a warmth familiar and foreign flowed into his breast.

His hand recoiled from the reactive rock. He'd not expected that. His heart was thumping. That said, it hadn't hurt. If anything, he felt a little better than before.

Lifting the thing again, he felt that warmth breathing within his breast. And, with it—*strength?*

And sleepiness. He suddenly felt weighed down by the long day's burden as anxiety melted; as when a statue, interspersed with ice that's seeped inside its cracks, is kept upright by the same stuff breaking up its solid structure, so when the warmth comes, everything collapses.

So fell the Beldrian limply to the floor.

Rather a perfect place to sleep, he reckoned, his mind going mistier by the second. Scanning for smooth, soft ground, he hardly had the presence of mind to stick the bright stone in his satchel, before he started bedding down.

Well, "bedding" might overstate the matter—it was stone—but heaps of feather pillows piled five-high couldn't have felt any better to Cor, right then, than flat rock floor against his back. He shut his eyes and, somehow, splayed out further.

And then, it wasn't long before the strange and dreamlike sights he'd seen, still lingering mirky within his mind's eye, had dissolved to mist, reforming into dreams still farther-fetched.

CHAPTER 4

Like a parade horse, blinders on its bridle, Celeste processed past orks of putrid green and rot-grey standing guard outside the throne room, shouting with faces contorted to smiles at fellows scarcely five feet off, all speaking at once, cacophonous and hardly caring. One idly slashed a portrait with its sword, slicing the centuries-old face of the fifth king.

Faring on straight-faced mid the giddy mayhem, Celeste secured her well-worn mental blinders against the glare of reality all around her: this fleeting ugly phase, from which would flow the promised future of freedom and equality. Fixing her mind's eye on that far off prospect, she stepped around an ork of warty white and through the daunting wooden doors of the throne room.

Lothar was slouched atop the King's old throne: one leg crossed over the other, with an elbow jutting out jauntily over the chair arm, so his head was somewhat lower against the back than it'd been shaped for, in spite of the cushion he'd added to the seat on his ascendance.

To Lothar's right, atop a somewhat smaller armchair of carven wood, was Clausiglade. Toadson, Lord Shattingway, stood at his usual perch to the left of Lothar; peering sometimes with satisfaction on a cufflink, shaped like a yellow lily, lying upon a cross of lily pads: the Toadson family emblem.

Spread out before them were several tense men in farmers' garb: loose tunics, belts, tight trousers. "We've scarcely enough crops left to live on, Sir." One of the farmers had worked himself up to speaking frankly, face a little red. "Gets worse each week. I told my kids, 'Just wait, the harvest's coming. Told 'em that since Spring. But then these guards of yours, they come and take some two-thirds. And they trample half the rest. Can't see how we'll survive the Winter, Sir."

Off to the side, the bald and twiggish Sulzdorf, that scuttled wreck of physiognomy, scribbled upon his notepad—hardly a half-foot from big and black-rimmed glasses—notes and plans for the next day's issue of the People's Press.

Last year, once Castle Norvester had been captured, the knights had fled, and, on the streets, some semblance of order had been restored by the orkish soldiers, Lothar had planned, first thing, to seize the press. *"He who controls the press, controls the people!"* he'd mused. *"I'll not have backward monarchists, sitting secure with* our *soldiers' protection, stirring up strife against their freedom's source!"*

The event had played out differently than planned. The next day after Norvester had been taken, they'd woken at sunrise to the sound of newsboys hailing the invading legions, led by Lothar, as "liberators," "topplers of the Tyrant," who'd "herald for our land a bright new day," with similar sentiments splayed across the pages of Sulzdorf's daily paper they were selling.

So, Lothar promptly had revised his plan and welcomed Sulzdorf into his inner circle. And he'd proclaimed that Sulzdorf's "People's Press," henceforth, would be *"the official paper of record for all our People's Commonwealth"*—a fact pointed out daily on the paper's front page, beneath the slogan that it'd since adopted: "Civil Society Soon Succumbs in Silence."

"Terribly tacky, but totally terrific!" Lothar had mused upon seeing the new motto.

As Celeste entered, Clausiglade smiled and gave a surreptitious wave.

She hid her smile and quickly hand-curled back a couple times. She wasn't much for open shows of warmth, but it meant much to Clausiglade. And for him, she'd happily cast aside her cool detachment. Owing her naught, with naught to gain, he'd given his happy solitude up to share his home with her: to rear a wandering orphan as his daughter.

Or, indeed, to do his best. He'd never fit the "father" mold precisely. More of an older friend: full of neat facts, practical pointers, and humor that'd hovered along the edges of her age's grasp.

Not to suggest he hadn't sacrificed for her. No, he'd enrolled her at the Academy with all his decade's savings as a scholar. Which covered half the cost. On top of that, he'd called in all the favors he'd accrued to get this unschooled girl a scholarship. He'd gotten Dean Gaudimorte to give a discount for one semester, see how Celeste did, and see if some department head saw fit to pay that scholarship and make it permanent. And, sure enough, Professor Starling had, after a mere month with her as a student.

When Clausiglade had inquired where all those funds had come from—"*how you physics sorts can somehow muster up money when we're all flat broke*"—Starling had shrugged and nodded down at Celeste. "*We save to spend on things that really matter.*"

She smiled. She hadn't seen the man in years. Not Starling, nor Aletheia nor the others, since Clausiglade—coming back from being the Steward of Reginald VI—had joined the Merchant's Caravan, and, at his invite, she had come along. The Merchant soon had heard a speech she gave to a crowd of wealthy clientele, which convinced them to buy a hundred casks of humdrum wine. Celeste had always had a way with words, rhetoric included, though she preferred poesy.

Say what you would of the man, but the Merchant recognized rare skill as soon as he saw it. He'd promptly introduced himself as "*Lothar*" to "*Clausiglade's youthful protégé, perhaps? Yes. Lovely way with words. Do you like wine?*"

The rest was history. But the whole way here, for twenty years and counting, humble Clausiglade had gone to pains to give her all he could, a girl with whom he had no bond of blood. She'd muster up a smile and wave for him if all the world were watching her and mocking.

"Not never have stores been so scarce. Nay, not never, Milord," a grizzled man in green was saying, burly and bearded, grim, with furrowed brow.

"Not never?" Lothar said, his lips curved up.

"Not never," affirmed the farmer. "Says my father, even as a boy, when second Winter struck Midsummer, wasn't bad as this, he says. 'Sometimes no food to sell, but never short of food ourselves,' he says. 'Nay, not in Norvester.' Not to say nothing of Norvester and such," he hastened to add. "But truly, Lord, the blame belongs, as I see it, on the blasted soldiers seizing our crops as soon as we can grow 'em. We've scarcely nothing left. Lose any more, we'll waste away midway through Winter, Lord. And not just us. The Kingdom's starving, Lord."

Lothar looked up at the vaulted stone ceiling, letting his eyelids sink, and loudly sighed. "When you say 'we' have nothing left," he said, "I wonder who the 'we' is. Not the soldiers and citizens outside: even now, eating supper at common kitchens, with the food that's taxed fairly from farms like yours. Do bear in mind: The land that you call 'yours' is only yours so long as *we* send soldiers to enforce your claim to it. Which is just a legal fiction. And all those fearless soldiers, Sir, need feeding. The Commonwealth has let you keep your land. We rightly could repurpose all your farms as People's farms, so all that food you grow would go wherever *we* might judge is just, rather than merely taking modest taxes. We haven't, though! We've let you keep your capital. Yet here you are! Suggesting we should change our generous ways and choose another course. Well! That, we can consider, though I doubt you'll like where that leads. Land rights are a privilege extended at the pleasure of the People. '*We've*' nothing left, you said. Sir, who's the 'we'?"

The farmer now looked sick. "Sorry, Milord. Meant nothing by it. 'We'—just meant some people. Women and men I know. And kids I know. They sit to sup, and nothing's at the table."

"'The *Kingdom's* starving'! says the landed gentry," Lothar declaimed, his purple cloak aswirl as he raised an arm in rhetorician fashion. "I see no 'Kingdom,' Sir. What I see, Sir, is one wide Commonwealth, together working toward one shared commonweal, from farms and swards to city wards; from all the pubs we seized to the old farms we've been pleased to let you hold. And I'll be clear. When I say 'you,' I'm speaking of *you* before me: burly men of means, who've found the food to keep your big frames fed, somehow or other, as you speak of 'starving.' *'Starving'*: it somewhat overstates the case, wouldn't you say? *'We're'* starving? Not that I see. You! Grubworg, yes?" waved Lothar to an ork. "Yes. Grubworg, are you *starving?*"

"Nope, not starving."

"Well, good! I'd hoped you weren't. Since this crew tells me 'the *Kingdom's* starving'; why, you had me worried!" exclaimed the Merchant, turning to the men. "To summarize: Our soldiers, here, aren't starving. You burly bunch aren't starving. *I'm* not starving; nor Sulzdorf, Clausiglade—Toadson, you're not starving? You've always been a slim sort. Starving, maybe?"

"Not starving," cuckled Toadson, "no, not starving."

"'Not starving,'" said the Merchant. "Over yonder, Celeste, you starving? No, not starving. Hm! So *who precisely*, Sir, is starving, Sir?"

The farmer flinched and faced aside. "Milord, I had to tell my wife and son last week we'd not enough for supper—"

"*So*, one evening, you skipped your supper. There's the price of progress! A hefty fare!" Arms high, he peered at Heaven. "You farm folk hunt, yes? Do you not eat deer? Did you not deign to try the common kitchens, as townsfolk do?"

"They're twenty miles away, Milord," the farmer murmured, eyes now flicking nervously toward the doorway. "And the deer—it's farmland, Lord. There aren't no deer on bare fields."

"Does no one teach these farm folk double negatives?" shouted the First of Equals; and they blinked. "'Not no one, no how,' I suspect! Well, Sirs, it's clear to me that, *contra* what you'd claimed—namely, that 'we' are 'starving' throughout the 'Kingdom'—there's no 'we,' no one's 'starving,' there's no 'Kingdom': in short, there's no *there* there. Now, to be sure, our taxes might have moderated somewhat the copious comforts that you used to savor: keeping your fertile farms with fellow kin, sharing their fruits with none, save for a fee. Well, now that's changed. And that *won't* be unchanging." His voice became more vehement by the word. "The era of equality, Sir, is coming. That's how the arc of history bends. I'll not unbend it. And nor shall you! Nay, not on Lothar's watch!"

"Just so!" Clausiglade jumped in, his hands clasped lightly, glancing at Lothar, whose glare now went wide at the interruption of his ardent climax. "Contrary to these malcontents' complaints and groundless criticisms, our constant goal has been to *help* the whole wide Commonwealth. Even those who'd wrongfully reproach our efforts! Ceaselessly have we striven to attain that end; even now, just moments ere these men arrived!" He paused an instant, peering at the Merchant, who, narrow-eyed, gave him an emphatic nod and flung a hand as though to affirm, *Go on.*

"In fact," the scholar said, "were we not speaking, *minutes* before this motley bunch marched in, of how we ought to have another day of free food at the common kitchens, Lothar? Where *all* the folk—including even these ingrates—can go and get some food to feed their families?"

The Merchant eyed the scholar for a moment, then shrugged. "That's right, of course. Well, almost. What I'd intended to announce, in fact, were *three days*, free of charge, at all the kitchens. I'd spoken of it with Sulzdorf. That's so, Sulzdorf?"

"Quite so," affirmed the newsman. "I recall your very words: 'Please, put it on the front page, so all the people see it and can partake.'"

"My very words," the Merchant reaffirmed. "'Partake,' indeed." He turned to face the farmers. "So! As you see, we're working to our utmost to make this Commonwealth—this common dream, dreamt by the People of this much-pained polity—a shared reality as our shining future; our far off destination, fixed by Fate!"

Celeste surveyed the five farmers. Some men now hung their heads. Others had ruddy cheeks, hot with a mix of shame, chagrin and choler. *More shame than guilt.*

"So, bearing that in mind, begone!" commanded Lothar with a wave.

One of the farmers' mouths fell open to object. But, as a big hand closed about his bicep, his breath caught. And he blinked up to behold the smashed grin of an ork guard staring back, ambiguously grey-green as a toadstool, and, louring to its flank, a warty white one.

"It's time to go now," Fungal Face said flatly. He half-dragged, half-led off the hapless farmer from Lothar's throne room, followed by his fellows, glancing at the ork guards suddenly gathered round them.

The ancient double doors of oak slammed shut behind the last of Norvester's country croppers, leaving the Commonwealth's leadership. "Ah." The Merchant sighed and smiled, slouching down lower upon the cushioned symbol of the kingship. Having held court with the day's last complainants by noon left Lothar in a marvelous mood, today as always. Turning to the south, he admired the radiant rainbow streaming through a stained-glass scene, commissioned by some king of storied Norvester; now, no more than memory.

Sol's white light slipped in through a single hole, left by a wanton ork when winning Norvester. The Glazier's Guild had offered to amend it, but Lothar liked to leave the imperfections, here and in all the landmarks that'd been harmed. *"Reminds you which way time flows. Only one way!"* What'd been burnt down, when Lothar seized the city, had been built back as simple blocky squares, with cement and any cheap supplies at hand. *"The plainspoken architecture of the People: equality incarnate; freedom's framework!"*

"So," Sulzdorf started with a studied lightness, "that story in the Press you spoke of. Shall I . . . ?"

"Yes, yes," the Merchant waved, "what's done is done. Anyway, not like it's out of our pockets! Three full days, free, at all the common kitchens. Let's make this count, though. In the front-page story, tell how our landed farmers caused this famine, conspiring hand in hand to cut their crop sales and drive up prices, maximizing profit, with no thought of the People's commonweal. As restitution for this crime against the Commonwealth, we'll redistribute crops: 'A fine and fitting fine for farmer-felons.' Say that."

"Excellent. Front page story, I'll see to it."

Clausiglade looked uncomfortable beside them, but stayed quiet.

"Also," Toadson said to Sulzdorf, "I'd like to order twice my standard order for Shattingway, so this important story is seen by all the people. As it should be: it is the *People's* Press! I'll charge the Treasury." He cuckled up at Lothar's laughless countenance, as Sulzdorf scribbled down the doubled order. "Free copies for the masses. Meet and fitting, to mark the prime importance of our free press!"

"'To mark the prime importance of our free press,'" the Merchant mused. "Yes, use that in the story, Sulzdorf. An excerpt from the official statement of Shattingway upon this sad conspiracy."

Lord Toadson shuddered with suppressed delight.

"And also, Toadson, I had meant to mention," the Merchant went on. "Our historians, studying some old deeds, strangely, found that your estates stretch somewhat further than was recognized in the unreliable records of the royals. In fact, your fields encompass—hm, those farmers, were they from Sterk or Stiarnhaad? Stiarnhaad, yes? Yes, Toadson, what the truer records show is that your estates encompass *Stiarnhaad's* croplands. I hope it won't be too much trouble, Toadson, heading the husbandry of Stiarnhaad up, and leasing back its farmland to the farmers currently squatting on Shattingway land."

"Those records of the royals—so unreliable!" Lord Toadson cuckled. "Absolutely, Lothar."

Taking a deep breath, Clausiglade kept quiet, but disapproval dimpled his facade.

"I'll have Professor Fictus on my staff explain Lord Toadson's title in the Press tomorrow," promised the newsman.

"You staff a historian?" Lothar exclaimed, then slapped a ruffled pantleg. "Why, Sulzdorf, you impress me more each day!"

"A 'scholar of all trades,' my team likes to call him," said Sulzdorf, shrugging lightly. "A historian; and doctor, lawyer, artist, sociologist."

"Ah. Economical!" approved the Merchant. "Well, I'll take twice my standard order too. You've earned it. Charge it to the Food Fund, Clausiglade!" The newsman made a note, the scholar nodded, and, leaning in his throne, the Merchant lifted his bulbous goblet to his lips, eyes closing on contact with the glass; then, glared and scoffed. "Heaven's sake!" Just as he'd craved that perfect sip, that crowning joy of noon, his cup was empty.

Abruptly, Lothar heaved himself to his loafers (*"I'd like to ban the pointless lace!"* he'd said), carefully clasping the stem of his cup in three fine fingers—keeping it upright a full foot from his torso, like he'd filled it right to the brim—and boldly strode toward the exit.

Lord Toadson likewise tried to stand in deference. But, being already standing, he instead puffed up and straightened like a songbird seeing a bigger beast; or maybe a nervous toad, breathing itself to twice its normal breadth before it croaked. He hopped along behind the Merchant, keeping close, but not too close.

"Celeste!" called Lothar, smiling as he neared. "Care for a glass or three?" He shook his cup. "Our tax collectors, shall we say, 'collected' a case of reds last Tievsday. Let me tell you, it's *terribly* lovely. Can I count you in?"

"Of course," she said. "But, while we're talking business, I ought to mention, near the marketplace this morning, something worrying that I saw there." She fell in stride by Lothar, who looked down with mild curiosity. "Some old knight, a cripple, was speaking in the forum to a crowd, forty or fifty, about his sons: two knights, together with those royalist sympathizers scattered across the Sightful Hills. And how, 'Soon now, the knights will come take back our Kingdom, from'—so on, so forth. And the forum *cheered*. We broke the gathering up, but." Celeste shrugged.

"The oppressed will wax nostalgic for oppression within a few weeks of their wished-for freedom!" sighed Lothar. "So, romanticism thwarts progress. *'Take back our Kingdom.'* Pah! By doing what, pray? Would they engage me *again* in bootless battle, with half the men they had when first we fought, while the ork throngs that defeated them have *doubled?* Or maybe Norvester's erstwhile steel-girt soldiery will try some subterfuge. Let's warn the gate guards to keep an eye out for some stern-faced, half-starved, unshaven, and grass-and-shit-smeared men in mail. Or maybe they'll disguise themselves as guards! Good luck with that, unless they've gotten *lots* uglier since last I saw them. Good old orks." He grinned. "No doubt they'll burn a bull or two to 'Eremon, the Fair and Kind,' and 'call upon his succor.' Hasn't helped much in the last hundred years. But *maybe this time!* If at first you fail, try, try again! Why, try until you die!"

Celeste said nothing, but raised her brow slightly.

"But," once more sighed the Merchant, "yes, you're right. We must make ready. We'll talk more of this. But come now! To the courtyard. Here, the air is—cloying." He cocked his head toward several orks standing nearby, sweat trickling down their folds. "And I can *hardly* wait to have that wine. Enough for all; even Toadson!"

Toadson cuckled.

"And brandy, too. A bit too much for me!" said Lothar, "but I know you like it, Celeste. By Heaven, this lass can hold her liquor!" he declaimed to all the castle's nearby denizens.

And, hearing that, her lips curved up a little; though Toadson's snorting titter spoiled it somewhat. Following a few steps behind her and Lothar, the minor lord excitedly spoke of something, losing himself sometimes to giddy giggles, and she and Lothar didn't listen. Passing some orkish squads and weary serving girls, they detoured briefly to the drawing room, where Lothar's requisitioned reds were waiting.

The brandy, too—"but I *insist* that first, Celeste, you take a sip or two of this!" The Merchant took two glasses, tipped the red. And now she had some wine.

She sipped it. Too sweet. Red fruit, two days too ripe. A noxious note. Not natural-noxious, like a farm. Like rot. "Not bad," she nodded, lips pursed with approval. Or so she hoped.

"Eh? Eh?" The Merchant sloshed the bottle. "More?"

She smiled. "I'll stick with brandy."

"Alas, Lord Toadson. She's too hard of heart for such fine pleasures," Lothar sighed. "How much?" He held a cup out.

"Just a sip," said Toadson. "A small sip. Reds have given me migraines lately." Pinching his narrow nose's bridge, he winced and rubbed away remembered pains.

"So be it! I never object to leaving more for me," the Merchant said, decanting out a dram that looked like dregs within the bulbous wine glass. "Can't have Lord Shattingway laid up with headaches." And Toadson, palm upraised to stop the pouring, accepted it and took a tiny taste, scrunching his face up and squinching his eyes.

Glancing at Celeste, Lothar shared a small smirk.

Minutes later, meandering from the dim halls into the courtyard, they came to a short stop as several orks passed by on peugs, patrolling. For centuries, orks had striven to tame the things—likely the longest-sustained of all efforts that orks had ever made—with some success, but not much. Mostly, they'd just made the beasts bigger and uglier, so their boar-like snouts and ferret frames had a mutant hideousness. They now lived half the lifespan of their forebears. But they were big enough to bound with orks atop their backs now, which was what they'd wanted.

They also stank. This, for a monstrous ferret, should have been no surprise, but always was at first sniff.

Lothar ughed and held his pendant of fragrant ambergris before his face. *"A keepsake from my birthplace. Quite a fine reek! Perfume's much easier than preventing foul smells, I've found in my profession,"* mused the Merchant to Celeste, when she'd asked about the object.

Two serving girls were standing by a well at the courtyard's center. One was drawing water to dump into a basin; the other, boiling some water from the basin over a blaze, then pouring it in various claycraft vessels.

As the two girls bent back and forth above the well and water pots, some orkish soldiers, patrolling here, had paused to leer a little, gathering around the pair.

"Hey! Yeah, you," bellowed one to a blinking girl standing just two or three yards off. A short ork, at four foot five, bald like a newborn baby, with downy pelage thin about its bare pate, which mostly had the hue of milkcap mushrooms.

Orks were a tall lot, typically, but much more varied than men. As though some scribe had copied the careful manual for creating man carelessly into a thousand error-ridden copies, which hapless Creation had relied upon: shaping the clay of life to smashed-up faces, strangely formed skulls and asymmetric features, and bones that grossly bulged from gimpish bodies at random. In a nutshell, orks were mostly taller than men, but more were tiny too.

"You wanna bend a little more? For me?" the bantam soldier catcalled to the servant.

The fair-haired girl said naught, instead redoubling her hard work drawing water from the well, as though her busyness might block the ork's advances.

But, alas, the ork advanced, craning its brow by her rump as she bent. "Not bad," it bantered. "Some o' that for sale?" The smirk of absolute impunity creased its pasty countenance.

"Clear out, please!" Lothar called, flicking his fingers. The gathered orks and servant girls were blocking the cobbled walkway wending cross the courtyard.

Swiftly, the servant girls gathered their pots and put them on the lawn a few feet over, so Lothar and his crew could stay on cobbles. Swiftly, but not enough to avoid a swat from a big ork with a boulder-like appearance: grey and ungainly, neckless, with a head that, from its wide chin, narrowed to a pate-point. It chuckled at her yelp.

"You heard the boss! Be movin' now, be movin'!" it admonished, as she and her companion struggled vainly to pull the vessels promptly enough to let the First of Equals fare unslowed on cobbles.

Never to be outdone by someone bigger, the short ork closed its fist and smacked the backside of the other girl, who—hefting high a vessel heavy with fire-cleansed water—cried on contact and stumbled forward, so the basin slipped from her fingers, falling sidelong to the floor and spilling half its slowly purified water. It mingled with the dust and soon was mud.

"Ha! That's what that's for!" Staring at her rump still, the bald ork bent its leer into a smile. "You belt 'em right, they squeal like so," it bragged to the bigger ork. "Be movin', now, be movin'!"

Having now halted to wait for the wenches to make way, Lothar sighed and shook his head, glancing upon his silver and gold-gilt watch. *"A wonder, what Vitulian artificers work up!"* he'd marveled when the watch arrived. *"Two decades till I need to wind it.* Decades!*"*

Not quite two decades old, the girl just decked had hastened upright, holding the half-spilt basin. But water now was seeping through a new crack, so what was left was dribbling to the dirt.

"Now look now what you've gone and done now! Naughty!" Striding beside the stunned girl, the ork seized hold and pulled her from the path.

The way was clear. So, with the sigh of one who's suffered through slow service, which, at last, is finally finished, the Merchant marched on, soon progressing past these lately liberated people of Norvester without a glance behind him; where the girl's behind, even now, was being whacked once again.

The short ork soon had hoisted up the girl, who balled her hands but didn't hit her captor. "She's light, see? Ha, she's glarin', see?" it gloated.

Noon's light, in Celeste's gaze, became a glare.

So, when the cobbled walkway finished wending about the courtyard, cutting off at the entrance to the old Queen-Mother's wing, she felt relieved when the Merchant opened the door into the darkness. "I rather like these rooms." He waved them in. "Far finer than that grumpy granite throne room!

Into the finery went Celeste and Toadson with Lothar in their wake; who, lying sidelong upon a chaise lounge, soon began to banter about the regions with the best red wines, the grape's importance, the superiority of pure varietals over blent varietals, and why a bulbous glass was best for *this* wine. At that point, he commanded that a case of reds be brought in. "Best to taste, not tell!"

Before talk waned into the weary blankness of several bottles wearing off—save Toadson, who'd tossed his first glass back and hit his stride just now, and started yammering something something about a funny thing he'd said on Sahng-day—aloft the fulgent sky, Sol had moved far. But those three hadn't.

"My, the moments fly!" mused Lothar, yawning lightly atop the chaise lounge, cutting off something Toadson had been saying.

The country noble hiccupped as he cuckled.

Off to the west through a grime-gloamy window stared Celeste, as the red of sunset spilled from a crack atop the top pane, not quite closed. She drank it in like red wine, craving darkness its seeping warmth would bring; wherein, perhaps, she'd finally find the light her day was lacking.

CHAPTER 5

Dawn reached around the East with rosy fingers—a waking lover flushed, clasping this loved world briefly before she'd have to flee it—but the Beldrian didn't see it, being cooped up inside a cave.

He couldn't tell the time but felt refreshed. *Certainly Dawn. At least.*

And suddenly the significance of the last day dawned on him, breaking through the bleary dimness and glaring red. *"I charge thee, Cor Volucre, to save what of the Elements can be saved; to resurrect what can be resurrected; to see, at least, that some of us survive."*

He grasped that Sun-shaped rock and felt its warmth, saw radiance seeping from his pouch's folds. Within him, too, he felt that warmth and light. Lifting the thing, he studied how those strange mists swirled on its surface: more akin to a world in miniature than any stone he'd seen.

After a moment, he realized the rock was bright enough to see by in the cavern. *Guess I won't need another torch this time.*

With one last look around the room, he left, walking around the corner, cross the clearing, and, with his newfound shining stone in hand, across the black abyss he'd almost fallen in. Soon, he'd repaired to the cliffside recess linking this cave with the wide world outside.

And Cor emerged to morning's ruddy colors, with pink still lingering in the welkin, and the low Sun casting westward shifting shadows. He scanned the landscape for the ferret-boars, but saw none save the one he'd lamed, now dead.

Well, time to head home. From the cavern's entrance, he hopped down seven feet to gravelly ground.

His footfall sounded; and at once, a snarl broke out behind a boulder to his flank.

Faster than conscious thought, he spun to face it: another of the beastly boar-faced ferrets, its maw maroon with blood. Was this one wounded? . . . *Oh.* He could see, in the corner of his eye, the half-eaten corpse of this thing's erstwhile comrade.

He found himself unsheathing from his side the longsword of the storied Beldrian warriors. Its keen edge seemed to catch and hold the Sun as he assumed the Ox Horn posture, blade beside his head, pointing at his opponent.

Squinting suddenly, it tossed its head, as though some tic had seized it, and barked; then, bore upon the Beldrian swordsman at full tilt, brown fangs bared behind its tusks, reaching its top speed in scarcely two steps.

He'd never faced a foe so swiftly advancing. But warm assurance breathed into his breast, and in a hot rush, trained technique took over.

Letting his longsword sag into the Key, he waited; then, juked right and went left, whirling just as the brawny beast was hurtling past him into the sideways slash of Wintersun, a true-edged crosscut, rising slightly and sinking.

Into the back of the thing's head it hewed, gold-gleaming as it severed bone and brain—and kept on cutting, so that Cor spun stumbling, much like a dancing partner loosed mid-twirl.

Getting his balance back, he eyed the beast—which now had half a head—and then his blade. It seemed no different than the day he'd gotten it. And yet, the way it'd passed through bone like butter . . . !

"What's mine is thine of power and puissance."

Looking upon the little satchel at his side, he raised the flap. The stone inside was shining.

Well. What a tale *this* trip would make, he mused, starting back west along the River Lysa. He'd have to tell his father. Who, by now, was bound to be worried about his son's absence.

Mists were meandering south across the river, as winds of Autumn brushed the warmer water. Stepping inside that wispy whiteness, soon he saw just ten to twenty yards ahead, depending how the mist swirled. He'd a strange sense that, till the moment that he broached those mists and saw what loomed there, *anything* might be there.

Some minutes hence, through a thinning of the fog, he saw some vaguely manlike forms ahead. *Moving, it looks like. Toward me, or . . . ? Yes, toward me.*

Crouching beside a boulder, Cor kept still, watching and waiting.

It was with relief that he heard the sounds of voices through the haze, bearing the faint forms of words: deep, rough voices, together with some clangs of steel on steel. *Soldiers?*

The shapes were fifty yards away now, but still obscured by fog. Behind its fellows, one of the figures was riding some beast: big and four-legged, but not wholly horselike.

A band of scouts? Squinting, he started toward his feet, then halted halfway, as hesitancy surged inside him.

"Get on your peug now, Groarg. We won't be pausin' to let you piss around."

"I'll get on, Jorngzor, soon as I want. You won't be bossin' *me*. You aren't my better. No one else is neither."

Through thinning mist, again, he fleetly saw the group's faint outlines: several on their feet, while others sat on steeds like he'd just seen.

"*Get on your peug*, I said. I'm bigger 'n stronger. I'll break your bones and eat your marrow, maggot."

"Eat shit, you yellow turd."

One sword unsheathed—faint from so far, but familiar to Cor—and swiftly a second followed, then a third.

"None o' you shiteaters won't eat no shit until I say so," spoke a third voice, viler with wheezing force than either of the first two. "Or, by the dust, I'll break

your backs and give you for flayin' to Lavezot. We'll be leavin' *now*, with Groarg
on peug or Groarg as food, you pick.

"I'm comin'."

"Thought so. All you other shits, I want those tents up by the time I'm back.
Or else I'll cut you down and cook your corpse to keep warm. All clear? Good.
Be back, you queefs."

Cor's face was furrowed at this strange exchange. Was this the famous "coarse-
ness of the conscripts," of which he'd read so much? The "foul-mouthed foot-
men"? The "soldiers' oaths"? . . . It didn't sound quite right. But who was he to
say how soldiers sounded? And what were "peugs"? He peered into the mirk.

A ray of sunlight pierced the fog and fell on two figures: one, a ferret-boar—*a
"peug"?*—and the other, something he didn't have words for.

The hulking thing was plainly humanoid: a head, two arms, two legs, a torso
clad in clothes and armor. And he'd heard it speak.

But where its face should be was skin like wax melted above a blaze. Its motley
colors ranged from corpse-grey to mildew-green to fruit-rot, like camouflage
for dwelling in a dump. Its sideways-slanted neck was wide and sinewy. Its
arms bulged, but in weird ways: not with biceps and forearms well-defined, but
tumorous bulk. He'd never seen a man even slightly like it.

And yet enough of "man" was in its mien that unlike, say, a mountain—grey,
green, brown, misshapen and big, but still sublime with beauty—the *kind* to
which his mind assigned this thing was man. And, by man's measure, this was
ugly.

And the "armor" it wore? No more than patchy plates of rusty iron, strapped
round its stocky torso by cords of leather, sewn through crude-cut slits, hanging
haphazard on its frame, so flesh showed under metal in a fractal mess. It would
have horrified the blacksmith Stalbart.

Orks. Now, the word came. This thing looked as big and ugly as the older
histories told of. And yet to see a hideous seven-foot monster, riding a monstrous
steed, was more than books prepared you for.

Perhaps the day would dawn when Cor would lightly battle bands of orks:
baring his steel to face whole hosts unfearing, with sunlight glimmering in his
eager gaze.

But that bright day was not today. He spun and sprinted off.

Heading back eastward, he mused on his plight. Orks! Armed orks! Blocking the only pathway home!

Here's your adventure. Hope it's all you hoped for.

He ran a good three miles in fifteen minutes, even in his boots: a feat that fleetfoot Cor might've been proud of on a normal day. But he was far too busy now considering whether those ferret-boars could sniff his trail; and, if so, whether he'd hear them as they neared.

Do they have hooves or feet? he idly pondered, slowing to a jog and scanning his surroundings.

He'd passed the Element's cave some time ago. The landscape, for a bit, had been familiar: landmarks he'd seen in the distance from Beldria. Now, almost all but the river was new.

Well, now he'd done it, eh? A single day away from home: already lost and lacking a way back. Hard to imagine how things could get worse.

Behind the Beldrian, metal clanked on metal.

He spun around.

The ork he'd seen on peugback was charging toward him on its champing mount, maw biting at the bit, eyes flicking madly from left to right. The rider's left hand, wielding a whip, snapped downward, so its rodent steed cringed and redoubled its careening onrush.

The ork's right hand was waving overhead a rusty scimitar, brown with unwashed bloodstains, and the arm beneath bulged hairless, muscle mingling with tumors in a metastatic mess. The thing was near enough to see through fog, still thick aloft the morning air. But how had he not heard it earlier?

Paws, not hooves, he noticed now.

And now he drew his sword. The sky was overcast, but, mid the clouds, that Beldrian blade found Sol and mirrored him brightly. A warm assurance breathed into his breast and bore the moment's butterflies away.

Studying the bounding gait of the ork's big steed, he let his longsword fall left into Tail Ward.

Waiting till ten feet lay between the beast and his blade, he broke forth into Morningway, a rising cut. It caught the peug's right leg, hewed through its hamstring and into its bone.

The beast plopped down, its belly bouncing once before it skidded to a stop, its rider rolling a few yards from its ailing ferret-boar.

Something in Cor decided he should dash toward the downed ork, blade held high, before it rose.

The fallen ork grabbed some gravel from its side and, snarling, flung it at the Beldrian's face, its strapped plates clanking as it climbed to its feet.

The Beldrian dodged but took some dust to the eye. Blinking away the blindness, itchy-eyed, he tried to study his massive enemy's stance, adopting Fool's Guard after an instant's thought, letting his blade hang low between his legs.

It took the bait. Barreling toward Cor with blade high, it slashed down wildly.

Well-honed instinct reacted. He swung up-left into a false-edged parry, and then a true-edged crosscut. Patient Traveler: one of his favorites, though it rarely fooled the Master of War.

He saw black blood was seeping from the ork's chest. It was nearly a foot-wide slit.

The ork was louring now with browned teeth bared, cautiously wielding its crude weapon crosswise. "I need a new peug, manling, and a breastplate." It slowly started to approach the Beldrian. "I'll chop you up to chunks of meat. With you, I'll feed my peug. I'll make your bones my breastplate."

Part of him pictured how that gear would work; the other part adopted Ox Horn posture.

He studied the ork: its eagerness to attack, the glare that wrinkled its repugnant mug. *Patience*, Aldartal would say, seeing that glare. *He'll give you an opening soon. No need to make one.*

So Cor—considering whether Glare of Day, directed at its brow, might break its guard—decided to maintain his guard instead.

Snarling asudden, the ork leapt forth and let loose a crosscut, wild with force. *And here it comes.* He sidestepped, so its swing went wide by a foot, and was about to follow up when his foe, raging aloud, raised its blade abovehead.

He smiled and halted the approach he'd planned.

The ork brought its blade down in something like Crownbreaker—Aldartal would have sighed and shaken his head to see such form—and Cor deflected with the standard parry, so the ork's scimitar slid down the slight diagonal of his own steel. When it was partway down, he pushed against it, converting its momentum to his own cut, while spinning on his front foot from the ambit of the ork's assault.

Thin Ice: another nice slice he seldom got to use against Aldartal, but awfully satisfying when it worked. *"Your defense turns his offense into yours,"* the Master of War had mused while teaching Cor.

His Beldrian blade had drawn a line of blood down the ork's bared breast now, crossing the other cut. His foe was fuming, as those whose passionate efforts are repaid with pain often do.

Cor flicked his sword in Gadfly, more to provoke it than in hopes of hitting.

But, wroth to wildness, the ork just let him slice its cheek, then roared and swung up from its side.

To call this "Talons Closed" would be to insult the slash that bore that title: a sudden and slanting upward slice from Fool's Guard.

Cor didn't bother to deploy a parry, taking a single step backward instead, then sprang forth into Daybreak, bladepoint golden.

It passed above the ork's crude plate and pierced its rubbery flesh, slipping within the space between two vertebrae.

Down it slumped at once.

Blood burbled from its mouth, which tried to snarl, but merely gurgled, spilling blackish streams that blent with dust beneath its now-limp body. Its gaze rolled, dwindled down, and now sagged shut.

And, just like that, a living thing was lifeless, and Cor had slain a sentient foe: his first. His nose went wrinkled at its nasty countenance, without the rush of combat to distract him: that smashed-faced sneer in death, those tumorous swellings.

His dreams of living like the Beldrian warriors always were tempered by the sobering prospect of slaying fellow men: real, feeling men. But, staring at the abomination bleeding before him—which had chased him down on peugback, blade bared, and threatened to make him meat and bonemail—he didn't feel so bad. He wiped his blade off.

Nice as it might have been to stop and savor it—this baptism of his ancient Beldrian blade—he was concerned more orks were coming soon.

The orks were riding east along the river. In retrospect, fleeing along that river probably hadn't been the wisest plan.

He turned and headed south. He didn't like to leave the shoreline, which would lead him home. But there was nothing for it.

Several hours he fared through yellow fields, faintly uphill, as Sol ascended till it hung before him. Cresting a slope a half-hour hence, he saw the whole south sprawling low on the horizon, where barley swayed, and Launlaufs Wood was looming.

Cor had surveyed those woods from Warden Knoll many a time, and from atop Moss Hillock. Indeed, in boyhood, he had found a boar there, while straying in that sprawl of emerald woodland. He'd seen it face-to-face at hardly five feet. It'd snuffled hot breaths for a bit, then walked off.

The huntsmen's brows had raised at hearing *that* tale. *"Most who meet boars that close get tusks, not tales,"* Hyrgalt, the fletcher, had mused, his head shaking.

Obviously, venturing into Launlaufs Wood was out of the question. He had no warm clothes, no map, no meals, no sleeping sack, and no bow. No, what he needed most was simply a spot where he could shelter for a day or so, and scrounge some food up.

Going westward, he would hit the Beldrian Boundary. North were the orks. And south was Launlaufs Wood. Which left the east.

"Now, fare east, Cor Volucre." The words came back with disconcerting clarity.

So, lacking any obvious better options, he did so, roving the vert hills for a couple hours without a wight in sight.

Pondering his plight, he almost missed a hill on the east horizon which, somehow, looked a little out-of-place.

Squinting, he cupped a hand about his brow. Was that a window? On the *hill's* west side?

A dozen steps confirmed it: someone dwelt there. He now saw several other circle windows upon this swelling of the sward. Nearby were a simple well, a single ruddy maple, and, in between the two, a laden clothesline.

It easily was the homeliest home he'd seen. He hardly could conceive that such a home could house an evil host.

But who could say? This wasn't Beldria. There were orks out here. And he supposed assumptions rooted in one's shared humanity don't hold with orks.

Slowly he stepped toward the barrow house, scanning its cozy stillness, hand upon his sword hilt. No sound disturbed the scene. He felt he'd strayed onto the pastoral canvas of a painter; and, any moment, he'd be brushed and mottled into a background of unmoving beauty.

He now was near enough to see the paint strokes running in tiny ridges down the round door: a blood-hued door of teardrop shape, its doorknob white as a child's arm's underside in Winter.

Reaching to grab it, he paused, seeing a pattern upon that doorknob, foreign yet familiar. He strained to see more closely what he'd reached for.

The door swung open.

What he first observed was her shamrock stare, with eyes curved clover-like; then, locks of sunset's shade, which, like Sol's beaming, fell straight until they struck her shoulders' surface, where they diffused in a reflective dazzle. Her ruddy hair hung over a tomboy tunic that hid her form, but the arm extending from it was lean, and it lacked any trace of tanning: a girl's arm. Likewise fair her face, except for its freckle dusting, with her hair's same hue. Amid that red, her gaze looked all the greener.

"Hello!" she beamed, briefly. She turned about as the sunny-eyed Beldrian blinked and searched for words, as a witless beast seeks shade in vain at high noon. "Gramps! Got a visitor!"

Back she spun and smiled: a girl of maybe seventeen, at most, without the mellowness that comes near twenty. "Well, you don't look much like the local folk! No farmer here, huh?"

"Not a farmer, no." His first words. "My name's Cor. I come from Beldria." Beldria: a hamlet surrounded by Boundaries, which she'd have zero chance of having heard of. "It's west of here." *Well. Charming introduction.*

Her mouth went wide, but, ere the words were out, an old man with a whitish beard emerged, hanging halfway to a belt at belly level. He wore a robe of royal blue, edged with cream hue. It hung to just above his buckled sandals. From foot to nose, he seemed a harmless elder.

Above that was a stare as sharp and pale as icicles. But his wrinkled ruddiness and wild white hair immersed that cold in warmth.

"Oh, hi Gramps," said the girl. "This here is Cor."

As she was speaking, the elder stopped and stared at the Beldrian, narrow-eyed, like one beholding some skyborne creature backlit by the Sun.

"Well. Who might you be?" said the old man. "Welcome."

"I just said, Gramps! He's Cor."

"I'm Cor Volucre," the Beldrian answered, hand extended. *Better.*

The elder sprang a smile, as amity leaked along his ruddy cheeks. And, just like that, he couldn't be more harmless. "I am Fyraett." Firmly, he took the proffered palm and shook. "I take it this one's introduced herself already? Told you all about her day too?" He motioned toward the tunicked teenage maiden.

"Of course!" began the redhead. Then, she blinked. "Wait, have I? No. I'm Brayleigh. Brayleigh Mirin."

He held his hand out; and, in two, she took it, grinning and nodding warmly. And the warmth thrilled from the touched hand to his flushing face. *Two-handed handshake.* This was something new. A small thing. But it sure felt big for him.

"Brayleigh," nodded the Beldrian. "Nice to meet you."

"Well, Cor Volucre." Fyraett faced the visitor, after a brief glance at still-grinning Brayleigh. "I'd ask what brings you to our humble barrow. But I sense trouble might have chased you here." The elder's little wave of hand swept in Cor's cut palms, scuffed knees, tooth-pierced boot, and sword.

"Right." The reminder of his recent travails doused his warm buzz like an ice bath. "Near Dawn, west of here, I was attacked by a—well, an ork, I think. Strange as it sounds. And 'peugs,' before that. Beasts like boars and ferrets, right?"

"Yikes! Bad luck!" Brayleigh said. "But why's that strange?"

Cor stared a moment. "Since . . . there are no orks? At least, where I'm from. Not for centuries now."

She eyed him like he'd said the Earth was flat.

"Where you're from?" Fyraett said. "Well, Cor Volucre. Welcome to Fernstead. This, we'll have to hear of: where you're from. First, though"—turning toward the house, he waved the Beldrian in—"you'll want some water. Some simple fare? A bit of bread and sausage? Brayleigh, be kind and fetch the water, would you?" He then spoke something Cor could not quite hear.

Well, no. He'd heard it. But the words were alien. Was this a different—what was that word—*language?*

Brayleigh replied with likewise foreign language.

To Cor, the concept of another tongue was strange and vague, like sight to a man born blind. In Beldria, speech had seemed a thing inborn, like smiles and blinks and rolling eyes and blushes. He'd not even understood what accents were, until he'd taken his first trip to the Fyrst Rocks and met a cowherd there. Strange speech, those folk. But nowhere near *this* foreign.

Heading into the homely barrow home, he followed Fyraett to a table of maple beside the window. This must be the glass upon the grass that'd showed him someone dwelt here. And now, its warm light was the only clue that there was a wider world outside this snug place; like light in the corner of a reader's eyes.

Cor took a tipple from his Sun-blazoned flask, a gift he'd gotten upon his eighteenth birthday. A fine old flask—more of a canteen, really—received the same day as his fine old sword. So, Cor's two thirsts in life were slaked at once. Life gives in spades; or, sometimes, drams and blades.

"Ah. Something brown, I hope?" said Fyraett, focused on Cor's big flask. "Just filled a board with bleu cheese."

One look at *that*, and Cor went watery-mouthed. By now, he hadn't eaten in nearly a day. "Brown, after eighteen years in oak? I'll say. You want a sip?"

"Mm, why not," mused the old man. "Eighteen? A patient people, then. Where you're from."

"Suppose so." Cor tipped out a liberal tot in Fyraett's cup, then took a bite of bleu. *Ah.* Hardly a day, and he'd forgotten food's flavor. He bit some sausage, bleu cheese still not swallowed.

"Ah. I'd forgotten the flavor. It's been decades!" The wizened man sipped the whisky. "Awfully strong, yes?"

"Straight from the barrel."

Brayleigh walked back in with cups of water, leaning toward the table; then, wrinkled up her nose. "That reek. What is that?"

Cor frowned, and Fyraett smiled. "It's called peat, child. Come back and try it in a couple decades."

"Hmph." Sitting in her seat, she leaned back far. "Sure, if I'm suddenly wanting nasty things, I'll let you know. You like that when you're older?"

Cor coughed, some sausage catching as he swallowed; then, cleared his throat as both hosts glanced, concerned. "This meat is top-notch. From a town nearby?" He hoped so. It'd be nice to spend the night at a proper inn, after the prior night's cave crawl. He reminisced on the Oldstorr bed and breakfast above the bluff, watching the foam-jawed waves below the Fyrst Rocks from his windowed room.

"Nope! Homemade, by the farmers here in Fernstead," replied the redhead. "Just past River Lahser, a bit northeast."

"The River Lysa?" Cor said.

"The River Lahser. Never heard of Lysa!"

"Hah! I have," Fyraett said. "Some sixty years since last I heard of 'Lysa.' My great grandpa: he called it Lysa. Said he'd called it that since boyhood, and 'I'm far too old to change just because all you young folk feel like changing.'" The old man mimed the wheezing of an elder, one finger raised reprovingly, then smiled.

"Was he from Beldria, maybe?" questioned Cor.

"Afraid not. He dwelt here, as did his father," said Fyraett. "I'd in fact not heard of Beldria."

"Beldria's where you're from, right?" Brayleigh recalled.

"Yep. Just a few hours west."

"'A few *hours* west'?" said Brayleigh. "But you can't walk west that far. You'd hit the Boundary long before—oh. *Oh.*" She turned to the elder. "*That's* why there are no orks, where he's from!"

"Yes, indeed," reflected Fyraett. And suddenly, the ice-blue stare was fixed on Cor, who faintly shivered with a chill. "Indeed." And then it passed. "I take it there's a tale there, of how you found your way to Fernstead?" Once more, the friendly flush of warmth was on his face.

"Well," Cor recalled, "it started simply enough. Walking along the northern Beldrian Boundary, I found a gap. Just dumb luck: flung a rock, it flew right through."

"A gap?" repeated Fyraett. "Hm. I had heard of such gaps. It's been said they're made by movements of the Wandering Stars, or the aspects fleetly formed between the Stars. If so, good chance the gap's already gone, if it was made by Luna. She moves swiftly."

Cor stared, mouth open, as the old man's words sank in. It'd not occurred to him that yawning gap might close; that it was *like* a yawn, and open no longer than this breathing world would need to catch its breath. "How long before it's back? Will it be back?"

"Who knows!" the old man waved. "How would one figure out such subtle things? Walk with a palm to the Boundary while watching the Stars?"

Is that what *he* would have to do? Feel his way back into the Beldrian Fragment? Harried by bands of armored orks on peugback?

"So, what next?" Brayleigh said. "You've barely started your story!"

Blinking at her shamrock stare and sunset hair, he lost his line of thought like a center fielder squinting at a fly ball against the Sun.

He forced the dazzle down. "Right. So, I'd roamed a mile at most to the east, when, at my back, some beasts like ferret-boars suddenly appeared."

"You called them peugs before!" she noted. "Must be peugs near Beldria, huh?"

"Hm? No." He shook his head. "No orks, no peugs."

"Now, let him tell his tale, child," chid the elder.

Glancing upon her Gramps, she slightly frowned, and then flashed Cor that special teenage eyeroll that says, *I'll humor him, though I don't have to.*

"Right," Cor went on, "so, there I was, just walking. A trio of peugs comes prancing up. Jaws slavering. Long-toothed. I see them there. So I take off. I try to beat them to a nearby boulder, climb out of reach. Came close, but one peug caught me."

"Fast beasts," said Fyraett.

"Yep. Nearly like horses," he said. "So—well, I slew it."

Brayleigh giggled. "Just up and slew it, huh!"

He tapped his sword hilt, shrugging. "So, after that, I climbed a boulder quick as I could. Managed to make my way to a cave. I—"

Suddenly, it occurred to Cor that perhaps it'd be best if he skipped this part.

His pause was not unnoticed.

"Then . . . you came here?" Brayleigh inquired.

And Fyraett's eyes were fixed heavily on him, like icicles hanging from a high story: perilous, hardly holding up, amid the warmth of what was all around them.

Cor shook a shiver off, brushing sandy hair from his eyes, and brushing, on his arm's way down, the satchel at his side. Within his breast breathed warm assurance, surging in from somewhere beyond his sense.

And, suddenly, he was speaking: "The Sun was setting, it was getting chilly, and there was still a pair of peugs outside. I thought I'd wait them out inside the cave's warmth. I went in, searched for somewhere I could sleep, and—well, I found this." From his leather satchel, he grabbed the gold-white stone and held it forth.

The elder's eyes went wide. "Do you—?" He halted, then seemed to strain to smooth his wrinkled brow. "What's that you have there, boy? Thing's awfully shiny."

"It's like ours, Gramps!" cried Brayleigh. "See the glow? Those swirling mists?"

The old man winced, palm forth, and spoke a few more words in foreign tongue.

But Brayleigh was already rushing off and calling, over the elder, "Be right back!"

"Brayleigh!" he high-lowed sharply. But the sounds of shuffling and shutting drawers were the only answer. And Fyraett sighed, brow furrowed, then faced Cor.

"Seen something like this?" Cor carefully asked, a little tense atop his corner chair.

The elder's piercing blues bore coolly upon him; then, melted into a rueful smile, as when a snowflake in the warm Spring, all at once, loses its crystal cold complexity and lets the lively season liquefy it. "Indeed, suppose I have. You seem a good lad." He paused and peered away, sorting his thoughts. "You've heard, I'm sure, the stories of the Elements?"

"Not till I met the Element this thing came from."

Till now, Fyraett had mostly been the master of his emotions. Now, his mouth fell open. "You 'met'—! You don't mean—was the Element *living*? You *saw* the change? From breathing being to—"

"A Fossil!" cried Brayleigh, as she came back to the kitchen, brandishing lightly a blooddrop-like rock: radiant, incarnadine, rounded and drooping, like it were frozen in falling from the wound. Swirling about her fingers on its surface were myriad mists, bright with a ruddy light. "And did I hear you right? You *met* an Element? Here I thought Gramps was just telling me tales!"

"Yes, I tell tales, and there's no 'just' about it! A proper tale is truth distilled and strengthened," Fyraett replied with a reproachful furrow, as Brayleigh gave another grinning eyeroll. "I hope you'll tell *your* tale: about the Element, and what he looked like, and his transformation from flesh to Fossil, and the things he told you," the elder entreated. "Take your time, of course!" he added, as the bleu-cheese eating Beldrian began to open his mouth.

Quiet Cor was never much for telling tales. But, as his hand closed idly round the Fossil, a recollected voice resounded in him: *"Be guided in thy goings by the inspiration that breathes warm in thy breast. 'Twill be my Spirit."*

And, having swallowed, suddenly he was speaking. "His name was Dievas. 'Master of the Skies.' I'd tripped and lost my light inside the cave, and couldn't see. I found Him by His light."

And Cor recounted everything that'd happened: that winged form, majestic, more-than-manlike; His stated fears about the foundering Boundaries and failing Elements; how He'd evanesced in waxing sunspray, leaving merely a stone; and how, before the brilliance bore him off, he'd charged the Beldrian to restore the Elements.

"And I accepted," Cor concluded. "So, now, I suppose I've started on a quest." The tone he'd tried for was the lightly ironic; but, being true, it instead came off mere fact.

And Fyraett nodded with a furrowed brow. "Astonishing. I'm sure your thoughts are spinning. Who would know what to think?" he finally said. "It's strange to find you're standing at the center of something vastly larger, something turning upon your little actions. Like the axle about which life spins. Still, be reassured: An axle only has to be an axle. The hands of higher Powers will supply the wagon, and they'll ensure that wagon's pulled the right way."

The stillman's son was unsure how to answer, and found his stare was flicking toward the girl.

She rolled her eyes a little at this gravity from Gramps. "Well, there you go. No pressure, Axle!" grinned Brayleigh. "Want some more bleu cheese? It's good."

Cor couldn't quite suppress his smile. "It is." He felt a slight flush on his face. "And, yes please." She passed the platter, and he seized some hunks especially blotched with bleu, eating one whole.

"Something about the young," the old man mused, watching the Beldrian scarf down well-aged wedges, as Brayleigh blithely observed and offered more. "Doing all the things time teaches not to do; but, in the end, the only ones who do what most needs doing. With age comes wisdom's fruits; but something barren too."

"You fuddy-duddy," said Brayleigh, lightly swatting Fyraett's hand. "Age is no more than a number and all that."

"Ha! Tell me that the day you're turning forty!" Fyraett replied. "Or tell my tombstone, rather."

"Oh, stop!" she scolded. "You'll be kicking, old man! You'll just be a fossil. Not a *Fossil* though," she giggled, holding up the reddish rock with shining mists aswirl upon its surface.

"That Fossil," Cor said, staring at its sheen. "Was that one formed by a dying Element too?"

"Yes, so it's said." The elder took the stone, which, as with Brayleigh, swirled about his touch. "The Fossil of Flua-Sahng: once possessed by Fyrir, my forebear, passed down to the first son since the Fragmentation, all the way to me."

"Flua-Sahng!" The Fossil's radiance waxed blood-red. "'The Consort of the First, who ringed the Ringed One and ordered Chaos, thus making Earth and Elements, and finally man, to rule this middle realm where mortal Spirit sojourns.'" Fyraett's voice had swollen with power beyond his fragile frame, eyes shining with the eminence of the sky.

But, with his final words, he hunched again, his robe hem sinking toward his buckled sandals. And as he handed back the stone to Brayleigh, abruptly, once more, he was merely an old man. "But what do I know. I'm just *telling tales!*" He raised his brow at the mercurial teen, who—not surprising—rolled her eyes and smiled.

Some minutes passed, and soon they all felt full, save Brayleigh—well, in fact, she felt full too, but she'd shoved down some more food just the same—and, swallowing, she yawned and shut her eyes.

Stopping mid-yawn, Brayleigh spun toward the Beldrian. "Wait. Hold it, Mister There-Aren't-Orks-Where-I'm-From. Forgetting something?" she accused, as Cor blinked at this blithe reproval. "*Where's the ork?*"

"The . . . ? Oh." Patting a palm against his sword hilt, he shrugged at her. "Suppose it's nowhere now."

"Ah. Story please!"

He smiled away a sigh; then, shared how he had slain the hideous thing, soon after daybreak, with a timely Daybreak. "Looked like a man made of moldering fruit," mused Cor, calling to mind its leaky corpse. "Knew they were ugly. But wow, was that ugly."

"Well said!" smiled Brayleigh.

"Yes, indeed." The elder furrowed his already age-wrinkled forehead. "Orks come in every color, huge and humble of frame. Some hairy, but with balding pates even by late childhood, lad and lass alike. From birth, they burgeon quickly, as a tumor swells swifter than the healthy life around it. Indeed, their bodies typically are bulging with half-hidden tumors by their teenage years. By that time, they've begun to make more orks in earnest, often bearing broods at once. Most that don't die to casual fellow-murder, or fall while warring in their frequent farm raids, die of disease by midway through their twenties. What we'd call cancer, they call growing up."

"Orks are like man minus manhood," he said. "Orks are what's born of spurning subtler beauties of Nature, groping low for grosser thrills, and giving total reign to the grotesque; foreswearing man's high faculty to sense the finer grace that's animate in Nature, for generation after generation; finally becoming oblivious to fairness, except as something lacked and therefore loathed."

"In short, they're ugly," Brayleigh smiled. "Like *you* said!"

And, lips bent up, the silent Beldrian shrugged.

"No orks in Beldria," Fyraett said. "I say, I find that fascinating."

"Well, there once were, hundreds of years ago, the histories say," recalled the Beldrian. "But our warriors beat them—once and for all, I suppose—once they'd pillaged and plundered Beldrian farms for several centuries."

"And, with the Boundaries bordering all of Beldria, well, that was that, I take it?" Fyraett finished for Cor. "How strange it seems! An orkless land!"

The Beldrian shrugged. "Never seemed strange to me, I guess. Just simple. Good, though just a bit small."

"Well, welcome to the big world!" Brayleigh hailed, holding her arms wide.

Smiling, Cor continued: "So, after that, I headed south, then east. I saw a hill with windows on the skyline, wondered what that might hold. And, here I am."

"So, where'd you see the orks?" she asked. "At first, when they were squabbling."

"Oh, two hours northwest. West, mostly. Why?"

"Wow. Awfully brave to wander in those parts!" Brayleigh said, prompting a frown and tilted head from Cor.

"He wouldn't know," said the old man. "What she means is, west of here is orkish land. More west, more orks. That far though—why, you'd be in the heart of the orkish lands. Rather remarkable you found just one band. In fact," he mused, "it may be more than 'dumb luck' that led you here." He eyed the glow of Cor's satchel.

"So," pondered Cor. "To get back into Beldria, I'd have to pass a bunch of orks."

"No doubt."

"Is there some other route? Across the river?"

"Equally suicidal!" grinned the girl. "Maybe a really good swimmer could swim it. But not with orkish arrows whizzing by!"

"How long before the orks clear out?" asked Cor. "I mean, they sometimes must be somewhere else, right?"

"Not really," sighed the elder.

"Well, but wait!" cried Brayleigh. "What about the Gurtag Jidh?"

"Ha. True, they ought to clear out then," he answered. "Typically not the type of thing one waits for with bated breath. And that would be some wait."

"What sort of wait?" Cor questioned.

"Well, a few months," said Fyraett. "Week or so past harvesttime. You know the Gurtag Jidh, yes? When the orks raid farms each Fall to fill their stores for Winter?"

"I know enough," said Cor, recalling the Annals' recountings of the annual orkish ritual that'd ravaged Beldrian farms. "Well. I suppose I'm stuck out here a while."

He wondered what his father would be doing. Worried all day at work, no doubt. And probably planning to go and start searching tomorrow.

Cor closed and rubbed his eyes. Barely past noon, and now he felt fatigued.

"Well, what if we—" said Brayleigh. But the elder fixed her a furrow so stern she went silent.

The Beldrian blinked.

And Fyraett's look was gone. Both hosts were staring now with sympathy. Maybe his bleary eyes had been mistaken.

"So, what if he stays here?" suggested Brayleigh. "Tonight, at least. No rush, right? Spend the night?" A friendly smile was lifting up the freckles fretting her cheeks like pollen over a field.

Shrugging, the elder nodded at the Beldrian and held his hand forth in an invitation.

Must've just been my tired eyes playing tricks. "I guess I've got a couple months to kill. One night, why not?"

"Wonderful!" Brayleigh beamed. "I'll fix the spare bed up in just a bit."

"And maybe I'll be spared a few quiet hours from this chatterbox!" Kind Fyraett's lips curved up, as Brayleigh swatted the elder's shoulder blade.

"So! Question, Cor," said Brayleigh. "I'm confused exactly what you *do* at this 'distillery.' You use a still? It sounds like you're an alchemist."

"Um, kind of. We make whisky, though, not potions."

"But what *is* whisky?"

Now the Beldrian blinked. "It's this." He held his flask up. "What you smelled. Like beer, but stronger."

"Stronger, huh? You sure?" She cocked her head and raised a dubious brow. "Like farmers say, '*Our* strawberry jam is strongest!' Do stillmen like to say, '*Our* drink's the strongest!'"

"Um, no. There's no debate. Distilling things, the whole point of the process—well, one big point is strengthening it."

"Uh huh."

"Sip it, you'll see. Clear at first taste. This stuff could clean a wound."

"Aha! I *was* sure that I smelled some medicine beneath the smoke! Makes sense now!" Brayleigh mused. "And here I thought you drank that drek for flavor!"

"I—eh." He turned to seek support from Fyraett—now sitting in a seat across the room and opening some old manuscript to page one—but the elder smiled and slightly shook his head, as though to say, *A few quiet hours, I said.*

"'To good health': *now* I get why people say that!" she went on, waving toward his Sun-blazoned flask.

Sighing away a smile, he let it lie.

So, Brayleigh kept the conversation up for several hours, the Beldrian serving as a sort of second to her waltzing lead, head spinning half the time, but hardly tiring even as she took him for whirl after whirl: "Do Beldrians eat with forks?" "If there aren't orks, do you have dogs?" "Do you have *different* things? Like rainbow-colored roses? Cats with wings?" "Do you like kale? I don't." "When you eat meat, do you feel *more* or *less* tired? I feel beat, but somehow better too!" And so she went.

Thus waned the beaming noon toward brooding nightfall. The welkin's radiance through the window, ruddying with pathos, marked Sol's westward march past prospect.

With mercy and amusement in his brow lines and bent-up lips, the old man had arrived to rescue Cor from constant conversation just before sunset, calling them to supper. "I've not had such a good read ere her bedtime in ages!" he had murmured. "Much obliged! 'Do you have *different* things.' Here, have some beer."

But, truth be told, the Beldrian hadn't minded. Birdsong is something of beauty, not interest.

A couple hours past supper, he was snug and supine underneath his quilt and covers, sinking toward sleep, even as his musings soared sky-high.

Quests! Orks! And Elements! What a world he'd wandered into! And with no way back. No more than when a Wandering Star departs its numinous domicile aloft the night, streaking toward strange signs, soon beyond the range where a retrograde reversal might return home. No, Cor knew, there was no way back but forward.

Amid such rapturous musings, Somnus stole upon the Beldrian; and, with arms unseen, bore him off lightly to the land of dreams.

CHAPTER 6

Celeste was feeling frail from last night's drinking. She squinted under a sky so bright it sparkled and winced against some street bard's brash refrain, rubbed wrong by all the city's friendly friction.

Not that these wending boulevards were busy. If, as the People's Press was wont to say, *"The People's Commonwealth is you, its people,"* well, now the Commonwealth was mostly enclosed behind brick walls, barred doors, and boarded windows.

A crow was pecking at a downed canary a few yards off. The smaller creature squeaked wildly and flapped. But, battered down by wingbeats and borne down by the bulkier bird, its efforts at flight were futile.

Celeste felt some sorrow for the small songbird. She *could* scare the crow off. But what would one such deed do, when the world was one where crows would always kill canaries?

Down from the firmament dove a fair osprey with trenchant talons stretching toward the crow. And, in a fugitive chaos of feather and claw, the black bird and the raptor both abruptly rollingly vanished from view in an alley, leaving the much-startled songbird, which winged off.

She blinked and peered, parsing what she'd beheld; then, shook her head and pulled her hooded cloak beneath her brow, covering her face with shadow. She walked the dirty way with pace redoubled to reach her destination promptly as possible.

An hour ago, she'd struggled not to notice, across the road, a pair of orks with peugs recklessly rooting through a farmer's cart, tasting and tossing the crops, which their mounts had nibbled at a bit, but mostly ignored. Half of the carted harvest had been scattered across the street. The farmwife had been flailing with balled fists ineffectually at one brute, which laughed a while, then shoved her into a wall, where, dazed, she'd gazed at nothing. And, defeated, unmanned, head hanging and humiliated, suddenly her husband had stared up at Celeste, with eyes that said: *What sort of world is this?*

Crops were crops, but she couldn't shake that stare.

"Consider growing up," Clausiglade had said, the day that they'd departed from the Academy. She'd asked what they would do with folk who said they didn't want the changes. When they'd set out, this "People's Commonwealth" had seemed both brighter and fainter, like a half-seen city afar. *"Suddenly, you're forced to follow others' rules: in school, working in fields and shops, and so forth. You do what others say, not what you want. At first, it's strange. Infuriating, surely! You feel you've shrunk from man to a machine cog. Yet, as you grow, you start to see the group more, and why it doesn't work when all are striving alone, to help themselves alone; and why, in the end, it's best when we can work toward* one *cause."*

All sensible, she agreed still. Yet that stare.

Such stares had scarcely crossed her mind, years past, when, all aferment with the moment, Clausiglade declared he'd joined the "Merchant's Caravan" to startled Celeste. And he'd bubbled over with blandishments about that motley band of tradesmen, massed from far-flung lands and led by the Merchant, Lothar.

"All the Merchant's men are equal; he is merely first of equals," the scholar had enthused. *"All things are shared. Their profits, high or low, all go toward one pot. They serve themselves from one shared cooking pot! There's neither prince nor pauper; merely a joint will to meet the public's mercantile demand and share the*

fair fruits of their mutual labor. And, best of all, the Merchant means to make the world this way: a world where men are equals."

She'd raised a brow. But in the end, his blaze was catching. What had won her over, really, wasn't so much his policies' particulars. The thought of being a part of something bigger, working to better life: *that* won her over.

"The Merchant": self-made man of fabled wealth, who always had precisely what you wanted and sold it for precisely what you'd pay, if pressed your furthest—which you always were, commercing with the Merchant—and employed a group of orks as guards and debt collectors. That's what was known to every Academy student. Only when Clausiglade had come back from Norvester, after his stint as Steward, had she first heard more flattering stories of the famous Merchant.

The scholar had been fuming in a huff about the *"bellicose and backward hegemon"* he'd served—King Reginald—who *"exploits his reign to stand athwart all progress for his people. They slave away today like centuries past, made subjects by a mere man, unenlightened; deluded, rather, out of recognizing what's wrong with the inequalities they live with!"*

But military matters made him maddest. *"The tyrant! He agrees, on my advice, to demobilize the Hergas—which was wise thrift, without a foe to fight, with starving subjects—but then he keeps his household 'Honor Guard,' that dismal den of backward royalist bigots. Hundreds and hundreds of the warlike louts!, who wheel about on horseback, waving weapons above the fondly admiring common folk, flattering the King's tyrannical tendencies. Disarm the Hergas of the Fellowfolk; but never Norvester's Knights! Worst of all worlds! Isn't that just what a tyrant would do though?"*

The sole bright spot in Clausiglade's dark depictions of Reginald's court was when the Merchant visited. He'd raved about the Merchant's forward mindset: putting material profit of his band above all else, and sharing what they'd won, firmly rejecting any faith or faction that might distract from their material mission. He'd lauded Lothar's fabulous charisma, and how *"he made his followers comprehend what's what, and made them see what's best for them, and made them want the equality we should all want."*

Months later, when the man himself rolled in with wagons full of wares from other Fragments—ready to arbitrage them at the Academy to well-heeled pupils, for a price five times what he'd paid—he'd seen Clausiglade there by chance, and recognized the former Steward of Reginald.

On learning that this scholar and former statesman had quit his post, Lothar at once suggested they sup together at the Grape Divine, a well-hidden wine and brandy bar in Oldtown. There, after a couple bottles spent bemoaning how backward Norvester had become beneath King Reginald—as the former Steward shared stories of how he'd striven in vain to modernize it—Lothar suggested he serve in the same role as Treasurer of the Merchant's Caravan, managing funds and maximizing savings.

Say what you would of Lothar, but he knew a bargain when he saw one. Clausiglade was a singularly overqualified Treasurer—a scholar and Steward who'd overseen a Treasury—yet hardly cared how much he made, so long as the cause was one he cared for.

"*On the spot,*" he'd said to Celeste since, "*I couldn't help it!, several cups in and not the stoutest drinker. I burst in tears! To think: me, managing the money of the Merchant's Caravan!*" Strange as this seemed for a King's former Steward, she'd understood: a distant, dreamt-of cause was what caused emotion's waves to swell in him, as distant Luna drives the seas to swell hysterical twice each day. "*And I said yes!*"

He'd told the whole tale over lunch the next day—hungover, he'd been lying in bed till then—and, eyes alight, he'd asked if she'd come too. "*I'd always been a bit ashamed I left you for that unfortunate stint in Reginald's service. Doubly so, once I'd seen the full depravity our royalty represents. And you'll learn more from one year of life than lifetimes spent in school. What was that punchy Goetsworth proverb . . . ? Ah: 'Those who would learn from books in lieu of life drink not the Sea of Wisdom, but the puddles past swimmers left behind.' Come, see the Sea!*"

Much as she'd liked the Academy—learning trivia had satisfied her leucocholic side, and she'd made several friends among the scholars—she hadn't had the heart to turn down Clausiglade. *And who knows?* she'd supposed. *He might be right.*

One thing had led to another, then another, and here she was: the Merchant's handpicked orator.

It was upon such thoughts the shriek intruded.

She spun to her left. There, sight was lost in shadow within an alleyway, between the butchery and seamstress' shop. But she could see an outline of hulking dark against the lack of light, louring above the sudden scream's unseen source.

She cupped a palm above her Sun-stricken gaze and peered into the gloom. An ork appeared, its big-humped back to her. It bent toward something, reaching its hand, and ripped. And, gripped in fingers fat with their beefy brawn, she saw a blouse of sunburst-patterned silk, flashing with Sol as the ork's arm fleetly strayed into the day.

Leaning again, it let the ruined garb loose. It fell like snow: a frail thing briefly seen, which once bedecked high beauty, and was fraught with bright and fractal patterns, but was now fallen to the floor and lost amid the lighting, melding and melting with what's all around it, destroyed and destined to be one with dust.

The ork bent down and, this time, brought up braids of burnt sienna, followed by a face twisted with terror and defiled with dirt, bent backward by the abrupt power of its pulling. It grabbed what garb remained about her back and ripped it to a swatch. A gasp wretched out at this brief constraint of cloth against her belly, cutting a shriek off as she coughed for breath.

Celeste surveyed the cityscape about her. Some passersby had heard the piercing cry and sensed what might be unfolding, judging by their little frowns, eyes flicking toward the alley. But none stopped; all kept striding, down a street where orkish guards were walking all around them.

She stared at the alley again. The ork was now pulling its pants down. Now, another screech came, but down its burly palm swept, and the sound broke off abruptly, like a ringing bell broken by its mallet. Fleetingly, Sol's glare lit the fell glee upon an orkish face like milky spit-up, chunky-white and stained. Its lower half wasn't quite concealed by shadow.

Her mind went blank at what it now beheld. What years had written on life's blank slate was wiped clean. What moved her now was not those paltry words jotted by chance and a jading environment, forming the manifesto of her mind, but the compulsive beckoning of her kind. Birds sing; squalls blow; trees grow; and Celeste does what Celeste now is doing, with dagger drawn and dashing toward the darkness, blade agleam and bright as the unbound locks alight behind her, billowing in the wind that bore her wayward.

She falls upon the fiend. Its form goes red, with sanguine spilling from its stricken neck.

After a shining instant, spurting red, the thing collapses to a crimson oneness. And all is right, and all is right again.

Now, Celeste blinked. She shook her head and blinked, breathing the moment of the moment in. A few breaths; then, she heard the unceasing shrieks from its victim, fallen back trembling to her bare back, viewing this violence on her violator with naked fear, cowering behind her crossed arms. Hysteria warped her wan face. *Twenty-five, at most. More likely twenty. Just out walking.*

She sheathed her dagger swiftly. "Shh, you're fine, you're fine." She started toward the fearful woman with one hand. But, beholding dripping blood, she blinked, withdrew her right and held her left out. The screams now waned to whimpers, now to tears. One moment more of hesitation. Then, she helped the dirt-fouled lady to her feet, still shivering from behind her folded arms.

Glancing behind her, Celeste saw an ork guard across the street and squinting at the scene. From that far, they'd be lost in shadow still—or, so she hoped—but it had heard the shrieks, no doubt. She grimaced as she scanned the alley, searching for some escape. *Aha.* "Go! Go!"

The woman followed Celeste's finger to the seamstress' shop, its back door slightly ajar; then, facing Celeste, backed away and nodded. "But you," she quavered. "How can I—"

"Just go!" She grimaced. Now the staring guard was waving at the alley, and a few more fellow orks were facing her, hands held above their brows and squinting toward the shadows. Now, swords drawn, they started stepping toward her. *No escape.*

A door slammed closed, lock clicking, to her rear. *Good.* She'd be safe, that twenty-something girl. As for herself?

"What's this!" a warty ork demanded, motioning toward the dead molester.

Despite the question, it was crystal clear what "this" was, with a bloody dagger wound and Celeste's bloody weapon-wielding hand.

"Cuff the cunt, Nauz," another ork commanded, shaking its head at the sanguinous scene. Blazoned on its paudron was an officer's badge. "He dead, Blugth? Bloody bugger! Got a beat?"

An ork that looked like it'd been doused in dried blood seized her and started to spin her around for cuffing; then, stepped back and let her loose. "Boss? This is Lothar's lady, right?" It squinted.

"No beat, boss," said an ork with flabby face and flesh the hue of olive-vomit, leaning to feel the fallen guard's neck. "See that? Not good. It's Ruptorg, boss. Remember? Lothar's Ruptorg."

She winced to hear the name. She knew it well, but hadn't seen the fallen ork's face till now. Lothar's "Left Hand," they'd called that leering hulk. Typically, Lothar found a fitting phrase or two to explain why what was needful also was rightful. But what even his rare charisma couldn't condone, his Left Hand did covertly. He'd served the Merchant nearly as long as Celeste.

"Kill her, boss?" questioned Nauz, her crimson captor.

"Can't. Lothar's lady. Maybe he'll say, 'Kill her.' Or, maybe he'll kill us for killing her," growled the officer. "Get her cuffed. But not too rough."

"Right, boss." Nauz pushed her breast-first into bricks and pulled her arms back. "If you try to break free, I'll break your arms."

"You're Nauz, yes?" Celeste said. "Yes. I'll let Lothar know that you're the guard who'd break his orator's arms."

"No breaking arms," the officer growled. "We're going to Lothar first."

"Fine, boss."

And off they fared toward what was once called Castle Norvester; now, the People's Place, with Celeste glaring, cuffed, in the ork guards' wake, cold as the Dawn, as her dark-louring captors called hotly at the crowds to clear the way, shoving aside each woman, man or child too slow of step, seeking the Merchant's justice.

CHAPTER 7

The call of amber-combed Electryone, hoarse as the day's first yawn, was what Cor woke to, beckoning him back into the waking world. Wafting in from the window was a warm breeze and, from the door, the warm aroma of biscuits. He'd half a mind to meander to the kitchen and yoink one now. But this was not his house, and he supposed that he should dress himself.

The Sun was halfway to its noontide height, the circle window showed. *Welp, someone slept in.* No wonder he was feeling so refreshed.

He slipped his tunic over his shoulders, stretched, fluffed up and ran his fingers through his hair, and, following his nose, he found a stack of still-warm biscuits by some scrambled eggs and apple cider in a pewter pitcher.

A handwritten note was nearby: *"Help yourself!"* The loopy writing left his limbs atingle. He found that he was smiling.

Sitting down, he sandwiched several eggs inside a biscuit and scarfed it down. *Delicious as it smells.* The subterranean room was cellar-cool, but with the sunlight shining through the window, the warmth was just right. *Good life here,* he reckoned.

He heard a snatch of high-pitched speech outside. That tingle again. He stood and shook his limbs. Washing the wooziness down with some cider, he donned his pack, breathed deep, and, through a door as red and round as sunrise, he emerged.

He saw a billow of red beside the well—the breeze through Brayleigh's hair—and, after a second, saw from her movements she was drawing water. Another second staring. Then, his eyes flicked left toward Fyraett, who had heard the creak and craned his head to face it. He was tending a garden full of gourds, fleshy and fat.

"Thanks for the biscuits," Cor called. "Best I've had."

The girl now whirled to face him from the well. "Oh no! You ate our biscuits for Miss Beatrice?"

Her lips bent up, as Cor's heart skipped a beat. "Just kidding!" cried the girl. "I'm glad you liked them."

"Now, be nice, Brayleigh," the ancient man admonished.

"The best part's after, when you burp," grinned Brayleigh. "Biscuity breakfasty goodness again!"

"Behave yourself, young lady!" Fyraett scolded.

Biscuity breakfast, indeed, had risen high in Cor's gullet now. He gulped the goodness back and forced a smart face. "Ought to head out soon. Make as much ground as I can during daylight."

"You sure you slept enough?" the girl inquired. "Give it another hour, you'll get lunch too!"

Cor grinned. "You've both been awfully good to me. Hope I can make it up to you someday."

"I'll hold you to it!" she said.

"So, where to now?" the elder questioned. "Do you know your way?"

"Well, I was hoping you all might help with that." He held the shining Sun-shaped Fossil forth. "The Element said, 'Fare east.' So, I'll head east." Speaking these words, he felt a warm assurance swell in his breast like a much-longed-for breath. "But I'm not sure what's there. Or what to seek there. If there's a map that you could show me, or. . . " He broke off, shrugging, in the Beldrian fashion.

"Well, we could scrawl a simple map, I think," said the elder, smiling kindly. "Back in my day, I did some wandering. You remember so much! Half the time, I forget breakfast by supper. Those sights I saw though: clear as at age thirty!"

His smile now saddened to something more sublime, as when declining Sol goes glorious red. "Young wanderer! You have many ways to travel. I sense it wasn't chance alone that led you from Dievas, Lord of Light, past orks and peugs, to our humble home ensconced amid the hills." His pale stare was pellucid now with sunlight, as when an ice sheet, windowlike, is backlit abruptly by a welkin-wandering brilliance.

Faced with that luminous stare, Cor simply nodded.

Reaching within his raiment's azure folds, Fyraett retrieved the radiant blood-drop remnant of Flua-Sahng. "Fossils. Rare indeed, and yet you found one. Then, you found another here. Fate works in weird ways. You'll find more, I sense. Most Fragments have a Fossil or two; at least, the ones where man and Mother Nature thrive. Most Fossils now are kept by kings and counselors, leaders and lords, and handed down as heirlooms. Some since the Pandaemonium. Like this Fossil."

"Since—what? 'The Pandaemonium'?" Cor repeated.

"You haven't heard of . . . ? Yes, I should suppose not," the old man mused. "Yes, Fate selects strange tools!"

Scratching an earlobe, the stillman's son shrugged.

"Well, every education must start somewhere. The Pandaemonium." Fyraett paused a moment. "In the Ancients' days, life and the world were different. There were no Boundaries nor Fragments back then. The Elements dwelt unknown in the umbral deep."

"In time, the Ancients stumbled on the Elements. Digging into the depths, they came upon some strange distortion sensed by their devices. They unearthed it. Simply a rock, it seemed at first, save for the faint red radiance from its surface. They'd found a Fossil." He held forth his blooddrop. "This very Fossil!"

"For all the things they knew, the Ancients had no notion what this stone was. In time, though, they discovered that directing more mundane forces through that simple stone released a power more volatile and violent."

"Some of the Ancients—my own forebear, Fyrir, among them—sought to bind that boundless power to some productive use. With some success. It's said they solved whole cities' need for fuel. Their artificers built bizarre devices, and they imbued them with the force of Flua-Sahng, devices doing the work we waste our lives on. They built a new utopia by Her power."

"Well, as they say: 'Wealth merely whets one's craving for more wealth.' With their Fossil-powered contraptions, they found some subtle signs of buried forces far livelier than the Fossil they'd unearthed."

"Tapping their Fossil to delve through the depths, they found the Elements. They'd been sealed away," recounted Fyraett. "But, for forward wits like Fyrir, breaking through that seal became a sort of life-quest. And they soon succeeded. Directing Flua-Sahng's fervid force inside, they stirred the sealed-off Elements into fury."

"The Elements broke the bounds of their immurement. They aspired to Heaven in shining spirals, roaring and soaring skybound, flung tempestuous flame and blazing rain upon the unready Earth. And in their wake was elemental waste."

"This was the Pandaemonium: when, in mere days, perdition wrought by a daemonic panic, and blind ambition, wasted what'd been built by man's prudent patience through millennia past."

"Among those still alive was Fyrir's crew of forward wits who'd caused this cataclysm. Driven to desperation, they used this Fossil to draw upon the power of the unbound Elements and, with it, build the Boundaries we now know. How did they work this wonder? Who could say?"

"What's known is, in a flash, our world was Fragments. And soon, those high Powers screaming through the empyrean were falling headlong unto fiery Doom, their once-abounding force now drained by Boundaries."

The Beldrian nodded, his beleaguered brain aswirl as it struggled to retain this exposition. *Wish I could re-read that speech,* pondered Cor. *Probably important to know things of that sort, if I'm to save the Elements.*

Such, his thoughts. But what he said was, "Well. Things make more sense now."

"You tell that whole yarn yearly, Gramps," yawned Brayleigh. "At least! I like the one with Arvek more."

"Young lady, it was not for your sake, this time!" harumphed the hoary sage.

The Beldrian smiled. "How many Elements are left now? Still living?"

"Nobody knows. At least, I daresay I don't," Fyraett replied. "Fossils are what we find now. If any Elements still live, I suspect they're found in other Fragments. For I wandered the whole of this one, in my earlier days. I also journeyed well beyond its Boundaries, with this."

From the azure robe's folds, he withdrew another red rock, roughly palm-wide, which, unlike the Fossil, lacked a misty radiance. Indeed, it seemed to absorb the beaming Sun.

"A Passagestone," the elder said. "By slow exposure to the eminence of a Fossil, some substances can be instilled with strange powers."

"Like steeping tea, but for a hundred years!" helped Brayleigh.

"Yes, young lady," Fyraett said. "This stone will part the Boundaries. He who bears this stone will walk the world as the Ancients did. Father to first son, this stone has been passed for centuries. I, though, who have birthed no heirs, bequeath the Passagestone to you, young Cor."

He handed it to Cor, who glanced at Brayleigh, then peered upon the reddish Passagestone. Somehow, it seemed too dim beneath the daylight. "I'm grateful," he replied. "I'll do my best to deserve it."

"That, I don't doubt," answered Fyraett. "You'll wander far, I sense, and you'll be borne by inspiration's breath and Fortune's winds on ways beyond this old man's meager fathoming."

Stowing the blood-hued rock within his robe's folds, suddenly the sage was simply a rustic elder, wizened and humble, squinting kindly at Cor. "That said," he went on, "when I was young and wandering cross the Fragments, I went once to an Academy to the east. No, not to study," Fyraett said, as Brayleigh blinked at this new fact, "but to stay a few nights. You see, they call the city 'the Academy,' after the school at its center. I saw there a library large as a farm field, with long rows of yellowed books like barley in the Fall: the cultivated fruit of scholars' study, awaiting harvest by the wandering reader."

"I should've stayed a while. What lavish wonders must lie forgotten there! But, busy and boyish, such books seemed detours from my daily life. Being old, I now know books are maps through life, which could have spared me many a winding way going nowhere. Such is wisdom, I suppose: that which one learns when it's too late to use it, except for others' sake," the elder said.

"All that to say, consider starting eastward, about two weeks, along the River Lahser; that is, the River Lysa," Fyraett said.

"Then that's where I'll go first." Warm certainty that this way was the right way swelled within him, as when a bird wings south for Winter on instinct. "I'll head back here in time for Gurtag Jidh, so I can stop at home. Although," it struck him, "the Passagestone would let me pass right now, wouldn't it?" He eyed Fyraett's mirrorlike eyes, reflecting him, hiding what lay behind them. "But anyhow, I'll still head eastward first."

The elder smiled. "That's swell. Yes, Cor Volucre, I've confidence you'll deserve it, by and by. A strong core, simple heart and sunny Spirit: swordlike in shining mettle and simplicity. You're what a world of winding, snakelike ways most needs, perhaps," the old man mused. "A straight edge."

The Beldrian blinked and searched for a response.

"Yeah, pardon Gramps," sighed Brayleigh. "He's so full of profundities, he always speaks in stanzas. You'll scare him off, you know!" she whined to Fyraett.

"Young lady!" the elder chid his teenage charge.

"So! What he meant was," she went on to Cor, wheezing it out in an elderly warble, "'Young man, it's been a fine time. All the best!'"

"That isn't even slightly how I sound, young lady," fumed the elder, furrow-browed.

"Before you go, you want another biscuit?" asked Brayleigh. "One of Miss Beatrice's biscuits?" She tittered as the Beldrian sighed and smiled. "'Miss Beatrice': ha! I've never met a Beatrice! And then that look was best! You see it, Gramps?" Her face went fish-eyed; then, she broke out giggling.

"You see he's standing right here still," sighed Fyraett. "What ever happened to 'just being nice'?"

"Have fun, Cor!" Brayleigh blew right over Fyraett. She beamed like sunset back home: eastward toward Beldrian simplicity as the pair were parted.

The simple Beldrian slightly shook his head. Why was he always thinking things not sayable? "Will do. I'll try to stop back soon." He smiled. "Be nice to swipe another couple biscuits."

"See, that's more like it!" she exclaimed to the old man, who sighed again, but waved with goodly warmth.

So, turning toward the half-ascended Sun, he waved above his shoulder, smiling faintly, and set off east. Without the faintest sense of what awaited him at this Academy and its unending stacks, or where he'd fare from there, he should be worried, he supposed.

But, swollen with warm assurance, and inspired with a sense that he was on the side of right—his prospects bright with the persistent beaming of Sol, and some remembered sunset hair—his pangs of doubt just didn't find much purchase.

CHAPTER 8

It didn't take Cor long to find the hazard and conflict he'd been unconcerned about that morning. He had hardly fared five hours from Brayleigh and Fyraett's humble barrow home when, to his fore, he faintly saw the shape of an ork on peugback, prancing straight his way.

He tried to turn and dash behind some birch trees before it saw him. But he wasn't halfway when, faraway, he heard a savage howl. And then the beast was bounding, and the ork was brandishing its blunt blade overhead.

Lips pressed, the stillman's son unsheathed his sword. *Gotta get used to this, I guess.* He studied the peug's long, loping gait, adopting Plow and planning his routine, while idly ruing his loss of naïve hope for a nice walk eastward.

The quick mount was a mere ten yards away—so close he clearly saw the moles and wrinkles upon the ork's sneering mug of moss-splotched pink—when, to his right, faint footsteps on the soft soil disrupted martial musing and dismayed him still more.

He spun and stared: a second ork, the tint and texture of a rocky road, hefting a huge flail in its upraised arm and sprinting forth. It had no second arm.

Warm instinct surged within his breast, and bore him straight for the first ork's steed.

The rider wrinkled its face in brief confusion at this courage, bordering on foolhardy fatal abandon. It brought its blade abovehead, as for Wrath Hew, roaring some bestial babel at its rival.

And then the Beldrian was *beside* the beast, an aureate blur: in range for merely a blink before he'd crossed beyond the ambit of the ork's blade. Jumping and spinning with sword out in Dust Devil, he slashed at the ork's bare back and cut through spine.

His foe's arms flung up in abject confusion, as, limp, its legs stopped clutching to its steed. The ork went tumbling backward, waving wildly in futile windmills till it hit the floor.

Cor couldn't quite evade the beast it'd ridden on. It bounced him backward, soaring, till he struck the soil. His hand hit hard; his sword went sliding.

He'd barely sat up when the second ork, some five strides to his right, had raised its flail for a spiky smash.

No time to stand. He heaved back, gritting his teeth against the impending impact of ball-and-chain against his ungirt breast.

A plane of air before him rippled red.

Rushing forth, furious, the ork roared—then broke off, wind blasted out by this red wall, bone crunching into crimson, smash-faced sneer becoming more smashed yet. It stumbled backward, staring a second at this half-seen wall, fading like sunspots from stray glance skyward.

Another wall of ruddy fulgence struck it, propelling Cor's opponent five feet high and further back. It flopped against the Earth. Its bare skull's crack was keen against bare rock, as when a pickaxe strikes and bares a vein aflow with ruby richness. And, just so, ruby was streaming from his foe's broken skull.

Um, what? The backbound Beldrian stared in wonder, then eyed the satchel at his side. *Was that . . . ?*

"Hi, Cor!" a girl called. "Good thing I came quickly!"

He turned and squinted, sitting on the dirt still.

"Sure would've been a short quest! One day's walk, and bam! You're orkbait!" Standing to his side some ten yards off, and beaming down bright-eyed, was Brayleigh, in a blanch-hued tomboy tunic, wearing a well-stuffed rucksack on her back.

Such was his first sight, hazy and half-parsed. Then, the Sun emerged from golden-flame-fringed clouds behind her, shining over a shamrock gaze, and freckle dust that gave her face some fire to liven its fairness.

Cor blinked back the giddiness, rubbing his eyes as though to blame the glare.

"Surprised?" she went on. "Had a hunch you'd want help!"

"'Orkbait'?" said Cor, now climbing to his feet. "That makes no sense. It's not like we go 'orking,' with orking rods and lines."

"Let's reel some orks in!" she giggled. "Give those buggers steel to bite!"

"All good," he said, "but then we have to eat them?"

"Hmph! Let's not take this too far!"

"'Waste not, want not'?" Cor questioned.

"Feed the flies! Think of the *flies!*"

"A noble cause." Cor still felt somewhat giddy; and more so, as she shook her head and heeheed.

"So, yeah, well done with Mister Bloodyback down yonder!" Brayleigh waved toward the other ork, even now exsanguinating in a puddle of spreading darkness, seeping into dust. Beyond it, faraway, its ferret steed was bounding southward toward the sunny skyline, its former rider seemingly forgotten.

"The second one—the one that red wall smashed," he slowly said. "Was that . . . ?"

"Was that yours truly?" she playfully finished. "Yep, for sure!" She pointed. And something solid bumped his back abruptly, sending him stumbling quite close to his savior. "You didn't think I had it in me, huh? 'Full of surprises, that Brayleigh!' they say!"

Standing two feet from the white-tunicked teen, part of him felt inclined to shuffle sideways. But this was outweighed by a swelling urge to stay right here. "Does someone really say that?" He kept the wryness faint upon his straight face.

"Well, Gramps does," she allowed. "And then it's more like, 'No more *surprises* out of you, *Young Lady!*'" She wheezed the words out warblingly, then tittered, as Cor's lips crept up in a stifled smile. "But yeah! You're not the only one to use these!" She held forth Flua-Sahng's Fossil, red and radiant. "They formed the Boundaries using *Her* force, right? Well, that same force of hers still makes more Boundaries!" She thrust a palm out, and a pale red plane shot forward, brushing back the waving barley.

"Well. Guess I owe you one." His mind was whirling, but more with what was beaming at him brightly this moment, than the weirdness of this mere girl wielding whatever had sent that last ork soaring. He guessed that after finding Boundary gaps, orks, peugs, an Element, and repeated combat in one day's course, strange powers were par for the course.

"Maybe you do!" she mused. "A debt to me: exciting! We'll need time to work out payment."

"That so?"

"Suppose you're handy with a sword. Maybe a bodyguard? Maybe an escort?" continued Brayleigh blithely. "You cut up that ork like—I don't know. A fish fillet!"

"Mm. Now we're back to eating them again?"

"Just getting in that orking spirit!" she giggled.

"So," Cor said, after a couple seconds' silence. "How'd you get Fyraett to let you come follow me?"

"Well, what could he do? I was halfway here before he got back from the Folfolds' farm!" She blithely waved Cor's dubious blink away. "No worries! Gramps will get it. Or get over it."

The stillman's son suspected this assessment was somewhat optimistic. Still, that said, he hardly was the one to be denouncing a sudden unwarned departure from one's home.

The way she'd phrased that, though. It made him wonder. "'Get over it'?" Cor said, staring at the girl. "Then you . . . "

" . . . are joining *you*, of course!" she finished.

He gazed at the mercurial girl a moment. A teenage tagalong had not been part of his hazy plan to put the world aright. Rather a lot to take on even past twenty. But then, being ambushed hours into his odyssey, and rescued by a red-wall-wielding redhead, hadn't been part of his masterplan either. The "plan" *was* rather misty, really. More like some long-term milestones, with the way to reach them only revealed in time by parting mists. Some clouds had cleared, perhaps, disclosing Brayleigh.

Maybe these weird and elliptical musings were what convinced him. Maybe it was more his growing giddiness, each time he studied her green-eyed gaze and grin.

The bottom line was, Cor found himself replying, "The more, the merrier." And that was that.

"Exactly right!" she cried, seizing at once both his hands and his gaze. "I feel the same way. Shared Fate, strange Fate, right?"

This sounded like a saying, but he'd not heard it. *Suppose that's no surprise. Sayings can't cross Boundaries.* So, he just smiled and shrugged and nodded, thus ensuring one reply, at least, was suitable.

This seemed to satisfy. She squeezed his hands. "So, where to?"

"That way." Cor inclined his head east; not feeling, yet, inclined to free his hands. "Along the River Lysa. Lahser, Lysa."

"I say potato; you say tornado," replied the redhead. "Welp, we're off, I guess!"

And off those wanderers went: first wending eastward between the hills, then bearing somewhat southward, forced from their sunrise-facing way by waters that slanted toward the woodland as they flowed.

Thus striding on the shore of River Lysa, idly, Cor wound up and whipped a small stone. It skipped six times along the wavy water before it breached the surface tension, sinking. Two minutes hence, he tossed another stone. *Three, four, five, six.* He grinned, his gaze gone wide. *Ha. Seven skips!* He preened in self-pleased silence.

"Some reason that you're robbing Mother Nature of all her rocks?" his companion inquired.

"You know," began the Beldrian, as her lips bent up, "I found the Boundary gap that way."

"About that!" Brayleigh said. "So, you were wandering along the stream, just slinging stones all day, watching them bounce off the red-rippling Boundary. One stone went through. So, you just waltzed on through?

"Um," said the stillman's son. "Essentially."

"Well." Brayleigh quavered as she pressed her lips, visibly pausing to compose herself. "Well. That sure took some stones." She heeheed crazily.

Cor glanced upon the girl and grimly nodded. He clapped two-fingered for his punny peer. Her giggle-fit redoubled, going strong for fifty yards or so before it faded.

Then: "So, this Beldria!" Brayleigh started. "Sounds—hm, how to say it nicely? Sort of boring."

"That's nice of you to put it nicely."

"Yeah, sorry, I'll try again," she tittered. "So! I gotta say, your throwing arm is good."

That drew a grin. "Eh. Guess it's all the baseball."

"Hm? 'Baseball,' was it? Throw a lot in baseball?"

The Beldrian turned and studied Brayleigh's face and found it straight. "You mean," he slowly said, "you're wondering what positions I would play? Like pitcher?"

"Sure, I guess. But first, *what's baseball?*"

It was this moment Cor came to appreciate how far and deep the differences in Fragments could reach. Not when he'd been pursued by peugs. Not when that lumpy ork was louring toward him. Not when he'd heard a new tongue from his hosts. It was when Brayleigh asked what baseball was.

He strove to explain the game for fifteen minutes. But after a discouraging string of questions—"What does the pitcher have to do with pitchers? What does he pour?" "Does stealing get you punished?" "Is it a homer since you win and head home?" "What happens if you hit it into someone? Are you allowed to try to?" "Why's the shortstop a person but the backstop is a thing?"—he let it go.

"I think I get it now!" declared the girl from Fernstead.

"You learn quickly."

They fared for days with clear skies, free of conflict, before they stood before the ruddy Boundary, shimmering above the barrows on the skyline.

"So," Cor began, as each stride brought them closer to a looming crimson light. "This Passagestone." Its dim heft, somehow, was disquieting. "Do I . . . ?"

"Just roll on through!" enjoined the spritely girl. "Get close, you'll see it creates a Boundary gap, all by itself. We'll have to walk like this." She clutched his frame, clinging around him close, drawing a blink and a nod from the Beldrian; then, drew back, giggling. "Kidding! It's a big gap. Big enough for a crew of Cors and Brayleighs."

He blinked again as, blithely, she continued. "Gramps and I'd go through four, five times each year. The farms there sell you stuff you can't get here: Goat milk. Good gardening spades. Good dolls." She glanced up. "Guess it's been years since I've been back there! Haha."

Cor peered, uncertain, at the half-seen plane. *Wonder what happens if the thing snaps shut, and I'm still halfway through? Or she's still there?* Nearing the crimson wall, and keenly aware of Brayleigh at his back, he forced himself to forge on full-speed even as instinct faltered.

Then, with a vivid flash, a gap appeared in the glowing wall. And Brayleigh was beside him, beaming her way through what was now not there.

Thus did the Beldrian first leave Brayleigh's Fragment.

"Thing's handy, huh?" The girl from Fernstead patted the Passagestone, which he was holding tight.

A week expired before they reached the bridge cross River Lysa. Guarding it were a pair of platemailed soldiers with heavy helms, their full-face visors down, wielding bardiches upright in one gauntlet. The triangle blazon on their black-backed tabards consisted of a quill pen, hoe and sword, each pointing forward at another's aft. Trapped in the triangle was a faceless fellow. The triangle was enclosed within a coin of shimmering silver, so its every vertex touched the circumference but never surpassed it.

"Good morning!" called the girl from Fernstead to the two guards.

"What's your business?" one replied gruffly in gravelly voice, lifting its visor. The blotchy brow and beady off-kilter eyes blinking within, together with its speech-tones, were obviously orkish.

Brayleigh blinked.

Cor stared at her: big-eyed and, for the first time since meeting him, seemingly at a loss.

The stillman's son stepped forward. "Not on business. Just tourists on a trip to the Academy."

"Can't go there," said the soldier. "Pass is closed."

"Closed?" questioned Brayleigh.

"Leitath's Pass is closed," said the other ork, "till Lothar says it's open."

Cor glanced at Brayleigh. Her befuddled face was open-mouthed and blinking. "That's fine," said the Beldrian. A breath of warm assurance bore the words out. "Then, which way to the closest town? We're hungry."

"Castle Norvester—I mean, the People's Place—is that way," the ork said, pointing with its polearm. "But, um." The guard glanced over at its partner. "You gotta pay the toll to cross the bridge."

"What toll?" asked Brayleigh, furrow-browed.

"What toll? Um. One silver," said the ork.

"One silver *each*," the other soldier clarified, smirking broadly beneath its helmet's beaver.

Brayleigh narrowed her green gaze at the guards, her right palm falling upon the Fossil hidden inside her pouch, as reddish radiance flowed from under its flap. She looked at Cor. He slightly shook his head.

"Two silver it is," said Cor, searching his satchel and giving each ork sentry a shiny coin.

"Good choice." A guard grinned toothily. "Go on, pass."

"Wait. Where'd you get this coin?" the other soldier demanded, peering at the silver piece. "Not Norvester. Not the People's Commonwealth. And not the Academy."

"Beldria," shrugged the Beldrian, after a single second's hesitation.

The ork guard glared back. "Never heard of 'Beldria.'"

"You wouldn't have. It's hard to reach from here," he honestly explained.

The soldier stared, biting the silver and squinting upon it, then shrugged. "Get going."

And so, the wanderers went.

She waited fifty yards before she whispered, "That was bizarre! *Ork* guards? To *guard* the bridge? Like hiring hungry dogs to guard your dinner!"

"I take it that the toll was new?" said Cor.

"Psh! 'Toll!' You should've let me smash those things!"

He smiled as she continued.

"Hmph. Ork guards! You used to see two knights, all silver-shining, nodding politely as you passed. 'Good day,'" hailed Brayleigh in what tried to be a bass but came out rather baritone at best.

"That breastplate blazon, with the coin and quill pen and so forth. That was, what, the sign of 'Norvester'?" the Beldrian asked. "And, by the way, what's Norvester?"

She stared a moment. "Now you mention it, that's *not* the sign the knights wore. With the crown, fist, flame and so forth. And that thing he said—not 'Castle Norvester' but the 'People's Place'—I've not a clue what that means!"

Nor did Cor. "So. Guess we won't be going to the Academy. Something about the way being blocked, he said?"

"Right, Leitath's Pass," she said. "On 'Lothar's orders.' Not sure who Lothar is. But Leitath's Pass is the only path from here to the Academy. Unless you want to wind in from the South, way down below the Skautfells. There's a walk!"

"Sounds like this might be harder than I'd hoped," mused Cor.

"We'll find a way! Let's keep going eastward, stop at some town and ask around," she urged. "Bound to be some supplies still to the Academy, crossing through Leitath's Pass. You can't just *close* it."

"So, try to hitch a ride with some old farmer? Hide in his wagon?" Cor said, lips curved upward.

"Hey! We can do this!"

So, they wandered on, leaving the river to shrink in their wake to a sinuous brilliance in the southern Sun.

The next few days were filled with Brayleigh's chatter. Cor wasn't quite the conversationalist that she was. But she had a way of melting those subtle boundaries barring him from speaking, and beckoning out the smile beneath his stoicism.

So, she was mentioning, one sunny morning, "this funny gourd that Mister Folfold grew. Shaped like a *hedgehog*, I swear!" she averred. And, from the foliage waving to their left, something whisked past her brow.

Before her lock of windblown red had landed on her forehead, the Beldrian had already spun to his right to scan the brush. *An arrow*, he could see now, sticking out slightly slanted from a tree trunk. And now he whirled left, with his blade in hand before his legs had finished. *Where . . . ? Aha.*

In two steps, he had started into a sprint; then, swiftly slowed, his offhand held up warily.

Four men emerged from tangled brush, two wielding nocked longbows and the other two with short swords, flanking the archers' far sides. All wore raiment ragged with gaping holes and smeared to swartness with grime. Their leering grins had three weeks' growth of ratty whiskers, thin and thick in patches. Well, three of four; the other had a facemask. That they were bandits couldn't have been clearer if they'd announced themselves.

Is this the end?

These days, he felt he asked that far too often.

"I'd lose the sword, were I ye," leered one archer. He wore a pointed sable cap, adorned with a sable plume, sticking from furrowed cloth with artless artistry. He bared a broad grin, browning like diced pears left out for a long day.

"Ye do as Raven Head says, ye might not die," added the archer on the opposite side.

"Or mayhaps we'll still slay ye," said the swordsman beside him. "But we'll surely shoot ye straightway, should ye not rid yerself of *that* right quick." He flicked his falchion toward the Beldrian's bared blade.

The final swordsman watched in silent stillness. He looked less ragged than the rest, and stranger, clad in a cloak of black and brown in swaths. Over his head drooped a hood, so the shadow hid his whole brow, and beneath it, his facemask concealed his mouth, so he was mostly unseen.

Cor largely ignored these details; for his focus was on the broadsword that this bandit wielded, and how his posture was a perfect Plow. The brute beside him swung his blade about like a twelve year old in self-indulgent swordplay. But this one with the mask was something more.

"Fine. I'd drop mine if you'd drop yours," Cor answered. *What am I doing?* A wordless warm assurance breathed through his breast and bore away the question, even as the band of bandits laughed and leered.

"So, shoot him, Raven Head?" the other archer asked.

The black-capped bowman waved away the idea. "Nay, nay. We forest folk are civilized, see. We use force only when we're forced, ye see. 'Save force for foes, not friends,' I say. Well, friends!—for so I take ye—my men need some silver. To feed themselves. And, ah, their hungry families." At this, the others snorted; save the masked one, who kept his silent Plow. "So, friends, I hope you'll spare some silver—as a friend would do!—for these poor souls. Whatever's in your pouches, save one apiece, should do. Be sure to keep one, so ye can get home safe and sound, my friends." He held a hand out to his fellow bandits. "We're civilized, see." He smiled. "So, what'll it be?"

The Beldrian's thoughts raced. Being robbed of their silver would spell disaster for his grand designs of faring east from town to town, with stops to resupply; then, staying at an inn at this Academy, searching through its archives for guidance on his next steps. Their supplies would last a week of travel. Maybe ten days, if stretched.

They'd have to head back, he supposed. Tell Fyraett things had fallen through at the first hard conflict that he'd faced. *You? Save the Elements?*

Hearing no answer from the stillman's son, the black-capped bandit spoke on: "Be ye short on silver, mayhap we can settle accounts some other manner. My men do need silver to buy their fare—big appetites, forest folk!—but, mm, we've other appetites wantin' sating." He lightly leered at Brayleigh. "What say, lass?"

And, just like that, Cor's thought to share their silver went up in smoke, and now his core was smoldering. "Leave now, you'll live." He assumed the Ox Horn posture, prompting a raised brow from the facemasked bandit, who looked prepared to leap forth. "That's what we say."

A roar of laughter burst from Raven Head. "Friend. Consider, for a spell, the situation ye find yerself—"

Beneath his feathered cap of black, a crossbow bolt squelched into a temple with sickening suddenness, pierced the other temple and stopped. And, smilingly, the thief collapsed.

The Beldrian blinked, then stepped between the shot's source and Brayleigh, scanning where the bolt had flown from. Over their heads gleamed another bolt briefly.

The bandits now stared wildly to and fro with wide eyes. Seconds hence, a second bolt punctured a bowman. And the three were two.

That was when Cor caught sight of the aiming ork, cursed with the countenance of a cauliflower, its squiggly eyes asquint at him and Brayleigh. Its loaded bow was leveled at them too.

"Duck!" cried the Beldrian.

And the crossbow twanged, as Cor collapsed ungainly to the ground, half-wincing as he hoped it'd miss his head and heart.

The awaited bolt blow didn't come.

Instead, he watched it plink against a wall of faint red, falling harmless to the floor.

After he'd wrapped his head around his fortune, he scrambled back to his boots.

"You owe me two now!" cried Brayleigh, flinging forth an open palm to block the next bolt. "Got you covered. Get 'em!"

The Beldrian veered in zigzags toward the verdure, half-wincing as a bolt whizzed by his breast, keeping an eye upon his enemy's crossbow. *"Watch the weapon,"* the Master of War had chastised, on drubbing him one day at age fifteen. *"The eyes can lie. The weapon never lies. It might mislead. But it will never lie."*

Amid his madcap haste and juking motions, he almost lost the archer in the thicket. Then, from its nocked bolt flashed a fleeting glare.

Hearing a rustle to his right, he glanced. A bunch of orks were barreling through the brush a ways off. By the time he'd slain this bowman, they'd be here.

Cor could feel his teeth grit tighter.

Yet, at the same time, sprinting toward the foe, he abruptly felt like one who, in a dream, weighed down by sluggish speed, suddenly can sprint.

And somehow, he was *there* now, with a blur of gold behind him, and his blade held high.

That cauliflower complexion just was wrinkling for some fell warcry when the Beldrian's sword cut through its crossbow with a leaping Lionpaw, sweeping from left to right and ceasing high.

Before the thing had even let go its bow—now halved to a handle—Cor's reverse-cut came, a Squinter, with the false edge swinging headward. It sliced right through the wan lumps like a chef making his first quick cut through a cauliflower.

Before that beast had slumped to its gnarly knees, he hurried toward his next foe.

Meanwhile, the other orks mobbed toward the two rogues. One launched an arrow from his longbow, laming an ork. The facemasked one stood still in Plow. These orks ignored the slender girl from Fernstead with neither arms nor armor.

Their mistake. The two orks at the forefront of the onslaught crunched to a sudden stop against a red shimmer. Another pair then smacked that half-seen plane, grunting and stumbling groundward in a daze.

"Grgh!" came a cry from his side. And the bandit wielding the bow had a sword in his head now.

The masked and hooded swordsman shook his head. "Useless." Sliding his offhand into his cloak, he whipped a knife out and, in one smooth movement, let loose. It jabbed an ork's eye, leaving jelly.

Ducking abruptly under a crossbow bolt, he drew a dirk and flung it at the archer, which, hidden behind the brush, screamed something garbled.

Now, short sword wielded warily in the Ox Horn, the dark-cloaked swordsman dashed toward two opponents.

A warty white one cocked its crossbow, aiming for scarcely a second, but was far too slow to shoot before a flung knife pierced its neck.

Sensing an opening, Cor shot toward a maced ork, first feinting left around a startled smash, then cutting true-edged right with Sol's Rebuke. Its slightly downward motion maimed the ork's offarm.

But the ork had brought its mace back for a downswing, which, with a wincing roar, it now let rip.

The Beldrian dodged it with a blind jump backward, so only his forward-flapping tunic felt the spiky weapon, snagging it and tearing. No harm. But now he was exposed to an archer, whose bow was nocked and leveled.

Then, the bolt launched. The Beldrian winced against the impending pain.

But the impact never came. A reddish radiance sprang into being beside him; and the bolt fell.

Now, out of Fool's Guard posture, Cor flew forth with Talons Closed, an upward crosswise cut. It sent the maced ork skipping back off-balance, leaving it easy prey for a Glare of Day. That thrust gouged through its brain and bone behind it.

He heard the bolt whiz past before he felt it, and, even then, blinked to find a widening line of blood upon his offarm.

Then, the burn came.

Forcing his focus back, mastering the moment, he burst forth in an aureate blur toward the archer. Nocking a bolt now, it was leering at him, too faraway by far to stop its next shot.

Or so it thought. He spanned that space in two blinks and, out of Roof Guard, reaved its bow and right arm with Fatherstrike. Both struck the forest floor.

A stifled cry reached Cor.

The facemasked bandit had just been skewered by a sharp spear through the breast. Shish-kabob-like he hung there; then, slid off.

Cor scanned the combat. Five orks standing still, two wielding crossbows and one aimed at Brayleigh.

"Watch—!" he began to warn. And then the bolt shot.

Her hand was flinging forth, her red hair flying. Around her sprung a dome of red, reflecting the sunlight faintly—and the bolt. It slid down. "I'll get the guys with bows! You get the rest!" She blasted her assailant with a Boundary.

"Got it!" Well, maybe. He was now surrounded by a trio of melee warriors, with a mace, scimitar and flail. They slowly advanced from three sides.

He adopted Iron Gate, arms forth, one foot forward. No good for dueling; great against a group. This posture's virtue was its versatility. You could go any way at once from Iron Gate.

Or, so the Annals claimed. No bands of bad guys to test it on in Beldria. Not this century.

Hoofbeats intruded on his martial musings. The orks now paused and peered upon the sound's source; and so did he.

Some fifty yards afar, a platemailed paladin atop his mount was coursing toward the combat with halberd lowered. His breastplate, blazoned with crown and fist within a flame of whitish vert, waxed silvery underneath the shining skies. Behind his steel barbute streamed hair of blond wildly awry, vexed by the whipping winds.

Leveling its crossbow, an ork launched a bolt at the cavalier, who crouched beneath its point, so it shot by over his shoulder. And he charged on, now seconds from the foremost of the foe.

Another orkish bowman now had nocked its weapon. But a wall of ruddy pallor bashed its bow backward, dislodging the dart.

The other still-surviving archer seized a bolt.

And now, the Beldrian seized the moment.

Darting to the ork before its bolt was nocked, he lashed out true-edged left—Luna's Lament—brushing the bow's tip just enough to jostle it, so the ork let loose with one hand. Then, Sol's Answer, tending up true-edged. And the archer's head was sliced in twain and spewing bloody brain.

The knight now reached the orks. His halberd rammed through one ork's throat: pierced by the point on top, decapitated by the blade beneath. The head rolled backward, balanced on the haft, then bounced awry, as the orkish body flopped and fell to a cross-limbed pile upon the floor: a marionette with all its strings snipped loose.

The knight's steed slowed now, faced by another foe howling with flail held high. And, from his flank, the third ork, with the color and consistence of a banana's flesh, was barreling forward with frenzied warcries, brandishing its blade.

Nearing the horse, it brought the scimitar back for a sweeping hew through its hind leg. But before the sword could swing, the alabaster stallion pitched forward to its front legs and, hind high, kicked the ork's cranium with an ironclad hoof. The skull collapsed in that spot, so the skin sagged inward. Dead upon its feet, it fell.

Spurring his stallion away from the fray, the horseman wheeled around his foe, with halberd pointing upon the empyrean, glimmering green. He lowered his polearm for a second sally, kicking his courser into a snorting charge: not toward the maceman, now, but the orkish archer, the last still living.

Even now, it was leveling its crossbow on the thundering cavalier; as, from the flank, the maced foe hurried forth to face this man dismantling the orkish ambush.

The stallion's gait grew faster, from a gallop to a mad sprint, adding speed to still more speed. With spit-spray round its bared teeth catching sunlight, it neared the ork.

And, in a blink, the knight stood, spun toward the second ork, shaking its mace, and, from his steed, at full speed, sprang and whirled with halberd held at full length. At its forefront, the big blade waxed asudden with vivid vert, swinging a wide arc toward the startled maceman, and, from its shoulders, cleanly cleaved its skull.

Meanwhile, his mount charged onward at the archer, which, having loosed its shot, now lunged aside. But leftward went the warrior's well-trained warhorse as well. Bounding at full pace into the ork's big frame, it blasted through that bulk. And the ork fell, broken.

Now, from his full spin, the cavalier landed and caught his balance in a crouch, his halberd outstretched still, as he heaved a heavy breath.

He hefted off his helm.

Beneath, his blond hair at once blew backward in a Summer's squall. "Well done," he called, waving to Cor and Brayleigh with one worn gauntlet, as he rose upright. Beneath a fair and manly mien, the morning glimmered across a gaze empyrean-pale. "Nothing like slaying orks to start a Tievsday!" Reflexive jovial irony filled his voice. "Or Armonsday, or Perkunsday, or whatnot."

The Beldrian—who had blinked at this display, lowering his blade and, speechless, shrugged at Brayleigh—now nodded at the knight. "We owe you one," he lamely advised the light-bespangled paladin.

"You know, not really! Thought it'd be a rescue, when I was watching the orks approach from yonder." He motioned toward a meadow-mound afar. "But," he went on, waving at bleeding bodies, "judging by *this*, you had things well in hand." His stare passed over a couple bolt-pierced bandits. "Hm. Hope those fine folk weren't some friends of yours?"

"Not even close!" confirmed Brayleigh. "In fact, these orks here sort of saved us two from *them*."

"Some gratitude!" the jovial cavalier said, gesturing toward the orkish corpses. Through his grin's curved lines showed boyishness and battle-hardening, as flower buds form above fallen leaves at Springtide. "Remind me not to save you two."

"Too late!" The girl from Fernstead balled a fist, belligerent, then giggled.

"Let's not punch the man with a six-foot polearm." Cor nodded at the knight. "I'm Cor Volucre."

"I'm Brayleigh Mirin!"

"Deliad Linvarum," nodded the knight. His halberd was, indeed, a daunting weapon. Daylight briefly waxed along the curved blade as it turned and tilted. His other gauntlet grasped a bone-hued warhorn, fastened to his waist beside a small, sheathed dirk. "Knight-Lord for Reginald VI of House Lofthungrian, Norvester's true King," Deliad declaimed, his lips bending up bitterly as he concluded. "At least, what's left of Norvester."

At his words, Brayleigh's head cocked in confusion. But Cor, for whom the whole world seemed confusing, outside his Fragment, merely nodded at the knight.

"We're grateful. Good to find some friends out here," the Beldrian said.

"Yes, thank you, Knight-Lord Deliad!" Brayleigh politely bowed her head.

"Just Deliad," gestured the Knight-Lord dismissively. "These days, only my men still use the title."

"Deliad!" she nodded blithely, holding out a hand and shaking his. "It's nice to meet a Knight-Lord."

"So. Where do you two hail from?" he inquired. "'Volucre,' 'Mirin.' Names I've never heard."

"From Fernstead," Brayleigh answered. At his head-tilt, she went on, "Little over a week's walk west."

The Knight-Lord frowned. "Awfully far west," he noted. "Is Fernstead near Langretta? Only hamlet I've heard of that far out. And that's days north."

At this, the pair of wanderers paused, exchanging a glance, then slightly shrugged. They'd not discussed exactly what was safe to say to whom. But both at once felt sure: this was a friend.

"Not north," said Cor. "We came across the Boundary. Fernstead is in the Fragment to our west. I'm from the Fragment west of that. From Beldria."

The Knight-Lord cocked his head. "Well. Now I'm curious. I know the caravans cross the western Boundary a ways north, at the gap. But you said 'not north'? And then another Fragment west of there? That, I'd not heard of. Then again," he shrugged, "watching the way you wield that sword of yours, at—what, a hair past twenty?—I was wondering who taught you. Must train warriors well in Beldria."

Chuckling, the Beldrian waved away his words.

"And you"—the cavalier nodded now at Brayleigh—"I can't begin to comprehend what *you* did. Whatever it was, it seemed effective though."

"It's simpler than it looks!" She smiled and waved absently, and a wall of red rushed westward.

Deliad laughed softly in disbelief. "No doubt."

"Plenty of firepower in that thing, I think." The Beldrian pointed at the paladin's polearm.

"You like the halberd?" He held up the weapon. "More of a spiked bardiche, I'd say. But someone called it a halberd centuries past. It stuck." Upon its flame-shaped pommel showed a glimmer of green, which, when the Knight-Lord grasped its surface, swelled into swirling mists, aglow and lively.

A Fossil?

"This is Hoarthaxe." Holding crosswise the man-high halberd, Deliad lightly mused, "Many a Knight-Lord met the foes of Norvester wielding this weapon. Now, that honor's mine. I pray, these days, that I won't be the last."

"This 'Norvester,'" questioned Cor, "is it a city? Or kingdom?"

"Both. A kingdom and its capitol. Or, anyway, it was." The Knight-Lord sighed. "Now Norvester's no more than an ailing king usurped of throne, our little band of loyalists who'd been his Honor Guard, and barren hills we hide on in the realm's northeastern reaches."

"That close to the Academy?" questioned Cor.

"The Academy? There's a name I hadn't heard in a long while." And the Knight-Lord's lip curled faintly. "Not near here, no. Nearly a week's walk south along the Gramsleith, just past Leitath's Pass. Which Lothar's band of half-men blocked off long past."

"You think there's any way they'd let us pass?" asked Cor.

"Not likely," shrugged the cavalier. "Not even the merchants make it past these days. They take the southern trail, or do their trading with Lothar's agents at a nearby town. Anyway," Deliad sighed, shaking his head, "what do a couple of good country kids want with that place?"

"We'd heard the archives there were the best we'd find," explained the boy from Beldria.

"With that, I can agree," nodded the Knight-Lord.

"You know another way that we could get there?" inquired the girl from Fernstead.

"I'm afraid not. Unless you're both as skilled at scaling mountains as battling," he replied. "Or, there's the option of walking through the orkish wastes down south, which make these knolls seem safer than a nursery."

Grimacing, Cor looked at Brayleigh, who looked back.

"You know," the Knight-Lord added, with an absence concealing care, "if you were wanting shelter—somewhere to stay, even for a short while, maybe—I'd happily have you housed in tents with us. Free food, free drink. Free company!" Deliad smiled a winning smile, with arms extended wide. "It's—well, a little less than luxury lodgings. But better far than sleeping in the dirt. And *that*," he said, "is speaking from experience."

The girl from Fernstead grinned and glanced at Cor. "Why not! Sounds like the way we'd planned won't work. Might as well make the most of it: go there, get food, get beds—my back's all bruised, you know!—and work out some good way to the Academy."

Well-said, supposed the Beldrian, somewhat glumly, wondering why every waypoint on this quest was winding ever further from its endpoint; and whether it was wise for two young wanderers, new to their quest, to team up with the crew of a throneless king, whose cause they scarcely knew.

But who could say what Destiny designed? What choice has man, confronted by the unknown unknowable, but keeping faith with feeling, borne by the warm assurance in his breast toward fated weal or woe?

"Why not?" said Cor.

"Splendid." The paladin spread his arms in welcome. "Well then. We've got a few days' walk to camp. As far as food goes, I've got fare for three." He slapped a saddlebag upon his stallion, which, seconds past, had trotted up beside him. "But, as for sleep, I fear we'll all be slumbering beneath the Stars, barring a cave or some such. We'll have to skirt past Loni to the South. Nice as the inn might be, alas, the Knight-Lord's not one to show his face in town these days."

"Well, more of what we're used to!" Brayleigh waved. "I like to camp. And Cor here likes to camp."

"Suppose I do," the Beldrian said, recalling that cozy bed and breakfast back in Oldstorr aloft the Fyrst Rocks, brushed by the breeze, facing the brume that roved above the sounding sea. *Sigh.* "What beats sleeping under starlight?"

"Right!"

Thus, two turned three, one plan replaced another, and off our wanderers went into the knolls near Norvester, where, apparently, some knights of that erstwhile nation and its erstwhile monarch were eking out their dismal days in exile.

Hovering above their wayward course ahead was shining Sol, still slowly culminating toward noontide's height, traveling halfway from one horizon to the other, just to ascend to his fated place aloft the far empyrean.

Likewise, it seemed Cor's course was straying wide of where he ultimately had to be, to achieve his high charge from the Lord of Light. But what a welkin-wandering Luminary must do, the Beldrian mused, at Fate's behest, so too must man sometimes to achieve his quest. If wandering round the world was what it took to satisfy his charge and save the Elements, he'd wander. So the best tales always went. And what's life in this world but a tale writ large?

CHAPTER 9

Celeste was walking in cuffs toward the castle. She tilted back her head and strolled serenely as best she could, being tugged at times by an ork and stumbling onward. Not entirely graceful, but her facade was proud and princess-like.

Inside, she felt more like a gullible princess who'd eaten a poisoned apple a moment past. *A moment? Or a decade?*

On she went, through Castle Norvester's gates and through the courtyard, through halls that monarchs made, through double doors of oak, into the former throne room of a fallen king.

Poised on the throne with one leg on an ottoman, while lounging leaningly upon a chair arm, cushioned as crimson as his pantaloons, was Lothar, waxing eloquent to an audience of laborers, shoulders slumped with hanging heads.

"And I'll not brook such backward creeping, and I'll not abide such self-ish—eh? How's this now?" the leader of the Commonwealth called out, peering upon his cuffed-up personal orator.

Out of his smaller armchair to the side sprang Clausiglade, trembling with a tight-lipped fury flowing from wide eyes. "How—how dare you! Guards—!" he started. Then, recalling these *were* guards, he said instead, "Unhand her! How? An outrage!"

Speaking this order, he stabbed with his finger to drive the point in; but in doing so, shivered and bent a little, like a fencing foil purporting futilely to pierce full plate.

The orks ignored him. "Boss, the girl killed Ruptorg," their officer said. "She stabbed 'im in the street."

The Merchant raised his eyebrows at his orator, studying her countenance in silence; then, shrugged. "My Treasurer Clausiglade gave you a command, yes? Cuffs off. And do dispense with all those chains. And all *these* too." He waved his five ringed fingers at the assembled audience of the citizens. "Matters of state to chat about. Chop chop."

"But—" spoke the foremost foreman, hand upraised as though to grab his high hopes back; but nothing. And out his crew was borne by orks in badges.

Nauz was unbinding Celeste. Staring on her captor, waiting, with serene imperium writ on her brow, fair and bereft of fear, she let her lips curve slightly upward. And, gawping, the ork now grasped its arm and quavered, glancing at Lothar. Who, indeed, was looking displeased with Nauz. Or maybe merely impatient.

Whatever it was, the ork stripped off the shackles and stumbled into a near-run from the throne room.

"Now." Lothar sipped his red. "First, thank you, Celeste. I'd started toward what would've been an *awful* headache, had I been forced to hear those"—waving, he rolled his eyes—"those *folks* who just walked out. 'Were walked out,' maybe? Anyway, your timing was truly impeccable. Had I to hear *another word* about our tax collectors, complaints of crime, bemoaning of the bandits prowling our borders—why, it'd drive me batty!" He tilted back his wine to wash the thought down. "Can't we just, I don't know, call it sedition? Ban it on that basis, spare me some stress?"

"A prudent choice," said Sulzdorf, scribbling notes for the next edition of the People's Press. "Populism is prone to inciting violence."

"Yes, populism, good term; or politics, if you prefer," affirmed the First of Equals. "Lord Toadson, I'd ask you to draft the bill."

"I'll have my 'folks' start drafting straightaway," tittered the minor lord to Lothar's left.

"Good, good. Be quick, don't worry about the wording," said Lothar. "Nothing matters but the name. Not like the *folks* will be reading the rest. Something, like—hm. The 'More-Free Future Act'? How's that?"

"Quite good," the newsman complimented. "Myself, I favor acronyms. I find they sell well. Say, the 'Populism-Ending Act for the Commonwealth's Edification.' Or 'PEACE,' for short."

"Oh, I *do* like that, Sulzdorf. I'll take it!" Lothar lauded. "'More-Free Future' has a fine ring, though. Celeste, you can use it when you announce the law.'" Lothar looked off with wondering wryness. "Ah, but what a name! Who could object to PEACE?"

"Well, no one, once it passes," Toadson cuckled.

The Merchant slapped the table. "Toadson, that's your best remark this year!" The minor lord cuckled again, speechless with satisfaction, as Lothar turned to Celeste. "Second thing: this rendezvous with Ruptorg. With the worms now, eh? Well, what's done is done. But he *was* useful, so I do have to ask you: Why? Some slight? He question a command of yours in public?"

"So we was—" started the orkish officer, still standing by Celeste, with a face as furrowed, withered and white as a mold-matted prune.

"Were you not listening?" Lothar asked the ork. "I said *you*. Meaning, Celeste, not—whoever you are. Heaven knows, my head already hurts. So, right, go on."

She smiled at the ork, eyes narrow upon its nervous stare, then looked at Lothar. "While I was walking through Oldtown today, I heard a woman scream, and, on inspection, I saw that Ruptorg was about to rape her. To rescue her, I'd no choice but to kill him."

He stared and waited for the story's end. Then, at her wordlessness, he held his hands out. "And, what? Some friend of yours? Some famous figure?"

"No. Just a woman, or a girl, out walking.

"Well. That's a shame." The First of Equals sighed. "You know what all the common folks called Ruptorg? 'Lothar's Left Hand.' And it was so well-said!

Catchy, concise, suggestive; why, even true! It's flattering being the subject of a phrase that others think up. Really, such a rarity." He shook his head in sorry satisfaction. "Well! No use crying of spilt milk. Or of spilt blood. Scarcely the end of the world. But I *will* say, I just can't have you killing my commanders and covert agents. Not without good cause."

"Rape wasn't good enough?" Celeste replied, tone flat, even as her insides turned with sickness.

"Good cause for *murder*, Celeste?" Now, the Merchant's fatherly air had taken a forceful tone: the one he saved for suppliants seeking audience who openly contradicted him. "Of course, had *you* faced danger, Celeste, that'd be different. By all means, self-defend! Defend a friend even! But, when our bystanders back random passersby, dealing out death by vigilante violence, why, what becomes of our civil society? What point to obey the law, if punishment be meted out by murder with impunity?"

"Now. Let's allow, arguendo, that your glimpse of these acts was accurate. *That's* a great assumption, as any jurist worth his salt will tell you! Well, Ruptorg was engaged in common crime: a sad and sorry thing we all aspire to end, and end forever. And we shall!, should we persist toward the more perfect union we all want dearly. But we'll never attain that crimeless Commonwealth by *more* crime, Celeste."

"Now. Say, in theory, that it might be needful, sometimes, to take life; say, to save a life. Not here! No loss of life was looming here! You killed him. Had you let the matter lie, merely let Nature run her course, my ork and your young woman both would still be breathing; indeed, most likely, none the worse for wear! You killed him. Should I sanction such a homicide, where would it stop? Should all who've sinned be slain? Where would the slaughter stop? Who would *survive*? Is this the ending that you yearn for, Celeste? Death, death, and more death, piled on top of death?"

"Well. *I* don't deal out punishments so lightly. And, in the long run, Ruptorg matters little." Like a skilled actor in between two scenes, switching his character scarcely in seconds, Lothar now doffed his righteous orator's scowl and donned a father's smile for a straying child. "Things happen! Life goes on! Mistakes are made! The only thing that I find somewhat strange—I'd say disturbing, but I'm still not sure—is that, instead of offering an apology for what was just a lively lapse in judgment, you offered a defense. And such a strange one! But I suppose the best of us, sometimes, are swept up in the moment? You misspoke?" With affable face and folded hands, he waited.

The *yes*—so simple—should have come so easily. Like all the other *yeses*, spoken and unspoken, she'd taught herself to not think twice about, throughout her many years beside the Merchant. But this time, somehow, something deep refused that ready answer. Something shook her head and shut her eyes. And from that dismal darkness swirled thoughts half-formed, finally allowed to form.

"This isn't what it was supposed to be." The words were borne out by a chilling wind, wending within her, from a place beyond her. "You said we'd come to stop the Tyrant's tyranny. You said we'd bring equality, end oppression. Instead, *we* tyrannize the innocent townsfolk unpunished, and ungoverned by the laws that others answer to. *We're* doing the oppressing. And everyone would say so, were they not so scared of us that they instead say nothing!"

"Celeste," warned Clausiglade, with a hand half-raised.

"And how do you suggest I solve this issue?" The Merchant's tone was mild, even talkative. But in his stare, unswerving, shone a strange zeal.

"Maybe we ought to rethink this whole business." The words were out before she'd worked the thought out. "Maybe the way things were, the way things are—well, maybe there's some happy medium. Maybe we just need moderation. Maybe that'd help. Help restore some of the hope that we started with. It feels so far off, now, so—I don't know." She shook her head. "I haven't worked this out."

"Well then! As long as you're working it out, eh?" The Merchant smiled and stared a moment. Then, he sighed. "I have to say, it's truly a shame. So many years we've striven, with hopes sky-high! And yet 'it feels so far off, now.' Yes, Celeste, you feel as I feel, in at least that one sense. A shame. Your company's good, your speeches better. But, like I said, things happen! Life moves on, and likewise Lothar," waved the wide-eyed Merchant.

Now the brisk wind within that'd borne her words out had ceased. And suddenly, Celeste felt a new chill, unlike the last one. "Lothar, I—I hadn't—I'd merely meant to make—"

"Guards!" called the Merchant.

"Now, Lothar, there's no need—" the scholar started.

"Yes, you two! Come, come," interrupted Lothar, as Nauz and Moldy-Prune-Face now raced in. "Seize that one. With the blonde hair, white blouse, yes."

"You can't be serious, Lothar!" Clausiglade cried.

The two orks stared a second. Then, on seeing Lothar was seemingly serious, they leered delightedly and seized her by the biceps.

"This woman is a wicked coconspirator and sympathizer with the oppressors' ways, who seeks to undo the good we've done, unwork the commonweal we've worked, and bring an end to what we've just begun!" accused the Merchant. "Who would believe it! Such a lovely lass. But 'beauty lies,' said someone wise. Alas, I just confronted her and she confessed. Go lock the lady in the holding chamber, while we consider a suitable sanction."

With Lothar's words, her hands had risen and clenched, her lips gone wide. But—like a stone that's lifted too swiftly from its slimy river lodging, slips from the fingers and plunks back beneath, even deeper in sludge than it'd been stuck before—she slumped and sagged. And, by his speech's end, only the orks' gross girth still held her up.

"Right, Boss," the officer said. "Come on, come on." It curled its hulking arm about her back, so starshine tresses graced its tumorous bulk, tugging her slack frame toward the double doors. "Come on! Stop draggin', now, or we'll start draggin'."

"Why don't we drag the bitch into the barracks?" said Nauz. "Some nice beds there. Might have to share." A wide grin warped the face beneath its warts.

At these words—like a sword that'd spent its days stuck fast within the smith's forge, with the fires that'd let it form now leaving it too limp for form to function, which is suddenly doused to steaming fury by a frigid downpour—the warm and wavering scholar from the Academy finally went cold and firm.

"Stop!" shouted Clausiglade, with piercing, pointed gaze and finger and voice.

The orks blinked, brows raised. But they stopped, at least, and looked to Lothar; who, in turn, now looked at the pointing academic, eyebrow arched. "Was there some point *you* wished to work out, Treasurer?"

"Why, I should say so!" countered Clausiglade, shivering with cold heat. "What you've ordered is—well, unmeet! Why, you would pluck the petals from the flower of the Commonwealth! The fruit that feeds our future! The seed from which our fledgling state will flourish!" With every metaphor, he waved his arm more. "Without this woman of words, this damsel of diction, where would we be? Indeed, where *will* we be? Back in the wagons, I fear, before long; without this one girl's grace to gild our purpose, and placate the impatience of the people, as, over time, we tread toward the utopia to which you'll lead us, Lothar!" Clausiglade piped, tone sinking like a teapot simmering down.

"Still a believer, I see?" Lothar smiled. "That much is good. But, Clausiglade, my dear Clausiglade, you make the matter much too complicated. A million words are spoken on, say, the seasons, and why they pass, and when and how they pass. But, in the end, *they pass*, despite the driveling of poets and dreamers. Likewise, laws are laws: They're passed, and when some trespass comes to pass, it falls to me to pass the lawful sentence. And so I shall. As Celeste said, she's 'governed by all the laws that others answer to.' The law's the law. Let's let this matter pass, yes?"

The Merchant held his arms wide winningly, as Clausiglade stared in fist-clenched silence; then, turned toward the small stone table with his wine, which, casually, he lifted to his lips.

The scholar seized the First of Equals by the shoulder, roughly spinning him around, so wine sloshed from his goblet, further reddening Lothar's already crimson pantaloons. "You free her, or I'll—or I'll make you free her!"

"No, Clausiglade—!" Celeste cried, her eyes gone wide, her hand out toward the humble man who, years past, had taken her in and treated her as daughter.

But Nauz now yanked her backward by the gut, relishing as she bent and gaped and breathed out, reduced from beauty to a bulge-eyed hunch.

"Aha! Our humble Treasurer shows some spine!" marveled the Merchant at his maven of tax, as, absently, he brushed some ruddy beadlets from ruffled velvet. "Spine, or something else. You scholars always struck me more as eunuchs than *actual* eunuchs. But it seems you pair might have a pair! Her, maybe more than you—by Heaven, the bitch knifed Ruptorg! I'm still reeling—but still, you've stepped up," Lothar said. "Alas, this raises some concerns. My rule of thumb is, anyone smarter than my orkish soldiers who has a sack, gets sacked."

"Well said, well said!" cuckled Lord Toadson, while clapping two-fingered, to keep from cutting off the First of Equals.

"So," Lothar sipped his red, "that settles things. Guards! Grab the gawky fellow." Several soldiers jogged up and seized him, jostling limbs in place for shackling. "Sympathizing with the oppressors. And insurrection too: just look at me!" He swept more red drops from his ruffled slacks. "And, mind you, lock him in a separate cell from Celeste. With the other oppressors, why not? Maybe some Knights of Norvester! Ha, indeed. No doubt they've much to tell the Merchant's Treasurer!" The First of Equals smiled upon the pains of his former fellow traveler.

"Fine then, kill me!" called Clausiglade, as the soldiers slung him off like a sack of flour: all empty white refinement, free of firm fiber. But the adoptive father of Celeste forced himself to one firm statement: "Torture and scourge me! Just set Celeste free!"

"Ugh!" parried Lothar, picking at a nail. "What sort of savage do you take me for? You think that I'm the sort to swing a *scourge?* You think that, Blugth?" he asked the ork beside him, whose slackjawed stare seemed unmoved by the turmoil.

"I think?" the ork repeated. "Nope, don't think."

"That sums the issue nicely," chuckled Lothar. "Still, isn't it sad," he went on to the soldier of dried-blood shade, and texture too, "that three—not one, but *three*—of what had been my best, most loyal lieutenants, are, in mere hours, lost! How does a fellow cope with such cruel Fate!"

"Sad, yeah," shrugged Blugth. It itched a fleabite.

"Sad. But that's my payback, making use of people! Given long enough, they'll always let you down," waved wistful Lothar. "Not like you lot!"

"Nope," quoth Blugth.

And, having heard this bantering drollery, the former orator of the First of Equals was hauled out cuffbound by her orkish captors, from the old and regal throne room of a sovereign she'd helped depose, down to the holding chamber.

CHAPTER 10

Led by the Knight-Lord through the rolling knolls northeast of Castle Norvester, Cor and Brayleigh kept up a blistering pace, pushing on tireless from when the flames of Sol's swift chariot first dappled the meadowscape with westward shadows, until the beaming of the Blazing One on the east horizon heralded the Dusk.

"That's forty miles today. The fires of youth!" the Knight-Lord yawned one night to his companions. "Myself, I'm somewhat sleepy." So he said; but he'd been walking with them, armed and armored, with all their bags being hauled atop his horse.

"So, who's this Lothar?" Brayleigh asked one day. "And who made him king?"

"Not king" said the Knight-Lord, curling his lip. "Lothar disclaims all titles, save First of Equals." Sarcasm filled that last phrase. "Which is to say, he wields power as completely as any king, with none of their nobility. He calls kings tyrants. Well then! What's a tyrant whose very title lies that he's an equal? What do you call a tyrant taking food from his common folk to fat his army of criminals, while telling them to thank him for equality?"

"I take it there's some story of how this tyrant came into power?" replied Cor.

"And a grim one," he nodded. "Not a tale I like to tell. Wounds haven't healed. Literally, in the King's case. But I suppose you'll need to know," he sighed.

"Lothar was known as the Merchant back then. A man of massive wealth, wandering the Fragments and buying here and selling there for profit. His origins, no one knows. Strange rumors though: That he was from some far off Fragment southeast. Fled here from foes in youth. And he's a eunuch!" The Knight-Lord laughed a little at the last.

"Supposedly. Whatever. What we know is, he studied at the Academy. In his time there, he inherited a fair sum from his father. Apparently, a fair and honest craftsman."

"Well, Lothar took those funds and started lending. First, little sums to friends from the Academy: his fellow students, fallen upon tough times. They'd sign some papers, promise that they'd pay and such. But buried in the boilerplate was Lothar's late fee: ten percent per month." He shook his head. "So, triple every year."

"His 'friends' found out the hard way, soon, that Lothar would never waive that late fee for a friend. The poor fools couldn't pay the fee. They'd all defaulted on the *debt*, forget the fee."

"So Lothar filed collection claims in court. But what *he* found out there was, all his lending was usury and illegal. Null and void, and totally uncollectable. And a crime! He claimed a lack of knowledge, and the court was lenient, let him off. But not the Academy. They expelled him!"

"So, away from the Academy, he slunk off to the slums. He found his orks there. Hired them to go collect on debts the courts struck down. And now, those students started paying. A debtor thinks of ways to pay his debt, when orks are waving bludgeons over his brow. So, Lothar came to be the local debt lord."

"Then, when the authorities caught wind of his scheme, he simply fled the city and kept on sending his orks as his 'collectors.' Some were caught; so he sent more! And Lothar made a fortune."

"His orks brought back all sorts of random articles from debtors: gold rings, deeds to family farms, silverware, books, and so forth. And he sold it. To locals first. But soon he figured out he'd make far more by selling to the gentry of far off lands, billing his goods as 'foreign.'"

"That's when he started wandering with his wagons, Fragment to Fragment, selling what he'd seized from students to the wealthy. And he bought things, hoping to sell them back home. Before long, his merchant business had become so big, Lothar made that his main job. Dropped the debt work. That's roughly when our man became the Merchant."

"The Merchant's Caravan, they called his wagons. It grew from month to month, amassing wares, getting more orks to guard them, as a tumor masses more swiftly as it swells."

"Well, in time, those were the orks that captured Castle Norvester."

The blight here, Cor observed, was like in Beldria, but if anything, even more advanced, with swathes of former greensward browning and yellowing, bare at the center.

"When your time comes, I'll say why."

With a slight shake of the head, he faced the knight. "Well, wait though. How did that happen? Some big battle?"

"Hardly! They strolled in through the open gate."

"Huh?" said Brayleigh. "So where were all the guards and knights and such?"

"Excellent question!" Deliad's blue eyes burnt like desert skies at noon. "How *did* it happen that Castle Norvester—the ancestral seat of House Lofthungrian, since the First King Sigram slew Mallarg Trollblood and dispersed his horde, and all the feuding families made him monarch—this citadel that stood unbreached for centuries, held against orks by the Honor Guard's brigades and the Hergas of the Fellowfolk beside them—stood guardless and with open gates at nighttime?"

"The story starts with Clausiglade: former Steward for Norvester's King, and now the Merchant's Treasurer. An old professor of Reginald's at the Academy, back in his days as Crown Prince. After his crowning, he made his teacher Minister of the Treasury: our topmost tax collector and fiscal counselor."

"Our King, during his at the Academy, was—how to put it?—steered by his instructors to a sort of self-destructive sympathy. Which comes when kindness tries to be more kind, but can't, so it warps to wanton license."

"So, when Clausiglade counseled that we adopt reforms for the commonweal, our newmade King was all ears."

"First came the holidays: Feast for the Commonweal, Everyman's Holiday, Worker's Week, so forth. And then there were the 'programs': solving problems by throwing silver till they went away. His subjects loved it. And His Majesty, who loved being loved, gave Clausiglade a promotion to Steward: his second in domestic matters."

"The troubles started when the Treasury ran out."

"Steward Clausiglade got the King to cut all funding for border sentinels. 'Pure waste!' said the Steward. 'They traipse about, harassing travelers, waving their swords; for what? To guard some fallow fields? We have our army and knights! What need for sentinels?'"

"Next came the Hergas of the Fellowfolk, who'd fought for Norvester since before her founding. 'Why waste our hard-won silver on part-time soldiers?' our Steward said. 'Let our shopkeeps serve as shopkeeps, our farmers serve as farmers. Not an army. Leave war to our knights, our full-time fighting force. Much more efficient.' And the King agreed."

"Then, sure enough, Steward Clausiglade came for us. 'A Program to Renew the Knights of Norvester,' he called it. What he sought to do, in short, was shrink us to a set of bodyguards: a couple dozen popinjays with pikes to stand in silence during ceremonies. 'We have no *need* for warlike men who wander the streets and menace working men with weapons, tempting our boys from more productive trades. Save money! Muster an army when the need comes!'" he reasoned.

"Luckily, I convinced King Reginald that leaving Norvester utterly defenseless would not be prudent. Reginald turned him down."

"So, was the issue settled? Not for Clausiglade! He sent his social terrorists to destroy us."

"With every brigand's death to a knight's bared blade, he accused us of undue brutality, riling huge mobs to riot against us, wrecking shops and, in the mayhem, leaving many dead; and then blamed *us* for bloodshed he'd incited. He called the criminals we arrested heroes. He spread false stories that our senior officers engaged in sordid stuff with serving women. He got his fellow scholars from the Academy to attack us with an endless stream of studies, claiming our 'excess violence caused more violence,' and so forth. Simple hackery; yet so much, who has the time to answer? We have *work*."

"Then, after ruining the Knights' reputation, Clausiglade approached the King again, demanding that he "at once disband the Honor Guard, which only heaps *dis*honor upon your reign."

"And I was there. And I said, 'Majesty, a man can see what's fair and feel what's right. You know that what's been said about my men is neither fair nor right. You know who we are. You know our accusers for the things they are.'"

"And, to his credit, the King said to Clausiglade, 'It isn't for the Steward to make 'demands' of his monarch, much less daft demands like this. Go get some sleep. Your ruffled spirits need smoothing.'"

His lips curved up. "The look that Clausiglade had! Like he'd not shat in weeks, and he was straining with all the world's weight. So, our Steward stomped out and never came back," Deliad beamed; then, darkened. "Well. *Never*'s not the right word, I suppose. Clausiglade came back with Lothar's orks behind him."

"It was the Feast for the Commonweal. Each week, they'd throw the Castle gates open and serve free food to townsfolk in the courtyard. Clausiglade's idea."

"That night, amid the shouting merry chaos, no one paid much mind to the hooded figures coming inside. The place was one big crowd. Even when the screams started, few thought much of it; at least, until the bloodshed had become a bloodbath. And by then, it was too late."

"Hundreds of hooded orks in Castle Norvester, all armed and armored. And they'd come to kill."

"I saw them there," the Knight-Lord said, his glare like Sol asmolder over barren sands. "The Merchant and our once-Steward, side by side. Breathing the same foul air, they stood so close! And I'd have killed them. I'd have died to kill them." He grimaced. "Duty didn't give me leave."

"I and my other knights circled the King. We cut a corridor to the stables through a wall of orks. We found some steeds amid the smoke, as fiery wooden beams fell down from above, and scattered straw was burning all about us."

"We kicked our horses to a headlong charge. Trampling and tripping through the dark, and showered with crossbow bolts we couldn't see, and dying. Norvester was red with the blood of my brothers that night. But, somehow, most knights made it out."

"And Captain Sigmund saved the King. His cousin. Carried him on his horse. But not before he'd taken a bolt wound to the bowels. Bad wound. Saved by our surgeon, but bedbound even now: waxing sometimes toward health, then waning ill."

"The townsfolk—would they ever fight this Tyrant?" the girl from Fernstead asked. "Revolt? Rise up? I can't imagine that they like this Lothar!"

"Maybe. But Lothar's like a summery drizzle, dousing the folk's fiery spirits with warm words," said Deliad. "And he's had a lot of help."

"What do you mean?"

"Oh, Lothar has some sidekicks," the Knight-Lord said. "Sulzdorf, the media magnate. Lord Toadson, from a line of lesser nobles who've toadied up to wealthy sorts for centuries."

"And then there's Celeste Daorbhean, both the fairest and foulest of the lot. His personal orator, whose batting lashes, long blonde hair, and rhetoric have turned the townsfolk's talk of armed revolt to quiet complaints. The worst fiend is the fair one."

His words and eyes were hard, but, as they crested a small hill, softened at seeing what loomed. "Behold! our regal residence on the Sightful Hills."

Scattered across the glen between two bluffs were tents, some fine but frayed, some rudely formed from hunted hides. Mailed men were roving round them.

"Why they're called 'Sightful,' I haven't the slightest, as there is *nothing* in these knolls worth seeing. Not much here, but we make ourselves at home. I hope you'll do the same."

"Welp. Beats more camping!" the girl from Fernstead said.

Cor's brow inclined. "Didn't you claim you liked camping? Not long past?"

"I don't remember that. Do you have *beds* here?"

So went our pair of wanderers, with a paladin expelled at swordpoint from his hearth and home, to face the future with his fellow exiles, led by a King now languishing near death; in hopes that, here, they'd hit some fated waypoint along their long path toward a farflung endpoint: to save the Elements!

Even now, after musing on Dievas' message over many days, it almost seemed to Cor too strange for story. Hardly a month past, his ambit had been mere miles of fields from Beldria to the Fyrst Rocks. Now he outwalked his former bounds each week. And, in so doing, he'd crossed the Boundaries. Twice!

He felt like some fixed Star aloft the sky set free to fare beside the Wandering Stars: with Sol and Luna, and, of course, the Daystar, lighting the first and last of each day's progress. What weird and Star-crossed prospects might await our Beldrian flown from Beldria, here beneath the shining aspects of these foreign skies?

CHAPTER 11

Accompanying the Knight-Lord into camp, they passed some sparring knights and brown-clad bowmen, and others chopping logs and leeks, and others dragging a cart that held a bloody bison. Some offered "hails" and "well mets" as they passed. He led them toward a large tent near the center, and, lifting up its flap, they followed him inside it.

Through the gloam of Sun-gorged gazes, they saw a map atop a benchless longboard. Studying the map with a narrow-eyed stare was a small but mesomorphic man with black hair. Youth's last bloom lay upon his brow, like Deliad, but lines of worry showed beneath his whiskers; at least a couple weeks' worth, mostly dark but dun in some spots.

"Knight-Lord." With a grin, the man stood straight, saluting. "Welcome back."

"Captain. Well met." The Knight-Lord clapped his back, but with a little bend of lip that spoke of the ironic brusqueness feigned by boyhood friends. "How are arrangements coming?"

"Almost ready. At least, as ready as we'll likely be."

"You got the sack then?"

"Shockingly, we did. We had no coin to buy the stuff, of course. But Foreguard Sithrik found a farmer, south some fifty furlongs. Called himself a 'King's man,' who'd 'never bow before the Usurper Lothar.' And he insisted that we have it gratis." The Captain grinned. "The cart came Govinsday."

Cor slightly frowned. If he'd just heard correctly, this crew was in such straits, it'd lacked the silver to buy a simple sack and marched for miles to find some soul who'd offer one for free. *A cart? To carry a sack? Or lots of sacks?*

"This world's hard, Orther, but it's full of fair folk," said Deliad. "Easy to forget that these days."

"Too true." The Captain now had turned to Cor and Brayleigh. "Speaking of." He nodded smartly. "I'm Orther Ormslik."

"Right then. Introductions. Orther, meet Cor Volucre and Brayleigh Mirin. Both from beyond the Boundary west of here, from hamlets neither you nor I have heard of."

"Beyond the western Boundary? Well, I reckon you're right," said Orther, reaching out to shake their hands. Calluses covered his fingers and palm. "A pleasure."

"Pleasure's all mine!" piped in Brayleigh, so Cor's mild "likewise" likely went unheard.

The Knight-Lord held a hand out toward his new friends. "This pair was fighting off an ork patrol when I came passing by. I planned to ride up and rescue them. It turned out these two wanderers had matters well in hand."

"Ah, warriors, eh?" Orther sized Cor up; then, somewhat more skeptically, glanced at the grinning teenage girl from Fernstead. "Seasoned in battling orks, boy? Cor, he said?"

"Well. Not quite 'seasoned.'" Cor shrugged. "Saw my first one scarcely a month past."

"But you'd never know it from how he swings that sword of his," said Deliad. "Daresay he'd best most men here in a duel."

"Oh? High praise." Orther peered upon the hilt jutting above Cor's belt, and how he held the pommel in his palm, even as they spoke. "High praise. But, merely a month past, found your first ork? You must've come from awfully far beyond the Boundary to our west," the Captain mused.

"Right?" replied Brayleigh. "I barely believed him. Like, 'I'm from Beldria. We don't have orks.' What?" She voiced her Cor quotes in a virile bass.

"So, here we have a seasoned slayer of halfmen?" smiled Orther, scanning Brayleigh's slender youth. "No axe? No halberd?"

"Don't be fooled, my friend," said Deliad. "This one thrashed those orks like—well, something you'd need to see before believing."

"See what?" Suppressed amusement showed in dimples beneath his sparkling eyes.

"Toss me that stone?" said Brayleigh, pointing at a paperweight beside the Captain on the big map's corner.

"Ahh. So, a sling then?" Now, in Orther's eyes, a spark of understanding showed. "Makes sense. A small man with a sling can slay a troll. Small man or woman!" Flicking forth his hand, he sent the stone weight spinning toward the teen.

She raised an open palm. From her fingers rushed a half-transparent plane of radiant red, blasting the rock and reversing its bearing. Missing the Captain slightly as it soared, it smote the furrowed fabric of the tent. The bottom flapped up and a breeze blew in.

He blinked, hair blown askew by a blustery swell.

"As I was saying," the Knight-Lord slightly smiled, "plainly, this pair would be helpful to have with us.

"'Desperate times,'" said the Captain, "'desperate measures.'"

"Indeed. So, friends," said Deliad to the duo, "we've hatched a plot, Captain Ormslik and I, to pry back Castle Norvester from the Merchant. Our moving moment will be Gurtag Jidh, when ork males venture out for violent looting."

"Well, it was once called Gurtag Jidh. It's now 'the Week of Taxing,' Lothar's labeled it. Under the banner and blazon of the Merchant, the same orks go in tribal groups to seize the same stuff that they took in olden times: 'From each according to his means!' the Merchant ruled from the King's throne. And, while they're collecting, any resistance is met with the same murder and rapine as in olden times: 'The Tax Department's delegated power of summary sanctions,'

Clausiglade calls that plundering. Progress! It's always awfully like the past, but with a bureaucratic badge and new names."

"Anyway, here's the plan." And he described it. The western wanderers listened, somewhat baffled but intrigued, as he laid the knights' plans bare from start to finish.

Then, he slightly shrugged. "It's not what one would call a fool-proof plan. Not by a long shot. But I've seen you fight. And I've a feeling, should you fight beside us, we'll have—well, more hope."

"Sell them harder, Knight-Lord."

Deliad dismissed this with a wave. "I won't deceive you two. There's danger here in droves. We're doing this since we'd rather win or die than be defeated. *But.*" He raised a finger. "I can assure you, should you come along, and we prevail, I'll see that you're repaid with wealth to suit a king, by Norvester's King."

The wanderers stood in silence for a while. "Well. I'm not sure that wealth is what we need," Cor slowly said.

"Excuse me?" Brayleigh inquired.

"There's one thing, though," began the simple Beldrian.

"How about two things?" the teenager broke in. "That satchel's looking low on silver, Cor!"

"We'll see to that," smiled Deliad. "You were saying?"

"'Who seeks, receives!'" continued Fyraett's scion.

"Right," said the Beldrian. "So, the pass is blocked, you'd pointed out. But if we help at Norvester, could your knights, once the Castle's been reclaimed, help clear the pass so we could reach the Academy?"

"Undoubtedly," said Deliad, scarcely pausing. "Can't have the enemy holed up in an outpost between our capital and a center of commerce."

"So! Empty out the pass and fill Cor's satchel," said Brayleigh. "How's that sound?" she asked the Beldrian.

Cor struggled to consider the issue drily and soberly; but, somehow, found the words rushing out with a warm spirit of assurance. "We'll help them. We'll need help with what we're doing. And one good way to get help is to give it."

"Good! I agree!" Her green gaze blazed with fire's sheen.

And it was done. The Beldrian blinked. *Did I . . . ?* He eyed the golden glow around his satchel.

But Deliad was already beaming. "Brilliant. We're in your debt; I daresay literally!" He motioned toward the Beldrian's modest satchel. "Well, we'll be good for it. With Fortune's help."

And so our western wanderers were ensnared in the schemes of Norvester's Knights.

Within an hour, the Beldrian was assigned to share a tent with several men. One was a new knight, Cor's age, named Arvaen. Seemed a kind sort; eager and green though. He got Cor to agree to spar that evening. Convincing Cor to spar was always easy.

As for Brayleigh, she got that bed she wanted. There were a few tents set aside for women, mostly knights' wives, with some infants still nursing. They welcomed her and asked about her home:

"It sounds so quaint!"

"Serene!"

"I *must* go see it."

"Do you have many knights there?" wondered one.

"Do *you* have any knights there?" grinned another.

"Since *lots* of them are here. And few of us!"

"So!" smiled the first, "how old were you again?"

And, soon enough, they'd offered up their spare bed. "Please, take it! These two won't. I've tried, believe me," one woman sadly sighed, while nursing twins.

Later, seeing Cor's cramped tent, kind Brayleigh noted that her tent had "not only a bed with blankets, but fluffy and feathery pillows! *Pillowcases!*"

"But not swords, I suspect!" the Beldrian parried.

Swords were indeed what filled Cor's next few weeks. That very day, he had his duel with Arvaen. He'd felt some nerves before it. *Here I am, fighting a knight. In front of other knights!*

It passed fast, that first fight. The knight's stiff Plow seemed feigned to Cor. *Who'd hold the sword like* that? *Unless he planned to suddenly shift his posture?* To try to suss out his opponent's scheme, he lashed out quickly into Luna's Question: simply a leftward crosscut, false edge leading.

His foe seemed strangely unprepared to face this standard start, mustering a shaky parry that pushed Cor's sword a little left and downward. *Why* that *though? What's he planning?*

Watching warily, Aldartal's pupil adopted Einhorn posture, gripping the pommel with his offhand, flipping his blade beneath his foe's and up around it. Facing Arvaen squarely, he shoved it forth, simply by shifting his weight a bit forward. A swift blow to the belly: To the Point, the Annals named that stab.

No parry came. The Beldrian's bladepoint jabbed into the jerkin of his unready rival, who, with wide eyes, now gasped and doubled over his prodded gut.

The Beldrian blinked—*that's it?*—then, forced himself to wear the casual face of one with friends, with nothing strange or out of sorts at all. "Huh, lucky me! It happens to us all," he lied.

The new knight nodded, weakly grinned, and brought his blade up. "Well then! Time for round two?"

Sadly for him, the second round was similar; save that, instead of doubled-over forward, he finished this bout falling over backward, when Down to Size—a quick and false-edged crosscut from Fool's Guard—clipped his kneecap. Down he dropped.

A pair of seasoned paladins now were watching, shaking their heads with chins in hand and smiling.

After a few more brief bouts with the poor man without a single blow upon the Beldrian, one watcher stepped forth, waved his junior away, and faced Cor. "Care to have a go? Good fighting. But you should find a fairer matchup, yes?"

Cor eyed his first foe sidelong, sympathetic for the achy and slumping swain, then shrugged. "Why not?"

"Good! My name's Ellrig," said the grizzled veteran. "I'm tasked with teaching him to swing that sword. Reckon it's fitting for us to face off. See if the master surpasses his student."

The two fought. And, in fairness, Ellrig *was* a sight more skillful with the sword than Arvaen.

Some cautious cuts and parries, jukes and jabs. Then, from the elder fighter, Fatherstrike from Roof Guard, slashing down and somewhat inward. A swifter sort of Wrath Hew, more a swat than the bodybreaking blow that it derived from.

Slipping beneath it, Cor sprang into Dust Devil, spinning around the elder and slicing backward with sinking blade, bashing his backside's starboard, so a slapping sound and stifled yelp ensued.

Now, Student Arvaen grinned and snorted; though at Master Ellrig's glance, he hid it hastily.

Seeing this display, more sparred with Cor that evening, and more the next day. By the seventh day, he'd built up quite a reputation.

That day, Cor found that he was facing Captain Ormslik, who'd heard he'd beaten Foreguard Dag that morning: one of the Honor Guard's finest few fencers.

"The art of it!" he'd heard Dag disbelieving, shaking his head at the wooden sword he held. "Like we're all workmen, dragging wood about to build our crude designs. But he's a painter, just brushing into being whatever he wants!"

Orther had raised an eyebrow in response. *"Not only is he an artist; you're a poet, eh? You plan to swap that sword out for a pen? I find you picking flowers, you're out, you hear?"* But, being intrigued as well, he'd challenged Cor.

Now, facing Orther for his twentieth bout, Cor was awaiting the Captain's next move.

Orther looked left, then lunged into a long thrust. *"The weapon never lies,"* the Master of War had told the stillman's son a hundred times.

The Beldrian batted it away and waited, dodged round another and parried a third. *"Your time will come in time,"* Aldartal had said.

And so it came soon, in a flash of steel and inspiration.

Out of Rage Guard, blade raised baseball-bat-like, he swung down-left with Wrath Hew.

The Captain stepped back, narrowed gaze agleam, and—*here it comes!*—he stabbed at Cor's bared stomach.

Now Cor, from Changer—with his hilt waist-high, his swordpoint near the soil and right foot forward—spun left and stepped forth further, so his back was bared, but, mid-stab, Orther couldn't strike him.

Now slashing with the full force of his full spin, just as his foe was bringing back his blade from its futile stab, Cor struck his ungirt thigh, eliciting from the loser a stifled curse. See the Roses, the Annals called that cut, sweeping like gazing eyes across a garden.

Chortles erupted from the watching crowd.

"One more?" asked Cor. "Or in a minute maybe?"

"Well. Let me breathe a little, nurse my wounds, then let you know," the worn-out Captain grumbled. "What are we at now? One and eighteen, was it?"

"Nineteen," corrected Cor. "Oh. You weren't counting the time I hit your hand, you dropped your sword, and . . . ? Sure, eighteen."

Orther sighed and stared up Heavenward.

"What's all this, Captain?" Deliad asked his second, bent low with hands on thighs and breathing hard. "A Captain of the Honor Guard—the Order of Gram!—is bested by a country boy? Sad day, sad day!" tsked Deliad.

Orther grunted. "I'd like to know where Country Boy here learnt the sword." He eyed Cor. "How you swing that thing like

you know my thoughts before I even think them."

"You did that same dodge every time I swung down," said Cor. "I thought I'd draw that out with Wrath Hew. It worked. So I spun past, did the See the Roses."

"'See the Roses'!" said Foreguard Dag. "More flowers!" He'd ambled up beside the Knight-Lord now. "Maybe I *should* go pick some flowers, eh, Captain?"

Indeed, upon the face of the defeated, a rosy flush swelled under his smile and headshake. "'See the Roses,' huh. We call it a 'crosscut.'"

"He who wins nineteen to one gets to name things whatever he wants," replied the Knight-Lord.

"Hmph. Touché," said Orther. "Well, I think I'm done. Or I'll be bruised too badly for our battle. Foreguard, you have my leave to go pick flowers."

"Will do!" Dag grabbed some poppies from the grass.

Now, *he* had been a challenge for the Beldrian. Dag had pressed Cor like the Master of War, minus some decades, minus age's dulling. With *those* fights, he'd had fun. Sure, eight of ten, he'd won; but eight were hard-won. With Dag, he'd worked to win; he'd played with Orther.

Such were Cor's thoughts. But what he said was, "Fine fights, Orther. Let's have a second go soon, huh?"

"Like that, a first-name basis with the Beldrian!" The Knight-Lord slapped his sighing Captain's back. "Nineteen and one! Reckon he's earned it, eh?"

"'Oh. You weren't counting when I hit your hand'!" quoth the disgruntled Captain. "'Fine fights, fine fights'!"

Most of these paladins *were* skilled with the sword. They simply lacked the finer points that came from studying the Sword Postures daily for nine years. The beauty of swordsmanship still showed here, somewhat, but like a fair face in a grimy mirror.

The Master of War had always stressed to Cor how much the Postures mattered. So, when Cor first beat him, with an esoteric parry-riposte routine he'd picked up from the Postures, Aldartal's proud approval had overbrimmed.

Sad, that a man who loved the Postures so much had never had a chance to add to them. Some notes, sometimes, but never a new technique. Not even his proudest, First Flight of the Cygnet.

"*That's not the way it works,*" he'd shaken his head, when Cor had questioned why he hadn't done so. "*Before recording something new in* this *book, it needs its baptism.*" The older man's bright eyes, at this, had waned a bit toward wistfulness. "*And when it comes to blades, just blood can baptize.*"

The First Flight of the Cygnet was a variant of Swan Approach, a standard thrust: a step and a half that ended in an upward point with leg and sword outstretched. In centuries past, it'd have been known to all of Beldria's warriors, as would its standard parry. But the Master of War had made it new again with First Flight.

"*Stutter the step, wobble the blade's approach,*" the man had coached Cor. "*Good thrust, good for closing. Like Swan Approach, but breaks the standard parry.*"

The move was hard. Much harder than it looked, with that misleading wobble and stutter step. But, after a while, he'd mastered it. And when he'd won a duel by doing a well-timed First Flight, Aldartal had been tickled pink. They'd gone out for supper that night, got some brisket, onions and aioli over at Sagriss' butchery. *Mm.*

Such musings made him homesick. How that life of beds and hearths, brown breads and martial arts, from which he'd once escaped to misty dream and musty story, now seemed flush with glory! From memory's welkin fell a light-washed image: the hearthside's heated roar; a peated pour, brazen with the cask, straight from his Sun-blazoned flask; savoring the day he'd had; and there, his dad, to say the meal prayer as he always had.

Memory came close to overbrimming in his eyes.

But, letting them fall from the skies, he found they'd fallen upon the vert-eyed beaming of Brayleigh Mirin, who was strolling toward him. It looked like she had something good to say, judging by how she was hiding her giggling. And, wondering what'd she'd come to share, abruptly, watching her glide, hearing her call, "Hi, Cor!" he felt that memory might make room for more.

CHAPTER 12

"Sack," of course, is a word with several senses: one being the lowly burlap sort that's slung about on backs; another somewhat lower. Then, there's a third sort, of a loftier spirit: fortified wine of white grapes, aged in oak.

Ranging from fino's fairness to the richness of the oloroso—from a lightness lighter than white wine, to the tawniness of whisky with decades in the cask—this potent potable goes well with almost any elegant meal. Its paler sorts suit delicate sorts of dishes: fino with fish or seafood, say. The darker match well with meat, washing dense flavors down with thick raisiny sweetness that exalts the savory.

All this to say, when Sithrik "got the sack," this didn't mean the saggy, slinging sort. Nor had the Knights of Norvester fired their Foreguard. Rather, a faithful farmer of grapes he'd found, moved by his fealty and troth to His Majesty, had given his visitors scads of vinous spirit, barrels and barrels of the blessed stuff. And then some fourteen empty casks as well.

In one of fourteen bumped and bounced along the Knight-Lord, smelling bold and vinous sweetness with every breath, struggling to keep his scabbard from prodding him a fiftieth time, and failing. *Could Captain Orther possibly, perhaps, avoid* one *pothole? Just one?*

He stayed silent.

Orther, in jest, had suggested their plan. *"I guarantee you, not a single soul would recognize this humble Captain here, clad in the crude rags of a rural cropper, rolling along on a rustic wooden wagon. Unlike our famous, fair and manly Knight-Lord, who's known to half the realm!"* he had proposed to smiling Sigmund, relishing the humor of reasoning the preposterous toward the plausible.

"Conceal ourselves in casks! Slip past the sentinels! Who could conceive such a cunning device!" Deliad had praised his Captain. *"Set aside, oh, half the adventure novelists this last century. But hey, who's counting? Not the orks, I reckon, nor reading neither! Bloody brilliant, Orther."*

Another bump, another blow to his pate. *Well, "brilliant" won't mend bruises,* Deliad mused, as they rolled along toward glorious reclamation of regnancy for Reginald VI.

"Can't have our metal helms clanking on casks!" the Captain had declared. And he'd agreed. "Our" helms. In Eremon's name, he'd not thought *that* through. His head had taken more trauma since this morning than during fifteen years of deadly frays.

"You drinking sack and driving there?" called Dag to the driver; who, of course, was Captain Ormslik.

"Was that a stone? You take some shortcut, Captain?"

"Sack's got him. We've been offroad for an hour."

"We'll find out, five hours later, he's been sleeping, we're in another Fragment—"

"Easy, Elsie!" The Captain's voice came clearly through the casks, and all went silent. Those words were the signal.

Now was the time their long-laid scheme was tested. Now was the crucial moment; now the crisis.

"Mornin', y'all!" the man drawled a moment later.

"What's that?" a gravelly voice growled. "In the wagon."

"Sack! For the Merchant. First of Equals, 'scuse me. First him, then any other folk who'd have it."

A pause ensued. "Don't see no sacks. Just barrels."

"'No sacks'? Why, y'all've not seen no sack before!"

"Tell us what sack is. Or we'll break those barrels and see."

"'See'? Why not taste?" rejoined the Captain in rural accent. "Sack! Like wine, but stronger. The Merchant's mighty fond of this stuff. Strong stuff! Man's liable to be lookin' for it now."

A second silence. "This is Lothar's sack?"

"Said so himself! Why, Hellfire burn my barley and britches if he didn't swear this stuff was—what did he say?—'a much superior spirit to mere white wine.' Man's got a way with words." Orther's approximation of a yokel quoting a cosmopolitan connoisseur was quite a performance.

"Yeah, that's how he talks," affirmed the gravelly growler. "So. Stuff's good?"

"Just the best sack this side o' River Lahser, I reckon!" Orther enthused, then lowered his tone. "What say y'all take a taste, and y'all tell me?"

The Knight-Lord strove to keep his smiling silent. This twang of Orther's was a sight more rural than any he'd heard this side of River Lahser.

"Um. Us, drink Lothar's drink?" The gravelly growler now sounded slightly nervous.

"Gotta taste it. We'll test for poison. We're *protecting* Lothar," a second said. A snorting chuckle ensued.

"Ha! Yep, I get ye. Gotta test it, yep," concurred the Captain. "You lot oughta like it! Here, got some bottled here. Y'all have a gulp or two, then tell me if we're good to go."

"I'll taste first," Gravelly Growler said, then glugged a few gulps down. "This *is* good!" it declared. "Beats weak wine!"

"What'd I tell you, what'd I tell you!"

"I'll taste now!" said the second. "My turn now."

"Here, have a bottle! Barrels more where that's from. I always say, 'Two things I'll never share: my darlin' Lilac and a bottle o' sack.'"

The Knight-Lord forced a laugh down. Eremon's name, he'd put his heart in this.

"No poison, eh?" proclaimed the Captain proudly, as the guard glugged down its bottle of sack. "No sirree Bob! Not if you keep it to a bottle or two. But hey, who's countin'? Call me a swindlin' liar if this sack ain't the specialest stuff y'all've tasted!"

"Beats wine. Way better," the other guard agreed. "Never drink wimpy wine again. Just sack!"

"Why, thankee, thankee. Y'all've gone 'n made me blush!" answered the Captain-turned-farmer. "In fact, y'all like my drink so much, let's make a deal. Promise you'll tell yer friends that Arty Armslee sells the best sack this side of River Lahser, I'll let y'all have a whole cask. How'd y'all like that?"

"Ha! Good deal."

"Guess this Gurtag Jidh be good!"

"Good, good. Y'all help me haul this cask here off, y'all drink away, and I'll be on my way."

Some sounds of steps and shuffling. Then, abruptly, next to the Knight-Lord, a cask was being clasped, oafishly manhandled—*orkhandled, rather*—and, amid straining grunts, slanted down sidelong.

"Just roll 'er down the ramp here!" called the Captain.

"Ha. So much sack," said Gravelly Growler, struggling with weighty, sloshing wine.

"Can't count those casks. So many," mused the second, likewise straining.

"Could take two. Three. Still lots left. Lots for us."

"Ha. Gurtag Jidh, right?"

"Gurtag Jidh!"

"Right! Ha!

Grimly, the Knight-Lord gripped his gladius hilt, steeling himself to spring from casked confinement with short sword flashing. In the extreme close quarters of sack casks, Deliad's burly band of knights had had to doff their usual glaives and greatswords in favor of short steel—let alone his halberd, the man-high Hoarthaxe—likewise swapping platemail for leather jerkins.

Just the lanky Beldrian had squeezed beside him, in his little barrel, a full-length longsword, leaning it aslant, wrapping his early-twenties slimness round it. Deliad admired the limber lad's devotion.

"These casks are heavy. Why not take the wagon?" the second ork was saying now. And the Knight-Lord faintly could hear a fellow fighter, shifting inside his barrel. Bracing now, no doubt, to spring out into a slashing pandemonium.

"Ha! Yer a hoot! Doubt Lothar'd like that, huh? Y'all crack me up," the Captain cheerily countered.

A pause. "Forgot," the second finally said. "It's Lothar's sack." And like a rolling stone, which, no matter how much massy speed it gathers, still crashes to a halt against a cliffside, so the ork guards' mad momentum suddenly stopped at Lothar's name.

"One cask," said Gravelly Growler.

And Deliad's grip went looser on his gladius. He heard them roll the barrel down the ramp, and felt their weight walk off the wagon's rear, and let the steeling of his limbs seep out in a slow sigh.

"Got it, y'all? You good back there? Good. Dandy. See y'all soon!" the Captain called.

Their only answer was the eager glugging of gifted sack, with periodic praise between long gulps. "It's good!" "We'll drink like Lothar!" "Drink sack all day!" "Ha! *This* is Gurtag Jidh!"

Forward the wagon lurched, wheeling its way from the ruts in the road into a bumpy roll. And with a bounce and rattle, and a bunch of bruises, swelling along with warm assurance in their breasts, casked in white oak, the Knights returned to Norvester.

They clattered over cobbles for a bit before they halted. Then, they sat in silence, fixed on the faint sounds of their former driver hopping down, patting a fidgety horse, stepping away from the wagon past earshot, then back again some thirty seconds later.

"Time to move, men," the Captain called outside.

He smacked the hated lid off, stood up slowly, stretched to his full span, then hopped from the wagon.

Rarely had Deliad so savored the daylight after some hammered hours in winey solitude.

"Knight-Lord. Enjoy the ride?" the Captain questioned.

"Well. First, I'd like to load you in a cask and roll you down the Ginnagonds right now," Deliad replied. "Assuming you survive, I'll see to it you receive a bust at Vestkirk for that performance you put on just now. 'My darling Lilac and a bottle of sack'!"

"What's that now?" Orther asked. "Why, I don't reckon I did naught, save for speakin' right King's Common to them there folk."

The Captain's cautious frown contrasted with his casual tone. He scanned the shady alley, walking to its far end.

Meanwhile, the knights were climbing from their casks, relieved and battered.

"Maybe a ride in hard oak—" Deliad began, but cut off at a raised palm.

"Man in a scarlet shirt. Saw me, I think." The Captain clasped his gladius, hurrying back from the alley's entrance. "Recognize him. Turpis. Merchant's man. Saw him last year. Take him out?"

"Stay. Wait and see. Don't make a scene," said Deliad.

They scanned the far off road for several seconds.

Then, into the alley came a silk-clad courtier, capped with a feathered and poofed up beret, his great paunch gaudy as a popinjay, testing two twiglike legs in sable tights. He suddenly spun to stare upon them squarely.

The peeping dandy pointed straight at Deliad.

Orther took off toward Turpis, sword unsheathed.

"Guards!" piped the top-heavy toff. "In the alle—!"

A shimmering red wall struck his backside, blasting the dandy airborne, waving ruffled arms.

His hands hit the Earth first. But his little limbs were no match for such bulk, flown fifteen feet. They splayed, and Turpis' bare face smacked the stone.

Cor gave a thumbs up to Brayleigh, who grinned back.

Deliad's men, baffled by this show of force with no apparent source, exchanged some whispers with wide eyes. Some stepped back from Brayleigh's raised palm.

"That's why," said Deliad, answering the unspoken question.

And Brayleigh beamed.

"Yep. Definitely Turpis," confirmed the Captain, bent beside the dandy. "Merchant's man. Came to Norvester with the Caravan."

"The man's a plum with limbs," the Knight-Lord mused. "Still breathing, right? Alright. Let's roll him in."

The Captain nodded. "Dag and Gertrand, all yours." And, as they struggled with the ungainly girth, he led the others through a little door.

It was a windowless and square white room. A two-chaired table stood alone to one side. One of the chairs, he grabbed and slid toward Gertrand, who slumped unconscious Turpis onto its seat. Dag tied his arms to the chair's back and gagged him.

And now, to wait. The next step came near sundown.

So, thirteen knights and two young wanderers waited for lurid day to fade to dusky grey.

The doorway's line of light had started dimming when sounds of far off mayhem first slipped in, first faint, then louder. "Just like we were hoping." He smiled to hear the clangor of steel on steel. "Let's go."

They'd started filing through the exit when, to their rear, a weak contralto cried, "Help! Knights of Norvester! Help! The Knights of Norvester!"

Somehow, the dandy had gotten his gag off.

The Knight-Lord spun with fist outstretched toward Turpis.

But Orther's balled fist was already blasting the fat toff's brow back. Off flew his poofed beret, and back his head bounced like a punching bag. Red spilled out from a smashed nose onto his gums, bereft of top teeth now and dripping drool.

"Nicely done," noted Deliad. "Let's be off."

They strode from the alley's shadows one by one, spreading across the street, casually strolling. *"Yes,"* said their faces, *"yes, I'm clad in leather. And yes, a short sword's at my side. Why not? Why, yes, I see that fellow over yonder, wearing the very same getup. And why not?"*

Meanwhile, Brayleigh and Cor kept up the rear, playing their part as a street-strolling couple. The way the green-gazed maiden clung to her man, holding his hilt and swaggering at her side, showed the authenticity of top-notch actors.

The easiest parts to play are who you are and who you hope to be someday, smiled Deliad.

Brawling and revelry showed down some side streets: the ork guards, cele-brating Gurtag Jidh. Their guttural hooting and the townsfolk's cries joined to cacophony. Sounds of windows shattering and women screaming soon became continual, as they advanced together toward the castle.

Its towers and turrets rose upon the skyline. As they approached, they saw more steel-girt guards. Half-ork, most seemed, with more of man's nobility in their brows. A hundred guards and more, the paladins passed.

Glancing at Brayleigh behind him, he nodded slightly—then, saw a guard was staring at him, tilting its head and squinting under a steel helm.

Tensing, he turned to scan a nearby fruit stall in roughly the direction he had nodded. Nearing it stiffly, sifting through the produce, he peered at fruits and studied them for faults, pretending to be pondering which to purchase: a smaller pear or bigger one with bruises.

The vendor, who was sitting on some steps a ways off, started toward this man in leather manhandling toothsome merchandise with soiled hands.

"Hey there!" he heard to his flank. "Nice day, huh?"

"Hey, fancy that. It's been awhile," he answered, setting the two pears back. "What's up with you two?"

"Well," Brayleigh waved toward Cor, "we're on a walk! Clearly. And you?"

"Whiling the day away." He stretched and yawned, then matched their east-ward stride. "Bit hungry. But the food here's not the best."

The vendor slowed and paused a moment, mouth open; pondering, perhaps, if he should seek the sale, musing on silver's many virtues. Then, deciding sloth's the better part of vice, he shrugged and ambled back to his lowly stoop.

Meanwhile, the watchful guard was glaring now at several orks with ales and swords in hand. They swung their weapons at whatever came too close, and kicked down piles of grocery goods, and shouted "Gurtag Jidh!" and garbled phrases.

It waved them backward from the castle. "Back off! Go do that down there!"

They ignored the guard. One grabbed a wagon wheel and flung it through a window. Women screamed as glass sprayed inward.

Hooting, the larger guard dashed toward the door and, shoulder lowered, blasted it from its hinges. More screams; more laugher. "Well, well! What's your names?" The other guard rushed in. "Ha! Gurtag Jidh!"

The wanderers and the Knight-Lord walked on past, until the walls of Castle Norvester loomed near.

"You ready, Brayleigh?" Deliad questioned quietly.

"Couldn't be readier!" she blithely replied.

"Remember. We can't have you getting caught. Stay safe. Stay inconspicuous"

"Yup." She yawned, stretching and scanning their surroundings. Nearby, the knights were stationed in the streetside shadows, watching and waiting. They knew what came next.

She started toward a nearby stall, then halted, as Deliad held a hand up toward the teen.

"And, Brayleigh?"

"Yes?"

"Distraction, not destruction."

"Yup!" Off she waltzed, looking for all the world like a harmless, happy waif with big things planned. *All true, except the "harmless," he supposed. Well, what will be, will be.*

He turned toward the other. "So, Cor. You're left, I'm right. If your side's blocked, you bail and back me up. I'll do the same."

"That's what we planned, right?" the Beldrian replied, hand on his sword hilt. "Ready anytime."

The Knight-Lord smiled. He liked this country lad who, somehow, had become a master swordsman, sparring and studying in rustic reclusion. "Good luck." He nodded at the lad.

"We've got this." Brushing aside some tan strands from his face, the Beldrian held a closed fist forth toward Deliad; who, frowning, eyed the clenching fingers.

"What's this?"

"Fist bump." Cor's hand sank slightly. "You . . . don't do this in Norvester, do you."

"Well, we do it now." He balled his hand and bumped. "That how it goes?"

"You got it." With a grin, Cor wandered west casually cross the empty street. He stopped behind some stacked-up crates beside a bakery.

Outside the castle, steel-girt guards were stationed, wielding big glaives, watching with blank belligerence. Within the gate stood several orks with crossbows, loaded with bolts and cranked, ready for firing. Making a mad dash doorward would be death.

As the others waited, Brayleigh was meandering among some stalls. She first approached a flower stand. A man of middle age was tending tulips.

Smiling, she asked something, hands clasped behind her. She listened like a schoolgirl as he showed her flower after flower, pointing out leaves and petals. And, when he grinned and glanced awry and spoke, she laughed and lightly slapped his gnarled hand's back.

Reddening, he looked away, then lifted up his largest flower—a daisy—held it forth and nodded.

With her lips fallen wide, delighted, she clutched the big flower close against her breast, said *that's so* something (reading from her lips), reached for her coin pouch and posed him a question. But he just shook his hoary head and waved. And, thanking him again, she wandered off.

Balban's balefires, what *is this girl about?*

Turning, Brayleigh smiled squarely at the Beldrian.

Then, strolling cross the street and speaking something unheard, she plucked a petal from her daisy.

A wagon wheeling toward the guarded gate seemingly hit a huge bump, bouncing up a full foot from the cobbles, crashing down and splintering. Wheel spokes broke; the axle split.

Ahead, the oxen harnessed to the cart started with terror at the clamorous crash and took off toward the castle's open entrance, trailing the broken-wheeled wagon behind them. Careening wildly as they barreled forth, their cart passed close beside some piled-up barrels and barely missed them.

Or, he'd thought it'd missed. But now the stacked casks were inclining leftward. Leaning precariously, passing the point of inflection, two big butts of aging spirits slid from the pile and plummeted toward the stones.

The girl from Fernstead now was glancing backward upon the bedlam, with her open-palmed hand closing upon a second sunlit petal and lightly plucking, as she spoke some phrase and fared on blithely mid the budding frenzy.

Striking the stone floor, the topmost cask shattered completely, so a flood of brandy burst forth, shone briefly in a spray of brown abundance, splattered aground and seeped through cobble cracks.

The second cask, in contrast, merely cracked, so a slender stream of brandy started burbling from inside, dripping to the stones undrunk.

"You! Stop right there!" a half-ork officer called, clomping in full plate from the castle gate.

Deliad's heart skipped a beat. But, as the officer stomped forth, he saw that it was staring at the wagon, still careening toward the castle.

Panic was warping the face of the driver. Yanking the reins of his pair of yoked oxen, his efforts only flustered them to mania.

Just as the orks came close to firing crossbows upon the crazed beasts, both abruptly veered right.

Too abruptly. Tipping now, the cart keeled over. The driver, hurled out headlong, hit the cobbles and spun two somersaults into a stall: indeed, the flower stall Brayleigh had been browsing.

Meanwhile, the glaived ork guards had leapt to action.

"We go secure the area!" one declared. The armed ork darted toward the downfallen driver, then past him, doffing its unwieldy polearm and bending down beside the brandy cask, still slowly burbling forth its brownish fluid. It stuck its gob against the stream and gulped, then raised a closed right fist. "Yea! Gurtag Jidh!"

And now its fellow orks, with lunatic laughter, were clomping toward the cask. They shoved and shouted, each of them eager to get a turn chugging.

"You! Stop right there!" the half-ork officer shouted, as its subordinates sprinted off to drink. It spun to face two guards still standing nearby. "You there! You two! You go and stop them drinking!"

But cold wind doesn't counter hot wind; rather, the contrariety causes storms. Just so, when the ork guards tried to grab their guzzling peers, this just provoked derisive jeers and pushing, and, in the meantime, more copious consumption.

Amid the chaos, none of the ork guards glimpsed the near-pellucid plane incarnadine that bopped the backside of the ork then quaffing, so its beige brow smacked the barrel.

In surprise, it swallowed cask-strength brandy down the wrong pipe.

Choking and coughing and abruptly standing, it caught its breath. Then, clenching one big fist, the ork unsheathed its scimitar. "Which o' you," the hideous hulk wheezed slowly, "smacked my ass?"

"Must've been Grobduk. Tried to make us stop!" one ork charged.

"Heard him say he likes big bums!" accused another.

"I saw Grobduk grab you!"

The relatively dutiful guard that'd dashed forth to halt the drinking held a hand up now.

But, far as the other ork guards were concerned, the evidence now was closed, the verdict set, and sentencing at hand. A scimitar swept, and dustward plopped the unpaired trunk and head.

And onward fared the guileless girl from Fernstead, plucking another petal and sweetly sighing.

Meanwhile, one opportunist pressed its maw against the spilling spirits as the others argued. But after a moment of excited swilling, another near-transparent ruddy plane flashed into being behind the boozing ork and pushed it pate-first into the emptying barrel, so brandy spilled upon its now-bruised brow.

"Grobduk shoved me too!" the bloodshot guard sputtered; then, blinked at the decapitated corpse of Grobduk. "Someone shoved me!" it corrected.

One half-ork, staring at the separate head and body, putting two and two together—or, rather, one and one—hypothesized, "Maybe it wasn't Grobduk, huh?"

"Who cares?" The beige guard grinned. "I never liked that Grobduk."

Its brethren roared with belly laughter.

"Me too," another barked. "I don't like Borbog neither!" And, with the sweep of a blood-befouled sword, shocked Borbog had become a font of blood, gushing in blackish heartbeats from its gullet. More laughter, laced with madness. "Gurtag Jidh!"

The giddy cry cut off. A crude knife stuck from its neck.

"That was my pa!" the stabber shouted, louring above its brother-ork's bleeding body; then, leered. "Just joking. Never liked you, that's all."

As merry murder burgeoned into bloodbath, amid the officer's ineffectual cries of "*stop right there*," more orks were rushing in from roads close by, lured in by sounds of carnage like wandering sharks that smell a spilling wound.

A glaive slashed, and a steel-girt arm fell groundward, amid much laughter at the lopped-off limb, still twitching slightly as it struck the cobbles. Howling, the one-armed ork half-hewed its maimer at midriff level and stopped inside the spine, so its top half tilted into a living "L."

As Deliad scanned this chaos in disbelief, he saw blithe Brayleigh, strolling still nearby.

A stray stone hurtled toward her. Up her hand flew, and, in a glimmer of gules, the missile halted and plopped down harmless.

Turning now toward Cor, she plucked the final petal and flung it toward him, speaking some three-syllabic phrase and smiling.

"In Eremon's name," muttered the admiring Knight-Lord, as riot and rumpus seethed. *Well, now or never.*

Turning to signal Cor forward, he found him already running.

Well, alright. That's combat. Can't always wait for the order. You just go.

Yet why was he approaching so far right, straight for the crenellated castle battlements? Why was the Beldrian openly *bolting* wallward? There's lightly improvising when you can; and then there's downright throwing out the plan.

Should I have stuck with Dag? mused grimacing Deliad. *Well, nothing for it now.*

He walked from cover with what he hoped was a convincing blend of disinterest and disturbance at the chaos. Closing upon the wall, he scanned for foes but found none watching.

Then, beneath the shade of the castle's crenellated overhang, hand on his gladius, he stepped toward the gate.

This was the part where he needed Cor's help. No way one man could charge that host of crossbows around the bend. But two?

No, probably not. Not unless all this bedlam caused by Brayleigh had left the guards off-guard. That was the hope.

But where was Cor? The way he'd sprinted toward the castle wall, he should've beaten Deliad here by far. Had he been held up? Deliad leaned and squinted.

And there was Cor: not skulking in the wall's shade, as they'd rehearsed. No, Cor was *climbing it*. He'd found a patch of furrowed stone and, scrambling from little ledge to ledge and crack to crack, somehow was scaling the bricks of the battlements.

Oh, no. You'd never do this to me, Dag. This was not part of the plan; nay, not even something they'd speculated on while planning. Probably since climbing into Castle Norvester was patently preposterous.

But the Beldrian, by now, was nearly halfway up the wall's height.

Now, there was nothing for it but to wait and seize whatever moment came. When Cor fell, no doubt some guards would go to inspect his outcry. He'd have to make his move then.

Teeth grit tight, he braced himself to barge a battle line of crossbows with his leather and little gladius.

But, seconds passed, the Beldrian didn't slip, and disbelieving Deliad watched him hop through the embrasure in between two man-high merlons, onto the ramparts and right down the stairway; whose layout, though unseen, the Knight-Lord knew by heart. He knew how many stairs and steps parted the castle door from fleetfoot Cor.

Counting the seconds and gauging by Cor's speed, he just had started to unsheathe his gladius and make his mad dash for the guarded gate, when cries and clangs of steel on steel began.

Grinning grimly, he darted for the fray.

Around the deep recession of the doorway, a clutter of orks with crossbows greeted Deliad, jostling and glaring and elbowing about as they strove to see this new threat in the courtyard. Just two of them—the officer and some slow chap, squinting and struggling to grasp what was going on—saw Deliad as he dashed into the gateway.

The Knight-Lord's gladius felled the latter first. Nothing fancy: a piercing of the windpipe, before the bulge-faced brute could bring its bow up. The short sword, after all, was not his weapon. Doing what he knew would work was good enough.

The officer took two jabs. The first one jellied its blinking eye; the second spilled its belly. Down to its knees. *Enough.* On to the next.

He cut two crossbow strings in one quick swoop, and swiftly counterslashed across one's neck. *You sure can swing this thing. No halberd here!* The other ork's big fist caught him in the ribcage. But hardened leather halts bare hands, at least, and Deliad countered with a downward bowel cut. So, from a neatly slit diagonal, shit spewed.

Parrying a punch with the sharp of his steel, he left the aggressor's left arm with a bone slit, and—seeing a dirk descending toward him—dashed straight at the puncher, pushing through and dodging: enough, at least, that the ork that'd tried to knife him scored only a slight hit to his angled elbow.

As the ork he'd charged tripped backward into an ally, bashing awry the bolt that it'd been nocking, Deliad slashed out with his sword at the dirk wielder.

This was a quick one. As the gladius cut close, the guard already had its dagger swinging.

But Deliad's sword, while short, was still the longer. It slashed off half the hand that held that dagger, and, as the ork eyed its wound, stabbed through its eye socket.

Really, he wasn't bad at this. A blade was a blade. That sneaking-in-a-barrel business hadn't exactly been the height of heroism. But wielding swords: why, here's the stuff of stories.

He thrust his gladius through a guard's grey midriff, unguarded by its motley array of armor.

Add every tale together of warriors wielding weapons besides the sword, and still you'd have more stories left of swordsmen than you'd counted.

He sliced a battle-bellowing ork to silence.

His softest spot would always be for Hoarthaxe, of course, and halberds. And that glaive he'd had, the one he'd gotten from Einnlund. Where *was* that thing? Well, anyway, he had a sword today.

He jabbed it into a runt that'd tried to jump him.

And maybe against these orks, against all odds, he'd have his life's highest glory with a gladius. If that were how the histories spoke of Deliad—"*the Knight-Lord who took Norvester with a short sword"*—he'd take it. Just so long as they all took Norvester.

He cut an em-dash into a crossbowed enemy, then quickly double-cut it into a Z. It stumbled back and stared at bowels. *Enough.* On to the next. He brought his blade back—

Ouch. A jagged scimitar, sliding off his jerkin, had caught upon his waist and cut a wide wound, instantly dribbling bloodbeads down his leg.

He whirled with sword outstretched and slew the assailant, clean through the throat. And, as it fell, he saw this was the one-eyed officer he had stabbed. *Eh. Not enough, I guess.*

Blessed with a brief lull from continual combat, he raced in round the corner of the gateway and, inside, got his back against the stone bricks; then, saw a pair of steel-girt guards on peugback charging at him across the castle courtyard.

Well. Not ideal. But one nice feature of walls, when facing mounted foes, was that they tended to stop such charges. And, indeed, the foremost oversized ferret soon had slowed to a trot.

Before the other peug could come that close, he hurled the trusty dirk he'd had since squiredom directly at its snout. It struck and stuck.

Snorting some bubbling blood, the big beast stopped: not badly hurt, it seemed, but wrinkle-browed like someone with a sneeze that won't come out. Its rider kicked it, irked at the interruption.

Now, the other foe was nigh. The Knight-Lord lashed out. But, being too short, his sword swept shy of the enemy whose snout he'd aimed at. And, exposed, his arm suddenly was inside the stinking beast's maw, which bit down on his bicep.

"Filthy, foul—!" curst the ailing cavalier, then drew a fist back and punched, full force, the biter's beady eye.

Now it let go. It blinked a furry eyelid over its blood-red orb, rather recessed inside its socket; blinked again, as Deliad stabbed up his gladius into its sweaty gullet, broaching the bottom of its cranial cavity; and, as it slumped to the Earth, blinked one last time before its shaggy lids sank shut for good.

Freed up, he risked a rapid glance at Cor—now fighting five orks in a circle of swords—and grimaced. *Gotta go help the kid out.* But first, he'd have to hurry and finish off the latter of this pair of peugbound orks.

Swatting the side of its steed with a spiked mace, it'd gotten the frenzied ferret going again; not so much charging as striving to escape, straight toward the knight.

The panting peug flew forward with terror-rolling eyes directly at Deliad. And, at the pace the knife-nosed beast was bounding, in seconds, he'd be blasted into a brick wall.

Moving aside and shouting at the mount, he got the thing to slow and swerve just slightly; enough that, now, the Knight-Lord managed spryly to slip beside the thing and slash its ham.

The peug, now fraught with injuries piled on injuries, finally collapsed into a twitching pile.

Meanwhile, the maced ork had leapt off already. Darting toward Deliad, it swung the spiked mace, missing his head by a foot, spraying stone shards.

"Can't have our metal helms clanking on casks!" Orther deserved to be decked. And with no helm.

He got his gladius back up just in time to swat aside the spiked mace whooshing toward him, then shoved the ork. He followed with a fast cut; quick but not long enough. His short sword whiffed.

The bludgeon swung now toward the off-balance knight. No way he'd step outside that swing. Instead, he heaved forth, and his shoulder took a haft strike. *Ugh. There's a bone bruise.* But it beat steel spikes.

Deliad retorted with a blow to its breast. But, being so light, the blade bounced off its ring mail.

The ork jabbed forward, and the Knight-Lord struck the haft before the spiky head could hit him. But, being so light, his sword just shifted the angle, so its sharpness grazed his shoulder bruise and gashed him.

And now the Knight-Lord knew: he hated short swords.

Fury sent Deliad's sword forth into the ork; but only an inch or so before it lodged in a big ring.

The ork responded with a swat that bruised his side and poked a couple spike holes.

"In Eremon's name!" he swore, hacked off the ork's hand, and jabbed his enemy—finally—through the eye.

Seems there is something that this sword can stab through!

Meanwhile, the Beldrian took a tall ork's jaw off, so teeth and all fell clattering to the cobbles.

Speechless—well, maybe "gobsmacked" was the word—the ork glared back and tried to roar. But Cor cut that off too. Its severed gullet gurgled.

And so his last of five foes dropped down dead, as Cor spun forth to fight more, faintly smiling.

Well, anyway, it seemed he'd not need saving.

The nearby courtyard was a sea of carnage, peaceful with Sun-glare partway through the storm. But, far off, foaming at the mouth, a wave of sea-green guards was growing and approaching. And, like a mariner marking in the seaspray a swelling wave, who hastens to act before he's heaved and washed away, so Deliad acted.

Hying to the gate crank, he gathered his strength and sliced its steel-link chain in twain, then shoved his gladius through the gears and spokes. It warped and malformed as he forced it through the metal.

He tried the crank. It caught on misshapen steel.

"The finest work you've ever done, my friend!" he hailed his hated weapon. "Fitting end."

The burgeoning orkish wave was breaking on the Beldrian by the time he'd hurried back.

As when the sea sweeps over a new volcano and turns to nothing with a steamy shriek, even as the molten terror grows ever greater, glaring with fervency, so Cor was glaring, erupting in an endless stream of swordplay.

Guess I picked right. Good call, Sir.

From a downed guard, he grabbed a fine glaive. *Looks like Brinsmyth's work. Stolen from the armory maybe?* At the feel of that haft's familiar weight and heft, he wondered why he'd not grabbed the first good glaive he'd found here, and thrown that gladius out. *Well, lesson learned.*

Lifting his warhorn to his lips, he blew. The sound that issued forth was so strong, so broad, the courtyard shook; and Cor cringed at the blast, almost botching a parry in the process.

"A bit of warning, next time?" said the Beldrian, running his last rival through at the neck.

"Have to be ready for anything, eh?" replied the Knight-Lord. "Let's go."

"Right behind you," came the ever-ready Beldrian's answer; first behind him but, in a hop and a flash, taking the lead by leaping over a tangle of guards and glaives.

Following him from the courtyard, he did his best to keep up. But the weight of his newfound polearm widened the speed advantage the youth already had. And soon, he saw a group of ork guards filling in the gap between them, blocking Deliad from escaping.

Grimly, he gritted his teeth to charge through. He lowered his shoulder and his polearm's point.

A plane of radiant red crashed into the orks, scattering them. And the way was suddenly clear.

Feeling a faint grin form against the grimness, he hopped that mess of maces, glaives and guards and ran toward where a ring of twelve bold knights was warring with a hundred foes around them.

"Go!" Deliad called to Cor ahead, spirits surging.

And, seconds later, both had joined that circle.

"Welcome!" said Orther, slicing down a maceman and sliding left to make room for his leader. "I don't suppose you've got some good news, Knight-Lord?"

"Well, 'good' here might be relative!," he replied, hacking a half-ork's hand off, "with a hundred guards trying to gut us. But we got the gate crank."

"Ha! Good enough. We heard that blasted warhorn." He pierced a peug. "The problem with that thing is, its 'help me!' sounds a whole lot like 'we did it!'"

"Don't knock the horn, Sir Knight!" admonished Deliad.

That band of puissant paladins battled on, together with the Beldrian: thirteen brave souls, battered by many more but standing strong, as one united front of spirit and steel.

One front of thirteen; then, it fell to twelve, when Ellrig fell.

Ellrig: a good man, good mind. He'd once had Knight-Lord Einnlund as his squire, and likely a dozen more since. A decent swordsman, at best. But maybe that'd helped make him best at tutoring their beginners on the basics. *"Ellrig would ream you for that!"* mocked the men, when duelists missed a parry or botched a blow, having been reared beneath that same stern rod: firm and persistent but patient and fatherly; a master with a heart. But now a pike had pierced that kindly heart. Down he collapsed.

The next knight lost was Gertrand. Grave of nature since squiredom, he had always done his duty. No excuses: Gertrand always got it done. He was the sort of man that no one knew, save those who'd been beside him many years. They admired how Gertrand went on working while the rest were resting, whether at sparring, hunting, planning for battle or pitching camp. Even in courting his now-wife: treating her to walks, fine wines, and well-planned trips and well-planned quips, showing a waggish charm he'd never shown. With Sibbe, he had two sons now, Cuin and Coenbehrt. He'd prayed that they'd outlive him; and they would.

Brayleigh, now battling from atop a balcony, was spared the wounds that Norvester's warriors suffered, but not their weariness. She barely managed to muster up the occasional shimmering Boundary to block a bolt that would've killed some warrior.

And now, saw Deliad, piling doubts toward Doom, a column was advancing from the castle: huge ork guards, girt in plate with heavy polearms.

He would've liked to die while holding Hoarthaxe. Blessed as he'd been to find so fine a glaive, it wasn't half the weapon Hoarthaxe was: that man-high halberd, flush with warm assurance, flowing from the flame-shaped Fossil in its pommel.

Yet somehow, that assurance swelled even now. And out it flowed as words as Deliad spoke, his deep voice booming from his bloody visage:

"Great glory awaits us, brother-knights of Norvester! For, should we slay the foe and claim the sige, and win back castle, country and fatherland, we win back all from naught. And should we die, now die we, brother-knights of mine, with Norvester! To a single grave we go: our blood becomes one with this hallowed burg, whose holy Earth holds our high Kings of old. Our Kings, we follow in death as life. For life and death! For Norvester!"

"For Norvester!" roared the bloody brother-knights, doing battle by their new-fallen friends and dying, with Sol's blaze in their blue gaze as they bled.

Faced with fair virtue and manly nobility, so manifestly unorkish, orkish faces showed slight uncertainty. Their onslaught slowed, and the encroaching column, clomping till now with cruel grins toward this group, stopped and regarded them with guarded stares.

And when the wave of ork elites went forth to face that levin-bright glare of Norvester's knights, lightning-like flashed those warriors' shining weapons and shocked the enemy to a scrambled welter.

An orkish limb flew here. An orkish liver fell there, and flopped atop old Ellrig's pate like a laurel wreath, with fillets running flankwise.

Thus, tempest-like, the ranks of Norvester raged and battered things beneath them, drowning them in furious clamor and fulgent strikes and fear.

Orther fought tooth and claw and fiercely as any. Within this storm, he was the foam-jawed waves, an avatar of the war dogs of Bangputys: teeth bared and panting, biting into his prey with piercing brutality. Sable blood spilled over him, and Orther's splashed face shone with sunlit grace.

One second, slaying foes; the next, knocked supine by a sword hilt to the brow, bashed half-insensible, blood drooling from between his teeth, still bared.

"Cover the Captain!" called Deliad. At once, the ring of men reformed around their fallen friend. Every man downed made those knights fight more desperately. He grit his teeth at the endless orks; then, blinked.

A huge hulk with a face of tumorous fuchsia—so smashed and swollen, it seemed some vandal's bludgeon had battered out its manhood—was advancing, shoving its way to reach the ring of knights.

A troll? The last he'd seen was when the old Knight-Lord had led the troops to war with Marblot Trollblood at Strig Farth, ten years past.

Trolls were gross things, massive and mostly mindless, save such vices as let them glut and lust their way through life. Said to be offspring of the orks themselves, bred to exaggerate the orks' basest traits, trolls were to orks what the orks were to men: a degraded form of a degraded form. The term "troll" was itself believed to be a degraded form of "thrall." For, being too slothful and stupid to survive alone, most trolls were taken in by the orks to serve as slaves.

Hefting a huge mace, the troll swung it batlike at Bayleth, a survivor of Strig Farth.

Fiery of mood and mien, wild and bright-witted, he was not one to get carelessly close to. He'd nearly been ejected from the Knights in squiredom, after slashing Sithrik's gut open while sparring. Had his steel cut one inch deeper, that hoary warrior would be six feet under. Later that year, though, on patrol with Sithrik, he'd saved his elder from a bandit ambush, slicing down five foes and biting a sixth to a bloody death with bared teeth. That was Bayleth.

But now, when Bayleth tried to block the troll's blow, it scarcely slowed. It bashed his sweaty brow in. And Sithrik saw his squire fall down to dust.

Death, death, and death. He savored breath. *So be it.*

A warhorn bellowed from the blinding west, borne on the Zephyr, billowing from afar.

As man and ork went still and silent, staring, he now heard horses' hooves—not padding paws of peugs, but charging stallions, champing steeds—pounding upon the cobbled path and closing upon the crowd in multitudinous myriads.

And with that martial harmony of hoofbeats mingled a roaring melody of men, with fighting Spirit full-swollen within their breasts and bursting into common battlecry.

A silver glimmer signaled, in the gazes of Norvester's Knights, the more-than-manlike stature of Sigmund, numinous with the Solar nimbus, wroth unto radiance like an angel of judgment, heading the charge of Norvester's horsebound champions.

Faced with this blitz of Norvester's native knights up Capitol avenues toward her very Castle, tilting at full tilt, lances lowered and roaring, the ork guards gawked, dumbstruck and horrified, and dove for streetside cover.

Doomlike neared the Knight of Norvester, dark against the glare of Sol, low-louring on the western welkin.

And woozy guards, giddy with wanton drinking and Gurtag Jidh just seconds past, now sprinted in crying confusion. But the crowds were thick, and there was no escape.

Those polearms struck with such dire power, they pulverized the bones they pierced between.

And mutual terror took the orks now circling Norvester's ring of knights. They spun and bolted, shoving fellow guards, screaming their futile way toward far off safety they'd never reach.

The troll—which just had ripped brave Rauthskegg's short sword from his startled hand, readying a blow that would've reddened his red beard—instead blinked stupidly at shining onslaught. It made as though to wield its mace against the storm and stress of their united movement, and opened its gob to growl some guttural scorn.

Instead, a bright lance lit upon its throat and silenced bestial baseness at the source. And wielding it was more-than-manlike Sigmund, leaning upon his charger in glaring furor, wearing his wolf-emblazoned barbute appalling, with light-doused locks abillow at his back.

The others. Like a lost and cave-lorn wanderer, so long submerged in mirk the Sun's forgotten, he gazed half-comprehending at the glory.

Cor laughed and, brushing off a bead of sweat, looked over at Brayleigh: wiping off her brow and, just now, scanning him, blinking and smiling, her hair abillow and red with western Heaven, illumined sanguine with the sinking Sun.

With eyes closed, Deliad breathed back combat's rush, forcing the daze and dazzle of Fortune down.

He faced his fellow knights. "Fine fighting, men. You're heroes of the realm. Should we survive tonight to see next sunrise, I'll see you wear the laurels and stars you've won here." He scanned the worn but smiling warriors swiftly. "We've still nine standing? Sithrik? Rauthskegg?"

"Aye, but short a sword," the ruddy redbeard said.

"You and me both! Consider it a blessing," rejoined the Knight-Lord. "Why not grab a glaive? Or flail? That looks to be a fine one, no?"

"That's Brinsmyth's work," a weak voice croaked below them. "I made him make that thing for fun. Years back."

Groundward the warriors' gazes went. And, grinning back at that bunch with wan brow, but bright eyes, was Captain Ormslik.

"Funny, eh? Right here, right where I fell," he said. "That same old flail! I stretched and damn near spiked myself. *There's* Fortune!"

"Some find their weapons. Some are found by weapons. It's meant to be, my friend. You're now a flailman." The Knight-Lord held a hand to the ailing knight, helping him flinchingly get to his feet. "That gash looks nasty."

"No doubt. Headache's nastier." He rubbed his head, then stared at scabby blood. "Ugh. Wish I'd had a helm a half-hour past."

"'Can't have our metal helms clanking on casks'!" said Deliad, full of karmic schadenfreude.

"Suppose I asked for that," the Captain sighed.

"Go get that gash dressed," Deliad told the paladin who'd planned this day. "You've done your part today."

"It's not so bad. The bloodflow's stopped. Well, slowed." The Captain crooked his head, then faintly flinched. "Alright. Alright."

Cor clasped his Sun-blazoned flask and held it forth. *He brought his* flask? *My man.* "You want some for the wound?" he offered Orther. "Burns like a forge-fire, but you won't get gangrene."

"I'm grateful, boy. Cor, rather," said the Captain, straightaway dumping some whisky on his wound, then winced again and grunted. "Eremon's name, what do you drink from this? Surgical spirits?"

"Cask strength." Cor took the flask. "Always drink cask strength."

"My man," admired the Knight-Lord.

Sipping whisky, Cor shrugged back. "Eighteen years inside a cask, then dumped out as a disinfectant. Hmph. I had to drink a bit."

"Back to the flask?" Brayleigh had made her way back from the balcony to the circle of knights. Wearing a big smile beneath shamrock eyes and wisps of sunset, waving with the wind above her freckle fret, she wagged a finger. "You know you've gone too far *when* . . . !"

"Have a sip?" suggested Cor. "This stuff's as old as you."

"Smells like it too! No thank you!"

Cor's lips curved up. "Smells like it . . . too?" He eyed the whisky and her.

"No. Not like that, Cor. I'm about to blast you."

"After all that work? If not for all your 'blasting,'" he said, "I'd have some fifteen holes in me."

"Yep! Much as I might like a slice of Cor-cheese, I like you best without a bunch of holes." She didn't miss a beat. "That's three you owe me!"

"Three. Well, I'll work on that. If I'm not sliced, or cheese, sometime before then," said the Beldrian, giddy but good, as early-twenties often are.

Ah, where's the time gone? By the bags beneath Cor's eyes and Brayleigh's, both were feeling worn. But neither looked fatigued as Deliad felt.

"Both of you battled like champions back there," he said. "Without you, we'd have had no chance."

They shared a brief smile.

Then, the Beldrian shrugged. "I wanted action. And I guess I got it." He glanced back at a gash along his calf. "A bit more, maybe, than I bargained for."

"Good thing I handled the bargaining, huh?" The girl from Fernstead finger-wagged the Knight-Lord. "The silver? And the satchel? Don't forget now!"

Now he broke into his own giddy grin. "Every penny," he promised. "Every penny, assuming we survive what's still ahead."

At this, they blinked and opened their mouths.

But Orther already had a hand raised, motioning east toward Castle Norvester. "Knight-Lord. Evening's nigh. We'll want to be inside before the raiders get back from Gurtag Jidh. Inside and set up."

"Quite right." The moment's gravity, momentarily unfelt by spirits flung soaring by success, swelled in his breast, as at the inflection point when someone high-flown starts to fall back Earthward. "Step one is done," said Deliad. "Now, step two."

"Step two?" said Brayleigh.

"Taking back the keep. And keeping it when Lothar's orks come back," he said. "But you two needn't worry about it. You've kept your bargain. Stay here at the base that we'll be setting up. It should be safe."

"While you go battle Lothar? Get the glory?" chid Brayleigh.

Frowning, he tilted his head.

"Not happening," said the Beldrian, steel in hand, Sol flashing on his blade and in his stare. "We'll see this through. Just show the way. We'll follow."

Brayleigh beamed. Deliad's doubtful brow inclined.

The Captain shook his head and chuckled. "Youth: When testing Lady Luck's a way of life! Feels less fun once you get your fifth or sixth blow to the skull. It starts to knock some sense in."

"Seriously, though," he looked now at the Knight-Lord, "I'd planned to join you on this part. But with this"—he brushed his bleeding head—"with double-vision and dizziness, I doubt I'd do much good. And half our band here looks as bad as me." He waved behind him at the bloody bunch. "Maybe these two, plus you, would be our best choice. Frankly, the way they fought, they'd help as much as any two of us. Even at our halest."

"Well." Warm assurance breathed into his breast and bore his Spirit above his lingering doubts. "Well, welcome then! We dared death side-by-side, and valiantly you vied against a fell foe not yours, but Norvester's. Thus you kept your bargain, bestowed the promised benefit and more, being partners to our cause. Now, not mere partners, you fight as fellows of the Knights of Norvester. Now, willingly, you hazard all for naught, except the fairness of our common cause. We won't forget it. Now, you're kith and kin. Your gains are Norvester's, and your good is ours."

At Deliad's earnestness, the duo from far west nodded and glanced, with the faint grins of those who go to a strange place fraught with peril and glory.

He faced the clangorous fray inside the Castle and waved forth, as the wind flung back his hair to fly toward blood-red Sunset. "Shall we, friends? Fate beckons, and the foe awaits our blades!"

"Born ready," said the Beldrian with a fist out. And this time, with a faint grin, Deliad bumped it. *Who* is *this kid? And why's he not a knight?*

"What's that?" the girl from Fernstead asked. "That punch thing."

"Nothing."

Together with the war-worn knights, the trio returned toward the open gate. Where a throng of orkish guards had harried them with bared blades mere minutes past, now silver-plated paladins were spitting straggler orks on polearm points.

"I'll see to it that the gate gets sealed again," said Orther as they went. "Then, work with Sigmund to man the walls and marshal our defense. We're short on arrows; hope the armory's stocked. Seems some of our ballistae have survived, up on the battlements. Glad they're not loaded—this last hour would've been a lot less pleasant—but now we've got to get some bolts. Some stones too, piled on the portcullis wall. Things work wonders when dropped a dozen yards. And I'll set up sentries to keep an eye out for returning raiders."

"All good," the Knight-Lord said. "And get that bandaged."

The Captain grinned and gave a sharp salute, flinching just faintly as he grazed his gash.

"Knight-Lord!" The lively call came from his flank. He looked.

And there was Hoarthaxe, held by Beran, a new knight.

Well, not *new*. The boy had been dubbed two weeks before the Merchant's Caravan took the Castle. Exile seasons warriors quickly.

"Your halberd, Sir. I ran the whole way here. And, here." He doffed the big pack on his back, handing it over. "A cuirass. Not quite full plate. But better than those glorified skins you all got stuck with, eh?" He grinned, hard-breathing, and nodded at the Knight-Lord's tattered leather.

Hefting his halberd's familiar wooden haft, he felt at once the old warmth welling in him, as, correspondingly, the flame-shaped Fossil upon the pommel waxed warm vert on contact. "Beran," he mused, "if I'm alive tomorrow, remind me to promote you. By the way"—he held out Brinsmyth's work—"you want a good glaive?"

The younger paladin sized the polearm up appraisingly, with some approving nods, as Deliad donned the armor. *Solid steel! Slowly the world of what once was returns.* "I've never felt so pleased to gain twelve pounds and lose a well-forged weapon. Well then, onward!"

"Yes, Knight-Lord, Sir!" saluted blithesome Brayleigh.

"Let's mosey," said the Beldrian, blade aglimmer and pointing toward their peril-laden prospect.

Thus went the lively wanderers, with the dead left in their wake, toward life and death ahead, where towering walls and trolls and troubles loomed, and the air was rife with Destiny and Doom.

CHAPTER 13

Night thoughts are the worst thoughts: night thoughts by night lights, unnatural lights that shine the Stars away. Recoiling from this false and lurid light, the mind is lured to false, dark, lurid places. And yet the Warlock stayed awake and read.

The First's own words: the Tomes of Doing and Undoing. He read each tome no longer than the time from one New Moon until the next: a deadline he always kept, though often with some reluctance.

As when a reader finishes a chapter and finds, with some frustration, that the next shifts to a foreign, faraway perspective, he always worried that he'd lose the thread, forgetting it before things tied together.

Yet what he always found was that, returning to an old Tome, he enjoyed it more, not less. And they enchanted him along, these Tomes, with poetic feyness. From the start he'd sensed it, haunting their language like a ghostly echo. The specter of poesy showed in misty moments, as wordplay drifted into rapturous rhythms.

Night thoughts by night lights: wandering, wondering thoughts.

"You, too, will have your pilgrimage through dark," Aislin had said. How truly she had spoken. How sadly ironic—tragic!—that a woman who couldn't suffer Sol for more than minutes had taught him all he knew of lighting darkness.

He wished he'd asked her more while he'd still had her. About her yearslong odyssey after winning the Spirit Trials, and the sites that she had seen: Glaukopis Garden. House Kohkav. Cremaste. She'd sometimes spoken of all her fellow wanderers: Her friend Koyeld. Liluri and Baldred's romance. And Lothar Gatapyl and his unmanning. And all the wide world that she'd roved back then.

Yes, her world had been wide. The Warlock's, though, revolved round something very narrow indeed. Vengeance was all he wanted from this world.

Lenvira. She'd been loathed as much by Aislin as he now loathed her. His vindictive nature made vengeance on the thing he loathed life's purpose. Aislin, in contrast, had handled Lenvira with equanimity he had wondered at.

His thoughts flashed back to when he'd fled the palace, when he had hesitated at that juncture where dead Riotha lay. And he had wondered who else might live and whether he might save them.

And then that boundless voice: *Forward, Chaos Progeny. The Fates will bring thee back. Await their beckoning.*

So, with the Fossil of the First in hand, and the ancient Tomes tossed pell-mell into a sack, squinting against the ruthless wind and world, he'd ridden the shadow into the unknown. And here he'd ended up.

Night thoughts, night lights, year after year. It'd been a decade now. Someday, it'd all come down to one great gambit.

Why not today? he often was tempted. *Right now!* What a relief it'd be: to take that animus that'd animated all he'd done this decade, brewing toward baleful might, and, homeward flying, smite his archrival and glory in her dying!

But no. He'd let the seasons work their work first. Her Summer, soon enough, would wane to a Fall. And in the Fall, the reaper does his reaping.

Stretching, he stood and walked outside the study, absently snuffing the lights with a handwave.

In moments, he'd emerged from bookish confines to a Sea of Stars he'd mapped on high from memory, shining above the subterranean sea. He stared awhile, blank as the midnight blue that separated all those sparkling points.

Suddenly, they sparked a memory he'd forgotten.

Boyhood. He had been bedbound with a fever, the way he'd always seemed to be back then. That afternoon, he'd learnt that Pyr and Dohren had had their Inspiration, leaving him the last in his year who had yet to do so.

Some buds bloom late. But others simply wither.

Aislin had run her pallid palm through his hair, as he lay sore and burning up, his book bookmarked and set aside; and, through the window, he'd stared upon the few Stars he could see.

"For all our fears, the Stars still shine unfaded, and still we approach what's fated," she had said.

That hand—paler than pale, which would be burnt merely by minutes in the light she loved—moving through hair, had passed his prospect's corner, where senses couldn't quite make sense of it; but, even so, could perceive it moving there.

"The morrow's wind will blow upon the morrow."

Faced with the subterranean sea's dark shimmering, he looked to Mother Moon, aloft beside the Gloamy One, lighting the blackness blue.

And, at the sight of those familiar lights, his darkling thoughts gave way to sparkling memory:

"When Winter looses Spring, new life springs forth fresh as ever, however late it comes. When boyhood burgeons and ascends to manhood, wistful, I'll watch my features fade from yours, as does the pink from the ascending Dawn. And, when the time comes, then your time will come, as mine did, as life's seasons ever come."

CHAPTER 14

Compression turns a comedy into farce. The slow sprawl of the good unto the great—striving through struggles and setbacks and thriving, burgeoning from lowly beginnings toward greatness, till goodness beats the once-unbeatable evil—that's comedy. But compress that books-long odyssey to one scene, where the lowly topple and stoop the mighty in a matter of seconds: then, a comedy skips and frolics into farce.

So, Cor smiled at the scene inside the courtyard: Paladins were pricking round the plain and jabbing joust-like at howling orks, who hurried round in futile circles, stumbling drunk and falling. Some lined-up archers stood outside a door and shot the orks occasionally emerging.

Some servants, led by knights and squires, were dashing across the courtyard toward the guarded armory, where cavaliers were setting up a compound. Bowmen kept watch behind makeshift barricades.

Passing a peug that was slumped on its face, the Knight-Lord leaned and, from its nose, tugged out a dripping dirk. He wiped the blood and snot off.

"Something you fancy about that knife?" asked Orther.

"This blade's beaten many a knight in many a match, Sir Ormslik," Deliad said. "Yourself included."

"Ha. *That* old thing? Ah, late nights throwing knives."

"It all pays off in time." He scanned the courtyard. "Sigmund! Fine work here. What's the situation?"

"Knight-Lord," Captain Lofthungrian nodded. "Well, in short, we heard your warhorn, rushed the gate, and found the guards were wasted on your sack."

"'Best sack this side o' River Lahser I reckon,'" said Orther.

"Right," smiled Sigmund. "So, we rode in and rode straight here. The guards were so caught up in Gurtag Jidh, they hardly battled back. Like hitting targets at a tourney. No lines of pikes, no barriers. Scarcely seems believable that these things captured Norvester."

"True," he nodded. "Their type is better at taking than retaining."

"That said," continued Sigmund, "they'll fight back when backed against a wall, as vermin do. We'll face a stiffer fight inside, I think." He eyed the keep. "I've sent some squads inside. Try to reclaim it one wing at a time. Some made it to the throne room but were beaten back."

"Well, we'll go try our luck," the Knight-Lord said. "You're in command out here. Go get that gate fixed. You'll find a gladius stuck inside the gears."

"Knight-Lord," the Captain nodded, and was off, kicking his horse to a trot toward the gateway.

The trio approached an oaken door of the keep, which was ajar. So, with a creak and quick scan of shadows up ahead, they went within and waited for their Sun-gorged sight to clear.

The courtyard's merry clamor faded quickly as they began advancing. But the clangor of steel on steel still echoed from afar, breaking the eerie hush upon the hallway. Occasional oil lamps lit a shadowscape, showing blue moss between the ancient stones.

Some men in mail lay face-down on the floor, and bloody servants, fallen upon their backs, terror still lifelike on their lifeless faces. And in their midst were multitudes of orks, strewn and splayed out in pools of glimmering gules.

A gasp intruded on the ghastly quietude.

A pallid serving girl was gazing on the trio of silhouettes that loomed before her. Hope in her wide eyes died to hopelessness. And, with a whimper, she spun stumbling backward.

The Knight-Lord quickly clasped her shoulder—"Wait!"—and turned her toward him. Now the blazon of Norvester, that crown and fist, showed clearly. "Come with us." And now her pent-up scream instead seeped out as a collapsing sigh and tearful nod.

On finding Foreguard Fundaem's squad soon after, escorting several servants toward the exit, he had her join them. And away they went.

The three advanced for several minutes more. Then, just like that, they stood outside the throne room.

"Well. Here we are," he said.

Strewn on the stones were corpses from a recent clash, still bleeding. A couple knights, one chef, and numerous orks. Beyond the bodies loomed two doors of oak, each twelve feet tall and reinforced with steel bands.

"A little odd." The Beldrian eyed the bodies. "I thought our knights were beaten back. But by whom?"

"That's just what Sigmund heard. Who knows what's happened since then?" said Deliad.

"I suppose." The Beldrian lifted his blade and scanned the slit of light between the big doors.

Deliad ambled toward them and tested one. Instead of bouncing back, blocked by a bar on the opposite side, it opened a couple inches. "Well," he whispered, "time to go get some answers. Be on guard."

Drawing a deep breath, Hoarthaxe held in two hands, he kicked the huge door open and dashed inside, with Cor and Brayleigh bounding at his heels.

The throne was empty. To its fore were five orks, arrayed in tight formation. Two had axes, with jagged edges raised near steel-girt shoulders. The rest had loaded crossbows, leveled doorward.

Before their first blink at beholding this, the crossbow triggers clicked, a trio of bolts were shooting forth, and Brayleigh's palm swung up to conjure a pellucid plane of crimson.

Not quickly enough. It blocked two bolts.

The third went skittering past them. But on Brayleigh's leg, blood beads were dribbling from a deep new gash, showing in red the route that bolt had taken.

Even as he looked back, the ever-ready Beldrian leapt into a sprint and readied a routine: *Swan Approach, Dust Devil.*

Then, red radiance flashed forth, sending the axemen stumbling into the archers, bashing their half-nocked bolts from upthrown hands.

And he was there. *So much for that routine.* Conspiring with the fugitive instant, Cor let inspiration breathe out through his blade.

From dead sprint into Daybreak, darting swifter than the orangish ork could sweep low with its waraxe. And so that sharp gleam disappeared in guts. His blade flashed as he unsheathed it from a body whose blinking lights, even now, were blinking out.

Right went his shining sword in Wintersun, cutting a bowstring in twain with a twang, waxing with daylike dazzle as it did so.

Another twang; and, on his side, a sudden pang. He felt warm moisture seeping down his side.

A halberd reaved the hands that'd fired that bow, and then the bowman's legs. The blade flashed vert as it maimed, and once more as it lamed the ork.

Planting his foot on a near-corpse, Cor vaulted above that falling archer. And from midair, in Tail Ward, he whipped out a Morningway. It rose and stained a startled archer red.

And Hoarthaxe heaved aloft the final axeman with flailing arms and axe, and flung the ork off. Doom was reflected in its downcast eyes.

A few feet from the floor, a shimmering Boundary blasted it backward to strike the King's throne. There, the corpse curled up doglike at its feet.

"Was that quite necessary?" Cor inquired.

"You never know!" the girl from Fernstead giggled.

"In Eremon's name, why is the King's throne cushioned?" The Knight-Lord stared upon the poofy pillow.

"So," Cor said. "Safe to say this was a trap?"

"No doubt," sighed Deliad. "Seems our 'First of Equals' is holed up elsewhere. If he hasn't slipped out."

"Well, we should find him fast then!" Brayleigh said.

"But where?" the Beldrian asked.

"I've an idea," said Deliad, striding toward the doorway. "Come."

The trio returned from vaulted majesty to vacant mirk. The half-lit hallways held some battle remnants: broken chairs, blades and bodies. But they were mostly immersed in shadow and stone.

"So. Where to?" questioned Brayleigh as they walked.

"The West Wing. With the dungeon. And the rooms of Queen-Mother Chelsyth. May she rest in peace," said Deliad. "Easy to defend. Secure. So, I suspect—"

Around the corner roared a scale-mailed ork with scimitar raised. It charged.

The Knight-Lord lifted Hoarthaxe, but its blade hit the support stones jutting from the ceiling.

Cor slipped beneath the halberd—and, in doing so, nearly was hewn at the neck—but got past it and got his sword up, leaping into Thin Ice.

A red wall whomped the guard aloft. It wailed and, grunting, hit its head upon an archway.

Meanwhile, Cor missed it and cut into stone.

"Ugh," sighed the Beldrian, eying his dented blade. "Was that quite necessary?"

"You never know what's needed till it's needed!" cried Brayleigh, blasting it once more for good measure.

"I'm pretty sure that wasn't," Deliad said, scanning the goo pool seeping round the guard.

"So, onward?"

"Hold a moment," Deliad said. He tried the handle of a steel-barred door at the hall's end, but it rattled and held fast. "I want to see who's in the holding cell. Wouldn't be shocked if it's one of my men."

"That, or a troll!" said Brayleigh. But she moved back.

Breathing deep, Deliad barreled toward the door. He struck as levin strikes an aged oak: splintering the centuries-old to a sudden conclusion with one colossal crash, slivery and fervent.

From inside came a cry—*an awfully high one*—but Deliad was already kicking down the half-hinged door, with Hoarthaxe high and ready.

Studying the cell through a sinking haze of splinters, Cor watched a figure form amid the mirk. *Nope. Not a troll. And not a knight, I think.*

Slim, hunched against the wall, long-haired, wan-faced, squinting through slits of ice-blue, she was holding a heavy rock. "Who are you?" she demanded.

"Ha! There's your knight!" laughed Brayleigh. "There's our troll! Don't worry," she assured the woman. "What's your—"

"Stop," Deliad said, blocking her with a stiff arm. If anything, his stare seemed harder now than if he'd seen a troll inside the cell. "Her name? Yes, I can help with that, I think."

The western wanderers blinked and studied her. Days in the high-heaped dust had dulled a blouse of saffron shade as ashen as her fist, darkened with dried dirt and clenched around her rock. The accents on her outfit—maybe blue once—were brown with gloam and grime. But their ascent in spires along her sides perfected in a pair of piercing eyes. Their celestial hue hardly could be more blemishless and blue.

"This, friends, is Celeste Daorbhean: scion of Clausiglade, and longtime orator of the Usurper Lothar. Ten thousand times a traitor to our true King."

As Deliad spoke, she drew her sharp stone higher.

"Oh, *please* do!" beamed the Knight-Lord through his bared teeth. "Give me the excuse to end *this second* what I've waited suffering years to stop forever!"

And now the stone sagged low.

"You asked my name. Deliad Linvarum, at your service, Lady: Knight-Lord of Norvester Kingdom, late and soon. Loyal liegeman of the Head of House Lofthungrian, His Majesty. Whose mandate you usurped."

A fair laugh left her lips. "Oh, that's just lovely." Bitter but fair. "What a beautiful turnabout! Isn't it just like I warned him? The hills, yes? The loyalists that were holing up out there? You snuck in, yes? Some subterfuge or other? Yes, yes, I see it in how you're staring. Well, Heaven's blessings, both on you and all your band. I hope you achieve here what you're hoping for. It's all deserved. Do what you would with me, so long as you do double that to Lothar."

"See how the sophist starts to spin her story!" The Knight-Lord shook his head at the detainee, Doom in his eyes, curling his lower lip faintly. "There's Us and Them; and she's with Us, not Them! Through ten years in the arch-betrayer's troth, amid the slaughter and seizure of my home, she's been a secret ally of our cause!"

"*'It's all deserved'*: it's awfully late to say so, after a shameless decade of deserving! *'Heaven's blessings'*: do you even believe in Heaven? Heaven implies Hell. I'd find that prospect fearful, if I were you. Particularly *now*." His halberd seemed to shiver with the last word.

"Believe me, if you'd like, or don't believe me," said Celeste. "But I *am* inside a cell, you see. I didn't shit inside that bucket for shits and giggles. I've been in this getup for—well, I guess for weeks. Ork guards aren't good at feeding detainees on a daily basis. Hence how I've shrunken from skinny to emaciate. My hair's a haystack."

This was false: the wisps waving above her brow were maybe flaxen, but in those light-stained locks was nothing stacklike.

"And I'm as dust-grey as the guard that smacked me each day he deigned to feed me." She held up her arms, whose sleeves slipped low along her slimness: marred by bruises from mauve to maize and blue.

"You'd put an end to pains I lacked the courage to cut off?" She held up her sharp stone. "Do so! But *do* slay Lothar too. And spare *him* no pains. You'll hurry, yes? He'll likely leave ere long, with all you knights so near. If not already."

"You know," Cor quietly said, "I doubt she's lying."

"Indeed. There's been some falling out, no doubt," said Deliad. "Now, she's turning on the devil who turned on her. An old tale. As they say, 'the traitor's retinue are repaid in kind.' She got her just deserts; and he'll get his."

"That's all I ask," she smiled.

"What did you do?" asked Brayleigh. "Why'd he stick you in a cell?"

"I slew his right-hand ork to stop a rape."

"To stop a—? Ah." Some seconds passed in silence.

"You ever gone together on a group hike," said Celeste, "searching for some scenic spot? You walk and walk, you check the map and walk. The landmarks look a little like they should. Or maybe not. It's tough to say. Time flies. Still, no sign of that perfect spot you're seeking. You wonder: *Did we miss it? Is it still there? Or was it ever?* No one wants to speak up. And, as the day is dwindling into darkness, someone declares, 'Hey! I think *this* is it!' You scan the wild wood, squinting through the shadows, worn, aching, wishing for that wordless thing that'd seemed so close. And you say, 'Hey! This *is* it!' You all agree. You slap some backs and grin. But, underneath that basking smile, you know: *It's not. It's not. Where are we? What went wrong?"*

The Knight-Lord pressed his lips and peered away. "Why are we wasting time with tedious musings? The Merchant's likely absconding as we speak."

Cor *had* once had a hike like that. "So, Celeste. You know where Lothar would be hiding here?" A hike through Launlaufs Wood at age fourteen, with four friends and a folded map, and hopes hopelessly high. *"Hey, look! We found it, huh?"* Vilhyg had cried, as day decayed toward Dusk.

"Queen-Mother's suite," she instantly responded. "And I might know a way there clear of guards. No guarantees on that, though, with this combat." The ring of steel on steel reached even this cell.

"Why don't you guide us?" asked the girl from Fernstead.

"Absolutely not," the Knight-Lord broke in. "Entrust the foe to help us find the foe? No, Madame Daorbhean should be manacled and marched off by the first free knight we find. Then, *we'll* check what awaits in Chelsyth's suite."

"You trust me on the one but not the other?" said Celeste. "Fine then, bind me. Do get going though. You're right: you're wasting time." Beswept with blonde wisps, wild and bright-stared, she seemed some darkling fey. "Plenty of time to execute me after! Or torture, toss me from the tower, whatever."

"Yes. You can guide us," said the girl from Fernstead. At this, the flabbergasted Knight-Lord spun to face her, but she went on blithely: "But! Before that, try to touch me. Yep, go ahead!"

Brow slightly wrinkled, Celeste started forth. She'd just held up her hand when, out of nowhere, a ruddy luster rippled through the air: precisely where her palm had stopped in place, its progress halted by some half-seen plane. Her fair face creased with faint confusion; then, disquiet as, pressing forward, she went nowhere.

A lamp's blaze, in the sheen of Brayleigh's green gaze, furrowing to a glare, began to flare.

And now that hovering blood-hued glow began to slide toward Celeste, slowly as the Sun drifts bloody away amid the death of day.

And, breathing, both hands up now, gaze gone wide, back stepped the First of Equals' former orator, and back again, and back. And now her back pressed back against her prison.

Still it came, incarnadine inexorability; until, face sideways to the solid stone, she stood stock-still, as hard light squeezed her cheek and both breasts flat.

And then the Boundary faded. And to her hands, breath heaving, Celeste slumped.

"So!" Brayleigh beamed. "I trust you. Just the same though, you take the lead. And I'll be right behind you! Be quick, but not too quick. You never know what you might run into!" Red flashed to her fore.

"Right," Celeste breathed.

The men exchanged a glance.

"Right," declared Deliad. "Lead on."

So, she led.

Down narrow ways they wended, with the deathsong of steel and steel forever close but unseen. Some of those shadowy passages seemed mere crevices and crannies till they'd entered, and most were thick with dust; some with moss too.

"I haven't passed through half these bloody holes since pagehood," muttered Deliad, ducking under a sagging bulge of stone bricks from the ceiling. His grousing held a hint of grudging praise.

As Celeste headed round a bend ahead, back flew her hand in a brief halting motion.

"Is—?" began Brayleigh.

"Guards!" came Celeste's call.

Cor's grip went tight around his hilt, as Deliad cursed quietly, glaring hatred down the hallway, crouching and holding Hoarthaxe at the ready.

"Intruders are ahead! Come quickly!"

"Yes, Milady," came a gruff growl. Bootsteps now, coming back toward the corner where the wanderers were waiting, squeezed nigh-helpless in a slim hall.

The Knight-Lord now looked wroth unto the verge of bursting violently around the bend with blade already swinging—first toward Celeste, and then the orks that she'd betrayed them to—but, frowning faintly, Cor held up a finger and grasped his arm. And now the Knight-Lord's glare fell on the boy from Beldria. But he halted.

The bootsteps grew to bootstomps. Then, two guards appeared ahead, with weapons at the ready and grim haste in their gait—and kept on going, with Celeste back a couple feet and following.

Passing their passage, she gave them a glance, and threw her hand forth in a frantic wave toward Lothar's two unwitting troops ahead.

Nodding back, fleetfoot Cor was off at once, with Deliad in his wake. He took the right, tiptoeing toward a poleaxe-hefting hulk. He leapt the last few steps, with Luna's Question flashing out leftward, just as the ork was leaning to see that faint sound's source.

Through nape and neck swept Beldrian steel. It stopped just shy of Celeste.

She flinched as orkish sanguine slimed her brow, flung by inertia from the swooping blade.

Then, Hoarthaxe smote the other, whirling backward just as its brain was being slopped off in twain. One segment plopped a foot from Celeste's foot.

She let a long breath sigh out swiftly. "Thanks. For trusting me. I think."

"Thank *you!*" grinned Brayleigh, brushing some goo from Celeste's ashen brow.

Heading down one more hall and up some stairs, they stopped at seeing huge double doors ahead.

"He's there," said Celeste, pointing. "We had planned to hole up in there if enemies breached the gates."

"A stupid place to pick for Lothar's last stand," the Knight-Lord said. "He'd try one final travail, facing his foe—in the Queen-Mother's closet? What, boldly wielding weapons from her couch? With thin walls? Windows opening to the courtyard? We'd wreck this room with one ballista bolt!"

"You could. But, bear in mind," she calmly countered, "*you didn't do that.* That's because—precisely as we'd predicted—you were so persuaded he'd copy your kings, hiding in the throne room behind a bunch of beavered guards with glaives, you'd surely not assault the queenly closet."

The Knight-Lord rolled his eyes. "Well, aren't we lucky we found a turncoat to correct our error."

"You know," said Brayleigh, "now is maybe not the best time for debating tower defense!"

The King's and First of Equal's foremost agents both glanced away, abashed; even grinned a bit.

"Well, anyway. One knight could knock these doors down," Deliad declared with a dismissive wave.

"Maybe before we bolstered them with steel bands," said Celeste. "Want to try and barrel through? Please do. But I'd suggest—"

"I have no time for this. Are you two ready?" Deliad asked.

"Always," Cor answered.

Brayleigh cocked her head and donned a cool and Cor-like posture. "Always!"

The former orator eyed the three, incredulous, but followed as they neared the reinforced oak.

"Oh, by the way." The Knight-Lord looked at Celeste. "Good trick with those two guards. Don't try that here. If it seems *slightly* possible you've betrayed us—well. You won't get the benefit of the doubt."

Lips pressed, she gave a little nod.

And now, he faced the doors and breathed: deep out, deep in. A low hum swelled about him, shivering stone, as his weapon waxed vert. Toward the doors he strode.

Hoarthaxe fell. With an emerald flash and fell roar, it slit the narrow space between the doors. Some steely shrieks of protest sounded, but the blade bore through and sliced into the stone floor.

And now the crew were kicking open the doors and dashing in to see what loomed beyond.

Two orks: beside the entrance, poleax blades thrown back, and stepping backward in their shock, whirling to face this metal-hewing hazard.

They never had the chance. Cor chopped one's head off, lashing out leftward with Luna's Lament, then slashing rightward into Sol's Rebuke. The latter left the sentry's helmed head tumbling, smacking the ground with jaw still going agape.

The rapid arc of Hoarthaxe reaved the other, right through a rerebrace into the ork's breast. Bleating sheeplike, the half-halved ork spilled sidelong, its liver flopping out and showing a big blotch upon its bottom left.

Our heroes hopped over the dying into Chelsyth's chamber.

Here, the decor harked back wistfully to a time that'd never been but always beckoned backward. Long-tasseled tapestries sprawled across walls, and oaken furniture was fraught with inlays, depicting fancied days of damsels fair and doughty knights: curtseying and clasping palms; weeping and watching, setting off on quests; daring the dragon's lair and black knight's bane; living out life's inherent love and war in ideal form for the actual to aspire toward.

"Wow!" gaped the girl from Fernstead in a whisper.

Beyond this beauty stood a hideous foursome.

The leftmost was a hunchback hulk: a monster, riddled with tumorous pro-trusions and skin stains. Its offhand was a hook. The other hefted a huge scimitar of sage and olive hues. Its platemail was a shamble of steel, stuck pell-mell together crudely in torso form and fused.

Monstrous, deformed; yet disturbingly manlike. The jaw upon that foul face was a square jaw. Its nose was merely a nose, if a mite bent. Its brow, though splotched mauve-black, was like the brow some drunken sculptor might've mar-bled forth, excusing faults as ruthless realism.

Beside it skulked a pair of shifty things. They matched that monster in some ways: hunched deformity; moley brows blotched with melanin; foldy flesh; and beady eyes, with soulless glassy gazes.

But they were three feet tall; twig-armed and stick-legged; so jittery they were jumping foot to foot. One had the hue of veins, the other arteries. But both had splotchy irises the shade of parched piss, flicking furtively about. Each sometimes giggled, as a moment's gravity sometimes can squeeze a giggle from the anxious.

And then the man himself. "Ha! *What* an entrance!" He clapped four-fin-gered twice, then twice again, face wrinkled with a grin of grand grotesquery, shaking his head at the hostile quartet: Cor to the fore beside Deliad, blades bran-dished in bright diagonals, glaring, crouched for combat; Brayleigh and Celeste behind to their sides with fists clenched, fair brows furrowed at the foe.

And from his chaise lounge, Lothar peered on high, where heroic saints in tempera paints basked heavenly. "Oh, I *so* hoped we'd have this scene!" he sighed, "with one of you: the Knight-Lord or my orator. But even I never *dreamed* that both might be here. They say the world is small; why, it's a marble! I hold it in my hand! How do you do?"

"Better with every breath and every death," smiled Deliad, lamplight on his blade ablaze and glaring in the skyscape of his gaze. "Poor present company. But I look ahead to leaving with a head held high soon. Yours."

"Oh, you *are* everything they said you'd be!" declared the Merchant with delight. "It does feel fine—flattering!—to know you have a foe who's such a pro. I'd feared you'd start this business with some 'surrender now, in Norvester's name,' what have you. Making me the chump who put down some second-level champion like a stray dog. Heavens, who would bother writing such a history?"

"But you bring company too!" the Merchant chattered. "The more, the merrier. What are you two? More knights?" He studied Cor and Brayleigh for a second. "No, no. The boy's too lax. The girl's a girl. This *is* the Knights of Norvester, not the Academy. So, not knights; knight-adjacents then." He smiled.

"I say, you did a number there on Nauz!" He flicked his ringed hand toward the headless corpse that Cor had hewn and hopped a moment earlier. (The lips of Lothar's orator curved up slightly.) "And you, Sir Knight: you chopped Blugth like a tree trunk! We'd shared some fine philosophy together, young Blugth and I; you timbered him. Too young."

"Well," Deliad said, "since we're all introduced now—"

"*And you!*" the Merchant sharply plowed on, cutting through Deliad's repartee and pushing it aside like dirt before the plowshare blade, his gaze agleam like rusty iron in noon's glare.

"Celeste Daorbhean: Most favored of my friends. The First of Equals' first. My fellow traveler, with whom I broke bread, tilted back the cup times beyond count. The fair-tongued wonder worker. Your words' work made it worthwhile: all that suffering, Summer after Summer and Winter after Winter, when we would wheel about on bumpy roads; feign flattery for aristocratic idiots; teach them the virtues of the various trash collected in that dump we called a Caravan; and, by the alchemy of commerce, convert our dirty dross to silver with a sale. All with your aid. You and me, me and you."

"Is it to kill me that you've come here, Celeste?"

The bone-thin orator eyed her former boss. "Really, Lothar?" she said. "You're taking that tack? The friendship tack? Well, I fear *that* ship's sailed—"

"Now, hold a moment, humor me." He held up a hand and shared a sympathetic smile, as might a father to a fuming daughter. "I'd hoped to have this talk tomorrow, Celeste, after your month of immurement was over. I'd meant to say: He'd earned his sentence, Ruptorg. Your retribution was—well, rough, but rightful. What's wrong is wrong and must be punished."

"Still, law must protect the process of the law. Above all, when we deal with life and death. Or so it seemed to me. So, just a month of jail—not execution—for a murder. A month. And, as you might've guessed, I told the guards to ensure that you were amply fed, had garb aplenty, had a pillowed bed, and suchlike. So I'm somewhat vexed to see you in such a state. Forgive me, but you're looking *awful* for someone so aboundingly beautiful. In Heaven's name, Celeste, *what* has happened here? A sort of hunger strike? If I had known . . . "

"A 'month,'" she smiled. "So sorry to surprise you ahead of schedule. But I *had* to show you how 'hunger striking' helped my figure. Fine, yes? How each bone makes its bony presence known? Doubtless, the bruises from my daily battering look less fine. But I've 'garb' to cover that; yes, garb aplenty! All that garb! Such garb, I carpeted the floor and covered walls with garb!"

"I'll give you credit where it's due: I orate for a living; you, for life. You could convince a slave she was a sovereign; then, get the girl to give you *her* last sovereign! Yes, you could get a burgher to believe that life's good lies in casting off his goods, to give them to the poor; *and* you're the poor! The Powers make life from naught; we, from the womb; but you! You've made a life from lies! Creation by the creative word: 'Let there be lies!'"

"Heartwarming, brilliant lies. Your words are like the rotfire on a fetid pit, which flares bright only as long as foulness lurks beneath it, feeding the lively flames with deadly fumes. Such is the gas light whose glare gives your evil some smoggy semblancy of goodness. Sickening: yes, I've been sick with you since girlhood, high on your flamboyant supply; with nothing higher to aspire to, from our lowly life of luxury, than breathing in the fumes of fiery lies and basking in the empty highs they bring."

"Your sermons on 'the oppressors' and 'the oppressed,' 'leveling what's high' and 'lifting up what's low,' 'the forward march toward future weal,' and so forth: just so much fervent haze for us to inhale, so we'd hallucinate a brighter future and fail to see your scheme for what it was. You'd kill a people and consume its corpse, as fungus first afflicts, then fells, then feeds. This city's ways, you've seeded with your orks, which first lay waste, then feed upon the waste, like fungal blight. And, at the blight's heart, *you!* Your cushions and 'collected' wines: a corpse, left by the city you slaughtered." She grabbed a guard's fallen glaive and faced the First of Equals.

The Knight-Lord now was looking Celeste over like he'd beheld some angel from above—or below—and he was still not quite sure which.

"*So* good!" the smiling Merchant marveled. "I swear, you could sustain a metaphor for a full *scene!* But then, that's all 'truth' is—a metaphor that sounds good—and the sort who seek the truth will stretch one metaphor forever farther to try to fit the world in. Folks like you. Myself, I'm fine with strewing motley similes, and making my realities as I go."

The wanderers from the backwoods west stared blankly.

"Ah, worry not." He gave a gracious wave. "That wasn't for you. Anyway, I won't dispute you, Celeste. Statesman's first rule: never debate before an audience of your enemies! They'll boo your wit and cheer for shit. And then, they'll tell the world you lost! And what's the use? I don't deny that I'm the man I am: living for moments, from moment to moment, finding my consummation in consumption.

"The way I see it, a city freshly fallen is like the fresh-fallen snow. We'll stamp it down and darken it soon enough to something dismal. But I'll sure savor its beauty while it lasts! And after that, well, there are *lots* of cities. Plenty of pleasures to last through my lifetime." He sipped a wine as richly purple as royalty.

The Knight-Lord's knuckles now were white with clenching his halberd's haft; his gaze, an azure blaze.

"Now, back to you." The First of Equals fixed a wide smile on his weapon-wielding foes. *"Here's* what I have for you. Some introductions, one great big brute to another."

"To my side"—he gestured leftward at the hunchback hulk—"is Shaetnoes. Shaetnoes! Don't you love their names? If Shaetnoes seems familiar, Celeste, well, he should. He's Ruptorg's relative! Lazy eye, those patchy things, the bulgy brow. I see it. Their mother was the same half-ork. Stayed busy: this big guy's father was a troll! One wonders, *physically*—well, I'll stop there. Ever seen how a huge snake slithers in the *tiniest*—no, I'll stop."

"So, Shaetnoes here inherited his father's size and strength; his mother's smarts (which is to say, he'll follow a simple sentence); and nearly a man's skill with that massive sword. Isn't that right?" He flashed a father's smile at Shaetnoes, which was scratching at its nose. "Really, we ought to rear a *breed* from your brood!"

Itching a flesh-fold, the great mongrel grunted.

"Anyway, we'll plan that roll in the hay another day," the Merchant mused, now turning to face the mini-monsters to his flank. "This puissant pair, right here, are Rot and Rut. These twins are *goblins*—get a load of that! This far north! Knight-Lord, you know goblins, yes? Smitten several, yes?"

"So, this dynamic duo—I daresay, these rambunctious runts—run faster than any fellow I've ever seen on two feet! And I've done lots of seeing. You ought to see the hellhole these sprogs spawned from. Well, you *won't,* but such is life. Or death, as it were." He shrugged.

"That is"—he showed one finger—"you'll see no more, unless you turn around and traipse on out! Mind you, I may just do the same. We'll see. Depends, frankly, if all my orkish friends are four miles out or fourteen miles. I've heard both. Orkish reconnaissance, need I say more?"

"What's certain is, a good five thousand guards, fresh from the Gurtag Jidh, are faring hither with all the haste their mangy mounts can muster. And, puissant as you pricking paladins are, I doubt that you're prepared to deal with *that!* Nay, Knight-Lord?"

"As for you." He smiled at Celeste. "All this, I do for you. Not good Sir Knight-Lord; who, candidly, has given me *lots* of grief. Insufferable, that spirituous chivalry and suchlike. As for you, well, I still like you. I won't insult the intelligence of a lady—things won't work like they once worked—but I *do* pray you pull through. Whether with this yokel pair and pompous paladin, or in other parts. Not at my side; nevertheless, alive. Maybe my mercy's friendship, maybe it's folly. Or maybe friendship's folly is made of mercy, like living means being made of blood that bleeds! In any event, it's yours, if you would have it."

"I'll pass on mercy, but I'll take the blood," said Celeste, staring rapt upon the Merchant. Behind the starshine of her brow-strewn hair, her gaze declined to a glare, even as her lips laid tooth and malice bare. And Celeste looked as darkly bright as desolated midnight: the glory bared by gloom. On gauntness lay a glamor fair and fey. Her mien was Doom.

"My soul's been bled from me by a decade's sins, being the mere means to your mordant ends. Now, I look without what I've long been within. See this? This ghastly skin cadaver-grey? The little death-spots wanly darkening limbs? The brow that lacks life's flush? These fingers: bones! You see? What lived in me is bled dry. Now, naught lurks within. And nothingness wants filling. What slow sin bled from me, I'll bleed from you." A glimmer showed the sharpness of her glaive.

"Bravo!" clapped Lothar. "Bravo. I've long felt that it'd be fine to go out with some fine words and fine red wine. And, Heavens, have we had one!" He sipped his purplish potable. "Now, the other. *Fine* vino. Celeste here can vouch for that."

The Knight-Lord stepped forth. "Now, if you're quite finished—"

"No, not quite yet," the First of Equals cut in, fiddling inside his furry cloak for something. He lifted up a foreign "L"-shaped object: a foot-long sable tube of fine-graven steel, with what might be a hilt of whittled wood aslant from one end.

"I *did* cherish, Celeste, the way we'd share our stories of the Academy. So little learning this far north! But yes, you know that spire not far from Grape Divine? The Hall of War? Where King Promethean found all sorts of ancient gadgets, way back when?" He waved back absently toward way back when.

"Well, *this* was part of *that* stash! Pretty penny, it cost me to procure the thing! It wasn't for sale. But, truly, all things are for sale, royalty and loyalty and relics alike," the Merchant mused, fondling the fine-etched metal. "Here's something even *you've* not seen, Knight-Lord, no?"

"Why are you wasting our time with this trivia?" the Knight-Lord asked, his halberd keenly alight.

"Here's why." He pointed the "L"-shaped thing at Deliad and pulled what looked a little like the tickler beneath a crossbow.

What ensued was not a bowlike twang but a stentorian bang: a fire-flare from the front of Lothar's sidearm; Deliad's dive sidelong, swift, but not as swift as flame-flung death; and, in the Merchant's eyes, a gloating gleam.

And then, a floating gleam that rippled bloody red. A metal pellet fell to the floor and plinked innocuously.

Now, finally, Lothar showed an honest feeling: the blanched face of a man who, having woken and left behind the nightmares of his long sleep, suddenly beholds their shadow to his fore.

"Like Aislin," murmured Lothar, near-inaudible. "An animist? *You?* But Lioss was . . . " Trailing off, he looked appalled on Brayleigh's bright-eyed blitheness. "Who *are* you?"

"Oh, 'the girl's a girl,'" said Deliad. "She's here as witness for an execution; witness or headsman. We'll see how things roll. What matters is, a head's about to roll." He moved toward Lothar, Hoarthaxe in his hands.

"Attack!" commanded Lothar curtly, flinging his half-full cup, which suddenly seemed half-empty, at Deliad, who deflected it with one hand, his deadeye stare not swerving from his mark. "I said, *attack!*"

At this, colossal Shaetnoes, its slack stare lighting up, lumbered and clanked toward the Knight-Lord, bellowing out a battle roar.

Faced with some five-hundred pounds of brute bulk, Deliad slowed down. He'd have to deal with this, then Lothar.

As the half-troll drew its blade back, then swung it in the expected sweeping arc, he slanted Hoarthaxe's haft forth for the parry.

As when a big squall blasts a sapling tree, whose trunk holds fast, even as its roots are torn from earthly moorings, so it tilts and topples, its hairy nether parts exposed perforce, its majesty abruptly made absurd, so Deliad toppled back. His top half fell even as his bottom seemed to spin and hover, with feet flown up and kicking toward a Heaven far, far beyond his reach.

He hit the floor breastplate-first, then his unarmored behind.

He rolled in time to dodge a downward slash, denting the stone where his head had been lying, then kicked himself to his feet with one quick leap.

The half-troll looked surprised its sword had stopped, instead of splintering through the halberd's haft. "I make man mash and dip my bread in you!" it bellowed, brandishing its big scimitar.

The Knight-Lord watched and waited, warier now.

Meanwhile, from Lothar's flank, the goblin twins flashed toward the wanderers impossibly fast.

Racing toward Cor was Rot, wielding a knife wavy and narrow. Red-faced Rut was dashing toward Brayleigh and whirling high a leather lash.

Waiting in Tail Ward, blade tip low behind him, waiting until his tiny foe came close, Cor swept up into Talons Closed.

But, leaning, the goblin sidestepped, hardly slowing its sprint, and now was close enough that it could stab.

Exposed, momentum twirling him away from his target, gritting his teeth, Cor kept spinning.

"Don't do an attack that leaves you no defense. But if you can't defend, at least attack," Aldartal often said.

From Ox Horn, spinning past his stabbing foe, blindly, the Beldrian sliced backward and down. Dust Devil. Risky. It would end a duel. It'd end a life. The problem was, whose life?

No one's, it turned out. Round the Beldrian's bicep wrapped a long lash and jerked his arm awry, exposing him to a jab from his opponent.

Desperate, yanking the lash and lasher with him, Cor dodged left.

Not enough. He felt that poniard puncture his vest and the flesh just beneath.

But, just as steel was slipping toward his liver, a rippling plane of red blinked into being and struck his stabbing enemy. Like a gnat borne off by a breeze, the goblin flew away.

Freed up from battling two foes now, the Beldrian whirled right toward Rut, tugging his lashed arm toward him, so his foe tripped forth.

The whip slipped off his arm just as he lifted his longsword in Rage Guard. And, one step shy of being in range, Rut stopped and spun to run away.

Retreating would've worked against most foes.

But fleetfoot Cor, flinging himself to a slash—Squinter, a falling, false-edged strike—caught flesh, severing some sinew and nicking its lung.

Choking a grunt off, the goblin jumped sideways, its side now seeping like a jammy egg, narrowly dodging Cor's follow-up Mountain Goat.

Cor couldn't chase it. Its brother was back, sprinting toward Brayleigh with its blade outstretched.

She sent a blood-red Boundary streaking toward it.

It dodged around it, canceled through its inertia and heaved itself into a stab.

It struck. Deep into Brayleigh's flank the dagger drove. A half-voiced shriek gasped out, her gaze gone wide.

And, as the wavy blade withdrew, she hunched with sunken head, hands upon her side, her freckles stark in the bloodlessness blanching her cheeks.

Before the mortal second strike could come, before his mortal sense made sense of the instant, the Beldrian blindly flung himself five yards. His blade was overhead; his foe, below him.

The goblin, blinking dumbly at this flying foe, dodged sideways.

Not enough. Cor's day-bright blade caught the thing's offhand, hewing off its top half. And, like Dawn, flinging forth her rosy fingers, a ruddy rush of sanguine splayed and sprayed.

Amid this clashing chaos sat Lothar's chaise lounge, still and untouched at the eye of the tempest, save a slight spot where blood-hued wine had sloshed. There, Lothar still was sitting, smiling mildly, unruffled, save his ruffled pantaloons.

Celeste loured toward him like a thundercloud. With wild-tost tresses, eyes like slits of sky amid the massing of the hosts on high, she seemed an agent sent from stormy Heaven to treat with dusty Earth.

"Well, how now, Celeste?" He held a hand out toward his erstwhile orator. "Finally! A chance for talking face to face; nay, friend to friend. No pointless, posturing nonsense. Straight to the point. Straight to the matter's heart!"

"The only point I'd make is with a glaive point. But, yes, the heart's precisely where it'd go," Celeste replied. "Prepare yourself!"

"Hold! Hold." He held a single finger high. "You get one point, I get one too. Fair, yes?" His unctuous tenor drifted over din like an oil spill over a sea.

"I *get* your point. The reality of our rule falls rather short of what you'd hoped—of what *we'd* hoped, in fact. Frankly, you're right, in fact. We *have* lost sight of why we'd done this. We've a lot to fix. So, what's the next step? Fix it? I would like to. Or let this Commonwealth collapse to a Kingdom?"

"They'd knock it down, those knights. You want *that* then? We strove to climb, but slipped. So, quit the climb? We took two steps, then backstepped once. So, run *back?* Call me a fond fool, but I say, step onward! To fix a Commonwealth gone wrong, do it *right.* Don't break it back to a Kingdom. Call me a builder!"

"Funny," said Celeste. "Far as I can see, breaking's about the only thing being done here."

"Oh, come. I'm owed *some* credit, yes?" cried Lothar. "Converting pubs to kitchens for the poor? Food for the hungry? Housing for the homeless? Misguided? Maybe. *Breaking?* Bit harsh, maybe? Give me some credit!"

"I'll give you my all, if it includes the misery you've given me."

"Ah!" Lothar leg-slapped. "I'll be stealing that one!"

"Go for it. See how it goes over down under."

"My, you're a *factory!* You make up your one-liners faster—" He lifted his sidearm and fired.

A blast erupted from the blackish barrel, and an explosive burn transpired her belly: one second, heat; the second, pain past sense.

Heedless of bright blood spilling from her fore, reduced to her contracting ken, her future contracted to a single loathsome point, she lunged and stabbed forth with her polearm's point.

It pierced the First of Equals through the throat.

Gurgling with wonder—gaze gruesomely wide and fixed upon a royal purple fountain, burbling about the gleaming polearm point, and mingling with the purpure majesty in which this merchant, kinglike, cloaked himself—from proud enthronement, poised aloft his chaise lounge, fell Lothar prostrate to the lowly floor.

So too, a snowflake in the Spring, fell Celeste: melting away before she'd made the wonder of sparkling fairness she'd been meant to make, into a pool proceeding from her ruin.

Deliad's resolve was dissolving as well. With flesh wounds aggregating gradually toward one great agony of weariness, he felt his frame object to every slash and dash. The half-troll pressed him harder and harder. Respites were rare; and each brief lull, like Somnus, beckoned him warmly toward a black oblivion.

Seeing a slight opening, he lunged forth and stabbed—not noticing, till half a second late, the way his foe was waiting, hook hand low with hunched knees.

Bending back with Deliad's blow so it grazed against a steel-girt breast and slid past, Shaetnoes hooked Hoarthaxe's haft and flung it flankward, leaving the Knight-Lord exposed and in range.

And now its sword was sweeping toward his neck.

He heaved himself into a backward bound, his upper half flying faster than his lower, the way that one leaps backward onto a bed.

It saved his life, but not the strip of sinew above his armpit, where the notched steel slid and brushed off flesh bone-deep.

He hit the floor, first with his back, then his boots and bare skull.

Beholding through a haze the Sea of Stars, he faintly saw the shade of some behemoth. Semi-insensate, Deliad dove away and, at once, heard a huge scimitar strike stone.

Heaving himself to his feet, a headache waxing as stupor waned, he pushed the pain aside.

Shaetnoes was on him at once, scimitar sweeping; like a big broom that's confronted by a dust bunny, which simply won't be swept up, but instead is brushed and blown annoyingly away, refusing still to be reduced to refuse.

Methodically, the monster swept its scimitar one way, then the other. Not exactly artful, but skilled enough that Ellrig would've shrugged and turned his tutelage to some other trainee. At eight feet tall, with arms and legs like tree trunks and nearly twice a man's reach, who needs art? Art's how the needy make do mid their need. When mere skill and a wealth of might will win, why waste time fiddling with fine points of art?

Deliad, for his part, artfully avoided the big sword's blows. But art gets arduous quickly. His breath grew short. Each dodge became a struggle. Sometimes, with balance off, he had to parry, nudging that notched blade just slightly aside. Each blow sent impact-shivers through his body.

He noticed, absently, the half-troll's onslaught followed a pattern: right-high; left-low; left-high; right-low; right-high; and so on. *Here* was something that Ellrig would've censured. "*I don't care* how *well you swing that damn sword. Fight in patterns, you get predictable, and then you die,*" he'd chid Squire Dag, who'd learnt that lesson well.

Biding his time, he lay low: all defensive, the way one fights when barely warding off a dire barrage. *Right-high; left-low; left-high; right-low.* He let the big sword barely miss him, letting his breaths heave loudly from his breast. *Right-high; left-low; left-high; right now.*

The blow came low and slow. And Deliad's blade was *there*, not nudging it awry with fine finesse: smiting it with the full force of his might. And, shedding vert-lit mist, his man-high halberd struck rusty metal and shattered it to shrapnel. His blade bore on toward Shaetnoes' nose and sheared it, together with some skull-bone underneath.

Shaetnoes blinked down at its bisected face, and then its bladeless hilt, a baffled "*how*" leaving its lips.

It didn't even try to dodge as Hoarthaxe halved its head and torso.

The Knight-Lord, overwhelmed with weariness, fell floorward, one hand forth to catch his weight. His eyes scrunched, burning salty with his sweat beads. The melee swam in circles. His whole frame ached.

Meanwhile, Cor chased the dagger-wielding goblin. Repeatedly, he outran it and was readying a fast cut—only to find it was swerving into some nook where his sword couldn't swing. Its hewn-off offhand dribbled blood behind it.

Giggling madly, it wiggled under a couch arm, so Morningway cut futilely into a cushion.

Thinking quickly, Cor tried to shove the sofa and crush the thing against the adjacent stones. But it'd already hopped atop the back and bounded off.

Sometimes, amid this madcap chase, it spun with stabbing knife outstretched, kicking off walls and flying, acrobatic, at Cor's face. Once, such a jab almost jellied his eye. Since then, he'd slowed down from a full-blown sprint.

And now a whip snapped, inches from that same eye. Throwing his head back, he halted midstride.

What? Smirking in the corner of his prospect was Rut, whip whirling circles over its head now, looking as hale as a rat in a rubbish heap. *How?* Last he'd seen that goblin, he'd just reaved it. Now, the only sign of that was scabbing blood.

Rot seized the moment. Darting toward the Beldrian with dagger raised, it tried to sneak a swipe in.

From Iron Gate, spinning from its short blade's ambit, he whirled on into Wintersun, his sword slicing right, rising and shining and sinking.

The goblin twisted to the side in midair. Cor's sword caught sinewy bonds between its ribs, but not the organs underneath.

The bluish foe backstepped, one palm to its blood-spilling side. It hissed at Cor some incoherent curses.

Crack. Sharp sound deafened his eardrum, just the left. At first, he felt a tickle on his neck's left; and then it felt both boiling hot and bone-cold.

And then he saw the leather lash flick backward, as red-browed Rut prepared another blow.

Within that second, through the bloody Beldrian, from somewhere, surged a burst of inspiration.

He was already spinning, sword outstretched, before the whip snapped forth. And when it came, nearly in slow-motion, he slashed through that coil.

Before it fell, he was already hying toward Rut.

Surprise began to register upon its brow. Its whip-arm now was rising, but much of what had been its whip was missing.

The swordsman now was nearing slashing range.

Rut's beady eyes went wide. It backed away.

Rust glimmered. And the goblin's brother Rot plunged at the Beldrian from a sofa's back. Its wavy blade was pointed at his heart.

Rot flattened on a faint red plane. It flew back over the sofa and smote the stone wall. It plopped down in a spindly heap and lay still.

And Rut was now within the Beldrian's reach.

The Glare of Day that glimmered from his longsword fleetingly lit the bounds of Chelsyth's chamber, as steel lit brightly on flesh and black blood spilled. The instant shone upon Cor's spirited stare, glaring above a grin of perfect sige.

The light of life went dark within its eyes.

And, in a flash, he whirled to face its brother. He bounded lionlike over a thick-stuffed sofa, his sword upraised to strike even as he soared.

Somehow, the goblin—again!—was now stirring, grabbing its dagger and starting to stand.

But down bit Beldrian steel before it rose: bit down with dread force, lionlike, severing brain from brainstem, lobe from lobe.

And down it slumped, as lifeless as its brother, both mere dust.

Strange stillness suddenly lay on Chelsyth's chamber. Some bloodspray shone upon an oaken inlay. Blood reddened the furry rugs beneath their feet. Some blood pools shone upon the ancient stone, dimly reflecting the firelight from dying lamps.

And, under Celeste, hunched now on her knees with hands upon her belly, blood was dribbling like water under a white birch after a deluge.

Brayleigh, too, softly held her bloody side. But she was flush with sanguine, and she rushed toward Cor like lifeblood back to a beating heart. "Wow! You were something!"

"Well done," Deliad said, holding a closed fist forth. "This how you do it?"

And Cor confirmed it was, bumping that fist.

"That *thing* again!" cried Brayleigh. "What's that punch thing!"

"Couldn't have done it without you," Cor answered, gingerly giving the girl a big hug.

And, freckles fading into a ruddy flush, she beamed back and forgot about her question.

"Hey." She withdrew and held his hands in hers. "That's four you owe me now." She giggled giddily.

"Couldn't have won without you *both*," said Deliad. He turned to face the fiery-spangled skies, shining through thin embrasures on their battle. "The rest of us were doing our oathbound duty. But you!—you hazarded your health and youth to make a dead realm's dreams of living real. You bled to fill the blot bowl of her future."

"Well! Far as we're concerned, you're all cool too," declared the girl from Fernstead, grasping Cor. She leaned a little on his firm left arm. "So long as Leitath's Pass gets cleared out pronto!"

The Knight-Lord laughed. "My friends—my fellow fighters—you'll find that Norvester never breaks her vows."

Breath caught on a constricted throat: a whimper, from where, with head hung low upon her knees, Celeste was hunched in blood, holding her belly.

The exuberance of their giddy win went grim.

"We have to bind her wound." The Knight-Lord looked about the boudoir, lifted Lothar's cloak of kingly purple and cut a lengthy swath.

"I'll help! I have some herbs to slow the bleeding. And purge impurities. Amaranth and campion, rattlegrass, cudweed," Brayleigh rattled off, while poking through her pouch and rushing over. "Gimme the cloth! I'll put together a poultice. It's good he had a glass of water here, not just the wine. I doubt wine disinfects well!"

"If, uh, you want some whisky?" offered Cor, extending forth his flask of cask-strength spirits.

"No need. The herbs will work for now," waved Brayleigh, readying their rudimentary bandage deftly and wrapping it round Celeste's bleeding belly. "And spilling whisky straight into an intestine might not be wise, you think?"

"Well. I defer."

The girl from Fernstead did, it seemed, know something of herbalism. She bound and tied the bandage. Its purple promptly darkened, bloodied wet. But, merely a minute hence, the bloodflow faded. The moist spot at the center stopped expanding.

"You think she'll be okay?" Cor quietly asked.

Curled in a lamplit crouch across the room beneath her wild-strewn hair, she seemed a Star with weak rays waning westward as the Sun rose.

"Good question. Never know with gut wounds. Deep ones are worst. Usually mortal, always painful," sighed Deliad at the suffering former orator. "Funny, the way when archfoes fight beside you, suddenly, you worry about their wounds like friends."

"Maybe that makes her a friend then!" mused Brayleigh. "*She* was the one who whacked Lothar, remember!"

The Knight-Lord blinked at Brayleigh, at a brief loss. But as his tight-pressed lips began to part, a woman's voice broke in. "Don't worry about me."

The Beldrian looked, then blinked.

Celeste was standing, one palm upon a chair, the other pressed upon her womb, squinting away her wound's pangs. "Just—let me grab a glass of water, please. And then I'll go wherever you're all going."

She started cringingly toward Lothar's table, where, undisturbed, a clear cup sat half-full.

"You sure?" The girl from Fernstead studied Celeste, tipping the cup back and cringing with pain. "Why don't you claim a couch, lie down a while? I'm sure they'd send the surgeon when they could. I know my herbs are good, but not *that* good!"

Setting the glass down, she drew some short breaths. "I doubt this surgeon has the time for *his* men. Let alone one of Lothar's crew."

"That's true. His hands are full," the Knight-Lord evenly affirmed. "For what it's worth, they say a righteous death redeems all wrongs. Perhaps it's for the best. If now's your time, you'll be remembered for your role today, and not the years before."

"Deliad!" cried Brayleigh. "Try to have a heart!"

"No, girl. The Knight-Lord's right. I'm grateful," said the former orator of the First of Equals. Her wistful stare was trained upon the Stars, but peering back on shadowscapes long past. "Some gravity suits the grave." She sipped her water, as wistful eyes went dim as Lethe. "Let's go."

She followed as the Knight-Lord led them out. Not that she didn't know the way. She didn't want them to see the way she hunched, and held her wound and winced, and leaned upon the walls, squeezing her hand upon the stony roughness. Somehow, its sharpness soothed her belly's pangs.

"So, where to?" wondered Brayleigh. "We all done here?"

"Back to our base in the courtyard," said Deliad. "The armory's safe. This area seems secure, but best to treat the whole wing as a war zone till troops have scoured the grounds for any stragglers, taken prisoners, and—"

"The prisoners!" whispered Celeste, palm to her lips. "We have to help the prisoners. The plan was, if the keep falls, kill the prisoners; don't let the enemy get them. Gaol guards know it. Some knights are there." Her voice, at first near-toneless, was full and forceful now: once more, the orator. "Knights. Liegemen loyal to Reginald. And the like."

"Well, guess we'd better hurry!" Brayleigh said.

"Yes." Deliad looked at Celeste. "Guess we'd better. How many gaol guards, Madame Daorbhean? Two?"

"Likely just one."

"Well. To the dungeon. I'll lead," said Deliad. "Cor, keep Celeste to your fore."

The girl from Fernstead scoffed. But Cor complied.

Scrunching her fair eyes and forcing herself, hand to the wall, along the dim-lit hallway, she followed by the sound of Deliad's footsteps and blurry shadow of his striding figure, seen through the agonized slit of her gaze. She grit her teeth against the gloom encroaching upon its corners when the pangs waxed worst.

None saw that grimace: not the western wanderers, watching her halting progress up the hallway with lamplit bloodspray in her tousled tresses; and not the Knight-Lord, loping at the forefront to find and save his fellows from confinement, scanning the grounds ahead with steel-sharp glare.

So, facing struggle past a struggling face, three heroes hastened from the harrowing fight that'd put away the People's Commonwealth, to help the harrowed people it'd put away.

CHAPTER 15

The walk across the West Wing to the dungeon wouldn't take long, with the Queen-Mother's suite being further along the same route from the throne room.

The grunts and cries of combat with the ork guards had died down—likely literally. What calls came echoing now, down corridors fraught with shadow, were warmly aglow with choleric sanguine: that familiar feeling from the sorts of men who make a living ordering chaos by force.

Coupled with this new lightness was the light of oil lamps, mostly ignited now, restoring to moody halls remembered majesty. That same light showed the fey and eerie splendor of motley shades of moss, from sage to seafoam, creeping from cracks in the centuries-old stone.

The same glow glinted on the sable goo spreading and seeping under orkish guards, like worms flushed out by a storm to face Sol's glare. It glimmered on the mail of men made martyrs, like Stars to count their people's future offspring birthed from the fertile blood they'd sacrificed.

It shone, as well, on Celeste's pallid stare through pain-scrunched lids, and on her belly's blood, still seeping through her poultice. Palely it shimmered as she progressed, and bright pain waxed and waned, like Luna moving through the midnight blue.

"This way," directed Deliad, down a hallway that ended in a bend ten yards away. "We ought to—"

Round the corner walked an ork: a spindly specimen, standing five feet flat, wielding what looked like a longsword gone limp and droopy, with a wobbly, leaning blade.

With drunken stumbling gait and sagging gaze, it took two steps. Staring forward, it stopped and double-took, and shook its head and squinted.

Already, fleetfoot Cor was hopping Hoarthaxe and closing on the groggy guard, blade high.

A red plane whacked it backward into a wall. Its droopy sword struck stone, breaking the blade off.

Not sure if it'd survived that flying impact, Cor finished off the Swan Approach he'd started, thrusting into its throat.

And heart-hot blood spurted directly into his face and doused him.

He spun and spat and retched. The skewered guard gurgled.

"Was *that* quite necessary?" Brayleigh questioned.

"The legendary bloodlust of the Beldrian!" Deliad declared. "No battle's won, they say, till a Beldrian fighter tastes the blood of foes."

"Ew," Brayleigh said.

Cor lifted from the fallen guard's belt a key ring, flaky and russet with recent corrosion. "You know which one?" He tossed it to the Knight-Lord, who sifted through the keys and seized the cleanest.

"Well. Start with this one, then we'll see," shrugged Deliad, continuing down the dim way toward the dungeon.

From round the corner came some muted speech, unclear, but in the smoother tones of mankind. A moment later, cell bars could be seen. The Knight-Lord and his fellow neared the prisoners.

As, from a tentative silence, an orchestra swells during tuning toward a common sound, so worried whispers swelled toward happy harmony: "It's him!" "It's happening!" "Knight-Lord!" "Eremon's name!"

Cor shook his head to see the prisoners' state: ribs caging forth; eyes drooping deep-recessed; unclad, save loincloths and, from top to toe, the sheen of sweaty months made dull by dust. In one far corner lay the forms of men strewn on the floor and moldering semi-fleshless. He grimaced but did not avert his gaze.

The girl from Fernstead did. She faced away, face wrinkling. Then, she raised her brow at Celeste; who, gazing groundward, breathed back all the black spots abruptly swimming in her watery eyes.

"Let's get them out." Cor glared like Sol Ascendant on crimes of midnight come to light with morning.

"Indeed," the Knight-Lord said, scanning the cells. "Just let me look first. There were felons here, murderers and robbers and rapists and such. Last thing we need is to let them out now."

"No. You can let them all out." Celeste looked down. "When we arrived, we emptied out the prisoners."

"'Emptied' them out?"

"Some, set free. Others . . . not."

The Knight-Lord looked at her and curled a lip. He sighed and started opening all the cells, beckoning the inmates out with outstretched arm.

Most of the haggard men who hurried out were Knights of Norvester, judging by the way they hailed the Knight-Lord, nodding and saluting.

"Men," Deliad said, "much as I'd like to tell you to eat some food and find some beds, and lie back, I fear we've got a few more hours till then. You don't deserve this. But I have to ask you to take whatever weapons you can find"—he waved toward where some spears were racked nearby—"and follow us to where we've pitched our camp: the courtyard, where we've fortified the armory. There may be combat on the way. I'll lead. I'll fight as many by myself as feasible, with Cor's help here, and Brayleigh's help. We'll fight. But I'm afraid we might need your help too."

Tears sprang from eyes that hadn't seen the Sun in many months, as dew begins to bead forth at Dawn on dry fields when a deluge looms. "Aye, Knight-Lord.

Aye, we'll do that," said the knights, steeling their thin-starved arms for wielding arms, and seizing spears in fingers skeleton-skinny.

"Clausiglade!" called Celeste suddenly to a prisoner.

The man was wearing what had been a gown of maybe mauve, before dust-grey had claimed it; as it had claimed his hair, hanging down thick with weeks of dust-dried grease around a bald patch. But, unlike all the knights, he had no beard.

Celeste's grin glowed upon that scrawny man.

On seeing that smile, his wan face warmly furrowed. "Celeste!" he gasped, clasping her two hands softly. "Oh! What alone has made my life worth liv—"

The Knight-Lord seized the scholar by the shirt. Lifting him one-handed, Deliad strode wallward and slammed him backfirst into stone-hewn bricks. His weak neck whipped back, and his head hit next.

"Gurgh!" came the guttural whimper from the former Steward to the King and Treasurer to the Usurper.

Dazed, Clausiglade's gaze declined toward fiery Deliad.

"Look who we have here!" hailed the happy Knight-Lord, "wobbling about in the spineless snake's way!" He shook his hand a bit to show his meaning, and, to and fro, his captive flopped compliantly. "*This* flaccid tube of flesh here fucked our Kingdom. *He* birthed the evil that was Norvester's death. *This* thing conceived those crimes against the Crown! Look at him, wobbling like a flame-licked wiener! What's wrong? You've come so far; don't flop short now!" To Clausiglade's throat, he held the tip of Hoarthaxe. "Well, here's one hard tip. Time for consummation!"

"No!" Celeste screamed. She shoved a path past Brayleigh and seized his arm and pulled. But nothing happened. She balled a fist and drew it back to punch.

Casually, Deliad blocked it with a bicep, then shoulder-shoved her, stumbling, into Cor's arms. "Restrain her, please," King Reginald's foremost paladin commanded, dominant as the Blazing One aloft the west, squared with a Wandering Star.

"No! You don't know—! You never—!" she was shrieking, struggling against the easy grip of Cor; who, unsure, glanced back at the girl from Fernstead.

"Hang on now," she enjoined the knight. "Who's this guy?"

"I'm glad you ask!" Doom lit the Knight-Lord's glare. "This sniveling, low-born, wormtongued, blacksouled mockery of manhood, quavering in my hand, is Clausiglade: the Steward that sold our Kingdom to the Merchant. This very Clausiglade, here, convinced our King to end the Hergas and the border sentinels. This very Clausiglade stood at Lothar's side, that black night halfmen captured Castle Norvester, standing so close they breathed the same foul air! This very Clausiglade stood and watched the orks savage my kin at the seat of our Kingship, wasting our women and men; even the monarch this very Clausiglade vowed, in Eremon's name, upon his life, to honor and uphold. *This—very—Clausiglade!*"

With the last three words, thrice slammed the scholar backfirst into bricks, head bouncing off, then hanging dazed and dull.

"Is that so?" Brayleigh asked Celeste, stare gone narrow.

"It's . . . " Celeste trailed off into a shut-eyed headshake, sagging in Cor's iron clasp. "His goals were good. He worked to stop the worst things. Lothar jailed him. He's not the man you think he is. His heart—"

"Oh, don't mistake me! He's no *man*," said Deliad. "On that, we're eye-to-eye. But 'good goals'? 'Heart'? Tell me this traitor didn't doom my Kingdom! Tell me he's not the heartless malefactor who left my motherland exposed and powerless, then pulled her legs apart for orkish rapine! Tell me my sight is mistaken, seeing that archfiend flopping in fear of rightful retribution! So tell me or stand aside. For I've beheld the blackness of his deeds and his designs, and you'll not lighten them with your fair-faced lies. So tell me now, or see the fury of Fate!"

He shoved the starving scholar stumbling floorward, falling on forearms too scrawny to stop his face from smacking stone. He hefted Hoarthaxe—that man-high reaver that had made this realm from blood and moil a half-millennium past—above the wretch who'd almost wrought its ruin.

"Don't!" Celeste howled hysteric. "Bind him! Beat him! Banish him! Make him a slave to your monarch! But don't slay *him!* The one man with the heart to—"

"No, daughter." Clausiglade, bleeding from his brow with hanging head, was holding forth a hand. "I felt a need to fix life's unfair flaws. But, doing so, I became the very unfairness I sought to end. Worse, only now, I see those flaws we 'fixed' were merely a broader fairness I didn't see, being blindered by belief. And, worst of all, my fair, frail, faultless child was misled by me to be a means for black ends. Don't strive to save me, Celeste. Just forgive me." He turned to Deliad. "Sir, I pray you, spare her. Celeste was simply a child led astray. She has a fair excuse. I don't. I'm ready."

"You'll face your Fate, at least, like something manlike. Fine! Maybe you'll find mercy in the Mists!" Deliad declared. "Doom comes. Prepare yourself!" Fire blazed upon the high-borne blade of Hoarthaxe.

Celeste screamed.

And Cor seized the Knight-Lord's left arm.

"*Yes?*" yelled the would-be executioner, whirling to face the blinking Beldrian.

"Don't you think," said Cor unsurely, "crimes against the Crown this serious should be dealt with by the King? You think he'd want to see the sentence done? Say something, maybe, to the man who crossed him?"

The Knight-Lord looked at Cor for ten full seconds; then, lowered his weapon. "What you say is true. Your motives? Misplaced. But the words are true." He turned to Clausiglade, holding Hoarthaxe's tip to his throat. "Step one foot out of line, you'll lose it. *Breathe* one stray breath, and it'll be your last," he said. "Heaven help me, but I hope you do!"

The former Treasurer for the First of Equals stood slowly, hand upon the skeletal ribs above his heart. "Much more than I deserve. Never too soon, though, to study deserving. And so I'll do." He turned to Celeste, sighing. "Maybe I'll make some small redress to you too."

She hied to the bedraggled scholar and hugged him, bawling, burying her sorrow in his shoulder, hiding her tears under starshine-hued tresses; but, as she clasped him close, recoiled at once, her hand upon her belly's bleeding hole, breathing away a dizzy spell of darkness.

"Celeste, you're—what this—?" cried Clausiglade and pointed, squinting through shadow at her seeping torso. "I'm no sage, but I know enough to know, that's serious! You need surgery! Stitches! Something!"

"That's where we're headed. But Celeste," said Brayleigh, "wanted to stop here first to free the prisoners."

He looked down at himself, with eyelids drooping and lips tight; then, peered forth with parting lips and fist held tight. "Let's hurry then! For her sake."

And so they hurried, from the dungeon's dankness back to the hallway heading toward the courtyard, where setting Sol was beaming through the embrasures.

Along the way, they found that Foreguard Fundaem, with several armed squires, had secured a storeroom fraught with ripe cheese and fruit from farms nearby, which they were piling into a couple carts. And, in a moment's mercy, Deliad sent his starving knights, set free from months' immurement, to guard those squires. "Make sure the food's still good. I order you to sample it thoroughly."

"Aye, Knight-Lord. Aye, we'll do that," grinned the knights, rubbing their concave bellies under bare ribs.

Rounding the corner as they left the room, passing a plaster bust of some stern king, with sentimental smiles and thoughts of supper, the last thing they expected was the ork facing them from the corridor's opposite end, holding a scimitar in its shivering hand. Its eyes rolled left to right in fearful frenzy, then halted on the humans down the hallway.

It paused, then roared and rushed upon party, its crude sword pumping and its platemail clanking.

Adopting Plow, Cor readied See the Roses.

A heavy object brushed beside his head—the plaster bust he'd passed a moment prior—and sailed beyond him toward their ork assailant. Smacking its brow, the kingly countenance cracked.

And, by the way it flopped back to the floor, a sheeplike "baa" escaping from its lips, the ork had likely done some cracking too.

Forth dashed the Beldrian to finish it off with Luna's Question, cutting open its torso. Its entrails spilled all over in shitty breach. Strangely, observed the Beldrian, versed in livestock, there didn't seem to be a liver inside.

"Who—?" Deliad blinked round. "Brayleigh, did you throw that?"

She shook her head. "Nope! It was him!" She pointed at Clausiglade.

Deliad raised an eyebrow.

"Bless me, but that was satisfying," the scholar said.

"Nice throwing arm," said Cor. And Brayleigh giggled.

"Extreme luck," waved the adoptive father of Celeste. "I do believe that that's the very first violence I've done on a two-legged being! I observed it like a rule even: 'Do no violence.'" He eyed the smacked, cracked corpse. "So much for that!"

"'Rule number one,'" said Celeste, smiling slightly. "'Never give up what's genius for the rules' sake!'"

"Ha! That's a Starlingism, yes?" recalled the scholar.

"He'd applaud you," Celeste said.

Onward they walked along the lamplit hallway, feeling a little weightless with this levity. Some mingled talk and merriment and laughter echoed along the corridor from the courtyard, where servants, knights and squires could finally savor the warmth of triumph as victory's violence waned.

"We did well, didn't we?" Brayleigh declared.

"That, you certainly did," the Knight-Lord smiled, "you wanderers from the west. A doughty bunch. May no man ever doubt it!" He faced Aldartal's student. "On that subject, while you'll still here, I hope you'll find some time to train my knights and squires some more in swordplay. If half my men had half your sword skills, why, we'd drive out all our orks like Beldria did!"

The boy from Beldria smiled. "The Master of War would love to hear that. He's the one who taught me."

"'The Master of War.' Man! Even your titles top ours," Deliad admired; as, to their back, a breath drawn sharply drew a glance from both the warriors.

They saw that Celeste, who had fallen a bit behind—being helped along in shuffling suffering by Clausiglade's scrawny arm—was staring backward along the hallway through the wavering shadows.

There, forming from the mirk, a five-foot figure was sprinting into sight, one long arm lifted.

No: one short arm, wielding a stubby spear. And under its blotched brow was a wicked leer, aimed squarely at Celeste's wide-eyed, wounded fairness. As was the spear.

She held a helpless hand out. Her other palm was pressed upon her belly.

Instantly, fleetfoot Cor was sprinting full-speed, his longsword throwing gleams off with his gait.

But even the fastest runner born in Beldria, a full twelve yards away from wounded Celeste, couldn't have reached her before that barbed iron.

Yanking her backward behind him and stepping before her, her adoptive father faced the charging ork guard; just in time to take its spearpoint in the center of his ribcage, right through the back, but stopping shy of Celeste.

Snarling, the halfman shook its weighted weapon, struggling to slide this wobbly skin and bone off. But it was caught in Clausiglade's bleeding heart.

Celeste was shrieking with eyes wide as Luna.

Brushing beside her, the Beldrian leapt into a long thrust with a longsword flashing fulgent: the Glare of Day, alighting in the gob of this growling guard.

It flopped upon the floor, reduced by a blinding flash to breathless dust.

So, too, flopped the adoptive father of Celeste, that hard spear sticking skyward from his heart.

"What's the—?" Brayleigh was saying as she turned to see the screaming's source; then, gasped and gazed.

Celeste was hunched with one hand to her gut and the other over her mouth. She faced the blood mirror forming beneath the man who'd been her father, after the murders of her mother and father. And, from the shifting flame-sheen on that blood, spilled from a man who'd held her in his heart, a carnival reflection of her figure waved, as it seeped from the world she could see toward one where all she wanted seemed to flee.

Amid the little wails that were her breaths, the others stared in silence, watching Celeste crouch toward the transfixed frame of Clausiglade, falling upon her knees in the issue of his heart. And, leaning over him, she seized his hand in both of hers, heart bared within her eyes.

Reflected in her stare, that wan face showed a weak smile, with its eyelids not quite shut. It moved no more. But was there something moved by her full-Moon stare, her tears like falling Stars, her Star-stained hair that fell upon that face like Dusk upon the dying day, departing that corse to join the daily westward course of Heaven eternal, guided by her gaze?

If so, that blasted body didn't say so. And Celeste's tears, like holy rains of Heaven, sank into dust and soon had disappeared.

All this beheld the Beldrian, dumb and blinking. What should one say, when any word one uttered would be like soil upon a still-open casket? There may be a man who could transmute the dust of mundane words to tear-dispersing water. But, if there were, he surely wasn't Cor.

Well, he would do what he could do. He watched for foes, one calloused hand upon his hilt.

Hearing a murmuring to his flank, he glanced at grim-faced Deliad, who was mouthing phrases just faintly audible over Celeste's sobs. He caught a handful—"Sol's spite, cleaving blades, night's shades as grieving Luna fades"—before the Knight-Lord looked away through an embrasure, where, beyond reach past the blackness, shone starlight.

In time, a troop of squire-attended knights, sent out by Orther to secure the West Wing, marched in upon this scene. So, Deliad sent a couple squires to fetch a suitable litter to carry off the corpse with. Such was done, as Brayleigh, made of moist-eyed sympathy, held Celeste's hand and spoke mellifluous words. They warmly washed upon the sands of sorrow like waning tides, which take some grains away, but always leave that bare beach no less there.

Eventually, an elder maid—assisting the exhausted surgeon with his ceaseless mending of wounds unending—saw the way that Celeste was holding one hand to a bloodsoaked belly. And, in a blink, that white-haired woman slipped an arm beneath her arm, and waved away her protests that the pain was not so painful. She led off Celeste, who was leaning on her.

Orther had strode in several seconds earlier, with words of import brimming on his lips and white gauze mummy-like around his brow. But, seeing the wounded woman shuffling off, he'd halted, with his head askew and squinting. "Was that. . . ?" he started, staring first at Celeste, then Deliad.

"Yes, indeed," affirmed the Knight-Lord. "The world's a stranger place than we imagine. They say 'the foe's foe is a friend.' But, Heavens, what do you do when the friend's the foe too?" Watching her hobble off, hunched, he winced faintly. "We'll worry later what to do with her. Anyway." Deliad peered away, then back at the bandages about the Captain's brow. "Fine hat you've got there."

"Got it custom-made, courtesy of the surgeon. Snug fit. Quite snug. But that's the way they're worn, he said," mused Orther.

"Least you won't lose it."

"Or my life."

"That too." The Knight-Lord's lips curved up. If he'd been told, half a day prior, he'd capture back the Castle—with fewer knights lost than when they'd *lost* the Castle!—and, in the flower of triumph, feel strangely sorry for two top minions of the treacherous Merchant, he would've decked whatever blockhead said so. "So. What's the status out there? Walls secured yet?"

"Secured and archered up. The city's sealed. With Gurtag Jidh, they'd kept a skeleton crew to man the wall walks. Now, they're all—well, skeletons," confirmed the Captain. "Save some straggler guards, fleeing from gate to gate, finding them shut, gradually getting shot down by our bowmen."

"Good show. And Sigmund's group?"

"So, *there's* a story," the Captain smiled. "His crew rode out to hunt some orks who'd fled the fighting in the city. Vanquish them now in their fragmented flight, before those ragtag bands reform to an army."

"So, Sigmund's men head out a half mile West. Lo and behold, they find *five thousand* orks, marching atop that same cliff that'd concealed our own men, while they'd waited for our signal to ride upon the city."

"So, he sees this. And what does Sigmund do? He gives the signal to charge: to ride right toward that ork-crammed clifftop."

"So, what do these five thousand fighters do? Stand up against a hundred men on horseback? Nope! In the black of nighttime, some bright fellow, hearing the hoofbeats and the battle cries, pisses itself in a panic and leaps from the blufftop. You know, fifty feet or so. And, like a bunch of lemmings, others follow! A few at first. But, as their numbers fade, suddenly the leap's looking better and better for all the rest. And then the riders strike, with screaming halfmen skewered on lances left and right. And promptly the other guards give up and take the plunge! Plop! There's an orkish *legion* lying with broken legs along that bluff!"

The Knight-Lord laughed and looked upon the ceiling. "Most triumphs, we have to work for all too much. Sometimes, the Powers make up for that like this."

Meanwhile, the Beldrian meandered down the corridor, more crowded now with crews of knights and squires, securing ever more of Castle Norvester from ever fewer and fewer ork stragglers.

Finally. He'd never felt even half so sore from fighting; none of those bruising months of trading blows with the Master of War. This weariness was keener, much as the steel that'd wounded him today was keener than the wood Aldartal wielded.

He smiled away a sigh. And, letting go, letting his wary stare sag briefly shut, letting the warmth of weariness indulged seep through the limbs that'd borne him through the struggle, he headed from the hallway into a side room: out of the way and small, with one slim window, where one could gaze upon the boundless gloam. That blue void beamed with peepholes from beyond.

At some point, Cor should probably see that surgeon—his wounds *did* hurt—but, at his core, he felt fine. Better with every smiling, shut-eyed breath, and every time his two eyes opened to Stars. Stitches and bandages could wait a while.

For now, the balm of memories old and new, mingled to unguency, would do: His memories of meandering mid the vert-hued hair of Earth, his blade's hilt in his hand, both back in Beldria and heading here with Brayleigh by his side. Memories of days spent dueling with Aldartal, sparring with Knights of Norvester in the circle, and battling for his every breath today. Memories of downing that first dram of whisky he'd helped distill, how hotly it'd hit his gullet while gracing him with superabundant scent, and how the girl from Fernstead's face went wrinkled whenever he opened his flask and took a tipple. Memories of sinking into a simple bed, whether within the big loft back in Beldria or in a tight tent on the Sightful Hills, and how the numbing warmth of weariness washed balmlike over his aches when eyes went shut.

Memories familiar and foreign, flush with feeling, mingled to something amorphous and healing. Such is the power of memory's panacea, to turn the strife and struggles of the day to consolation in the dark of night.

"Hey," called a girl behind him. And he turned.

The pallor of Luna lay upon her face. The corridor's lamplight left her red locks coruscant. Her green gaze bore a queenly blaze. And yet those mirthful eyes were girl-like too. She seemed—not hesitant. No. But waiting for her next step.

Warmth breathed within his breast and through his limbs. "Hey. Care to stargaze?"

"Watch the Stars with Cor? Of course!" She slipped beside him at the embrasure.

Silent, they stared for a moment. And then, "You think we're safe here?" Brayleigh softly asked.

"I think so."

"Oh? How do you know?"

"I know."

She stared at him, then snuggled into his side. They stared together on the blue beyond, as when a pair of seabirds light upon a lone rock to regard the sounding sea: one foot of land, two beings of air, and broad sea.

"Hey." Brayleigh now was beaming up at Cor. "There's something on your neck. It's sort of purple. A smudgy thing." She pointed, and he felt it.

"That's where the whip hit. Back in Chelsyth's chamber."

"I *adored* that room," she sighed. "But yeah, that neck welt. Know what it looks like?"

Glancing downward at the girl, he found a puckish, puckered grin upon her face. He smiled away a sigh. "I think that I can guess."

She giggled happily. "You know what'd make it less conspicuous, Cor?"

Shifting his shoulder-length hair so it hid the blotch, he pointed. But she shook her head.

"No. This." With puckered lips, she leaned in neckward, lifting her palm and closing it toward Cor—then, whispering a *wha-chik*, she cracked an air-whip and tapped his neck's far side. "A matching set!"

She teeheed happily as he shook his head. "You need some help, just let me know! I'm here!" And Cor could hardly help but chuckle quietly.

"One way or the other," she spoke softly, "I'm here."

He stared at her. And in her glimmering gaze, facing him with the window at his back, he glimpsed himself, reflected with a glow: one mere man stretched to fill a Sea of Stars.

Reaching, he clasped and held the hand she'd raised. "A matching set," he smiled.

And so did she, with all the beaming beatitude in her aspect brimming within the Wandering Stars above: paired across blank blue distance past conception to light our lives with blessings past perception.

He felt that heavenly grace within her hand; and felt, then, all the world was going as planned.

CHAPTER 16

Luna had waned a ways west across Heaven, closing with each hour on the watery Crab, as the Evenstar sank beneath the skyline's blue, before the western wanderers saw that surgeon.

"Yikes, lass. You slip and take a tumble on your sewing scissors?" he had lightly asked, on seeing how far that steel had pierced her flank.

"Gimme those surgeon's scissors and I'll show you *exactly* how I slipped!" she'd lightly fired back. "Or, better yet, a big old rusty knife!"

"Ay ay ay," smiled the man sadly and sighed. "You're likely younger than my daughter, lass. Bad enough seeing a bunch of knights with holes. This breaks my heart. We'll get you sewn up straightaway."

Celeste, as well, had been sewn up by starlight. And, given the severity of her gut wound, they'd offered her a rare spare cot to sleep on. But she'd begged off and waved away the bedding. Now, she was seated with her back to a birch tree, hunched with a hand to her cloth-covered torso.

Hard to discern if her eyelids were shut or simply sagging with an Earthward stare, from here beside the bonfire, Cor observed.

A half hour earlier, Brayleigh had suggested Celeste come join them by the jovial blaze. But, like an ailing cat, she'd looked away and slunk back further in the birch's shade.

"I'll need my knights, this next week, to defend the walls of Norvester from the waves of ork guards going home from Gurtag Jidh," the Knight-Lord noted, rubbing his hands warm by the radiant woodpile. "We'll also have to escort the King here soon. The man's still bedbound on the Sightful Hills."

"Then, straightaway," he nodded at the wanderers, "I'll see to it that a squad is sent down south to liberate Leitath's Pass from Lothar's forces. If they're not gone. Orks gladly plunder and pillage, but only guard with dread of death to goad them."

He turned to face the faint austerial gusts. "And then, unless you'd like to join the Guard—the offer stands!—you two can take your trip to the Academy. Why you'd want to go there, good kingsman kids like you, I've not a clue." He grinned. "Still, as I said, we keep our word."

"That works," the Beldrian said. "We'll want a break, after that business." He thumbed toward the castle. "Mind if we borrow a room or two meanwhile, once we get settled? Just a place to sleep."

He laughed. "Cor, you could have a suite for life, with 'Cor Volucre' engraved on gold outside. Yes, you'll receive a room. And you too, Brayleigh."

"Watch out, we might just accept that first offer!" Brayleigh said blithely, eyes flashing mercurial. "Like, could I have that cool room Lothar had?"

"Queen-Mother Chelsyth's suite? Um, I suppose it's unused. May she rest in peace," he mused. "Anyway, we'll be sure to find you something."

"'Who seeks, receives!'" affirmed the girl from Fernstead.

The simple Beldrian shook his head and smiled. "So, how long is that trip to Leitath's Pass?"

"Man on a mission, eh? A few days' ride," Deliad replied. "Then, you're at the Academy. What brings fair folk like you to such a foul place?"

"Wow, you sure hate it, huh?" said Brayleigh. "Why?"

"Eh," waved the Knight-Lord, "you'll see soon enough."

"We need the Academy's archives," answered Cor. "The reason why is—well, a longer story."

The Knight-Lord eyed the bustle all about them and shrugged as though to say, *We have all night.*

Cor reached inside his satchel and retrieved the Sun-shaped Fossil of Dievas, shining aureate, aswirl with mists. And now the Knight-Lord's brow raised. "It all began when I was back in Beldria, walking along the eastern Boundary, when I found a gap: a way to leave the Fragment."

He told it all: how he'd been tailed by peugs, taken shelter overnight in shadowy tunnels, discovered Dievas, and been charged to bring back the Elements. He recounted how he'd roved east, run from a band of orks and battled one, met Brayleigh and Fyraett, and been told to seek more insight into the Elements at the Academy.

"And so," concluded Cor, "we went that way till bandits ambushed us, and then some orks. And then some cavalier coursed in and saved us."

"Lucky you, eh?" said the Knight-Lord. "You know, that stuff about the Elements: Schoolkids learn that, or learnt that, here in Norvester. How the Elements, in old times, flew through Heaven and flung down flames, wiping the Ancients' world out. How, since then, they've faded into Fossils for the most part. Funny, they say before the Pandaemonium, there were no orks, no peugs, no trolls, no goblins. What a weird thought, eh?" He waved at the carnage and corpses littering Castle Norvester's courtyard.

"Well, not for Mister Beldria-Doesn't-Have-Orks!" Brayleigh replied.

"True. Heh. And we were proud too," said Deliad, "when we drove the orks far north—scattered them through the knolls and sent them screaming, flying into the farflung wastes beyond—a decade past, beneath my predecessor, the Knight-Lord Einnlund. But the things bounce back, if left alone. Your Beldrian way was better."

"Anyway." Deliad eyed the Fossil of Dievas. "It's said that as the Elements died and dwindled, some strange things started happening in some Fragments. Fragments without any Elements or Fossils. A blight began to creep across their crops, leaving land barren. Beasts began to change, with each new set of offspring slightly stranger: deformed, defective, uglier. And the worst were somehow the ones who bore the future broods, which ended up even worse. And, as went beastkind, so mankind went, from noble man to halfman—that is, to ork—in those unfortunate Fragments."

A sky-clear memory flashed through Cor's recall.

"A miracle. Just sprung right up at Springtide. Like she'd just had a nice long sleep. Five years!" said Morty, smiling at his barley stalks, waving anew on soil that'd once been barren.

Cor's father nodded at the eager farmer, as, bored, Cor looked off toward the baseball field.

"And if she looks a mite bit bleary, well, who wouldn't? Five years! Bless me, but it's fine, eh?"

That eagerness—he felt a little sick.

"Sad stuff," sighed Deliad. "Fascinating stuff. But, truth is, we don't dwell upon it too much. Too busy battling orks to ponder past times."

"'Ye Children of the Mist would yield your world to the Children of the Dust; who soon would die, being creatures of consumption, not creation,'" spoke Cor, with words borne forth by warm assurance. "'Death, vileness; then, eternity devoid of both: this be thy world's weird, absent the Elements.'"

The Knight-Lord looked upon Cor's captivation. "What's that now?"

"What the Element warned about. The reason that we have to help the Elements," recalled Cor.

How had he recalled that whole quote?

"Right. So I'd figured, right around 'thy world.'" The Knight-Lord's lips curved up. "Well, *there's* a quest. A worthy one. Though I won't say I envy the pressure. Guess the Guard is off the table?" He grinned at Cor's apologetic shrug. "Who knows! When work winds down, I might just join you," he joked; but in his eyes was more than jest. "Like the old knight-errant on his sacred quest!"

Cor smiled and stabbed the campfire with a stick, glancing at Celeste; then, blinking and squinting.

Briefly, she'd seemed to be staring at them beneath those sagging lids; like Sol's eclipse, glaring around the edge of Luna's shadow.

Blinking again, he saw a wounded woman slumped by a birch and staring at the stones. Looking away, he slightly shook his head. *You're seeing things. Just a suffering, sorry woman.*

Fixing his stare on the Star-dimming flames, he let the hazy warmth waft over his sense and senses, leaving sleepy satisfaction.

"Knight-Lord," hailed Orther a half hour thereafter. "Some word from Foreguard Fundaem. He's just finished flushing the last few orks out from the East Wing. We've beds enough for all our knights and more. And, no doubt, you're all keen to claim a few."

"Quite right." The Knight-Lord stretched. "Been quite a day. See to it our barrel-riding band get first beds, together with the wounded ones. They've earned it. Including you two," he went on, now turning to face the western wanderers. "You pick first."

"Yay! I could use a break from crying babies," said Brayleigh. "So much *crying* in that tent!"

"And 'fluffy and feathery pillows. *Pillowcases,*'" said Cor.

"Yes, well." The girl from Fernstead waved.

"No crying *or* pillowcases in the knights' tent!" Cor pointed out. "And lots of swords."

"Yes, well!"

"You two go to then," smiled the Knight-Lord. "I'll be here for a bit. Alas, the burdens of being the Knight-Lord. You, though, Captain Ormslik, have strained that battered brain for long enough." He eyed the gauze on Orther's bloody brow. "Can't have my Captain keeling over on me. Go get some shuteye, eh?" He slapped his shoulder.

The Captain, searching for a clever counter, found nothing. So he rubbed his head. "Will do."

"You coming?" Brayleigh called across the courtyard to Celeste, slumping in the birch's shadows. "We'll help you up the stairs. Well, Cor can help you. I'd probably drop you down some spiral staircase!"

Her droopy eyes lifted halfway to their heads, as flowers on snapped stems strive and fail toward sunlight. "No, I feel fine. I'd like to lie here longer."

"Okay. You're sure?" confirmed the girl from Fernstead. "Okay. Well, get some sleep. That wound was awful!"

Celeste said nothing and stared at the grass, bereft of Luna's shimmer amid the smoke.

Sharing a brief glance, Cor and Brayleigh shrugged. They shuffled off to enter Castle Norvester once more, some of their earlier sanguine lost now, yet still a bit more sanguine than they'd been, by the arcane alchemy of the human heart.

CHAPTER 17

Under the Dragon's Tail and dying down from Heaven's height, Luna's lidded eye looked east. There would the Dawnstar signal day's ascent, after these dark-mantled hours had marched off. But she'd not see it, being part of dark's procession beyond the skyline's blue.

Celeste's gaze sank to where the bonfire's embers now were waning. They'd warm away her shivers if she approached. Why bother though? They'd dwindle soon to dust.

Her hand upon her belly felt the blood that'd soaked the surgeon's futile bandages. The throbbing in her torso waxed and waned: a heartbeat signaled not by sound, but pain. Sometimes, it bent her forward, and her eyes would squint the anguish back. Then, it'd recede, and she'd sag back against the birch behind her.

She saw the laughing, loping beings at play about the bonfire. Strange to think that, hours past, she'd been like them: traipsing about on two legs, measuring their lives by laughs instead of minutes.

Now more than ever, she felt what it is when a foreign feeling makes you unfamiliar: the intimate abstraction of a thing you feel throughout your fulness, you alone, that you must placate with your every move—that melancholic need to serve some second purpose beyond the primacy of being!—to which the sanguine world would be oblivious.

She'd hid it well once. It was harder now. What use, such work, in such a world as this? Why not just sit unseen in shadow instead? Suffering can show the leer in every laugh. And, from the fervent laughter of firelit triumph, concerned looks made her cringe with consciousness. Why not just vanish from their violent sight?

She stood.

And now that suffering overflowed and blent with the surrounding fervency, became one boiling boundlessness. And Celeste, a ruptured boat afloat on rapturous sea, let the old blue bear her off toward her destiny.

Out of the firelight went the unmoored woman, out of the radiant raucousness and welter toward shadowy submersion, where the summons of silence wafted from outside the courtyard, where color and care alike were drowned in darkness. From shores of consciousness, she fared a few steps into the lapping of the dreamy nightscape.

The vague words of the gate guard went unheard. Just whispers of the same wind that was moving these swelling waves; mere breezes over a mere, unfelt beneath the asphyxiating billows.

"Don't worry. I'm going out, not in," some voice said inside her head—or maybe aloud? She smiled, as waveborne seaweed smiles itself to a wave's shape, moving the most it's ever moved, as, meanwhile, its moving impulse wanes. She wasn't worried.

Luna hung high and waned aloft the sky. Broaching a narrow gap between the buildings, her rays lit glaringly upon the ground but stopped there, short of Celeste. Through the shade, she roved toward River Stiarna—where, reflected, the Sea of Stars shone, infinitely far from the celestial depths above—and walked above it, leaving the watery lightscape in her wake. Only the shadows left by Luna's absence stretched around Celeste toward the deep blue distance, which gloomed, alluring, in her gaze unwavering: her destination and her destiny.

A haze was hovering over the empty ways she walked, bereft of life and lively laughter. But, through that black despair of pain and wear, she seemed to see a semblancy of Lothar: a pierced corpse, bleeding purple from the throat, cackling atop his throne and calling her. And at his right side stood, as ever, Clausiglade, watching her with an old man's infinite sorrow, seeing the life he'd lived to leave behind was wilting. *Why so sad? I'll see you soon.*

A band of burly, shouting shapes ahead. She heard their happy cries from six feet under the watery depths removing her from their world. She hardly heard the words of the upbeat warriors, marching in merry triumph through Norvester's gate. They were just gestures toward a waking world she wasn't in, submerged in selfhood's mere: the merest details needed for her life-dream.

Through Norvester's gate, she wandered, toward the nothing that loomed for her beyond this noisome something, past guards who glanced and peered, but didn't press. Out of that noisome mass of noisy mankind, into a country of Star-bespangled silence.

The night winds whispered of a longed-for end, which rustled through the reddening elms and ashes. She heard their vow: oblivion from the pain blighting all things beneath the Sea of Stars. There was no suffering in the swelling now. No, here was Heaven's light, breaching cloudy life to reach *her*. Here was the beyond laid bare.

Was it an hour she wandered the umbral ways, with naught to guide her gait except the prickling of tall grass tickling at her hands and legs, and dirging nightbirds, beckoning from the distance toward an existence higher than human reckoning? One hour? Three hours? Did time still flow for her?

Two trees loomed high atop a hill ahead, an ash and elm, both fraught with age's wizening, bare with the Fall. And through the gap between them, the celestial Wanderers sparkled with allure: an earthly gateway to the welkin's ways.

Lured by the boundless, Celeste wandered toward it, watching it swell with every upward step.

And suddenly, blinking, she returned to *that* day.

She'd seen the haze above the skyline's hills first from the forest's edge, ascending grey and giving puffy clouds a gloomy countenance.

Over the hill she'd hurried. And from there, she'd traced the dark smoke from tenebral skies down to a smoldering mound of stone and timber, strewn with the blackening orange of straw near-burnt.

Watchful and wondering, she had neared the smoke. And, at the bottom of her blinking prospect, beneath the beams and stones that'd been her house, she'd seen the blackened bones and a pair of skulls.

A child will work out, after a while, what's what.

And so she had: The fence, now sagging splintered. The many bootprints in the muck nearby. The missing bags of barley and salted meat. And then, of course, the other corpse she'd found, half-claimed by flame, but clearly inhuman—hideous—and, driven deep into its head, her father's harpe.

"Oh, soon enough, you'll use it. Yes, you'll use it," he'd told her when she'd asked: her earliest memory. *"And then you'll wish for when you didn't have to!"*

Numb to the noontide Sun of Noversday, even as her eyes scrunched narrow against its glare—*"Those fair blues! Once made me squint too. But you! Why, you're more loth for sunlight than the Moon is!"* her smiling mother had marveled more than once—from meadow's brightness back into the mirk of the Elding Woods had Celeste wandered, dazed.

Down wending ways she'd walked, and through a maze whose bends she knew before they loomed in view, so many days she'd happily whiled away there, and then beyond. Through timberland and thicket, she strayed till Sol had sunk beyond the skyline; and Somnus stole away with her at nightfall.

She'd woken to a host of shadows stretching toward her from spiky trees as tall as she was small. Onward she'd wandered. And a day had passed before she'd found herself at forest's boundary and peering over a plain beswept with breezes, where Earth's long hair was waving flaxen-fair.

Into the head-high sward she'd hied, and cried wordless and witless, letting Luna guide her across these darkling ways where all was absence, and lonely lights were strewn about the distance.

So had she ranged and roved, through grange and grove, till, outlined in the light of westering Luna, two gloamy trees had grown within her gaze: an ash and elm, both fraught with age's wizening, bare with the Fall. And in the gap between them, where celestial Wanderers sparkled with allure, she'd seen a gateway to the welkin's ways.

Back from the faded past to a fading present, she blinked again upon those same bare trunks, flinging their branches futilely toward the Heavens. *The same place ...! How...?*

The dark of deep blue space dimpled her face. *How absolutely fitting.*

She took the gloamy path she'd taken back then: between the trees, and through that twinkling pass to darkness where the celestial massed; then down to where the wheatgrass thickened to a thicket.

Struggling to pass that prickly, piercing brush was nasty now as twenty years ago. Much stronger now; but not a willowy waif of eight, who'd slipped so easily through these gaps. They tore her now, those briars. *But this will pass.*

She shoved away the web of wood and burs bare-armed and bleeding, brimming with impatience for imminent release from life's vexations. *Release!*—it sprawled before her like a shadow of intervening Fate, which blinding suffering casts blackly upon the silver screen of sense. She thrust her frail frame through the final thorns, letting them take their toll in strips of skin.

And there it was: that Star-flecked waterfall. Beyond the woeful waters was a crevice upon the crags, where, once, an eight year old had fled the fell touch of the Falltide elements.

Into those depths of darkness, Celeste pressed, with black spots swarming in her squinting prospect, like starving flies that smelled forthcoming Fate.

She had to squeeze and scrape her way inside, losing a layer of skin. *But so what? The flesh would weigh you down from where you're flying!*

And now she slipped out from that skinny cranny to nothing: blissful, black and blessed nothing! She flung forth blood-wet limbs of bone and skin and felt the nothing there: nirvanic nothing! *Yes, life is pain. Life's purpose is to end.*

Stepping with blind abandon into nothing, she savored every fleeting step and second, out of the blue of night into the blackness, deeper and deeper toward the end of things.

And it was then that, lacking sight, she saw light.

She strove to blink it back to the black of night. But no: those greater depths just grew more bright. And she could see it now, slight but still clear.

No ... ! You're not here! But this was mere denial of what she'd feared.

And, sobbing, Celeste fell. For she could see *Him* now: sparkling reflected from round the umbrageous bend. Just like the last time.

Tearful and dream-taunted, fearful and shade-haunted, dazed by the light, she crawled around the bend.

And there it loomed: the Starlike thing that'd doomed her to all she'd suffered in these twenty years.

Nearing the Fossil, she fell to her forearms.

"Why did you save me?" Tears left starry trails. "For this? To grow up yearning to undo all evil, learning too late that I'd strew the same upheaval that I'd rued and hated? So I could watch a second father die? So I could blotch what innocence I had?"

She slackened and let her forehead fall to the Earth. But, even there, Celeste saw the Fossil's eminence and how it threw forth shade from jutting outcrops. Yes, blades of shade that darkly fell upon her.

"Dear Daughter of Luna; Daughter of Mine." The bass tones boomed through the room, pregnant with doleful pathos and soulful power.

Up from the gloom peered Celeste.

Luminous before her, looming like a shadow in negative, was Dusk's grace given a face. Back from His head's height curved a pair of horns. Flaring and pulsating round them was white hair, flaming aethereal round a numinous face. Down flowed that hair over His shoulders and bare breast, translating the empyrean down His torso. Unfurling full-size to His rear were webbed wings.

"Dear Daughter of shining Luna and of mine," He spake again. "Thine endless pilgrimage through dark shall have its end; and it shall spark such light and life as shall transcend thy sorrow. The Daystar goes at night but brightens the morrow. So thou, fallen darkling, soon shall spring anew and, out of rue, bear sparkling forth new fairness."

She stared upon Him, stained by tears and light. "Why? Why live life like this? Why not just die?"

His glow eternal lit a smile paternal. "Incline thyself to Me, where I'm enshrined within thy breast. Consign thy cares to Me."

Celeste beheld Him, her hand to her belly. With worn mind on the wane and blind with pain, she whispered—she was not sure what. Pure feeling, perhaps. And yet whatever phrase lapsed forth from Celeste's haze of incoherency prompted a smile of infinite sympathy.

Sleep, Daughter, fair and deep as prayer can keep thee, that vast voice sounded, through a boundless void of winking flares in which she'd started sinking, with sense and senses shrinking by the second. And soon, her heart and thinking part had strayed far from the chthonic shade they'd longed to fade in.

Yet, even here, felt she a familiar shade in a Starscape dreams are made in, bodying forth forebodings fair and new, ominous and blue, true as the Lodestar leads north. Here, in swarth oblivion hidden from view, yet shining hence from just past sense, where pining flew, was—*who?*

She knew not. Yet a single word resounded throughout the unbounded, mingling midnight blue and swirling white to whirling starlight: *You!*

On fared she past all dreaming into a teeming mass of fair Mists; and, in their midst: *You! You!*

PART II

DOWN FROM THE SUMMIT

CHAPTER 18

When Dawn flicked out her fingertips of rose over the wine-dark water of River Stiarna, so its spray was sparkling ruddy with her glee at fresh day, a slumbering redhead didn't see it. She was still fathoms deep in dreams of Fernstead, which she called home; then, wandering through the gloam of ghostly woods, which also felt like home.

That's odd! she pondered; then promptly forgot it.

Stretching upright from her first proper sleep in many Moons, she squinted toward the Sun and let a yawn sing forth, so long and tired that even amber-combed Electryone admired it.

Bed's big enough for two! mused teenage Brayleigh, feeling a fervency thrill from her core through sore limbs with a sprightly little tingle.

Closing her eyes to savor sleep's last sediment, drinking in sweetness clinging to her sentiment before the flow of bright day washed it down, she sighed another yawn out.

Then, she stepped from her courtly castle suite to seek the privy.

Half an hour hence, she was waving and hailing a stillman's son and paladin, eating pork and standing mid the sward of Castle Norvester. "Hey Cor! Hey Knight-Lord Deliad!" Brayleigh called.

She crossed the courtyard as they waved and watched, feeling the fresh breeze billow through her hair and beaming as she neared her new peers. "Morning!"

"Morning," said Deliad, eying the Sun at Midheaven. "Well, maybe morning."

"That how they do their hair in Fernstead?" Cor's lips curved up.

"Yep, redhead bedhead!" Brayleigh felt it—*yikes*. "Woke five minutes past and walked straight here! I'm *famished* though. I'm feeling empty as tripe! So, care to tell me where you got that grub, Cor, before I eat you up?" She smoothed her hair and hoped her wordstream washed the sight from memory.

Of course, the "where" could hardly have been more obvious, what with the big lively bonfire from last night blazing nearby, converted now to a cookfire with several small pigs spitted overtop.

"Well. In the interests of not getting eaten," said Cor, "I'll show you. And I'll go get seconds."

"That's fine, you pig, as long as I get firsts!" She sweetly smiled. More evidence for her theory that, if you want to make a man change subjects without him knowing, just ask an obvious question.

She smoothed her hair once more.

A minute hence, the pair were munching sizzling slabs of pork, with Brayleigh's being as big as Cor's and Deliad's combined.

"Ahh." She could feel the melted fat congealing on her palate, down her gullet and into her swelling gut. And it was good. "Farewell, my friend!" She curled her fingers twice at a half-carved piglet. "Yes, your life was brief; but what more lofty end could pigkind long for?" Savoring the belly of the beast, she swallowed.

Looking at Brayleigh, Cor coughed out a laugh.

Feeling that all was well within the world—pig in her mouth, and her pig-pen-like bedhead forgotten by all those present—sighing contented, she scanned the courtyard.

Oh, hey! Shuffling close by, that sweet old serving woman she'd seen earlier was faring toward the food. She smiled and waved.

The elder nodded nicely back. "Hello dear! You find that privy in time? It's awfully hidden."

Frowning upon the chambermaid who'd helped her find that humble chamber—and just in time—she blushed and peeked upon the blinking Beldrian. She mimed a chewing mouth, so speechlessness might be mistaken for ladylike politeness.

She faced the elder and said, with widening eyes: *Speaking from woman to woman,* why *say that?*

Or so she hoped her blazing gaze would say. But the ancient servant simply smiled back slightly and waddled off.

That's right, old lady. "Waddled"!

"So," she spoke, having pretend-swallowed her pretend-mouthful, "where's Celeste?"

Cor looked over and shrugged at Deliad, now strolling up beside them. "You know, Knight-Lord?"

"Assume she found a room. Just sleeping in, I reckon. With the wounds and such," said Deliad.

"I'm not so sure. I worry about those wounds!" said Brayleigh. "We should see if she's alright. Since, who else here would think to check on *her?*"

"Well, speak with Beran. He was sent at Dawn to go record who's where in all the rooms, and who needs watching. As for me," he went on, "I have a hundred gravely wounded warriors, each of whom I'd sooner check on than her."

"I'll do it," said Cor. "I've pigged out quite enough." He flung some fatty scraps into the fire.

"Good man," the girl from Fernstead grinned. "Get going."

It turned out, though, that Beran had seen no one matching the Beldrian's simple sketch of Celeste: "fair, trim, blonde, twenties, not too tall, but not short."

"Well, not that no one looked like that," explained the junior Knight of Norvester, smiling slightly. "Not by a long shot. But I know their names now. Spoke for some time with several. Heh. No Celestes."

The Beldrian slapped his back and started off.

"Let's spar again sometime," the young swain called. "Just not when they're around to watch, okay?"

Nor had the surgeon or his nurses seen her, Cor learned some minutes later in the courtyard. "Which worries me a bit," the surgeon went on. "Bad wound. I gave her fifty-fifty at best."

After an hour of scouring Castle Norvester, Cor had given up, and now the girl from Fernstead was lobbying for the Knights to launch a search.

"You ever think she wouldn't *want* us searching?" replied the Knight-Lord, after several minutes of brushing Brayleigh's questions off. "You realize, King Reginald will be coming from our camp, right? He may well have her gaoled for life. Or hanged. Maybe she didn't want to 'hang' around, huh?"

"Uh-huh." Her keen gaze showed a green blaze. "Well, *you* ever think a terribly wounded woman, who lost a loved one only yesterday, and turned on everything she'd thought was true, and suddenly disappeared amid the darkness, might've gone off to do something more dire?"

Sighing and staring skyward, he was close to sending a couple squires to search outside—if nothing else, to get a break from nagging and be polite to a savior of the city—when, through the wide gate, who should walk but Celeste, serene of face, straight-backed and smooth of gait.

"Well! Would you look at that." The Knight-Lord pointed. "Seems all our fears were unfounded. She's fine, see?"

Yes, hearty and hale; but "fine," the three soon saw, might overstate the matter.

Celeste's garb, already grimy from her month's immurement, was ratty and ripped up now and strewn with slivers. Her belly bandage was a single big scab, soaked through with blood dried to crimson and crumbling. Brambles adorned her blonde hair like barrettes. She looked, in short, like she had spent the night rolling around in briary brush and bleeding, save that her limbs seemed strangely free of scratches.

Brayleigh hied over. "Celeste! Yikes! How are you?" Nearing, she clasped the older woman's hands within her own. "We're *so* relieved to see you."

Blinking at first, the former orator shrugged. "Best that I've been in a while." She smiled weakly.

"Your wound." The Beldrian pointed at her belly. "How is it?"

"Healed, I think. I'd strip the bandage, but I'm afraid that it's the only thing holding my outfit together at this point." She pointed toward the torn and punctured cloth.

"Ridiculous," said Deliad. "You were shot through. I saw the hole. Rather like Reginald's wound: the one that's kept him feverish for a full year."

"Well, no such luck," the Merchant's orator mused. "You see"—she stripped the bandage just enough to show some pinkening of her belly's smoothness, where yesterday had been a hole—"it's healed."

The Knight-Lord squinted, blinked and shook his head.

"Of course, I had some help," she added softly, withdrawing from within her shirt a stone that shone like starlight through an evening mist.

"You too?" The girl from Fernstead's eyes went wide. "Where in the world did you find that thing, Celeste?"

She looked away. "Long story." With her lips still parted, she seemed close to sharing more, so no one spoke.

Then, after a couple seconds, she turned to Cor. "Last night, I heard you talking. About the cave, the Element, and the task He set for you: to save the other Elements. To stop this world from falling into foulness."

"Yeah," he said. "Sounds a bit out-of-this-world, huh."

"Well, maybe. Or it might be we're too worldly," Celeste replied, brushing hair from her brow. "How much that makes this world of ours mundane is merely our willful spurning of what's higher? We call this world of ours a 'cruel world,' 'small world,' and 'world of hurt.' Good is 'too good for this world.' That's the 'way of the world.'"

"But who but us has made it so, and who should make it better? Not man alone. I've learnt that much the hard way. But maybe man with the aid of Powers above. Man can't make Heaven of Earth. But maybe Heaven can, through man."

"All that to say"—the orator breathed in—"I'd like to join you and help you, if you'd have me."

The Knight-Lord raised a brow.

"Yes," Cor replied with strange assurance, nodding swiftly and smooth-faced without a blink. "The more, the merrier, right?"

He didn't blink, but Brayleigh did. *Well! That's weird.* "Well, that's great!" she declared a second late. *"The more, the merrier"—he said that to me too!*

She'd felt obliged, till now, to shelter Celeste from the severity of the Knight-Lord's censure. Now, she was not so sure. *That instant "yes!". . . He paused for me. He wasn't sure at first sight?*

Running her right hand through red locks, she smiled. "So great! A third. We'll have fun! Welcome! On, then!"

So great. A third wheel: have fun! Well, come on then.

Even Celeste seemed a bit surprised, but pleased. *Pleased, huh.* "I'll do my utmost to deserve this." Running her right hand through fair locks, she looked down. *Your hair looks fine!* "I've quite a lot to atone for."

Deliad seemed keen to speak, but bit his lip.

"What better way to atone than save the world?" the Beldrian mused, as smooth and sunny as noon. And Celeste slightly smiled and nodded back.

Grr! Gonna be like that, huh? Guess we'll find out how Blondie fares against a Fernstead redhead!

"Bad guys, beware: there's three of us now!" she said.

So, in a blink and batting of some lashes, both red and blonde, our pair of western wanderers became a trio; and, by a twist of Fate, the foe of yesterday became a friend.

Friend? Frenemy? We'll see! Don't mess with me!

Within this friendly space, the wanderers spent the next week idly: resting and recovering, savoring the hearty meals served at the mess hall, raiding the kitchens between their meals, and, in Cor and Brayleigh's case, roving the castle.

For country folk, this limestone-cut colossus was quite a thing to wonder at. And while they'd seen a fair amount of it their first day, looking for Lothar, they'd been much too busy doing valiant deeds to admire the vaulted arches, tapestries livening whole walls and long halls, the majesty of the monarchial chambers, and leagues-long prospects from the parapets.

Castle Norvester, of course, was in such shape as over a year of orkish occupation will leave a place, with plenty of shattered glass, pulverized plaster, slashed paintings and garbage, strewn mouldering in the crannies of the corridors. But even a week went far toward fixing that. Most of the menials and servants had stayed here throughout the Merchant's rule. They'd soon scrubbed off the stains, removed the paintings for repairs, and gotten rid of the gross debris and rubbish.

By week's end, Castle Norvester looked quite livable; and right on time to welcome Norvester's ruler back to the seat of his new-restored reign.

Not that he'd sit on that throne right away. He still was suffering from his year-long fever, and his infected wound remained inflamed; so weak, his only semblancy of kingship was waving from his carriage as he wheeled by the clapping townsfolk.

But a feeble King was still far better than a First of Equals. The worst of tyrants is the one who feigns kindly equality with the common folk, and forces them to tell that flagrant lie, even as he rules and lives by different rules. That was the Knight-Lord's opinion, at least.

The coming of the King to his long-lost homeland wasn't all handwaves and happiness though. On seeing the ruin a year had wrought on the Old-town—smashed statues, stained glass shattered in the shrines, centuries-old oaks in sacred groves made stumps, and blasted monuments and burnt memorials—he fell into a bleak mood under his blithe mien.

Upon remarking on the widespread wreckage, he listened sadly as an elder servant, who'd suffered through the last year under Lothar, recounted how, when ork guards got too riotous, Lothar would let them lay waste to some old works. That'd keep them happy for a week or so.

"Valuable resource, monuments," the Merchant had mused. *"We mustn't spend them all in one week!"*

By nine that night, the King was in a black mood, propped up upon his bed beside the window and staring cross the lone and level courtyard on old King Osmand's trunkless legs of stone.

"With every statue wasted, we lose faith that what we've wrought will weather terrible time," the ailing monarch brooded, baleful-eyed. "And so we start to fear to make fair things. Such is the sinister end of iconoclasm: abortion of what's fair before its birth."

Meanwhile, the Knight-Lord stood beside the bed, silent, letting the sick man say the things that he himself had thought but fought on through.

"Whole realms have been bereft of beauteous art for ages, where the orks and orklike sorts, by wanton wastage, have persuaded people that there's no future for the subtle and fair: for motley minstrel's chime and metered rhyme; that life's a lowly span of thrusting pleasures and parrying thrusting pains until we cease."

"You've had a hard day, Majesty. A hard week. You've earned some sleep, yes?" Deliad finally said. "With Dawn, what we beheld at Dusk looks brighter."

Noting Reginald's dismay, the Royal Historian had gotten together a host of master guildsmen to start restoring what had been laid waste. Even now, a crew of theirs was carting statues of kings forgotten to the Shrine of Eremon the Fair and Kind. The scent of burnt meat wafted over their work from within. As they drew near, those marble monarchs seemed alive again, processing toward a feast in praise of them.

Predictably, Cor soon resumed his sparring with the Honor Guard. And so he found himself, one day, facing the hardest foe he'd ever fought.

Sigmund Lofthungrian—close kin to the King and Captain of the Knights of Norvester—peered through sky-hued slits of blue, his huge sword held forth in Plow, and planned his next barrage of blows.

Weeks ago, Arvaen had raised the idea that Cor and Sigmund spar. But Deliad's Captain had claimed to be too busy. He was not one to make fools of his fellow men wantonly. *He* surely had no need to prove his prowess. Indeed, the squires already whispered of it.

But when he'd heard that Cor had bested Dag, eight-two, *that'd* caught the attention of the Captain. Dag was the only knight, other than Deliad, that Sigmund bothered sparring with these days. No showoff, Sigmund, but he loved a fair fight.

The Beldrian had befriended Dag. They both were men in their twenties who lived by the blade. One day, he'd asked Dag whether "*Sigmund, you know, is any good.*"

Dag had glanced over at Cor. "'*Any good'?*" Shaking his head, he'd grinned. "*Good* luck, *my friend.*"

Good luck indeed. He'd come on like a wolf, but bigger. When his blade came biting down, that first blow, Cor had coolly blocked it head-on—and, shivering head to toe, ears ringing bell-like, he'd nearly dropped his sword at the utter impact.

He'd gotten a few good cuts in. One came close. But, that first bout, he'd never quite recovered. It'd ended when the Captain bashed his bicep, leaving a bruise that'd last at least two weeks.

That was a painful lesson. But he'd learnt it.

Bout two, he'd been more cautious. All defense—mostly dodging, at that—till Sigmund dashed toward the Beldrian with a head-high slash. And, ducking, smiling, he could see what'd come next as clearly as in a crystal ball.

First, Gadfly, swatting at Sigmund's flank. The huge man lurched left, snarling and wolflike in instinct's perfection, and Cor's point whiffed by.

As he'd foreseen. Next, Peacock Tail, his sword flashing in front of his foe's face, distracting.

The big man, well and truly off-balance now, threw his head backward and backstepped.

And Cor, from Longpoint, stepped forth into Swan Approach.

The Captain had no answer to that blade thrust to his breast, save a grunt at the blow.

That, and a more respectful wariness upon those sky-slit eyes, when round three started. It went a full five minutes, as did round four. The former went to Sigmund, powering through a parry with a slash to Cor's left shoulder. The latter went to Cor, with Down to Size—a knee-high slice from Fool's Guard right to left—canceled abruptly into Lionpaw, pinging the big man's breastplate with a rightward cut.

By now, it seemed like half the Knights of Norvester were watching. Half the servants too, including—with bated breath and sparkling, batting eyes—those Beran had been telling him about.

The crowd's suspense, swollen huge with waiting, popped like a pricked balloon two seconds in. Sigmund had led with a charging slash leftward. That was the opening that'd jarred Cor in round one. He didn't try to parry or dodge it this time.

Instead, his sword flicked out in Gadfly again, striking the huge man's hand square on the knuckles.

His fingers flicked out, and the sword slipped free, flying in whirling arcs toward Foreguard Fundaem, who—blinking—blocked it with a couple bracers.

Unarmed, his arm kept swinging with momentum sideways. And by the time he'd brought it back, the Beldrian's blade was pressed against his breast.

"Touch," Cor concluded.

And the crowd applauded and laughed. And sparkling gazes, fixed on him, sparkled still more.

Sigmund, that wolflike warrior, was rather sheepish now. "Brilliant technique." He shook his head and glanced at Foreguard Fundaem, burnishing out a new scratch on his bracers. "And so fast. That's a fight I'm fine with losing."

"Well. You're as good as anyone I've fought," said Cor. "In fact, I thought you had me back in round four. You could've parried out of Hanging Guard, right near the end. Riposte—Luna's Retort, or some quick thrust like that. You could've had me."

"I don't know what that means," replied the huge man. "I'd like to though."

"Why don't I teach you now?" suggested Cor. "Let's just go grab some water."

Deliad laughed quietly as Cor tilted back a waterskin and Sigmund walked away. "'You could've parried.' Heh. How does it feel, besting the scion of Sigram Lofthungrian?"

"Who?"

Deliad simply smiled and shook his head, patting the Beldrian's back.

As Cor was sparring, country-girl Brayleigh was wandering the city, something she'd never gotten to do at length.

As she was headed out to do so one day, Celeste approached her, Star-shaped Fossil in hand, shining as pale as the Daystar at Dawn.

Aha. The moment comes. She makes her move! mused Brayleigh, staring at the looming lady. *"Get rid of redhead girl, then get the boy!" Well, Blondie, we'll just see now, won't we!*

Smiling, readying herself to let loose such a red blast as would've broken a troll to bits, she waited.

"I don't suppose," the pallid woman said, waving politely and walking beside her, "you'd like to help me learn to use this thing?" She eyed the Fossil. "Can't quite figure it out."

The girl from Fernstead let the awesome forces surging within her, sadly, wane away. "Of course I'd like to!" *Only problem is, who you like too!* "Takes three to save the world." *We'll see if one world's big enough for three!*

"Thanks. I can sense it. But it just gets hairy, sorting the strands out and keeping them straight," said Celeste, running a hand through her fair hair, as Cor and Deliad walked by in the distance.

Your hair *looks fine!* "No sweat! I'm sure you're fine. In fact," she went on, "maybe you're too focused on strands and such. And looking in the wrong place! I'd keep it simpler. What you need's inside you, and not out there!" She waved across the courtyard, where Cor was stretching yawningly, arms bare. "Just you! I think you'll find things simpler that way."

Celeste seemed somewhat puzzled by the advice. "I—well, I'll try. It feels, though, like I'm trying to tie a knot. And it's too complicated."

"Oh, *definitely*, you don't need to tie a knot!" she cried. "In fact, if I were you, I'd untie whatever knots you might've started tying!"

The older woman blinked.

"I mean," said Brayleigh, "it's more like mist. You don't tie mist. You form it, by enclosing it in who *you* are inside. And then you let *that* out. You make *that* real. You don't 'tie knots' with someone—I mean, something."

"Somehow, it just isn't working for me. Hard to explain. But I'll keep tying. Trying."

"Yep! Like they say: 'Just try until it works! Easier to make a baby than explain how.'"

Celeste blinked at her. "Really? Someone says that?"

"Everyone! Well, every farmwife in Fernstead."

Of all my folksy sayings, why'd *I pick that?*

And that was the extent of Celeste's progress.

After that first week's passage, as he'd promised, the Knight-Lord sent some knights to clear the pass to the Academy.

"Thanks again," said Cor, watching those knights and wagons vanish south. "I know you need what knights you have these days."

The Knight-Lord waved. "Something we had to do. Whether we did it today or in two weeks, we'd have to take back Leitath's Pass. That pass is what kept the southern orkish hordes down south. Sooner we claim the pass, safer we'll be."

"Meanwhile," he said, "I suggest you wait here another week or so. Wagons are slow. Won't want to catch them ere the pass is captured. Well, not unless you want another battle?" He grinned, as Cor and Brayleigh shared a glance and felt their scabby wounds. "No, I should say not."

"No need to justify it!" said Brayleigh blithely. "You like our company that much, we'd be happy to hang out here a little longer. Right, Cor?"

"Well, charmed, yes. But—" began the Knight-Lord.

"Sure," said Cor. "Where else could I do so much sparring?"

"And I'm not finished wandering through the city!" added the girl from Fernstead.

Deliad grinned. "Alright then. Yes, it's nice as any city. But see the Nature too. Go see the Ginnagonds! Fine views from there of Norvester. Or the farms! Our native engines of nativity!"

"I've seen a million farms. But just one city!" said Brayleigh.

"I've spent decades seeing farms," said Cor. "But just a few weeks dueling knights."

"Well. En garde, then, I guess."

It worked out well, waiting that extra week. That week, the monarch's year-long fever broke. His seeping gut wound scabbed and sealed. His gloom gave way to a brightening zeal, as he beheld statues and monuments honoring his ancestors starting to be restored toward regal glory.

He called in Deliad often for conversation: sometimes affairs of state, but just as often seeking out somebody he could be frank with.

"It now occurs to me," King Reginald noted at one such meeting, "that I haven't thanked you. Or those two western wanderers that you've spoken of."

Those two were set to leave the city at Dawn tomorrow, joined by Celeste. Which was good, since someone soon would surely ask the King what should be done with Lothar's former orator.

"No need for thanks, Sire," Deliad said. "Continue recovering. Sit upon the throne of Norvester. And guide our people again toward greater prospects. That would be more than thanks enough for me."

"Indeed," continued Deliad, looking down at the courtyard, where some serving girls were scurrying, and gardeners were replanting trampled gardens. "I bear the blame for failing to turn back the Merchant's forces, when they took the castle. What I've done since is no more than atonement."

"Pah." Reginald waved. "Don't lie politely, Deliad. You were the one man who tried to warn me away from the mistakes that led us here."

"Sire—"

"No, I know things rightly now," spoke Reginald. "I'd come to believe the arc of history bent in Norvester's favor naturally; that all I had to do was keep the people happy, and, sure enough, prosperity would follow."

He shook his head. "Delusive optimism. Born of an easy boyhood, schooled by scholars who'd never faced a hard choice in their lives."

"Now, I know history arcs darkly toward downfall; unless we bend it up ourselves toward brightness, and make hard choices that will bend it that way."

"Ending the Hergas and the border sentinels? Rewarding sloth and worklessness? Strewing silver upon the streets in endless feasts and festivals? Opening the castle's courtyard up to crowds?" He shook his head. "A wounded year in exile has one perk. You can suddenly see stupidity for what it is."

The Knight-Lord held a hand up to disagree, but Reginald waved it down. "No, I know this is spoken fairly and rightly. 'A man can see what's fair and feel what's right,' a wise man told me once." His lips curved up.

Clear enough whom he meant. But Deliad's memory jumped back much further, to a boyhood walk beside the River Stiarna with a friend; who'd just impressed his younger peer by chopping in half a birch bough with his whetted glaive. He felt his own lips curving now.

And now, he knew he had to say what he'd been thinking for several days, but never said aloud.

"So, Knight-Lord," said the head of House Lofthungrian, "I'll trust you—as I should've trusted you, these last ten years—to lead the restoration of Norvester's Hergas of the Fellowfolk. Do as seems fit to make it fit for war."

"I'm—honored, Sire," said Deliad after a pause.

"And," the King added, noticing that halt, "should you seek something else, just name it, Knight-Lord. And by my mandate shall I make it so!"

"There is one matter, Majesty." He drew a deep breath. "Those two wanderers from the west, the ones we spoke of."

"Yes." King Reginald snapped his fingers. "Right you are. I'll see that pair receive fit recompense for their heroics."

"They're—on a quest, Sire. Strange as such things sound, in dismal, lowly times like those we've lived through." A swell of warm assurance bore the words out. "A quest. Conferred upon them by an Element. Like in the stories: Arvek Devilsbane. Stragus Daemonis. A quest to restore the Elements from their thousand years of fading, dying to Fossils." Here, he glanced at Hoarthaxe, leaning nearby, its pommel glimmering green.

"And, Sire, I feel I'm called to join their quest."

And now the words were out. No changing course.

The King did not respond at first. He stared, his sunny countenance clouding, like an island that's used to seeing more rain than shine; but still, savored that little shining while it'd lasted.

Finally, he sighed and looked out at the sky. "Why don't you tell me why you think so, Deliad?"

And so he did. He shared what Cor had told him of Beldria and its Boundary's newfound gap; of Dievas and the quest he'd given to Cor; of Fyraett and his forebear and the Fossils.

"And, hearing what he said, I knew for sure—as surely as eyes can see and ears can hear—I had some part to play in these events." These thoughts were half-formed till they'd left his lips.

"And that part isn't here with kith and King?" The monarch held a hand up as his Knight-Lord began to answer. "Isn't that the way of things? Right when the long climb ends, one looks ahead, and what does he find but a rough, rocky trail?"

"Sire—"

"Say that I accept this quest is real. Not simply a figment of a rustic's fancy," the King said. "Much of me is wondering, Knight-Lord, why in the world I'd send away my *Knight-Lord*, in some small band, to fight small sets of foes. I have whole droves of knights to do such things. And I've *one* Knight-Lord, who, in leading them, doubles their value, doughtiness and valor. Would sending him away not seem unwise?"

"Of all my knights to send out as a sort of knight-errant bodyguard—tending to a boy and girl who, good of heart though they may be, have chosen to give their lives to chasing legends—to send the *Knight-Lord?*" said the recovering King. "When I could send a few fools wielding axes to do the same for a sliver of the cost? The impracticality, Deliad! The illogic!"

"I'd simply have told you 'no,' two years ago, when Clausiglade's counsel ruled my way of reasoning." King Reginald fixed a gaze gone firm on Deliad. "And I've still half a mind to tell you 'no,' and 'stop being swept off by romantic fancies.' But that's the Clausiglade lingering in my mind. And such minds do away with monarchs, yes?"

The Knight-Lord, who had opened his mouth to answer, let his lips close.

"I'll ponder your request," King Reginald said. "Pray tell me, though, precisely what you'd request of me."

"A leave of absence," Deliad replied.

"Indeed. How long?"

"Indefinite."

"In Eremon's name!" The convalescing King stared at the Dusk descending on his Kingdom, reclaimed by a miracle merely two weeks past.

Some fifteen seconds passed in darkening silence.

"Tomorrow afternoon, come back before me with them: this Cor Volucre and Brayleigh Mirin," the King commanded. "And you'll have your answer."

"Sire, as you wish." The Knight-Lord lowered his brow and briefly shut his eyes.

"That will be all."

"Your Majesty." He bowed and, lifting Hoarthaxe, whose Fossil now was faint, he turned around.

His gaze ahead was falling into a grimace even as he took his first step toward the shadows lurking beyond the doorway leading out. They obscured what loomed for him in winding hallways, leading away from his King, fraught with nightfall.

Where I am going? He followed where his feet went, wandering through gloam. *And who will lead me there?*

CHAPTER 19

The next day, Sol hung high aloft Midheaven, and Cor and Brayleigh both were getting anxious, each glancing often and quietly at the other.

The King "desired their presence in the throne room," Deliad had told them, midway through their last meal in Norvester, just as they were raring up to savor a casual day of walking south.

Now, standing just outside King Reginald's throne room, Cor had a lump in his stomach much larger than when he'd last approached these double doors, wielding his sword. And it wasn't the food.

He felt a burp form.

Well, it was the food too. He'd not have had that eighth egg if he'd known that, in a half hour, he would meet *the King*.

He forced it down. They'd almost reached the doorway.

"Is Celeste coming too?" Brayleigh had asked upon the announcement of the royal summons, holding a hand out toward the eating orator.

She, unlike our two western wanderers, looked like someone who'd converse sometimes with kings: queenly and calm, garbed in a walking gown.

"I would suggest that Celeste not apprise His Majesty of her existence here," Deliad had answered evenly. "I'd suggest that she keep quiet until she's far from Norvester."

She'd stared at him. "Then, you're not going to tell . . . ?"

Deliad had met that look levelly. "My friends, here, will be rewarded for the pains they took for Norvester's gain. So, I suppose, shall you."

Neither the Beldrian nor the girl from Fernstead had seen a king before now, much less met one. Nearing those double doors of arching oak, both felt like every blink and step betrayed that they were country bumpkins, straying far from their native fields and folk and folksy things.

Brayleigh had wanted to find some fine clothes. "Like—that!" She'd waved toward Celeste's silken finery, flowing in bleu-de-ciel waves down her form.

"Not necessary," the Knight-Lord had waved. "He's spent the last year in a tent. With knights! He's used to dented armor and dirty tabards."

Having her clothes compared to a dirty tabard had not completely calmed the girl from Fernstead. But it was far too late for a wardrobe change.

For Deliad now was pushing wide those doors, baring that tense pair and their travel gear to the serene and lofty majesty of Norvester's King: his crown ablaze with noon, shining through stained glass and highlighting Heaven's mandate.

Oil lamps were lit along the chamber's walls. Tapestries hung between them, showing battles: huge sprawling scenes of axe and mail and mayhem; battles by men now buried under time's sands, in which this monarch's forebears fought and won.

"Come," the King beckoned.

Clad in robes of vert, lined with ermine, a man of middle age was facing them. His hair was fair but greying: blonder on top but, by his thick beard's bottom, completely grizzled. On his shoulders sat a purpure mantle, blazoned with crown and closed fist within a tongue of flame. A chain of gold rings encircled the emblem.

Wounded grandeur lay upon him. Forth he hunched, favoring his torso. But flashing eyes and flushing cheeks exuded rejuvenation swelling toward robustness.

Nearing the King and falling to a knee, the Knight-Lord lowered his head. "Sire."

Cor did likewise, hoping that this was something he should do, not just a knight thing.

Brayleigh, too, began to go to a knee, then seemed to reconsider. She crouched and lowered her head and grabbed her pantlegs in what might be mistaken for a curtsey, by someone who had only read of curtseys.

"Rise," the King said. His voice was deep and strong, but had the quiver of one suppressing laughter.

The three complied and faced the monarch's throne, minus the cushion they'd last seen it with. Carved out of stone, it was covered in inlays that, from afar, looked much like leafy branches, swirling and interweaving into a thicket, but, up close, showed a host of tiny symbols: spirals, horned circles, trefoils, eight-spoked sunbursts, octads and triads, and eight-pointed stars.

"Sire," Deliad said, "I bring upon your summons those we spoke of: from Beldria, Cor Volucre; from Fernstead, Brayleigh Mirin."

"At your service!" piped shaky Brayleigh.

"So I've heard," smiled Reginald. "Stalwart service indeed, my Knight-Lord tells me. And yet so young," he mused. "Well, as they say, with age comes wit, but youth has heart and will. And I'm more sure of the latter than the former. New friends of mine and friends of Norvester: Welcome."

"We're honored, Sire." Cor hoped this was the right phrase, as Brayleigh triple-nodded earnestly.

"We want to thank you both—we, King and Kingdom—for what you've wrought, together with our knights," the King went on. "Deliverance of our nation; salvation of our folk; renewal of Norvester: we owe these things to you. Not native-born, you vied for us with all the might and valiance of our most vaunted heroes. Words can't match this. Material prizes cannot recompense this. But we shall do our best. Come, Cor Volucre."

The Beldrian, breathing in, approached the throne. Then, unsure what to do, he knelt again.

The King unsheathed an emerald-pommeled sword, broad of blade and riddled with glinting runes. He held it over Cor's right shoulder. "I, Sovereign of

Norvester, Head of House Lofthungrian, dub thee"—he struck Cor's shoulder with the sword's flat, and then the other shoulder—"honorary member of the Order of Gram and Knight of Norvester, with all appurtenant privileges and rights. Sir Cor, thou art created. Rise before me."

Cor stood, eyes wide.

"You're one of us," said Reginald. "Henceforth, when Norvester wars for Norvester's sake, she fights for you. She backs you as her own. Your good is our good. And your quest is ours." He spoke the last with special emphasis.

"Of course, we'd scarcely let our savior leave without some sort of trophy," Reginald went on. "Wherefore, I've charged my finest blacksmith, Brinsmyth, to grant you, Cor, the finest mail he's made. I've been advised you're a man of the sword. I trust you'll find it suitable for swordplay. That, and a tabard. Can't have Knights of Norvester clad in just any rags." He waved at Cor.

Brayleigh, begarbed in travel slacks and tunic, glanced at Deliad. Her wide green glare was audible: *"He's used to dented armor and dirty tabards?!"*

"'Tis a trifle," the King apologized, "but you will not find finer mail."

"I'm grateful, Your Majesty." The words still sounded awkward to Cor, but he made sure to speak them firmly.

"Now. Brayleigh Mirin. Let me ask you first," began the monarch, "how you've liked your lodging at Castle Norvester."

"Crazy nice!" she squealed. "I mean." She steadied. "It's been simply lovely!" Her nervy exuberance was a sight to see.

King Reginald couldn't quite keep down his smile. "Good. I'm advised you've taken a special liking to my late mother's suite within the West Wing."

"Maaybe," said Brayleigh with a giddy grin, followed by a blink and a ladylike throat-clear. "Your Highness. No!—Your Majesty."

He chuckled. "Well. Though those rooms are, by long use, reserved for the monarch's mother, her regrettable passage has left them vacant. And there won't be another to fill them for a long, long while. Heaven willing. Wherefore, I hereby create in your benefit a life estate in the traditional suite held by the Queen-Mother; with, of course, all appurtenant privileges. In other words," he went on after a moment, "you can live there."

Brayleigh, for once, was speechless. First, she stared. Then, "'Appurtenant privileges'?" she finally managed.

"Yes, all the privileges." At Brayleigh's blank face, the King continued, "Dedicated servants. Tailor and seamstress. Service from the kitchens. And so forth."

"Y—Your Majesty!" she squeaked. "Thank you!" She shook her head. "That is to say, I am most grateful, Sir. Sire!"

Reginald laughed.

Then, turning to the Knight-Lord, "As for you," he said. And now that regal brow was stern. "This past day, I've been pondering your request for a leave of absence to assist this pair upon their farflung quest. I've made my mind up."

The western wanderers blinked and looked at Deliad.

"It's with a heavy heart I give this answer, and grave spirit." Reginald looked upon the ground. "Your prayer is granted, Knight-Lord. Be at leisure to assist this sacred effort as you would."

The foremost Knight of Norvester lowered his head, lips curving up as his eyes closed. "I'm grateful, Sire."

"It'd not be meet that deeds of such import be done without an emissary of Norvester," King Reginald said. "I trust that, in the interim, you'll delegate your duties suitably."

"Sire, Captain Orther Ormslik will assume command of the Honor Guard's administration and all strategic matters. Captain Sigmund Lofthungrian will take tactical command and lead our knights upon the field," said Deliad.

"Fine. I approve," said Reginald. "In your absence, we'll fix all this." He waved up at the window of stained glass with a single hole, still broken from when the Usurper's orks had seized the city. "Yea, we'll fix every bit of it. We'll better it. We will make such a city as men shall speak of a thousand years from now. We'll spite the orks and orkism, which have sought to smash our faith that the future will preserve what's fragile and fair. Men shall see Norvester and know man's nobility!" That deep voice brimmed with vigor and majesty.

"By Eremon, may it be so!" the Knight-Lord said.

"Last, Knight-Lord, is the issue of your halberd: my house's heirloom, handed down since Mannus," the King said. "I've determined you should keep it for now. You'll be beyond the bounds of Norvester, but I've full faith you'll serve the cause of Norvester, wherever you may wander. Use it well and honorably! As you have always done."

He bowed his head. "You honor me too much."

The Head of House Lofthungrian shook his head. "You, Deliad, are a first-rate friend and Knight-Lord. And that's a lesson I learn more each year. Eremon be in your breast and at your back!"

"Your Majesty." He went once more to one knee.

Cor quickly imitated, crouching low.

And out slipped that suppressed burp.

Brayleigh choked a giggle down, as Reginald's eyebrows rose.

And, on that note, they parted Norvester's King and headed for the city gate together, with one more wanderer having joined the wanderers.

Celeste was waiting there. "Come for farewells?" she asked the Knight-Lord.

"Yep! Farewell to *Norvester!*" said Brayleigh, as the orator's brow went furrowed.

"I like to think, where I go, Norvester goes," the Knight-Lord mused.

"We have a fourth," said Cor.

The Knight-Lord spread his arms forth winningly.

"Well." Celeste's face looked much like Brayleigh's had when Cor had welcomed her among the wanderers. "We're growing by the hour."

"'The more, the merrier'?" said Brayleigh, smiling straight at Cor, who blinked.

"What's an adventure without a good halberd?" waved Deliad, Hoarthaxe gleaming on his back.

"More of a bardiche, right?" inquired the Beldrian.

"Touché."

"Your mail, Sir Cor!" A squire ran up, bearing a bundle. He handed it over.

"Ah, right. Forgot that." From within, he lifted a chainmail vest, with wider bands of steel woven to a carapace of shining webs. It scarcely weighed more than the leather vest he'd worn when taking Norvester.

"Wow," said Cor.

"Lucky." The Knight-Lord eyed those glimmering loops. "At your age, I wore mail from Brinsmyth's students."

Doffing his pack and tunic, Cor slipped into a slim-cut gambeson and the gleaming vest, and finally a tabard with a crown and fist.

"Now *everyone* is better-dressed than me!" lamented Brayleigh, staring at her slacks.

Cor swung his arms a bit as though in swordplay. "Supple. Like leather. Stalbart would approve."

"Well, tell this Stalbart, this is Norvester mail," said Deliad.

"I'll sure miss it here in Norvester," sighed Brayleigh. "Feels like yesterday we got here!"

"You're telling me," the Knight-Lord quietly affirmed, facing the home he'd longed for for the last year.

"Beautiful place," said Cor. "It's what I'd hoped that cities were. Before I'd seen a city."

"You'll like the Academy." Celeste brushed her blonde hair. "More interesting, and just as beautiful."

"It's prettiest when the river ripples *red* at sunrise, right here!" Brayleigh loudly observed. Her green gaze had a blazing sheen Cor blinked at.

"The River Stiarna? Yes, I like it too," sighed Deliad. "Well, farewell to hearth and home. And off to the Academy! Where the men wear gowns, and think that villainizing valor makes them clever."

At this, the adoptive daughter of Clausiglade frowned and stared, but kept her silence. Perhaps, like Cor, she saw the depths of sorrow shimmering beneath the Knight-Lord's sea-blue gaze.

But why is Brayleigh smiling *now?* he wondered. He sometimes felt he saw in three dimensions, while women saw a fourth, fraught with strange feelings.

"Knight-Lord!" hailed Orther from beside the gate, some fifty feet away, with Captain Sigmund, Foreguard Fundaem and other knights. "A word?"

"Of course," the Knight-Lord called. "I'll be right back."

Cor couldn't quite make out their conversation, which spanned two minutes, save one last remark by Deliad as he left them: "Maybe a mile. But not so close you're caught."

And Sigmund nodded. "Safe travels, Knight-Lord."

"Let's make sure there's still a kingdom when I come back, eh?" said Deliad, and the other knights saluted.

"So," he started a moment later, nearing Cor, "my men have cleared the Gramsleith up to Leitath's Pass. They're camped outside it as we speak. By next week, when we arrive, it should be won and done."

"Good." Cor considered asking what that "mile" was—*something about the Pass?*—but let it lie. He trusted Deliad. And his way was, trust or don't trust. There was no halfway for him. He didn't test his friends: If friend, then trust.

"Been nearly a fortnight since I've swung this thing. I'm feeling downright rusty," Deliad said, drawing his halberd from his back. "I trust we'll find some time for sparring as we travel?"

"You trust correctly." Cor exchanged a fistbump.

"Go team!" The girl from Fernstead held her fist out.

But Cor and Deliad must have missed it, being too busy being borne forth by a Boreal wind along the way ahead, winding through oaks southeast toward summits haunted by the mists.

Down from the summit of their heady triumph in taking Norvester, they proceeded now toward new peaks looming large and needing climbing.

Celeste clasped Brayleigh's fist and squeezed it softly. "Go team!" she affirmed in sweet, melodious tone.

Brayleigh smiled back but sighed. "Well, thank you, Celeste. I'm not sure that's quite right though."

On the team went, savoring the Autumn wind, toward westering Sol, as high and out-of-reach aloft Midheaven as the elusive and half-fathomed hopes of four companions on a common quest.

CHAPTER 20

A whole week passed before they hit the Pass. Grey summits grew upon the southeast skyline from vague and gloaming forms to an icy wall, louring titanic all across their ken.

"We're going to pass through *that?*" The girl from Fernstead tugged her tunic. "Should I have brought a jacket?"

"Patience," said Deliad simply.

Celeste smiled. "It's far less menacing from the other side."

Brayleigh's brow rose. "But first, we have to get there!"

Sometimes, while walking in silence that week, Cor seemed to hear some voices from afar, echoing amid the oaks and many hills.

"There," he declared one day, as they were drawing close to the snow-capped heights. "Anyone hear that?"

"Actually, yes." Celeste was staring backward quizzically, where the way was lost in trees.

"Not me," the Knight-Lord shrugged. "Strange echoes here, with mountains, hills and such."

"The Skautfells sure look bigger here than back home!" Brayleigh said.

"'Skautfells'?" Celeste replied. "The Scoffa Range?"

"Aren't these the Skautfells you can see from far west?" asked Cor.

"Same mountains, different name," said Deliad. "Rarely hear 'Skautfell' now except from old folk."

"I've never heard that. And I grew up next door," said Celeste.

That afternoon, they'd emerged from the woodlands into a sprawling sward—marred by broad spans of blight and barren dust, lacing the gusts—when they beheld a wagon wheeling toward them.

A bearded fellow in green robes held the reins. He had the muscled paunchiness of one who loved his meals, but also liked hard labor that burnt them off. Beside him was a woman with auburn hair afrazzle atop her head. Her figure was a good deal like the man's, minus some muscle, plus some curves up top that clearly showed beneath her purple robe. Well into middle age but well-preserved, they both wore half-moon spectacles, rimmed silver.

Their conversation quickly came in earshot: an animated argument about the Moon's role in producing weather patterns.

"Dear, even if I allowed that one could treat the Moon, for certain purposes, as matter—which, mind you, still rests mainly on speculation!—that leaves the far more fundamental problem of matter exerting influence from afar." The man's right hand was motioning as he reasoned.

"No, no." The woman's auburn frazzle bobbed as she shook her head. "Your premise is the problem: that we're a bunch of isolated Things, and in between us is a great big Nothing. I think that's wrong. I think that there's one fabric beneath it all, even if our eyes can't see it. Think of a rug in a room full of blind people. They'll never see it. But if you should tug it, they'll still go toppling when it slides beneath them! Even if you 'exert that influence' from afar!"

"But what's your *evidence* there's a rug to tug?" the man retorted.

And she rolled her eyes. "Well, what's your *evidence* that there's not a rug? And, for that matter, what *evidence* exists that we're a bunch of billiard balls, as you imply, not moving till we're bounced by another ball? The Moon moves, then the sea moves, then the winds move. The rug analogy fits. What more is needed? As Aislin said, 'What's truth except a metaphor that intuition found to fit the facts?'"

"Quote Aislin at me, will you?" laughed the man. "'Truth is merely belief pursued and caught. Don't mock belief. That's what Lenvira does.' More wise adages in her early twenties than any old man I've met! But I do miss her."

"Likewise," the woman sighed sadly.

She looked up as Celeste called out, "Hey! Professor Dexios! Professor Aletheia!" jogging past her fellows and waving at the pair of wagon riders.

The bearded man was squinting. "Say, is that—?"

"Celeste!" the woman exclaimed in delight. She hopped down from the wagon as it rolled. Hiking her robe up, she bounded toward Celeste, her frazzle bobbing and her figure bouncing beneath her robe, her ruddy smile ebullient: a figure of gravity-flouting buoyancy.

Nearing, she hugged the adoptive daughter of Clausiglade. "Oh, Celeste! It's been so long."

"Much too long, Professor!" Celeste suddenly looked far younger. Her smile was wider now than back in Norvester.

"You're finally headed back to the Academy? The bird returns to roost?" At Celeste's nod, the woman smiled. "Good! Never should've left, never mind all those giddy plans of Clausiglade's. How is he anyway?"

"He passed away, not long ago." She looked away.

"Oh. Dear, I'm so, so sorry," said the woman, as her companion climbed down from the wagon. "Well. Seems you made some friends, out in the wide world?" She waved at the other wanderers to her rear. "Will they be studying at the Academy too?"

"Not if you paid me," Deliad muttered.

"Visiting," Celeste said. "Spending some time at the library. But I should introduce you!" she declared, as the other wagon rider was approaching.

The woman was Aletheia, Master Alchemist and Celeste's former instructor at the Academy. The wagon's driver was her husband, Dexios, a geographer and navigator, and cartographer and meteorologist: a jack of all trades in the study of travel.

Both amiably hailed the western wanderers. "Can't say I've met a man from that far west!" said Dexios. "I should show you two my maps. Maybe begin to fill that big blank space in."

But meeting Deliad drew a stronger reaction.

"*The* Knight-Lord?" said Aletheia. "And the halberd. That's *Hoarthaxe* then? Why"—she brushed back her frazzle—"I'm suddenly wishing I'd worn something nicer! It *is* an honor, Sir."

"The honor's mine," he answered. "Don't mind me. I'm used to seeing more dusty tabards than dresses and doublets."

"Just like the King?" the girl from Fernstead grumbled.

"What, coming straight from speaking with the King?" Aletheia lightly asked.

"Well, yes," Cor answered.

Aletheia laughed, then blinked at Cor's straight face. "Oh. Oh, you really mean that?" She spoke faintly. "Celeste, you *do* make fascinating friends."

"Oh, well, enough about us," Celeste waved, a little uneasiness beneath her smile. "But how are you two? How's the Academy been?"

"We wouldn't know," said Dexios.

"We've not been there in two years now!" Aletheia's voice was light but shaky, like a bird with wounded wing.

"We're exiles," Dexios said, drawing a chuckle from Celeste, fading slowly into a stare as the Professors failed to join.

"You don't—what, *exiles?* Really?" Celeste asked.

"That's why we have this wagon. Full of potions," said Dexios. "We go round from town to town, selling what Allie makes. I map the routes, maintain and drive the wagon, tend the oxen, and so forth. Big change, eh? But we get by."

"Potions?" The girl from Fernstead's eyes were glimmering. "*Real* potions? Not just like medicine? Like, love potions?"

"I've yet to find a way to induce true love!" Aletheia sighed. "But maybe it's not love in *that* sense that you meant?" Her lips curved up. "There's *lots* that I can do to loosen the lips, make dry things wet, put chilly things in heat—"

"How old were you again, girl?" Dexios broke in, frowning upon his wife, who waved and shrugged.

"Let's chat more later!" Brayleigh winked back blithely, pointing two fingers back and forth between them.

Delighted to! the middle-aged woman mouthed.

"So, yes, my Master Alchemist of a wife makes potions," Dexios said. "And mighty fine ones."

"Suppose 'the spirit of the Gnos' is with me, as Xenia used to say!" Aletheia mused.

"But wait," said Celeste, "wait. The exile thing. You can't just say *that* and then change the subject!"

The two professors shared a glance.

"In short," said Dexios, "there were things we disagreed with. Things that the Dean did. Suffice it to say, my temper got the best of me. I told him—"

"No, no, I'm not about to let you do that!" Aletheia said. "The story starts much earlier. And I, alas, am the protagonist."

He sighed, as Celeste stared. "What do you mean?"

"Well. So." Professor Aletheia took a deep breath. "It started with some students. Called themselves the 'Resistance.' Just annoying at the outset. They shouted slogans: 'There's no education without emancipation!' 'Education without equality is frivolity!' 'Your suppression of our truth is our oppression!' They had some strikes and sit-ins and the like."

"But what they wanted never was quite clear. Seemingly, all the things Dean Gaudimorte's gang had done for decades—turning the Academy to a sort of hub for anti-monarchism, deemphasizing the pursuit of knowledge—is what they wanted. Only fast and furious."

"Which makes one wonder: are they a *Resistance?* Or just the front lines for the people in power? Doing their dirty work? Clearing the way for them to do precisely as they'd planned? Dean Gaudimorte and his Governance Committee certainly haven't stamped out this 'Resistance.' They've given it an official advisory role!"

"Anyhow, I'm just a girl who brews potions. But I did think this stuff was awfully silly. And then I had a funny idea. 'How funny,' I thought, 'if I should write a sort of tract on *Resistance Alchemy.*' Simple satire, really. A send-up."

"I'd explain that every chemical is equal. And the toxic traits that some show are just a product of our preconceptions. And, if corrected, we can taste their true traits."

"And so, I dashed a draft off in a week!"

"I explained, for instance, potions we call 'laxatives' are simply those which 'we're acculturated to spurn and to expel.' But, 'by suppressing those preconceptions, we can turn a laxative to a curative elixir.' And, 'to test for alchemical bias, imbibe some antimony and see how smoothly it stays down.'"

"So," she said, "I wrote that, and I showed it to some friends, who might have mentioned it to other friends. One day, I found my manuscript was missing. So, I forgot about it for a month."

"Lo and behold, one night, I'm walking home and passing some Resistance types, all shouting something or other, handing pamphlets out. And what do I see stacked there but *my tract!* They're handing out *my tract!* Resistance Alchemy!"

"Somehow, my manuscript made it to them. They read it. And they thought the thing was genius! They took it, every word, as gospel truth!" She tittered. "And that laxative test? They tried it!"

"In other words," said Dexios, "she had first years shitting their pants in the name of equality."

"Ahem!" Aletheia forced her laughter down. "Next thing you know, the Resistance demanded the Governance Committee add my tract to *the alchemy curriculum!* It was added to the agenda for their monthly meeting!"

"Sadly," she said, "it seems some friends of friends let slip that my tract might not have been quite serious. And, more importantly, *I* wrote the thing."

"Oh, they were mad then, those Resistance types. They accused me of *attempted poisoning!* My little, private, obvious-send-up satire!" She sighed through a smile. "The Governance Committee sided with them. Or, I should say, they voted. It was a tie. And the tie-breaking vote of Dean Gaudimorte was to ban me from the Academy."

"So, as I'd started mentioning," Dexios said, "I had some choice words with the Dean that day. I might have made some injudicious statements about his judgment, intellect, and—mother." Aletheia giggled as he cleared his throat. "So, I was added to the lifelong exile."

"That's—quite a story," Celeste said.

"That's crazy. Didn't you say Academy sorts were smart?" Brayleigh asked Celeste.

"One would think so, yes?" Aletheia said. "Even Clausiglade would have laughed! And he was always *friendly* with that crew." She grimaced after a second. "Sorry, Celeste. I wasn't thinking."

Celeste waved it off.

"Sounds just like the Academy I remember," said Deliad.

"Did you study there?" asked Celeste.

"I spent a year there as a teen," he answered, "together with some other squires from Norvester. We spent a year being told by spiritless pedants to unlearn what Nature teaches us from birth: that you can see what's fair and feel what's right. And we were taught to hate our King and Kingdom."

"I think that you're exaggerating slightly," said Celeste.

"Slightly, maybe," shrugged Alethea.

"Well, anyway. I'm sad for you," said Celeste. "But it was their loss."

"Yes, entirely their loss," said Dexios. "Not me, mind you, but my wife. You'll find no Master Alchemist matching *her* outside Spelungagnost."

"Oh, stop," she waved.

"No, no, I'll say precisely what I'd like," he answered firmly. "As for me, this exile suits me just fine. I'd yearned for another journey. You know we met upon a journey?"

"Mm. Our life-quest," smiled Aletheia, looking skyward.

A moment passed in silence. "Well!" she said. "Why don't you take a break and have a bite? I thought I'd miss the meals at the Academy. But farmers out here *pay* for things with fresh food. It's not so bad!"

"Sounds just like home!" said Brayleigh, rubbing her belly. She'd walked toward the wagon before the others even could get a word in. "What's on the menu? Pumpernickel maybe?"

They ate for two hours, as the two professors regaled them all with stories of their wandering these last two years. And then, in turn, Cor told what *they'd* just done in Norvester; leaving vague some parts involving Lothar's personal orator.

"And so, the King's restored and Lothar's gone," concluded Cor.

"Remarkable," said Dexios. "Seems there's some good in this world after all!"

"Had I been Aislin, I'd have killed that scoundrel decades ago. And saved the world some trouble," Aletheia muttered. "Anyway, good riddance!"

Shortly thereafter, they were standing up, stretching their limbs, and savoring final bites of gouda melted over pumpernickel.

"Delicious," Celeste said. "We're really grateful. And—well. It's great to see you two again." Her eyes were suddenly shimmering. She looked young.

"The joy's all ours! It makes a lass feel young, being with the young," answered wistful Aletheia.

"What is it, thirty-five years since our journey?" asked Dexios.

"Yes, in seven weeks and two days! Counting from when you proposed to me, Dear."

"I knew that."

"You had better!"

Dexios nodded, then turned to Cor and Deliad. "Listen, friends. You think the game of courtship's won and done with marriage. Wrong! That's just the end of round one."

"Wise words!" the teen from Fernstead told the greybeard.

Aletheia smiled and squeezed his calloused hand.

Soon, the four wanderers were walking off east.

While he was waving, Cor glimpsed his companions. Celeste looked happy and troubled and sad. Brayleigh was patting her belly and grinning. Deliad was tossing his dirk up and catching it. And Cor? He sipped his flask and eyed the Sun, declining low along the western welkin.

Their lengthening shadows stretched toward Leitath's Pass, which now could be made out between the mountains: a sliver of sky, piercing the burgeoning Earth. What would they find there?

"Fare east, Cor Volucre. There shalt thou find thy passage cross this plane."

That must have meant the Passagestone. What next? Would he fulfill his quest here, browsing books? Or would he have to save more kingdoms first? Or find more ancient wise men, ancient Fossils, breached Boundaries, unplumbed caves, and unplanned perils?

Who knew? He had a hunch, though, that whatever he found here, he would have to do more wandering, and that his life's tale still had many pages, before he reached his destined destination.

CHAPTER 21

With Leitath's Pass now dwindling in their wake and the Academy's shining spires ahead, the wanderers were surprised to see that something vast and metallic was standing between them.

Well, "standing" wasn't quite the word. The object—egglike in shape and shade, with sunlight glimmering upon its polished curves—was in the air. Nothing that they saw was holding it up.

"What in the name of Eremon . . . ?" murmured Deliad.

Nearing the thing, they saw it had four fins of gold, which streaked back from the floating egg to sharp points in its wake. Attached beneath was something like an ocean-faring ship, but with the egg atop instead of sails. Fastened to this apparent "deck" were cables, stretching diagonal from four corners groundward.

Across the white egg, in calligraphy of midnight blue, was written a single word: "SOJOURNER."

"I know what this is!" said Celeste, excitement and remembrance rushing through her. She'd been a teen then, barely Brayleigh's age, and hanging round the Observatory after her class had ended, as she often had done. Her present focus faded into memory:

The day's last light of grey was streaming in. Those little birds of brass were whirring by abovehead, nearing glassy walls and swerving just in the nick of time, then flapping onward.

"But I have bigger plans," Professor Starling was saying, after Celeste had applauded and wondered at this artifice for a while. "Much bigger. Birds can fly without my help. For man to fly though: that *would* be a marvel. The *Sojourner*, I'm going to call her. Someday."

"I think it flies." At the others' puzzled faces—eyes flicking toward the object, plainly floating—she shook her head. "No, not just hovering there. I think it *flies*." She waved a hand toward Heaven. "A ship that sails the skies. And you can ride it."

The Knight-Lord raised an eyebrow.

"Can *we* ride it?" asked gaping Brayleigh, day's sheen in her green gaze.

"Maybe they'll let us once we save the world?" suggested Cor.

"Let's take our time," said Deliad, studying the airship with some skepticism.

"Or maybe sooner," Celeste said. "I know who built this. Know him well, in fact. I'll ask him."

The girl from Fernstead's face lit up like Dawn.

Passing the *Sojourner*, they saw three figures in scholars' gowns approaching on the Gramsleith, clad in three colors, walking with a hunch. Each of the scholars had grey hair or no hair. But age's dulling hadn't reached their faces, which had the sharpness of a craggy cliffside. Their smileless chatter wasn't quite in earshot.

Beside them was a silent man. He wore a cloak of motley colors over black mail, belted but otherwise loose and flamboyant. His hair was long and black; his eyes were black; his face, the hue of desert sand, and faintly grinning at something that no one had said. Strapped to his back was a short lance, and sheathed at his left side was a wicked-looking knife.

He eyed the wanderers briefly one by one—pausing for slightly longer upon the Beldrian, whose hand was resting on his hilt—before looking away with undisguised disinterest.

One of the scholars stepped ahead of the others: a bald and beardless man, with drops of sweat dribbling along his bulging neck and dampening his colored collar. As he neared, he bent his craggy countenance into a winning smile. "Celeste, my dear! How wonderful to see you."

"Dean Gaudimorte. It's been so long." Celeste smiled politely.

He approached and, hardly pausing, hugged Celeste, leaning over his ample belly. Then, smile still fixed upon his uneven face, like he were posing for an unseen artist, he stood up straight and held his arms out. "Ah, our prodigal child comes home. And with companions!"

The Dean's smile swept across the three of them, although Cor noticed that it never paused upon their faces.

"Friends of mine," she said. "Everyone, this is Dean Gaudimorte, the head of the Academy—"

"Merely the first among equals! I make no pretense that I'm more than that!" the black-gowned Dean broke in. "Malvolio Gaudimorte, forever at your service." Once again, he held his arms out. And the smile was still there.

"Beside me are Professors Liv Vitodium"—a woman with a curled lip, close-shorn hair, and squinting gaze against the Sun—"and Zell Phobios"—a long-necked man whose Adam's apple looked larger than his chin. "Both pleased, I'm sure."

Nodding, they made some sounds of idle agreement.

"And at my other side is—what was it? Loginos, yes?" asked Gaudimorte. "Yes, Loginos!" he went on, as the man in motley cloak silently nodded. "From another Fragment, far to the east, he tells me. Ha! What times."

Cor scrutinized Loginos. He seemed, somehow, vaguely familiar.

Brayleigh's eyes went bright at this talk of hailing from a far off Fragment, and she'd begun to open her mouth and point at the Beldrian. But at Celeste's brief sharp glance, she shut her mouth, then turned it into a cough.

Good. Celeste didn't want to tell the story of how their group had met, much less to Gaudimorte.

"Anyway," Gaudimorte glanced at Brayleigh and Celeste, "it's good to have you back. And how is Clausiglade?"

"He passed away not long ago," said Celeste. "Killed by an ork in the recent retaking of Norvester."

"So the tales are true! Retaken. 'Wagons and history alike will roll backward at times,' they say. Well, I'm just glad you're safe," said Gaudimorte. "What a shame though. Terrible shame, that such a forward wit should pay the price for the backward ways of royal reactionaries. He will be missed. We'll keep you in our thoughts."

The Knight-Lord's eyes went narrow. And, at once, the man in motley cloak had turned to face him, tilting his head inquiringly, one hand holding the hilt of his wicked-long knife. But Deliad kept his mouth shut.

Celeste looked down. "Yes, he'll be missed." A moment passed in silence.

"Now, do my eyes deceive me," Gaudimorte said, "or is your friend behind you not *the Knight-Lord?*" The bald man's eyes gleamed brightly as his sweat beads.

"Forever at your service," Deliad said, arms folded over a blazon of crown and fist.

"Well. What a marvel. Celeste and the Knight-Lord! And so soon after—mm. Well, anyway." Dean Gaudimorte's gaze had drifted to the airship. "So nice to have you back. We'll have to catch up."

"Of course," said Celeste. "Nice to see you too."

The trio of scholars soon were out of earshot, as they continued toward the Sojourner.

Celeste was first to resume walking east.

"Are all your friends that charming?" Deliad asked her.

"Oh, stop," said Brayleigh.

Deliad held his hands out as though to say, *I'm simply asking questions.*

"Clausiglade was never too fond of Dean Gaudimorte," Celeste responded evenly. "Which seemed odd, since they agreed on most things. Still, I valued his views. I've always kept the Dean at arm's length, despite the benefits friendship would've brought me." Her voice was cool and level as the tundra. "In short, you're wrong to say that he's my friend."

"Unlike the way she told him *we're her friends!*" Brayleigh said pointedly.

Celeste said nothing. Neither did Deliad, but he looked away.

She led the party through the city gate. Here, near the walls, the neighborhood was somewhat seedier than anywhere in knight-fraught Norvester, let alone farmer-filled Beldria or Fernstead.

"Do ladies at the Academy dress like that?" asked Brayleigh, gesturing toward two women, wearing very short scarlet skirts, boas round their necks, and too much make-up, standing at the corner. They scanned the streets and posed for passersby.

The Knight-Lord tried and failed to force his laugh down.

"Just the most fashionable ones," answered Celeste.

"Is this the Fashion District?" Brayleigh asked, as Celeste led them quickly past this district, and Deliad quietly chortled to himself.

The shabby structures crammed along the streets soon were replaced by rows of family homes, still somewhat tightly packed but nicely tended. Many had flowerpots and gardens with herbs; even vegetables, sometimes, in small square beds. Some children ran along the strips of grass.

The girl from Fernstead nodded with approval. "How do you like that home?" she questioned Cor, pointing at one especially fine stone house.

"It's, um." The Beldrian blinked. "I like the house. Maybe I'll have to see more of the city. But I think Beldria might be a better fit. Or Norvester. Or, um, Fernstead."

"Mm." She smiled, glancing sidelong at Celeste. "Yeah, me too!"

"Give it some time," said Celeste. She felt vaguely that justifying this place would justify herself. "The beauty's deeper inside. You'll see."

She felt a bit disheartened at the black look that Brayleigh gave her in response. *That bad?*

Cresting a hill, they caught their first clear view of the city's shining spires: obelisks of white, dazzled with day and soaring toward its source, each of them tall as Norvester's tallest tower.

"One of the few things here worth seeing," said Deliad.

"Well worth the price of admission right there," mused Cor.

"I understand you saved the Kingdom purely to clear the pass so you could come here," said Celeste. "Quite a price!" Being prone toward big thoughts, she wasn't much for small talk. But she'd try.

"The joy is in the journey, right?" said Brayleigh. "It's whom we meet along the way and all that!"

"Indeed," said Cor. "Beautiful place here, Celeste."

"Good place, good people," she replied. "Deep down."

"The things one does for beauty!" Deliad said.

Even *he* was not so openly hostile now. She felt some small hope swelling warm within her.

But that black look from Brayleigh again! It saddened her. The girl had seemed to be her first new friend here.

The next ten minutes passed in gradual progress toward the Academy's many shining spires. Along the way, they saw security guards in growing numbers, strolling two by two and scanning their surroundings. Many looked, beneath their vests and visors, oddly large and bulky.

Must be investing in safety, Celeste supposed, a bit surprised at this. Dean Gaudimorte hadn't liked the Academy Guard; which, likewise, hadn't liked his deanship much.

The strangeness of the guards had never struck her in youth—she'd grown up seeing them—but it did now: Those dull grey vests they wore, as light as leather, deflecting even direct blows from a blade. Those little canisters of smoke they carried, which burst on impact, promptly blinding whole crowds, choking out breath, setting their bare skin burning.

Most striking was the weapon that they carried. A "stunner," it was called: a slanted tube of silver with a single dial and button. Pressing the latter sent what looked like lightning jagging out wildly toward what it was aimed at.

Centuries ago, when King Promethean's men unsealed the spires, they'd found a stash of these in what had since been named the Hall of War, stored in a closet on an upper storey. Without quite grasping how they worked, some scholars had found a way to replicate the firearms, rebuilding them component by component.

Their foremost limitation was the fact that they'd only fire a hundred times—or fifty, when dialed to full power—till had they to charge. The only place they charged was in that closet they'd come from. And the scholars never had found a way to replicate that little closet.

The sight of a familiar house ahead dispelled her reverie. "Here we are," she said, pointing upon the homely thatched-roof cottage of faint blue, with its faded yellow door. "Drop off your things inside. If we get split up, make your way here and we'll meet up at evening. It's easy. Follow the road from the gate."

"This house belong to a friend of yours?" asked Brayleigh.

"It's Clausiglade's. Or, I guess, it's mine," she said. "You can share my room, Brayleigh. Cor and Deliad, Clausiglade has only one bed. But it's big."

"I call the bed," said Cor immediately.

"Arm-wrestle for the bed. Loser takes floor," Deliad at once replied.

"Fair," Cor affirmed.

"But she just said it's *big* though!" Brayleigh observed.

The Knight-Lord and the Beldrian stared a moment.

"Arm-wrestle for the bed," repeated Cor.

"Yep."

Brayleigh sighed and shrugged at Celeste. "Boys!"

Celeste proceeded to her room by habit, but seeing it caught her off-guard. There was her bed: the guest bed Clausiglade, twenty years ago, had offered to a tousled orphan child, dressed with that heron-patterned quilt he'd had. There was her wood-carved heron on the dresser, gifted by Clausiglade on Yuletide one year. There was her tome on ornithology—he'd "checked it out" indefinitely from the archives, as professors were permitted—open to a page she'd been reading at eighteen, back when the world had seemed as wide and open as what a heron on the wing beheld.

"I take it this is yours," said Brayleigh. "Cute birds!"

Celeste turned sideways to hide her eyes' shimmer. "Indeed." Feigning a yawn, she blinked it out and quickly brushed the moisture from her face.

"Should I just set my bags right here?" asked Brayleigh. "Happy to sleep on the floor! You have blankets?"

"Bags can go anywhere. Right there is good. And don't be silly. This bed's big enough for both of us." She forced some sanguine up. "Unless you'd like to test your strength right now!" She held a clenched fist forth, then giggled faintly.

After a blink, Brayleigh joined her. "Let's do this!" She put her dukes up; then, threw back her arms and fell back laughing onto Celeste's bed. "Ahh. I'll be up in just a minute. Maybe."

Leaving her room a couple minutes later, they found the Knight-Lord rubbing at his wrist.

"Hey there! Who gets the bed?" asked Brayleigh happily.

The Knight-Lord grimaced. "Shouldn't have agreed to best of three."

"Yep. Quit while you're ahead," replied the Beldrian, yawning as he stretched.

Soon, they were back on the street and approaching the city center, where the rows of homes were replaced by a marketplace; or a bazaar, really, with all the cluttered carts and peddlers hawking their fine wares from every which way. What space was left was filled with browsing shoppers: a mix of townsfolk, students wearing tunics of brown, grey, black or white, depending on seniority, and scholars wearing gowns, colored according to their fields of study.

"Do we have time to stop here?" Brayleigh called from behind the others. She was staring wide-eyed at an array of motley herbs and spices, strewn in a colorful mess on a cart.

"You'll have all afternoon," responded Celeste. "But we should catch Professor Starling now, before he leaves for lunch."

"This marketplace—is it this busy every day?" asked Cor, sliding between some crowded customers.

"Six days a week. It has to close by law on Sahngdays," Celeste answered. "Well, it *had* to. The Dean had hoped to do away with that. Eke out more taxes from the increased trade."

"Sounds like a scholar," the Knight-Lord affirmed. "No higher concerns in life than taking money that others make to redistribute it." He frowned and balled a fist as someone bumped him. "Yes, who needs holy days, when you could have *this* for seven days a week instead of six? In Norvester, there aren't 'markets'; only shops, neatly arranged, where no one shouts or shoves you. All closed on Armonsday. How backward, eh?"

Celeste refrained from answering, but her eyes rolled, as Cor laughed quietly. Brayleigh didn't hear, being busy gawking at some life-sized statues of beasts from far off Fragments, carved from plaster.

Eventually, they emerged from the open-air market into a neighborhood more civil and spacious. The boulevards here were broad and lined with mansions of stone, half-hidden by fences, walls and hedges. Vines hung along these homes from high aloft their windowed pinnacles and parapets.

"Wow. Do the nobles live here?" Brayleigh asked.

"Some Norvester nobles, yes," responded Celeste. "Though not as many now. It's mostly merchants. Also, of course, the Governance Committee."

"You mean the ones who exiled your two teachers?"

"One and the same."

As eminent as these homes were, they didn't hold a candle to the spires shining Sun-bright above the busy skyline. Strikingly smooth with a metallic sheen, these obelisks seemed both alien and aloof from the host of homelier towers aspiring toward them, like ideas in a crowd of instances.

"Did the Academy build those?" questioned Cor.

"No. They'd been ancient back when King Promethean unsealed them," Celeste said. "In fact, he founded the Royal Academy as a place to study the spires and what they held. That's where we come from."

Still "we," a decade later. Should've stayed here.

"And here we are," she announced, halting before a brown stone building. "The Observatory." Above its entrance soared a winged figure of tarnished bronze.

"Like Dievas," murmured Cor.

She led them through the oaken double doors into a hallway partly of paneled wood and partly of the same grey stone outside. Oil lamps of brass were spaced evenly and flaming. Hanging between them were portraits of men with long grey hair in academic gowns, typically caught in forehead-furrowing thought.

"So there are classes here? Not just the spires?" said Brayleigh.

"Yes. I took one here," said Deliad. "Favorite of mine, in fact."

"Oh?" Celeste said. "You know Professor Starling then?"

"What's all this about Professor Starling?" someone called back.

Rounding the bend was a middle-aged man. Wearing a navy blue jumpsuit trimmed yellow, his frame was svelte but broad around the shoulders. A birdlike bounce was in his step. A light brown combover lay on his slightly creased forehead, still thick but losing color along the temples. In one hand was a gadget built from gears and crisscrossed rods. In the other was an apple.

"Professor Starling!" Celeste dashed ahead and clasped his wrists, then leaned and gave a hug, grinning up childlike.

"Celeste. Fancy seeing you." He shared her smile. "Been far too many years. What brings you back here? You and all your friends. Need a refresher on physics?"

"Not quite," she answered. "We're here for a few things. But I should introduce them first." She did so.

"Pleasure to meet you, Brayleigh, Cor. An honor, Knight-Lord." He nodded at each. "I'm Dirk Starling. You're all forbidden from calling me Professor, Celeste excepted." He glanced over his shoulder. "Why don't you all come join me in my office? Looks like you all could use someplace to sit."

Absently, Celeste wondered who would stand. His office, last she checked, had fit three chairs and only barely. "Perfect," she replied, and turned right.

"Where you headed?" Starling called, after she'd taken several steps from the others.

She frowned. "Am I remembering wrong?"

"You're not. I moved." He walked the other way. "Come on."

They followed Starling up a spiral staircase, and then a second, third and fourth, emerging into another hallway of wood and stone. The lamps were sparser now. No portraits hung here, but tarnished old devices were displayed on sideboards, worked with barley twist and inlays. The occasional doors were windowless and unmarked.

The scholar opened one and began to climb the shadowy staircase looming just beyond it. The door atop was carved with constellations—the Ram, the Bull, the Twins, the Crab, the Lion, and all the ecliptic crew—and Celeste knew why.

Opening the door, Professor Starling strode in. They followed him into a large round room, domed at the top, with a big tube of brass angled to face an open slit in the ceiling. Starling had told her it was called a "telescope"; a name no eight year old from rural Norvester was likely to encounter.

Starling patted the pedestal beneath the brass machinery. "Caught a good glimpse of the Dawnstar this morning. Good way to start the day. Not superstitious, but something in her shining rubs the right way."

"Ah." Celeste smiled, as Cor and Brayleigh wondered at the bizarre brass contraption and big dome: her, scrunching up her eyes and pointing up, then turning to him happily; him, head tilted and peering at the prospect, then at her.

How much more like *them* might Celeste have been, if not for Fortune's whims? Was that how life worked, weaving one's future from whatever's nearby? Or would the little golden thread of her life have woven itself into a darkened tangle no matter what weird mishaps intervened?

She shook the introspection out. "Not bad, Professor."

"Quite an upgrade, eh?" he agreed, sweeping a hand at his observatory.

Several large tables and desks were piled high with leather books and loose notes, scribbled top to bottom and along the margins too with formulae and figures. Metal gadgets and gizmos like the geared thing in his hand lay on the papers, many half-assembled. Some birds of brass were glimmering in their midst.

"Sit down and stay a while!" He tossed his widget atop some rods and, biting into his apple, plopped in a wheeled chair of burgundy leather next to the biggest and most cluttered table. As promised, there were plenty of chairs to choose from.

"I'd been stuck downstairs a decade or so, and long past due to pick another office." Starling leaned back in his overstuffed seat. "But Gaudimorte and his Governance Committee put me off year after year. This past Winter, Dean Gaudimorte joked that the only room he had to give was the observation room itself. I told him I accepted his proposal."

"Do you sit in for the astronomy classes?" asked Deliad, studying the telescope idly.

"They're taught downstairs now," the Professor answered. "The Governance Committee is of the view that the astronomy that matters is the theory and math—not 'spending nights staring at Stars.' Never mind what the department head thinks!" He sighed. "Anyway, that's what brought me here. What about you?"

"Well, first, what's new in these parts?" asked Celeste, clearing papers from a seat and sinking into it. "You, the Academy, so forth."

"Hm. Everything and nothing," Starling said. "I've reached and touched the Heavens, and fallen back down beneath the burdens of the earthliest things."

She smiled. "Is this about the Sojourner?"

"What? You remembered? The one time I mentioned . . . ." He stared and shook his head. "Indeed. You saw her, heading here from the pass? A beauty, eh?" Nostalgia lit his face, lifting his lips. "She's just as I imagined her: each curve, each feature; fair and buoyant as a cloud; that little hum of hers. Just like I dreamt of and spent long decades longing for." He looked a little wistful. "You remembered, eh?"

"That first time you were showing me your brass birds," she nodded back.

"Indeed." He shook his head. "I should've known. That memory: like a transcript of everything I told you. Ah, what promise. And then you picked *humanities!* The waste!"

"Hm, what? I didn't pick humanities." She frowned. "I left the Academy halfway through."

"Same difference," waved the Head of Physics. "So, your question: Yes, this is about my ship. Alas, these days, most joys and woes of mine arise from her."

"How so? The woes, I mean."

"Well," Starling said. "You saw her. She's been built for some time. Fully finished, primed for flight. For *flying*, mind you, not just floating there. I did the labor, with Professor Logi and several students. The material costs? All paid for with discretionary funds scrimped up by my department through the years. While others frittered all their funds away, we saved ours up to spend on actual science. What's left is what should be a technicality: the Governance Committee's final signoff."

"Sadly"—his tone took on an acid note—"the Governance Committee, after months, can't seem to muster the simple 'yes' needed for science to make her largest leap in centuries. There's always something, some inane concern: 'Raise the rails higher'! 'Change the cabins'! 'Add *carpets*'! As soon as I address it, they find something else to be worried of. Week after week!"

"And so I wait here," Starling sighed, "and wait. I'm keen to give her such a maiden voyage, she'll shiver to remember it after her hundredth. At this rate, though, she'll be an old maid by then, and I'll be shriveled dry. And what's the point then?"

Deliad frowned slightly at the scholar's phrasing.

"So what are their concerns now?" Celeste asked.

"Well, till a few weeks past, they cited safety," said Starling. "Which was ridiculous really. It isn't half as dangerous as a ride on horseback. I prepared a whole report to prove it: tests and tables, charts and figures. I spent a month on that. They took one look, then tossed the thing aside and raised new issues."

"Now, it's the ethics: 'Whether it's appropriate to expend our funds upon the pointless luxury of flying birdlike, while the poor still suffer in poverty.'" Professor Starling sighed. "'The poor': misused to villainize valor in science! Imagine if, years past, we'd halted science till poverty were gone. We'd have *more* poor. We'd still be clad in pelts! Living in caves! Most good new things in life are 'pointless luxuries'; till, suddenly, we can scarcely live without them."

"I hope you told Dean Gaudimorte that," said Celeste.

"Something like that. Though somewhat more polite." He shook his head. "Dean Gaudimorte pointed out that we have wagons, which can cross the Fragment in weeks. 'Which, most would say, is fast enough,' he said. Hmph. Give them a few years of flying, then ask what folk consider 'fast enough'!"

"You know," said Brayleigh, day's sheen in her green gaze, "we have a Passagestone. It opens the Boundaries and lets you pass. What if you mounted *that* inside the ship? So it could fly from Fragment to Fragment? So much for the Dean's excuse, huh? No wagon's gonna do that!"

Cor held up the crimson stone, which seemed to absorb the light.

Professor Starling raised an eyebrow. "Really? A 'Passagestone'? A stone that parts the Boundaries? *That* would be something." He glanced over at Celeste, as when a child has told a farfetched story and one peers questioningly at her parent.

"I haven't seen it used yet," Celeste answered, "but I believe it works as Brayleigh said. She—knows a bit about the Boundaries."

"Oh?" Starling regarded the teen girl from Fernstead. "Someone who studies the Boundaries these days? They're there. That's all our scholars learned through centuries of study. That's why none study them now. Did you take courses somewhere? With a tutor?"

"Nope. I learned all I know from Gramps! And testing."

Starling smiled kindly. "Well. What did 'Gramps' teach you?"

Brayleigh glanced over at Celeste.

"Go ahead," she said.

The girl from Fernstead raised a palm.

A semilucent blood-hued Boundary struck the back of Starling's wheeled seat, so he abruptly was rolling cross the room with arms thrown up; only to halt just a few feet from Brayleigh, bumping against another half-seen Boundary. It rippled in the scholar's face.

"You see," said Celeste, "Brayleigh knows a bit about the Boundaries."

"Ah." Professor Starling blinked. "You've always had some fascinating friends, Celeste." He faced the girl from Fernstead now with greater gravity. "So, this Passagestone. I assume that it emits a field of some sort. Something disrupting the Boundaries. If so, the question is, how far this field extends. Wide enough for the ship? And other questions: Whether it's altered by altitude. Whether it fluctuates with the weather. Hard to test. I don't know how I'd detect such a field."

"Well, what if I could tell you where it was?" asked Brayleigh excitedly.

The scholar shrugged. "That would be that then. I suppose it's possible." He paused, a gleam appearing in his gaze. "Certainly, if she could *fly through the Boundaries*, that'd speed the signoff process up. It'd have to. Who would let red tape block what Boundaries won't?"

"So, right. It's like a field around the stone," said Brayleigh. "Stretching, oh, fifty-odd yards."

"Ah, perfect," Starling said. "That's plenty—"

"*But*," Brayleigh went on, "it weakens as it spreads out. It's only strong enough to breach the Boundary five yards or so each way. Not fifty yards."

"Ah." Starling frowned. "So much for that, I—"

"*But*," Brayleigh went on, "the Boundaries weaken up high, the farther from the ground you go. I've felt it on hills. And by the time you hit the sky, I bet they're barely there!"

"So weak this stone might make a gap that fits my ship?" said Starling.

"One way to find out!" declared Brayleigh blithely.

Starling frowned slightly. But it soon gave way to that glimmer in his gaze again. "To cross the Boundaries, we just have to hit the sky first. Well, she and I can get you there, my friends."

The wanderers shared a glance. They'd spent a week walking between two towns within one Fragment. How many Fragments would they have to cross upon their quest? With Winter coming soon? It wasn't lost on them that Starling's ship might be a way to save some travel time.

"You know," said Starling, "I should head out now. Dean Gaudimorte and the Governance Committee were doing a walkthrough of the ship this morning. Signoff could come at their meeting today. Just have to tell them how we'll cross the Boundaries."

"I mean, I'm maybe sixty-five percent certain that this should work, but . . . " Brayleigh trailed off.

Starling dismissed this with a cursory wave. "What things worth doing start out with certainty? We'll do this." He was beaming now. "Indeed, we'll make this work. Or, if we fail, we'll try another way, and try another way, and, testing how we fare from way to way, we'll wayfare finally to the place we're seeking." His fist was clenched around his half-eaten apple.

"And if the Governance Committee rules against us—well," said Starling, gaze gone narrow, "science never stops, no matter how hard scholars struggle to stop it."

"Right! Who needs their rules?" cried Brayleigh.

"Aptly said. Rule number one: Never give up what's genius for the rules' sake," Starling declared with one finger held high.

She couldn't help but smile. This was the Starling that she remembered.

"So," said Cor, "this ship. Assuming that the Passagestone works out, think you could fly us a few places maybe?

The skyward-gazing scholar smiled. "My friends, I'll fly you round the world and back again, if, thanks to you, the Sojourner gets signoff. I've reached that age when picking my priorities becomes a pressing thing. 'When if not now?' one wonders. Yes, I hope to have some good flights, before I fly away from little old Earth."

"So?" Brayleigh asked the Beldrian. "You're in charge! What do you say? Get the Passagestone mounted?"

Cor blinked, then nodded, lips curved up. "Let's do this."

"Excellent." Starling faced the girl from Fernstead. "So, Brayleigh, was it? You can sense this field around the Passagestone? And Boundaries too?"

"Mm-hmm!"

"Alright. Let's meet tomorrow morning outside the airship. Bring the Passagestone. You'll have to help me find a place to mount it. And you can tell me if you think this field spans far enough for us to fit."

"Will do!"

"For now," he said, "I'm off to the Committee. Without their signoff, all this work's for naught." He stood and strode toward the exit, with a birdlike bounce in his step. "Been a pleasure, you all." He stepped outside, then leaned his head back in. "Why don't we reconvoke at Dawn on Sahngday? Over at the Hall of Ages, by the board where they post their meeting minutes. You know it, Celeste. That's where we'll learn if they voted. And how."

"Sounds good," smiled Celeste. "Glad that you're on our side."

"Always!" The scholar vanished down the staircase.

"Suppose I should've asked you all beforehand," said Celeste.

"No, that's perfect," Cor replied. "So we have, what, five days before we hear back about the Sojourner? We'll want that time for browsing the library, right? Big place, right?"

"Vast. You'll be amazed. A whole new world," said Celeste. "I'll show it to you."

"Oh, for Flua-Sahng's sake!" the girl from Fernstead muttered.

The others faced her with quizzical stares.

"Just stubbed my toe!" She forced a smile through her apparent pain. "Yowch! Bad stub!"

"So, you can maybe show us where to search. Or where to start at least," said Cor to Celeste.

"Of course, yes. I know every nook and cranny." Celeste was eager to show she had *some* worth, being the only wanderer lacking skills in battle. "Some that you probably could spend a whole night in and not be bothered by a single visitor!"

Brayleigh was muttering again. *Must be a bad stub.*

"What did you want to study first?" asked Celeste. "The Fossils? The Elements? Dievas?"

"I think our first priority is to find out where any living Elements are," said Cor. "If anyone would know a way to bring back the other Elements, I would think it's them."

"Sounds like a plan!" Celeste tried to smile sweetly; something she'd rarely had to do this decade.

More muttering. *Ouch. Poor girl.*

"I am impressed, I have to say, that you can read the Eldscript," the Knight-Lord noted to the western wanderers. "It took me several months to pick it up here. Do you have schools back home? Or is it tutors?"

The pair of country-dwellers shared a glance.

"The Eldscript?" questioned Cor. "What is this 'Eldscript'?"

The former Academy students shared a glance. Celeste's brow furrowed, as Deliad's face sank.

"Alright then, Celeste," Deliad glumly said. "It looks like this is going to be in our hands. I assume that *you* can read the Eldscript, yes?"

"Can you wield halberds?" she replied. "Of course."

"Wait. You mean everything at the Academy is in another language?" asked the Beldrian.

"Not quite," said Celeste. "It's a lot like our tongue, but how they spoke it many centuries past, back when the Royal Academy was created. You'd likely understand it, spoken aloud; well, some of it. The issue is, the script looks nothing like our script. Rather more runic. Our scholars kept on writing in the Eldscript, even as it disappeared from daily use, so anyone could access all our archives by learning just a single script and language."

"Which means that nine in ten tomes here are Eldscript," the Knight-Lord finished grimly.

"For the old ones, it's more like ninety-nine percent," said Celeste. "And it's the old ones that discuss the Elements. They're not exactly studied much these days."

"So," Brayleigh said. "You mean that Cor and I can't help you two? You'll have to browse these books, and Cor and I will have to—something else?" She blithely shrugged and waved that *something else*.

"Well, you'll be helping the Professor work on the Sojourner tomorrow," Celeste said. "Cor, I suppose you can study some maps, after we have a sense of where we're headed, and plot out how we'll get there. In the meantime?" She shrugged. "Have fun."

"Yeah, you just go and have fun," grumbled Deliad.

Cor grinned. "Not much for books?"

"I'm Knight-Lord of Norvester, not a librarian."

Out of the skylit serenity of the Observatory, down the grey stone stairways and hallways went the wanderers. They emerged to a bustle that seemed twice as bright and loud now. Into that urban hubbub disappeared the pair of rural westerners, one dashing back toward the market and its motley wares, with red hair and the other in her wake.

The older duo went the opposite way. Sol beamed from Midheaven on the fair and lofty heights of the Hall of Ages, where, in cluttered darkness, the wisdom of the Ancients waited—stacked in leather tomes, with leaves of paper and parchment formed out of lives long gone, and full of words unspoken for several hundred Springs and Falls—waiting for life to bring them back to light. Perhaps a few would see that brightness soon, thanks to the lively and brilliant spark uniting these wanderers with the fair designs of Heaven.

Chapter 22

Sol glared from Midheaven on the heaving moil beneath the skies' serenity, churned up by the manic appetites and libidos of the open market. There, with Celeste's blessing and Deliad's grousing leave, the westerners prepared to dally away the livelong day.

"Lovely scarves!" "Love lockets!" "Potions for lovers!" The signs and shouts pervaded the overrun streets and, lief or loath, the thousand passersby, leaving them like this place in mood and mien. Here was a trio of students, tasting samples and trying to make a free meal out of it. There was a guard on furlough, haggling over the fishing pole he'd spend his next few weeks with.

Brayleigh's green gaze had gone bright at first scent of street food, wafting from the ways ahead. She'd darted toward it, slipping through the droves of passersby with slender, smiling ease. Being rather broader, he'd been forced to follow by rudely shoving through the assembled shoppers. He'd tried to grin apologetically, but mostly just got glares back.

He had lost her for almost half a minute, when he finally—catching a glimpse of some colorful piles of powder, and remembering her excitement—found Brayleigh browsing herbs and spices with a big smile.

"Ooh! That's Fluxweed! And some Woundwort. We'll want those, don't you think?" she questioned Cor, sensing his presence without looking somehow. "Some Cinquefoil to soften it. Tormentil."

"Ah. Will we?"

"We don't have to. Just don't ask *me* to mend you, when you get sliced up again!"

"Okay, let's get some. Good idea."

"I know, right?" She looked at him and waited.

Oh. He lifted his satchel and withdrew a silver piece.

"You want enough to save your life a few times or every time?" she asked, eying the lone coin.

"Well, when you put it that way." He retrieved two more.

"Yep, that should do!" She waited as he paid the vendor from his dwindling savings. "So nice! I've never seen so many spices and herbs, outside of Misses Folfold's pantry. Probably not even there! I could spend all day just *buying* stuff and never getting bored!"

Cor winced. He wondered what it must be like in Brayleigh's head.

"This light's so bright!" she noted.

Bright as a silver piece, light as my satchel. "Which one's your favorite?" questioned Cor. "Of the herbs."

In fact, the girl from Fernstead still was feeling giddy and gleeful at her stroke of luck: that there was "Eldscript" and they couldn't read it. Just her and Cor! And, meanwhile, Mister Third Wheel and Goldilocks were buried deep in books, in dim stacks, thinking heavy thoughts. *For days! Or weeks!* She smiled a bright, light smile at Cor.

Then, she remembered he'd asked her a question. "No, no. It's not like that. You can't have favorites. Like asking what your favorite tree is!"

"White oak," answered the stillman's son immediately. "You can't age whisky in maple or pine. Gets gross."

She frowned and pondered. "Think of the Sword Postures. Like asking what your favorite Posture is! You favor one, you're doing it wrong. Right?"

"Hm." He peered upon his sword. "Good explanation."

She smiled. She might not be Academy-taught, and might not know a simile from a metaphor, but she could teach a class on *this*. "I try!" Nature and Fernstead farmwives were her tutors; and what they taught, they taught well.

"Hey, what's that?" She lightly seized his fingers, felt them tense up, and tugged him for a second toward a table of something or other—that wasn't important—and then released. *Scarves*. "You like scarves?" she asked, running the hand that'd held his through some silk.

Making their way west through the market, Brayleigh zipped in mercurial circles round the Beldrian, casting her bright gaze briefly on all the goods sparkling among the constellated booths. Cor kept a rather more constant pace west, but with a sunny face and smile, she observed.

The street cooks seemed to like to give her samples, and didn't mind that Brayleigh wasn't buying; especially when she loudly announced delight at their deliciousness. She could oblige. In truth, she'd likely have done it anyway.

As for the hawkers of clothing and trinkets, they weren't as big on handouts. Still, they puffed up with pride whenever Brayleigh affirmed the beauty of some fine ring or bracelet and requested to try it on, and said "of course, of course." And then they'd look at Cor, and sometimes ask if he agreed. And, bless him, he always did; though sometimes with his eyes upon his satchel.

She felt that things were going the way they should.

"I'm thirsty!" She'd learnt early in life that being the kindly random one, who keeps things moving and never boring, made the small talk better. And small talk was a big deal on a first date!

"Those things look tasty. Want to taste one, Cor?" she asked, already strolling off to sample some sort of milky iced tea with black bubbles. Better to be a ditz, laughed at *and* with, than be a bore who never laughs at all!

A much-maligned term, "ditz," and most unfairly. Many make small talk out of things of interest; a short supply that's always soon depleted. Only the ditz makes her small talk from *anything*. She's like an alchemist of the human heart, converting *everything* to conversation!

Yes, Brayleigh could compose an ode to small talk. But it would likely change the meter and subject after a stanza or two. And be better for it!

"*So* hot for Fall!" She tugged her collar forth a few times, airing out, as Cor—with clear view—now blinked and glanced politely away. *Good heart! Too good? We'll work on that.* "Nice blouses here! How's this one?"

"This one" was a crop top, cut to bare the belly button and ribs alike. And maybe a couple more things.

Brayleigh tittered.

Cor blinked and—*Hey, is that a blush? So cute!* Mission accomplished.

Now, back to the tea.

Dozens of sample cups lay on a counter, in all the rainbow's hues and many more, strange and pastel, ranging from chalky yellow to mellow lilac. "So, you thirsty, Cor?"

He blushed again—*but why?*—before he saw her hand held toward the tea.

"Try something new?" She smiled as sweet as lilac tea must taste.

Cor looked a mite concerned. "Um, maybe a sample?"

"Of course!" the overhearing vendor called back. "This one's called taro. Top seller. Here, try it."

Cor took a tiny sample cup and tasted. "Oh. Huh. That's good." He held it up and sniffed. "A little sweet. And strong. But I want more."

"Like me!" She beamed. "Well, like the farmwives say: 'The first taste's sweetest! Savor it while you can!'"

Cor coughed some tea out.

"What?" she asked him. *Heehee.* "Wrong pipe? 'We're made with two pipes for a reason!'" *Heehee.*

Cor looked a little flushed and flustered, but clearly wanted more. "I'll take one taste—" He coughed. "I'll take one cup please. Of the same stuff."

"And I'll take that one!" Brayleigh pointed blithely. "The cream-pie-colored one." She seized the cup of pearly off-white fluid with scarcely a pause.

"Two for one silver," the vendor replied.

"Thanks, Cor!" Kind Brayleigh smiled preemptively.

The Beldrian looked inside his little satchel and found a silver piece. And, having paid, he took a deep gulp from his purple drink.

He choked. He scarcely shut his mouth in time to keep from spewing taro all over Brayleigh, and, even so, dribbled some along his chin.

She threw her red head back and cackled happily.

"What in the world was *that* thing?" Cor coughed finally. "All slimy and almost solid. Big!"

"The bubbles! Did you forget the bubbles, Cor?"

"Not bubbles. These things are *balls*. I'm drinking *balls!*" he wondered, staring wide-eyed upon his cup.

"Fine, balls then! Forget to swallow when the balls came, Cor?"

"That sucked," he said. He wiped his messy face.

"Too busy sucking for swallowing, huh!" sighed Brayleigh. "Well, I won't make *that* mistake." She closed her lips around her straw and sucked and swallowed.

Then, she bared her pearly whites in a big smile. "Yum! I'd drink this every day. Can I taste yours?" She sipped. "Jeez, twice a day!"

"Why lay it on unless you lay it thick?" the Fernstead farmwives said, while buttering bread and teaching farmgirls the art of buttering up.

She wandered on toward where her whimsy led. She was a honeybee browsing a field flush with wildflowers: lured in by a sweet scent one moment, beckoned by bright hues the next. And, the whole time, buzzing her happy song for all to hear.

If she was buzzing, Cor was bumbling: dodging awkwardly round the passers-by and booths, pursuing her through thick crowds, always careful not to bump others. That's how Beldrians were. So, every time some feckless local bumped him, without even looking back, much less saying "sorry," his forehead furrowed more. From time to time, he gulped his tea; but only from the top, and not the bubbles oozing at the bottom.

Brayleigh, now feeling delight overbrimming, spun to the Beldrian and let it spill over: "Isn't this great! If I get used to this, I might just give up saving worlds and such!"

Cor chuckled wordlessly.

Uh oh. "You . . . like it?"

He briefly looked away, then back at Brayleigh. "I sure like spending time with you," he answered.

She felt her cheeks flush. "Right response," she murmured, grinning, her eyes falling floorward.

She gathered her wits and faced his sunny gaze. "Now, your turn! Let's go do something that *you* want to do."

He shrugged and smiled. "Alright."

She let him lead: a brisk walk west, as far from cluttered booths as could be managed, barely even glancing.

She wondered how he had the heart to do that: To pass these pleasures with a calm, straight countenance! To leave them there, unvisited, unsavored! Whole new conceptual categories formed in her head to fit this oddity. *What's this called, the way he walks right on and I just can't?* Lacking such words as "stoic" and "epicurean," she settled after a while on "man" and "woman."

As booths began to thin, she idly observed that they were walking back toward Celeste's house; then, not so idly.

Brayleigh took a deep breath. She felt her heart start fluttering. She glanced over at Cor. That sunny and confident gaze and stride.

Facing straight forward, she brushed a stray hair from her face, then ran her hand through it again. *Maybe I laid it on a little* too *thick . . . ?* Suddenly, his haste to pass the market's pleasures made sense. All too much sense! *Oh no oh no.*

Cor stopped abruptly and turned to her. "Let's do it."

Drawing a deep breath, Brayleigh opened her mouth, not sure what she should say, looked up at Cor—and saw that he was pointing at a field.

"Um. Cor," she started. "Is this really how . . . ?"

And then she saw the vendor at the field's edge, standing beside some balls and clubs of some sort, which Cor was gazing at with gleaming eyes.

"How what?" the simple Beldrian boy replied.

She smiled and hugged him briefly. "Perfect pick!"

He looked confused but happy to be hugged.

Beyond the vendor was a sprawl of dry dirt, riddled with patches of yellow-green grass. A laborer-looking fellow with a club was standing near the vendor. On the field, a lanky mustached man was facing him.

The latter lobbed the ball forth underhand. The laborer swung his club and barely nicked it, sending the ball spinning backward and sideways.

"Some sort of game you've played?" she questioned Cor.

"This is baseball." Cor beamed. "Remember baseball? I taught you all the rules."

"Oh, right. Of course!" she bluffed. "Just pictured it a little different!"

"Better to show than tell, right?" said the Beldrian.

"So, someone stands there, throws the ball. You hit it." She scoured her memories. "Weren't there other people?"

"Yeah. There's more to it than this." His eyes were alight: that look he'd had while sparring with the knights. "But I see what they're doing, I think." He strode forth.

"Lead the way!" Brayleigh called happily behind him.

He approached the vendor, who was heavyset, half-shaven, and had the face of one who'd spent decades emoting to the point of wrinkling and dimpling. On his head was some strange billed hat. He clucked his tongue at seeing the club whiff by another throw. "All right. That's three. You're out. Buy one more round? No? Fine."

He turned to Cor, as the defeated laborer lumbered off. "Hi there. The name's Bub Roth. You here to play?"

"I am. How much?"

"One silver piece, three hits. You played before?"

"Of course. It's baseball, right?" said Cor.

"'Base ball'?" Roth's wrinkled forehead wrinkled further. "Nope. No 'bases.' Why don't I tell you the rules, son?"

"Sure, go ahead."

Bub Roth pointed at the field. "He throws the ball. You swing. You hit it past that first sign, get two silver. Past the second, you get ten. You get three hits. Missing's fine. But miss three times, that uses up a hit. You got it?"

"Sounds familiar. Sure," said Cor. He opened his satchel and drew one silver out. One of the last, saw Brayleigh, now beside him.

She suddenly felt a little guilty. "Hey, why don't you let me pay? You've paid enough!"

"Wait, you have silver too?" His head was tilted.

Uh oh. "Um."

"Anyway, no need. I've got this." He handed over a silver piece. "Don't worry."

"Where this thing from?" Roth squinted at the coin. "You call this silver?"

"Sure," said Cor. "From Beldria."

"'Beldria'?" Roth bit the coin, eyed it and shrugged. "Whatever. Pick a club, kid."

Cor stepped forward and started lifting clubs, swinging them halfway, shaking his head, and testing more. He finally settled upon a grainy shaft of birch. "Good bat."

"It's called a club," corrected Roth, as Cor walked past without replying.

"Hmph." The vendor turned to Brayleigh. "Picky, isn't he?

"Maybe those ones weren't as good!" she said lightly.

Roth shrugged. "A club's a club."

Cor gripped the bat with two hands, wielding it behind his head. His feet faced sideways from the mustached hurler. His knees were bent. His eyes were on the ball.

"Looks like he's held a club before," Roth grunted.

The thrower lobbed it underhand toward Cor, lofting it in a gentle arc.

Cor caught it, shaking his head.

"No, no. You have to *hit* it," called Roth. He looked at Brayleigh. "Little slow on the uptake, eh?" he muttered. "Save your silver."

"Throw it like this, okay?" Cor told the thrower. He flung the ball back overhand.

It whizzed directly at the mustached man, who flinched faintly at catching the ball with his bare hands. "Sure, kid."

"Good arm, though," Roth acknowledged quietly.

The hurler wound up and released the ball. His motion looked more awkward than the Beldrian's. The ball flew straight though, and it wasn't slow.

Cor swung his club. *Crack*. Far into the field the ball soared, arcing past the second sign and rolling several dozen yards beyond it.

"Well. Guess he gets that silver back," Roth murmured. "Must've been true about playing before."

"Guess so, huh!" She felt happy.

Muttering something, the thrower grabbed another ball by his feet. Facing Cor, lips pressed, he wound up and pitched.

This time, Cor slugged it a little more left, but roughly as far as he had hit the first.

Bub Roth was nodding now and faintly grinning, arms folded over his chest. Beside the field, some passersby had stopped—perhaps at hearing the cracks like thunder coming from the Beldrian—and now were watching in a growing audience.

"Throw it a little harder, next time?" Cor called.

The hurler looked disgruntled. "Yeah, you got it." He wound up and released, his right hand reaching so far his fingers nearly brushed the ground. His right leg swung forth wildly as he let loose.

The ball zipped low and outside. Cor was ready. He leaned and *swung*.

Somehow, his birch-carved club caught the Sun's glare and flashed golden on contact.

The stricken ball, like a ray of daybreak, shot from low on high. It scattered as it flew, shedding the whiteness wrapped around its core. Its remnant soared aloft the blue serene, a sinking silhouette. Then, it vanished westward into a far off grove of ash and elms.

"What!" Roth was shouting. "What! You're kidding me!" He wildly laughed. "What's that? Two hundred yards?" The ball had flown about two times as far as the second sign. "Ha! Girl, you got a keeper."

The girl from Fernstead giggled.

Meanwhile, the audience, grown rather large now, eagerly applauded.

Cor blinked and glanced at the unexpected clamor. Walking toward Brayleigh and Bub Roth, he looked a bit embarrassed, staring at the dirt, his bat slung over a shoulder.

Brayleigh noticed how doing so made his biceps and broad shoulders—already quite pronounced—pronounce themselves even more than usual.

Good pick, Cor. She smiled and waved like some celebrity were coming.

Bub Roth grinned widely and nodded at the Beldrian. "Boy, I've been doing this for a long, long time. And that was half again as far as I've seen."

Ballplayer Cor itched an ear. "Homer's a homer."

Brayleigh and Bub Roth shared a glance and shrugged.

"I don't know what that means," declared the vendor, "but you're damn good at this. Here, have ten silver. Worth it to see that! Find your girl some flowers."

Cor flushed. His stare—which had been fixed on her, she now saw—flicked off toward some sagging clouds.

Blushing! At that! And here I thought...! She tittered.

"Also," continued Roth, "you can have these. Just promise me you'll use 'em." From his pocket, he handed over a pair of leather gloves: thin, light brown, lacking fingertips. Their feel was soft and supple, like a well-worn mitt. "Wear these and you can swing a club all day. I know. I used to use 'em. Then, I took a line drive to the knee. And here I am."

"You sure?" Cor slipped a glove on. *Soft.* It fit like—well, like a glove. "They're nice, but if they're yours—"

"The nicest. Yours now. Tell the world you got 'em from Bub Roth."

"Well. I will then."

And with that, they waved and went back toward the marketplace.

Sol had sunk low along the west by now. Already it'd started flushing faintly, as its farewell neared. Beneath its faded beaming, some vendors had begun to gather up their goods and cart them off.

On seeing some meat pies tossed pell-mell from a tray into a jar, she felt her stomach rumble. She'd not eaten a bite of food since breakfast, save free samples. And they don't count. So she was downright starving.

"I'm famished!" she announced. "If I don't eat soon, this breeze is going to blow me away!"

"Can I come?"

"What? How about, 'Let's find supper'?" Brayleigh cried.

"After those samples, you're still ... ?" Cor trailed off. "I mean, sounds good. It's always supper somewhere."

"There! That's the spirit."

She strode off toward the street that'd had the best food, passing several ped-dlers of lesser snacks. This was no day for fried dough or caramel apples! ... Not that she expected filet mignon with wine from market vendors. But she'd show at least some class to Cor, some standards.

Maybe a nice big sausage? She could taste it!

So, on they fared for fifteen minutes more, led on as much by scent as sight.

She rounded the bend where all the tastiest booths had been—and saw that every single one was empty or shuttered.

Brayleigh blinked. She scanned the street. *Closed. Closed. Those weisswursts, weren't they . . . yes!* She sprinted toward where the sausage booth was . . . *What? Oh no!* Her bottom lip slipped forward.

"Closed," she sighed, as Cor caught up.

"What about that?" he asked, pointing beyond the food booths toward a park. A painted sign said "Sausage Eating Contest." Big-bellied men were shuffling toward the site.

"Cor," Brayleigh calmly said, "are you suggesting that we conclude our day by having *me* stuff myself silly on sausages publicly?"

"Um," Cor replied.

"Since, if you are, then *yes!*"

She could just taste those sausages already!

She strode off toward the table, piled with weisswursts, bratwursts and knock-wursts. *Time to try them all!*

"Sagriss, our butcher, used to do these sometimes," called Cor behind her, jogging just to keep up. "My sword instructor won it once. Ate nine."

"Well, maybe soon you'll have two famous friends!" Brayleigh replied with a pat on her belly, stepping straight up to a man in an apron blotched red, who weighed at least four hundred pounds. "Excuse me! What's the price? I'd like to enter."

"Three silver. Five back if you win," he answered. His lips curved upward with the second sentence.

"Hm. That's a lot." She eyed Cor. "Can we afford it?"

"Hey, just the sausage costs that much!" the man said. "You get a good meat dinner out of this. Here, tell you what. You enter, and I'll throw in free sausage for your friend here."

"Deal!" cried Brayleigh.

She turned to Cor. "Good thing that Bub Roth guy gave you that silver, huh?"

"Good thing," he smiled, glancing off skyward as he opened his satchel.

"And who knows!" she continued. "I might win this!"

"We've seen unlikelier things."

"Yes! That's the spirit."

The butcher-vendor smothered laughter. "Good luck."

"Hey, I can eat a lot! I'd go for *days* with barely a bite, when Gramps and I were walking from farm to farm. And then I'd make it all up in one meal! And I looked like *you* by the end!" She pointed at the butcher's aproned belly.

"Lad, if you need some help rolling your winner here home, I'll lend a cart," the man told Cor.

"Go get it ready!" Brayleigh called, already advancing toward the table of contenders.

The sausage heap was huge, as were the men seated along the longboard on a bench. She'd never seen such neck folds, guts and jowls gathered in mutual gluttony. Even their fingers resembled sausages! They grinned and grunted. There were no plates; just personal slabs of wood. Utensils? Not a chance.

She sat down daintily between the fattest and the baldest fellows. "Pass me a platter?" she called to a contender whose neckbeard almost hid his bulging neck flab.

He raised his brow—as much as he could manage beneath its weight—and slid a wood slab over.

"Much obliged, friend!" She shook her shivering arms. *Alright! So hungry.*

"Well folks," said the butcher, now shambling toward the longboard. "This is it then. Most of you know the rules, I know. You take one wiener, eat it, then you take another. First to twelve wins. If no one gets to twelve, the highest wins. In a tie, the first done wins. You puke, you're out. You stand, you're out. Make sense?"

Some guttural grunts of affirmation followed, along with one "Sure does!," a bit higher-pitched, although she tried to keep it gruff.

The audience—some thirty townsfolk, notably bereft of scholars—leaned in with anticipation.

"Alright then. On my mark." He raised a cleaver, then smacked it into a tree stump.

And with that, the competition started.

Brayleigh dug in, devouring one whole weisswurst in ten seconds. *Delicious!* Fat flavor filled her mouth. *Worth it!*

She felt proud. But she paused a moment now. *Awfully rich, huh? Let's let this sausage settle!*

She watched and waited as the others ate their seconds, feeling slightly disappointed she'd not take home the prize. But this was tasty, so who cared? Cor would likely laugh. *Well, let him!*

She started on her second with a small bite, and then a bigger one before she'd swallowed. *Boy, these are good!* And then she knew that two, at least, would not be a problem. Munch, munch, munch.

Things took an unexpected turn soon after, when Baldy, who'd been winning, suddenly set down half of a sausage, shook his head and shoved his slab away. "Not worth it." He stood up. "Not worth it." And with that, he waddled off, wincing and holding his gorged gut in both hands.

Then, Neckbeard—who, at five, was far behind—brushed off his hands and belched. "Nice eating, Feitman. I need a beer." He stood and shuffled off.

That left the fattest fellow at Brayleigh's side.

"Twelve! Twelve! Twelve!" chanted the spectators giddily.

Feitman seemed ready to oblige them. Or else he still was hungry after eating nine. In any event, he started on his tenth, as Brayleigh finally polished off her third.

Strangely, she felt a little hungry still. *Thanks to whoever's helping me up there!*

"Good knockwurst! Like the garlic!" she called out to the butcher-vendor, and the audience chortled. She'd be a lovable loser at least.

Brayleigh had nibbled her fourth about halfway and felt about as full as full can be—perfect, in other words—when, at her side, Feitman abruptly froze. His face was scarlet and swollen as Misses Folfold's ripe tomatoes.

He spun around, quite quickly for his size, and vomited.

"Aw!" moaned the crowd. "So close!"

But that means . . . Brayleigh's eyes went wide. *Dear me!* She spun toward Cor to announce the news, mouth opening.

Out slipped a big burp.

She sealed her lips. *Oh dear!*

Cor failed to choke back laughter as he clapped. And now the audience was applauding too.

"The wiener-eating winner!" hailed the butcher.

Standing, she beamed and tried to smoothe her skirt. Her belly felt like she was three months pregnant. *Worth it!*

The butcher handed her five silver. "Fine eating. Wonder where you put all that."

Polite. She felt precisely where she'd put it, pushing her too-tight shirt out. "Could you get me that cart? Might need it! You ready to roll, Cor?"

"I'll never doubt you again," declared the Beldrian.

"Wise words!" She led him from the clearing, waving a few times at the audience in their wake. "Oh, by the way. You didn't hear me burp back there. Right, Cor?"

"What burp?"

"Exactly right. Since, if you had, I'd have to launch you sky-high!" She snapped and sent a Boundary flashing forward.

"Hm. Can't have that. I owe you four still, right?"

"Right, four! Can't pay me back from way up there!"

"Besides," he said, "burps happen to us all."

"Heehee. That's right. At least no king was here, huh?"

"I think you took the crown from Feitman."

"True," she said. "I have to say, though, when he barfed, all out of nowhere like that, I think *someone* up there was helping me! Like Fate or—um." Her stomach suddenly heaved and churned. She lifted three fingers to her lips, swallowing it back. "And *I*, will have to go sit down! How's that spot?" She pointed at a statue on a platform.

"About to pull a Feitman?" Cor replied.

She tried to titter and hold it down at once.

"Let's go." He led her toward the marble platform.

She strove to focus on the statue's features, and not the turmoil in her tummy. Holding her belly's weight with both hands, she surveyed the figure of stone: An armored warrior. Not like the Knights of Norvester, shining in their steel plate. More like the leader of some wandering war band, with battered mail and billowing cape, and, wielded high in one hand, a pike still wet with blood. The other palm was by his face, perhaps hailing his soldiers or shading out sunlight.

"I'd like to learn to pose like that," said Cor.

"'Heithbrand, the Foremost of the Line of Kaesiad and House Lofthungrian, Conquering Savior of Beregin,'" read Brayleigh from a plaque upon the platform. Upon the stone itself was an inscription she couldn't read, carved in some ornate script.

"Could we be Norvester's 'Conquering Saviors'? Please?" asked Cor.

"We should've asked for that!" said Brayleigh. "The pass; the satchel; conquering-savior statues!"

She eased her new bulk on the statue's base. The crisp breeze felt nice. *This must be how bears feel when Winter comes!* She felt like hibernating.

"Technically," noted Cor, "we conquered Norvester *and* saved it right? Too late to ask, you think?"

"'Who seeks, receives'!" She curled her hand and patted the spot beside her, beckoning him. He sat there.

Silence ensued. They watched Sol redden and sink.

The west wind was alive tonight. Each time it spurted by, it brushed some itchy strands over her eyes. She'd sweep it to the side, only to have it blown right back.

She sighed. "So long! Annoying. Should I get it cut?"

"Like clipping petals of a flower for being long," the Beldrian said. "What's natural is what's beautiful."

He'd spoken at once. But after a second's pause, he blinked and went wide-eyed, then glanced at her.

But Brayleigh—she was absently aware—was now the blushing, blinking one. "Okay. I'll leave it then." She smiled and, reaching over while looking at the ground, she grabbed his hand.

Silence again. The last sunlight was waning, as Luna waxed aloft the eastern welkin. Neither felt speech was necessary now; which was a normal state of things for Cor, but rare indeed for Brayleigh.

"This feels nice," Cor finally said. "We're always walking, working. Just sitting's nice."

"Mm-hmm." She shut her eyes and yawned. That food had left her feeling woozy. *Worth it.* "It got late, huh?" She leaned her head on Cor's left shoulder.

It was somewhat hard, bone under sinew. Far from what she'd hoped for, stuffed drowsy as she was. She suddenly wondered what he was thinking. And what *she'd* been thinking.

She felt him tense and turn; then, loosen and lay an arm around her shoulder, so her head lay in the soft spot formed by their connection.

Funny how such slight things change everything. Her head and belly and life felt perfect now.

They ought to head back soon to Celeste's house. Neither knew quite how to get there from here, and night was falling. Yet, in warm entwinement amid the cool winds, watching red Sol wane as Stars waxed, and the sprawling sky went blue, neither felt ready, quite yet, to return.

CHAPTER 23

Deliad's first day in the stacks was more pleasant than he'd expected. He was never a scholar, but had a workman's intellectual spark. To work his work with fervent potency, he'd fuel it with the wisdom of the past. He therefore had a soft spot for old histories of war, and warning tales of waning kingdoms, epics of conquest and heroes' biographies. Like coal deposits left by former conflicts, waiting for future men of war to mine them.

That brave old world, he was well-heeled to travel, whether in body and deed or mind and word.

"I'll take the war histories," he had suggested, "you take philosophy?" This suited Celeste.

So, for the first day, and the second even, it felt fine. Like a stroll through scenic lands, familiar and lively, after decades' absence.

Warm fuzzies, by day three, had started waning. He wanted nothing more than sunshine now, and cool Fall winds, and scents of fallen leaves, trampled beneath his boots, and Hoarthaxe on his back. His breakfast, eight hours in, was still a lump inside his stomach. Both his hamstrings hurt. The only "fuzzies" now were fuzzy eyes. No wonder those professors all wore glasses.

"So! Wander through the market for the morning, then lunch, then see the spires?" Brayleigh asked Cor, as the four wanderers went out for their fourth day.

"Sounds good," he said. "Except my silver's low."

"Well, that won't stop us! I can treat today."

"No, no. I'll not have Cor be shamed," said Deliad. He searched his coin sack. "Here. It's on the house." He handed Cor two coins. "The Kingdom's Treasury, that is."

Cor opened his mouth to thank the Knight-Lord, glancing down—then, he blinked. The coins were gold.

"To 'empty out the pass and *fill Cor's satchel.*' That's what we promised, yes? We keep our oaths," Deliad affirmed, patting his bulging pouch. "Although I think you'd spoken of silver, not gold?"

"We'll take this deviation from the deal's terms!" declared the girl from Fernstead, giddy-faced. "You see?" she cried to Cor. "'Who seeks, receives'!"

"Well. Thank you to the seeker. And to taxpayers, I guess." Cor eyed the gold. "I'd never seen one. A gold coin. Just in stories, back in Beldria."

"Trolls, castles, combat, spires, and flying ships; and you're still goggling at a gold coin? Really?" she said.

Shrugging, Cor flipped the coin and caught it.

"Well," grimaced Deliad in a jovial gloom, "while you two wanton in the breezy market, sampling gourmet Academy cuisine, I'll be savoring the dusty scents of Eldscript."

"Your sacrifice is much appreciated!" consoled kind Brayleigh.

"Come on, you big baby," said Celeste.

So, the two young souls traipsed off. And off went Deliad, with his former foe, to read books.

Entering the Academy archives, he saw and felt the gold of day sealed off as huge doors shut, plunging him into darkness. He sighed and waited for his sight to adjust.

Nor had his spirits become brighter by the evening, with bleary eyes, a stack of skimmed-through books, and naught to show for it. From the unread pile, he picked the skinniest left and started reading.

"Ah. Perfect." Deliad smiled.

"Hm?" Celeste said. "Found something helpful?"

"'Master William tosseth the branch unto the straying canine; which, straightway, doth hie thereafter. Whereupon crieth Master William, 'Hasten, dog, hasten!'" he read. "Don't write 'em like they used to, do they, Celeste?"

Her lips curved up. "I doubt the Elements show up in that book, Deliad."

"Keep an open mind, Celeste!" He tossed the tome aside and seized another. "'Of Fey and Wondrous Deseridata, Logged by One Who Wandered Many Moons and Miles.'" He flipped through. "Looks like an encyclopedia."

She leaned and looked. Each page was overflowing with illustrations—literally, with drawings spilling across the text into the margins.

"Deliad, is that a sea snake?" Celeste read: "'Tis said the Ur-Serpent spawned in Liossian waters; but, slowly burgeoning larger, wended westward, by stream and lake, passing betwixt the peaks and through the Boundary into fiery Balban. There, for a century, it grew unto greatness in Sea Gyvidurys; whence, become too big for even those deeps, it swam Pehuson's River across Vitulia to the Sea of Night. The Ispiri say it dwells there even to this day, spinning up maelstroms, swallowing one in ten ships that seek to cross.'"

"What is this?" chuckled Celeste. "Wanted to search the children's wing today?"

"It's quality, Celeste. Quality's what it is." He turned from *U* to *E*. "Ha! Here we go." The silhouette of a horned, majestic man, misty and hard to make out, filled the page.

"'Element,'" quoth Deliad. "'Not to be confused with such base substances as lead and iron, nor with phenomena like fire and water, which we also label elements.' Ha!" he gloated.

"'Scholars still largely concur that the Elements, mythic though they may be, are also a matter of historical record. Plainly, they were present to wreak the Pandaemonium on the Earth. And they persisted after. Children's rhymes, it's said, record the whereabouts of some; most famously, the following, which we all know:'"

I sing of Seven who fell from Heaven:
The Lord of Light, where warriors fight

The halfman droves and huge bulls rove.
The Lord of Twilight, on a white height

Far northward, perched beside the birch.
That same fair starkness, seen by darkness

On Sveitfyl Sward, the Starry Lord.
In Fernstead, Chaos' Consort bled

By Lysa's stream, where Fyrir dreamed,
Before she wept and lay and slept

By an apple tree near Balban's sea.
Guarding that garden fell the warden

Of Ausrine, mother of king and queen.
Her heirs enshrined the Fair and Kind

In Beregin Shire among the spires.
The First is last, who fell and passed

Where Sol is split by a moonlit summit.
Wander again, you Seven from Heaven!

"We have it on the authority of Ellric," read Deliad, "that this rather humble rhyme records the Elements' whereabouts. For instance, he asserts that 'Sol is split by a moonlit summit' far east of here, where 'Heron Summit' stands. He claims the kingdom there knows much of the Elements."

"But Ellric's answers merely raise more questions. How could he know this? Who could cross the Boundaries to travel there and learn such truths? Indeed, how would one learn where some seven Elements lurked, to write a rhyme about them? Most today concur this rhyme is merely a fancied myth; perhaps with tidbits rooted in the truths about our past we'll never know completely."

"And that's how the entry ends," he said. "Not bad for the 'children's wing.' Eh? Eh?!"

"Pipe down," smiled Celeste. "Here, let me see that."

She studied the rhyme, line after line. "The Lord of Light—that's Cor, right? That what he called his Fossil, Dievas, right? And Fernstead, with the Consort—Brayleigh, right? The Fair and Kind in Beregin Shire—that's Eremon. The Fair and Kind, you call Him, right? And Norvester began in Beregin, the old name for the Academy. And Eremon's Fossil—well, *you* know it well."

"Huh." Deliad called to mind his halberd's pommel, flame-shaped and vert, warm and aswirl with mists. "Which leaves, what, four of seven?"

"Three," said Celeste. She raised a Star-shaped Fossil from her robe. It shone pale blue. "Fair starkness, seen by darkness on Sveitfyl Sward, the Starry Lord."

"Aha."

"Sadly, I see two problems with the last three," Celeste went on. "One: All the listed 'Elements' may well be Fossils now—like those we have—rather than living creatures who could help us."

"Who knows though? Dievas wasn't dead," said Deliad.

"True. Fair enough," she said. "So, second thing: Who knows what those descriptions mean? They're vague. A 'white height' with a 'birch'? An 'apple tree near Balban's sea'? I'd never heard of Balban; except we say 'when Balban freezes over.'"

"'By Balban's balefires' too, right? But that last one." The Knight-Lord had a faintly far off look. 'Where Sol is split by a moonlit summit'—that one. I think I *know* that place."

"A peak that touches the Sun?" She raised a brow. "I'll have to see this."

"No, no," he said. "I read some travelogue, back as a student, by a mountain climber. He came to the Academy just to climb Ginnagond Bluff. Got me to do it too, reading the thing. Rather inspiring book."

"You *climbed* the Bluff? Where did you find the time?"

"No one cares much what grades the Knight-Lord gets," said Deliad. "Anyway, that book. It said something about the Sun being split by a summit. Some local lore that if you looked far east from the peak near Dawn, you'd see Sol split in two. That's why he climbed, if I recall correctly."

"So, when I climbed, I looked for that. I *saw* it. Must've been hundreds of miles off. A mountain much taller than the others round it. So tall, it split the sunrise into two."

"Huh. Maybe," said Celeste. "Quite a trip to take on 'maybes.' More than one Boundary to cross, I would bet."

"That's what the Passagestone's for," replied Deliad. "And they 'know much of the Elements' there, he said. Seems like a logical target to start with."

"Uh-huh. Well, we should write this down, at least," the former student said.

"And then set off? Or take a few days off first?" Deliad yawned.

"Deliad, do you intend to take a *journey*, hundreds of miles into Fragments half-known, without even *slightly* studying what we'll find there?" said Celeste mildly, writing down the rhyme.

He yawned again. "Give me a map, I'm good."

"We'll want at least a week of careful research," she went on calmly like he hadn't spoken.

"Well, anyway," he grumbled. "I'm going home. Done for today. You coming?"

"I suppose," she said. "We ought to speak with Starling though. Might have some update on that ship of his."

"Fine."

As they fared toward the Observatory, they heard loud speech afar before they saw the speaker: "What we call 'truth' is consensus, no more. There's no true truth. We build word structures, like 'good and evil,' 'fair and foul,' and so forth. We slot Ourselves on one side, and the Others upon the other. And we cite these structures to validate our oppression of the Others. Well, not us. No more!"

The ardent tones were nasally, but charismatic: one who wasn't born with much, voicewise, but made the most of it. The speaker wore a scholar's gown of black. His head was wholly bald. He had no beard, and barely any eyebrows either.

"Thank you! It's youth like you who make our movement possible," he hailed a student, who was tossing silver into a half-full hat beside his feet.

His audience was a mix of males with manbuns and hardly any hair. Many weren't shaven, but few were bearded. Necks and arms were skinny. Their wrinkled shirts were tighter round the belly than at the breast. Their gazes glimmered feverish, like the energy they could've spent improving their physical forms were burning in their glares.

"Idiots," said Celeste.

Deliad's lips curved up. "Not what I would've expected to hear from you."

"Professor Traditor. He makes his money denying truth to those who hate the truth, since truth has nothing good to say about them."

"Careful, you'll sound like me," the Knight-Lord said.

"True, can't have that."

They stepped around a corner—and into Deliad strode a guard at full speed. Both bounced back.

Ugh. Big guard. "Apologies," he offered, though it really wasn't his fault.

"Watch where you're walking, lily-cheeks!" the guard snapped.

He blinked. That gravelly voice. And, showing slightly beneath that visor, flesh more grey and green than any man he'd seen.

An orkish guard? At the Academy? This was something new. He was too busy being surprised and pondering to offer a reply. So, the ork just sneered and sauntered by, with blotchy fingers curled to a fist around the stunner at its side.

"So. What was that?" he asked a minute later.

"I've not a clue," the former student said.

"Dean Gaudimorte getting guards for cheap these days?"

"I'd noticed some guards looking strangely large. And hunched and slouched."

"And grey and green, it seems."

Upon arrival at the Observatory, Starling was hunched and slouched and staring into the eyepiece of his telescope. He held a pen in one hand, with a piece of parchment upon a nearby table dense with scribbling. He clasped an unbitten apple in the other.

"Evening, Professor." Celeste found a seat.

"Ah, good to see you, Celeste," Starling said, not seeing her, since he still was peering at the faraway celestial. "Dawnstar's out. Best thing about the Fall. You see Stars earlier."

Celeste's lips curved up as she calmly waited.

Deliad yawned loudly.

"How's the view?" asked Celeste.

"Splendid."

Pointedly, Deliad yawned again. *Four full days in the dark, squinting at books. Finally, I finish in time for some daylight; and this is how I'll spend it. Waiting here.*

Stretching both arms, he let a third yawn loose.

Starling turned round to him. "Here, have an apple. Might wake you up." He tossed it to the Knight-Lord, then turned back to his eyepiece.

Deliad caught the fruit and promptly flung it over his shoulder. It struck some high-heaped gears and metal gadgets, scattering them cross a table.

Starling frowned and turned around. "Well, make yourselves at home." He sprawled back in the largest leather seat. "You know that Stars, and everything up there, follow the same rules of physics as right here? Same unseen forces, moving Stars and apples!"

"Of course," said Celeste. "I did take your courses."

"Of course, who wouldn't know *that?*" Deliad mumbled. *Sun's sinking as we speak.*

"I should've known," smiled Starling. "Top-notch student. What a loss for science, your leaving. Speaking of," he went on, "that young girl—it's Brayleigh, yes? What a natural mind for mechanics she has! In one day, that girl grasped the things I struggle to teach my students for a whole semester! I've never seen another student like her."

"That so?" the former student asked politely.

"Indeed!" he affirmed. "With her help, we'll be flying across the Fragments soon as we get signoff."

"Speaking of which," said Deliad, "what's the status?"

"I told the Dean that she could cross the Boundaries. He seemed surprised. Intrigued, perhaps?" He shrugged. "One hopes. We'll find out soon enough on Sahngday, when the Committee posts its meeting minutes."

"Another question," Celeste said. "Just now, we met an orkish guard. That something new?"

Starling strolled over to the open door and shut it. "Yes, that's fairly new," he said. "When Norvester's border sentries were disbanded, we started seeing more orkish raids around here. Some burnt farms, first; then, merchants' wagons looted."

"The Academy played it down. But it got worse. Food and supplies were short. Winter was coming. Some said our guards should mount their own attack. Wipe out the wandering ork bands," he recalled.

"Instead, Dean Gaudimorte had the bright idea of hiring the orks as guards. 'For cheap! Good deal!' he said. And the Committee agreed. So now, whenever orks come, they get hired as guards."

"Perhaps you've noticed how the Oldtown's worn down, roads aren't repaired, and new-built buildings now are uglier than the old ones? And you've wondered where all the money's going? Well, now you know."

"Meanwhile, more crimes are caused by the orks than solved. But," Starling sighed, "at least the raids have stopped. We'll see how long that lasts. A lot of guards aren't happy about it. Fighting side by side with the same orks that would loot your farm and kill you, needless to say, isn't good for morale. And Gaudimorte fired their captain for objecting."

"Sad. What are laws and leaders for, if not to keep the enemy out?" the Knight-Lord said.

"A lot of guards aren't happy," he repeated, staring away for a moment; then shrugged. "So, anyway, I watch the Stars above, which don't get worse with every passing year, unlike most other things," concluded Starling.

They left the Observatory soon thereafter and met with Cor and Brayleigh at Clausiglade's house. There, they recounted the rhyme that they'd found, and Celeste's insights on its meaning.

"So, we have some leads but only one that's clear," she said. "'Where Sol is split by a moonlit summit.' Or 'Heron Summit,' as they said it's called."

"A straight shot east," said Deliad, "more or less."

"Well, great! Good work," declared the girl from Fernstead. "We leaving then?"

"We should soon," Deliad nodded. "Wait a few weeks, we'd be snowed in for Winter."

"But what about the Sojourner?" said Cor. "Won't be snowed in with that. And flying's faster."

"We'll learn tomorrow if the ship's approved," Celeste replied. "If so, then after Starling finishes doing his upgrades, we can fly off. Till then, we'll try to study Heron Summit."

"Assuming she's approved," the Knight-Lord said. "If not, I say we go. We wait much longer, and we'll be wintered in."

"Well, let's just see what tomorrow brings, then make the call," said Cor.

No one could argue with that. So instead, they let these heavy matters lie and turned to lighter things: first, Celeste's fond nostalgia for seeing the snow-capped peaks around the Academy, which Deliad shared; then, Celeste's happy memories of whiling Winter away within the archives, which he did not; then, Celeste's offhand comment that "Norvester wishes it were like the Academy."

"Oh! Playing with fire!" boomed Deliad. "Two can play. Let's talk about that 'Fashion District,' eh?"

"You spend much time there, Celeste?" Brayleigh inquired.

"No. Bear in mind I left at barely eighteen," said Celeste. "Didn't have, or need, much money."

"Never too late to begin!" Brayleigh urged. "Deliad, you got some gold for Celeste's satchel?"

And so it went. The dimness waned to darkness outside. But here, the hearth-light crackled bright, melting away past pains and future fears, leaving those four in the present's warm sensescape, where, ultimately, all of life occurs.

CHAPTER 24

Professor Starling stared upon the papers, pinned to the bulletin board. His face sagged; his squint drooped.

He was standing in the foyer of the Hall of Ages. To his rear, two rows of stone-carved columns stood. The floor was tile, massive white squares of marble swirled with grey. Spaced evenly on the side walls were a series of somber busts, which, in receded wall nooks, caught the light somehow despite being in shade. The ceiling, too, was stony and white, except an eight-spoked sunburst blazing at its center.

Cor would've marveled at it more—and still did, a fair amount—but he was focused mostly on Starling's grimace.

The professor grabbed the papers and, unpinning them, began to scan the second page. He shook his head, as the others crossed the foyer, and closed his eyes and closed his fist, crumpling the stack of papers.

"Tied vote. He broke the tie by voting nay." He opened his eyes and glanced at them. "Dean Gaudimorte."

"He sounded like the sorta guy who'd do that!" sighed Brayleigh.

"Why though? Why would Gaudimorte care?" asked Cor.

"You want his reason or his rationale?" said Starling darkly. "Gaudimorte and his gang resent each silver piece being spent on beauty, rather than one of their partisan pet causes. Waste silver, they won't care. But build some beauty, and they'll seek ways to shut it down. Like this."

"As for the rationale?" Celeste said.

"Right. That." Starling uncrumpled the papers and read: "While, from the outset, the Sojourner Project, we do not doubt, was driven by a sound desire to further science and physics, the Committee, upon deliberation, have determined that, in good conscience, we cannot permit the Project to proceed. While flight is, doubtless, a thrilling aspiration of many, now—when hunger and homelessness still plague our poor, and much of sickness still surpasses medicine, and many of our young have little learning—is not a time for us to seek out thrills."

"'Us.' Classic Gaudimorte," Starling said with curled lip. "The poor, the sick, the young, and Us against Them."

"So, what's our next move?" asked the former student. "What do they want from you? What would appease them?"

"You haven't heard yet how the statement ends." Professor Starling's tone was bitter as Boreas.

"Hmph. They sure beat around the bush," said Brayleigh.

"'We acknowledge that the necessary capital to build this 'ship' is largely spent already.'" The scholar's brow was wrinkled as the papers. "'Should we permit the Project to proceed upon that basis, though, this might encourage others to engage in surreptitious squandering of the Academy's funds on personal projects. To avoid this moral hazard, with regret, we have determined that the Sojourner must be dismantled.'"

"'It is with reluctance that we have settled on this strong response. But, in the end, we simply could not countenance such science for science's sake; which would reward adventurism and may result in more. Better to make a difficult choice today than wait and deal with many more tomorrow.'"

"That's crazy!" Brayleigh cried. "You're going to *fly*. You shouldn't have to explain why *that's* worth doing. Like having to explain why life's worth living!"

"I'm glad that someone feels the way I feel. Without an explanation," Starling smiled. But underneath that grin was total gloom.

"Maybe it's time to stop explaining then," said Celeste. "Sometimes, the only source of power for those doing wrong is that we seek their signoff before doing right. Why give an explanation? Why bother coaxing bad sorts to be sensible, over and over, when you could instead deprive them of their power by simply leaving? Why not make foes of foes and friends of friends?"

The Knight-Lord now was nodding, lips curved up, some admiration showing under his stern brow.

"Celeste," the scholar said, "are you suggesting that I just fly away?"

"In a word, yes," she said. "Why not just fly away to Norvester? Offer your ship in service of the King. Technically, this is his Academy, no? So this is his ship, no? You think he'll see this, and hear how it could carry knights cross Fragments, and say, 'You'll have to give this back to Gaudimorte'?"

"That's not what he would say," affirmed the Knight-Lord, nodding in open agreement now.

"Fair points," said Starling. "But before I left my homeland, and friends and family, and department chair, I'd have to think a bit about priorities."

"Yes, that's the choice you always face," said Deliad. "But, should you choose to leave, sooner is better."

Now it was Celeste's turn to nod.

"Indeed. I'll give it thought," the scholar said. "You're right. There's something base about this place; at least, what it's become within my lifetime. And now it's bearing down on me. I've fallen down from the summit of my dreams and striving, to a place where low sorts weaponize their words against what's lofty and high."

"That said," he sighed, "I think I'll have to bandy words a bit more, before I fly away."

"Could you appeal this?" asked Cor. "Could someone overrule them?"

"No one," said Starling.

Deliad frowned, crooking his head.

"Well, what if you went back to them," said Brayleigh, "but changed up your proposal? All that stuff about the 'poor,' the 'sick,' the 'young,' and so forth.

What if you called this a 'Project for crossing the Boundaries to bring food and medicine back'? Make it a class, something that students help with. And call it 'the Committee's Air-Aid Program.' Not that they really care about that stuff! But you'll make clear your airship is on their side."

The scholar stared. "Your sense for how the politics of the Academy function is impeccable."

"Brayleigh, you think like Lothar." Celeste smiled.

"That's 'First of Equals,' please!" the teen replied. "Think it'll work?"

"Who knows?" responded Starling. "But, out of several bad options, it's best."

"That's the spirit!"

"Why don't we do a demonstration?" suggested Cor. "Load up the ship with food, supplies and so forth, and invite the Dean and his Committee for the inaugural ride?"

"Good call," said Celeste. "Maybe being in the air will put them in a loftier spirit. And all it takes is one changed mind to break the tie."

"Well said," affirmed the scholar. "We'll do that then."

"And I'll go speak with Gaudimorte," Celeste said. "I saw him the other day, and he'd suggested we catch up. So, I'll see what's new with him, and be all friendly-friendly, and I'll see what the Academy's working on these days. And then we'll make sure we present this 'Project' as something that advances his priorities."

"As I've said, Celeste," mused Starling, head shaking, "you should've been a scholar here."

She smiled; and, briefly, looked like a precocious student upon being praised by a renowned professor.

"Come help me load the ship then?" Cor asked Deliad.

"Can't right now. Something I'd like to look into," replied the Knight-Lord, peering off and pondering. "Starling, could your assistants handle loading?"

"Of course," he said. "But what's this that you're planning?"

"I'll explain later," said Deliad, already striding away toward the door at a quick clip.

His fellow wanderers traded glances, shrugged, and followed him outside to start the tasks they'd set out for themselves. The Sun was still ruddy with sleep and hardly above the horizon. But they already felt that much of morning had slipped away, and they'd need all the day to make much headway toward their farflung hopes.

CHAPTER 25

Being Sahngday, there was not a wight in sight as Celeste progressed through the Hall of Equality. The whitewashed plaster of the walls reflected the glare of the artificial lights that lined them.

"Fitting that this Academy's forward progress toward an enlightened future be well lit!" Dean Gaudimorte had declared when they'd been added.

A decade and a half ago, the Dean had moved his office from the Hall of Ages here, upon being appointed to the Deanship. In doing so, he had done away with the old name this lofty spire had borne—the Hall of Fairness—dubbing it henceforth the Hall of Equality.

"'Fairness' was fine, but a bit too ambiguous. Let's make clear what we mean. Let's be more modern. Is life fair? Who knows! But it's sure not equal, so long as some unfortunates starve and languish, while wealthy nobles feast and fete themselves," he'd said in his inaugural address.

He'd also plastered over the ancient stone, covered with esoteric signs and symbols, with plain white. *"Empty hogwash! Pure baroqueness! Mere frills and finery, signifying nothing! It's time we moved on. We'll waste no more time on obscurantism. Mystic mumbo-jumbo! What can't be spoken plainly is not worth speaking."*

The new walls hadn't mixed well with the firelight, so he'd installed these artificial strips. They sought to replicate some softer lights recovered from the spires, but never quite glowed with that old nimbus, glaring instead. Rather a nuisance, like having the Sun shining in both eyes' corners at the same time.

Near Dawn, she'd stopped at the Office of the Dean but found the door shut and the office empty; which, being a Sahngday, wasn't a surprise. She'd scoured the whole spire, then the Hall of Ages, but had no luck. Likewise, no dice at noon.

Now, nearing three o'clock, she'd come once more. One final try before accepting failure.

This time, the Dean's door was slightly ajar, and from the opening came a crack of light.

A tingle thrilled through Celeste's limbs. At once, she started running through the lines she'd readied; a habit she'd developed as an orator. Not that you tried to memorize these things. The key was having one or two good comments for every likely line of conversation. Make two good points per topic, you were golden. The rest would fill itself in.

Hearing voices, she halted. *Should I . . . ? No.* Best not to knock. He seemed the sort who might be annoyed at that. She'd wait for them to stop. If nothing else, she'd have few more minutes to rehearse.

"Good morning"—no—"good afternoon, Dean Gaudimorte. I've waited for a chance all week to catch up! And I was passing by, and . . . " Oh, I hate this.

Speech snippets reached her as she worked her words out. "The first two funds are fully exhausted now?"

"As of this morning, yes, till next semester."

"Which leaves us only with the Charity Fund. Not where I wanted to be before Winter!"

That voice was Gaudimorte. The other seemed familiar as well. But Celeste couldn't quite work out where she'd heard that nasally and pedantic tone.

"That's never held us back before, you know."

"'*Before*,' we didn't have five thousand orks to feed!" retorted Gaudimorte. "And a month before the next semester's silver rolls in!"

"A contract is a contract," answered the other. "Keeping a contract's like keeping a secret. Once you let one slip, the rest . . ."

"Yes, yes, yes! One and a half. So be it!"

"Good. I *have* earned it. What would you do without the law on your side?"

"You know I've never quarreled with you on that," replied the Dean. "Look. That just leaves the timing. They say King Reginald soon will be restoring the royal subsidy for Academy research. Within weeks, some are saying. Wait till then. We'll get our subsidy; then, you'll get *your* subsidy. And, meanwhile, we'll maintain some minimal spending on charity, as we all agreed we must."

"Well, yes, but could we cut it back a bit? Who really needs the *Second* Sahngday Feast? Stew Kitchens twice a week? Why not just once?"

"It would be noticed," the Dean declared firmly. "And, you know well, the last thing that we all want—the one thing that would ruin this for us all—is if we're noticed."

The other sighed. A chair slid. "Fine. I'll wait. One month, I'll wait. Then, I'll expect my fair share. Whether or not the King's 'subsidy' comes through."

"Fine, fine! We'll hike tuition if we have to."

"Just blame it on our monarch's wasteful wars."

"He's barely back in power a month! . . . I love it. The wars, his army, tax cuts for the wealthy. We'll cite it all."

"Just say it till it sticks."

"It's awfully nice being the arbiters of truth! Alright. Well, this was good." A drawer slammed shut.

"Indeed. Till later, Gaudimorte."

It was now that Celeste, wide-eyed, realized she should go.

She spun and tiptoed round the closest corner, and—scarcely out of sight—she heard the door creak, then slam shut. Footsteps followed, slowly fading. A second set of footsteps came and went.

She hardly could believe what she'd just heard.

This can't be what it seems. Things aren't that simple. And yet, she'd learnt well in her time with Lothar, evil can cloak itself in long, fine phrases, but the ugliness beneath is plain and simple.

Cautiously, Celeste stepped back toward the office and snuck a peek inside. She tapped the door—no answer—and, glancing behind her back, she slipped inside.

The Office of the Dean was wide, impeccably pristine and modern. A simple, square desk, glaring with the false light shed by some ceiling strips, stood at the center. Atop it was a sphere-shaped paperweight, not holding any papers, and a pen was poised aslant upon a pedestal. The chairs were shaped to feel like they were padded. A fake tree, tall and trimmed straight, livened one corner. An abstract sculpture towered in the other corner. One wall had one square canvas splotched with colors. Another wall displayed the Dean's diplomas. And that was it.

She stepped behind the desk and, eying the door, slid open a drawer. Unused supplies and knick-knacks were inside and, among them, one black diary.

She started reaching, stopped and looked outside. No one. She pressed her lips; then, opened the diary.

It looked to be a ledger. Dated entries reflected payments furnished and received. Each one was labeled as "Research, "Historical," or "Charity." Payments received were a mix of mostly tuition, taxes and donations. About a third of payments furnished went toward departments' educational initiatives. The rest were simply labeled "Overhead."

She leafed through Gaudimorte's ledger, scanning the entries. Each page looked similar, save the dates' progression. She reached the present and the entries stopped. She stared a while; then, shrugged and set it back.

Or meant to, anyway. Her finger brushed the drawer's sharp corner, and she dropped the booklet. Opening midair, it plopped down, pages creasing on contact with the floor.

She winced and grabbed it. Scanning each page, she strove to smoothe the creases; then, winced more when she accidentally smeared a Research payment entry.

Should be fine. The entry was from last year.

She was shaking, as—carefully—she put the ledger away.

She'd started for the exit, nervous now, when, glancing one last time at Gaudi-morte's office, she saw a slip of parchment on the floor; not far from where the ledger had fallen earlier.

Lifting the little sheet, she looked it over. It must've been inside the ledger somewhere. A simple chart was at the page's center:

Overhead

Overhead: 5

M.G.: 2 ~~2.5~~ 3

F.T.: 1.5

C.D.: ~~1.25~~ 1.5

L.V.: 1.25

Z.P.: 1

J.H.: 1

B.J.: 1

Ork Guards: ~~2~~ ~~3~~ 6

She peered upon the cryptic text and pondered. Most of the ledger's expenses were "Overhead." This seemed to break down where that money went. But why, then, did this table of "Overhead" have "Overhead" as one of many entries? She guessed it wasn't odd to track "Ork Guards" separately from the other expenses listed. But what *were* the other entries?

Then, she blinked. "M.G."—*Malvolio Gaudimorte?* The other initials—*are these all names?*

She eyed the "1.5" next to the "~~1.25~~." Could it be the "one and a half" that Gaudimorte's visitor wanted? The initials listed next to that were "C.D." *But who's "C.D."?* She'd spent too long away. The list of scholars' names she knew had shrunk.

Scanning the entries again, her eyes caught on "Z.P." *Zell Phobios.* One of the professors with Gaudimorte, when they'd passed him on the Gramsleith; the long-necked man with the outsize Adam's apple. And then that woman with them—*Liv Vitodium!* She felt a flutter as she found "L.V." *And all these other names* . . . She stared and wondered, her sky-pale gaze going wide at the implications.

Is all this just a big conspiracy theory? Celeste was all too aware of the way the wishful mind could link together the unlinked, seeking a common scheme in mere coincidence. Two coins flipped long enough will land the same way seven times straight, without the game being rigged. The unlikely is inevitable, given time.

And wouldn't *she* look silly if "M.G." were "monetary grants," and the others likewise!

And yet she felt such innocent explanations were far more farfetched than a simple scheme of powerful men and women moved by greed.

This would explain, she realized, why the Dean was reluctant to approve of Starling's Project. Each silver piece being spent on honest science was one less he could split with his conspirators. And, if he approved of one, how many more would be inspired to seek their own approvals, seeing mankind fly, being moved to chase their own dreams? Shut it down now, and dreams stay put in dreamland, and silver keeps on flowing where it should.

She realized she was glaring through a cold haze, as when the heat of breath frosts forth through cold and clouds away the clarity of one's prospect.

She glanced outside—no sign of passersby—and pocketed the ledger and the parchment. Who knew if she would have another chance? What if they took apart the ship this week? This ledger might just get it off the ground. Literally. And they might even a get a new dean, more sympathetic to the love of learning that'd led to this Academy in the first place.

No time to dwell on "do or don't." She'd done it, and what was done was done, and that was that.

She stepped out, peeking through the half-open door, and strode away. In seconds, she'd departed the corridor and descended to a lower floor. And no one now could know where she'd just come from.

Passing a window, she peered to the west, where Sol was hovering over a stream-lined egg with four gold fins, trailing to points behind it. It floated high above the dirty floor. Indeed, it seemed to yearn and strain even higher, above the winging herons, white and hoary, toward where the cirrus glowed with backlit glory. And yet that yearning couldn't overcome the tether tying it firmly to its stake, fixed amid faded weeds in dusty wastes.

CHAPTER 26

"Perfect, Professor!" Brayleigh shouted back.

She'd promptly taken to the "Professor" moniker, right over Starling's protests. She was nowhere near the man's age; indeed, less than a third of it. Playing the student felt perfectly natural.

Plus, she was not about to let sweet Celeste primly address the scholar as "Professor," batting those blonde lashes every which way, lingering on Cor, all cutely deferential, while Brayleigh was reduced to gruffly growling a mannish "Starling" at the grizzled man.

"The whole ship's in the field now!" she continued.

"Excellent!" came the call back from below deck.

Brayleigh faced Cor and beamed. "Good call! We owe you."

Hours earlier, wheeling in a cart of food, he'd casually inquired why they were mounting the pedestal to hold the Passagestone left of the airship's center. At the time, Starling had doubted him. But, on redoing his math, he'd found the Beldrian was correct.

Cor shrugged and smiled. "My meager contribution to aviation. Moving food and stones."

"Hey, what good's flight without some food?" she said, waving at the unbound welkin; then, she blinked. "Woah! Just like that!" She pointed at a heron winging its way above a waterhole, holding a flopping fish inside its beak. "You see that? Ha! Yum!"

But, before the Beldrian had finished turning toward the hungry bird, a crow dove down and, flapping next to its neck, began to claw and bite around the fish.

The heron whirled and batted with its wings. But, in a flash, a flock of swooping crows had fallen upon the great blue heron, fighting to take it down and feed upon its fish, confusing it with ravening caws on all sides.

"Yikes! Poor thing! Good thing Celeste's gone," sighed Brayleigh. "She's a big heron fan, right?"

Hearing the "yikes," the Knight-Lord—who was climbing the walkway to the deck even now—looked up.

The heron now let loose its flopping fish and, with a burst of furious flapping, batted and spooked the crows away, then soared off eastward. Meanwhile, the black birds feuded madly over the fallen trout.

Witnessing this airborne brawl, Brayleigh forgot to ask the Knight-Lord why he'd walked up from the west and not the city, which she'd observed a couple minutes earlier.

"How's the ship coming? She ready to fly?" he questioned, turning away from the fight.

"Should be!" She shook the ominous scene away and beamed back. "Whole ship fits inside the stone's field. We're pretty confident we can fly through Boundaries."

"'Pretty'? How would we find out if you're wrong?"

"Crunch!" Brayleigh clapped her hands and beamed more broadly.

Deliad's lips curved down. "We could go by horse. Unmount that Passage-stone, get past these peaks, and we'd be on the plains before the first snow."

"And walk through snow all Winter?" questioned Cor.

"I'm more than 'pretty confident' we'd survive," he muttered.

"Live a little!" Brayleigh waved back.

"My first concern is to continue living."

His hesitance notwithstanding, Deliad helped them load up the airship with the last supplies. Even Starling joined soon, rolling wares about in a wheelbarrow with his usual birdlike bounce.

They'd just stopped, and were brushing blistered hands off, when they saw Celeste coming from the Gramsleith to climb the walkway.

"Hi there!" Brayleigh called. "Have any luck?"

"You could say that," said Celeste.

"What was the Dean's response?" demanded Starling with glimmering gaze.

"We didn't speak," she said.

The scholar frowned. "Go on."

"I think Dean Gaudimorte has been embezzling funds from the Academy. That's why he doesn't want to pay for *this*, and things like this." She pointed at the ship. "The more that's spent, the less that's left for him."

Starling had blinked a couple times by now. "I take it there's a story here," he said.

"I overheard him talking in his office," she nodded. She recounted all that'd happened, then lifted Gaudimorte's ledger from her pocket. "And here's the proof. The last page in particular. The slip of parchment labeled 'Overhead.'"

He browsed the leather ledger front to back, brow furrowing as he reached the final page. "'M.G.' Malvolio Gaudimorte. Triple share, of course. The crook. The scoundrel! All those years of villainizing science for science's sake, and preaching how our funds could feed the poor—and he's been robbing the Academy blind! You found this on his desk?"

She shook her head. "Inside his desk. I'd heard him shut the drawer."

"What do we do? Deliad, can you arrest him?" asked Brayleigh. "Have him hauled before the King?"

"That's not the way we do things here," said Starling. "Not this last century, at least. At the Academy, legal complaints are lodged with the Committee, for matters touching on Academy business. They hold a trial. And that decides the matter."

The Knight-Lord raised an eyebrow. "The 'Committee': the Governance Committee? Led by Gaudimorte? With Liv Vitodium too, the last I checked?"

The scholar nodded. "Yes, it's not ideal, but it's our only option. I believe the Dean, at least, will be required to recuse. I'd be inclined to accuse just him for now, and leave out the others. Liv and Zell, you'd mentioned. 'L.V.' and 'Z.P.' aren't that much to go on. But you heard Gaudimorte's voice. That's good enough."

Day's remnants dwindled swiftly, as the wanderers pondered this turn and made plans for the morrow. Celeste and Starling discussed how they'd lodge their accusation, what would follow next, and what they'd have to do. So, by the time they left the ship and headed for the city, Luna was looking over the east horizon, and, at Midheaven, the Red One hotly glared against the tilted luster of the Scales.

At daybreak, Starling formally convoked a special Governance Committee meeting; a rarely used privilege of department heads. The twelve Commissioners thus convened near noon within the Hall of Ages. Some were curious, others just grumpy.

"This had best be important, Starling," Professor Seint Vitran remarked. "My classics students will be wondering where their teacher went."

"As will my physics students," Professor Brenna Himinn said.

"No doubt! I wouldn't bother you with minor business," he said.

"Well, we'll all have to judge that, won't we?"

The rest of the Committee soon strolled in, as did its leader.

"Morning, everyone! Or is it afternoon?" Dean Gaudimorte greeted. "Liv. Calvor. Felix. Zell. Professor Jarble, you're just in time! Pleasure to see you all."

"Now." Gaudimorte eased his ample girth atop his ergonomic artificial chair. "Why don't you tell us, Starling, what's the occasion?"

"All here? Good." Starling stood. "I'm here to lodge a formal accusation of misconduct."

Some brows raised; more incredulous than impressed.

"This must be a very serious matter indeed, for you to bypass the ordinary process of filing papers—as the law prescribes—so we could meet on merely a few hours' notice," a skinny and wrinkled scholar drily observed, hands folded over his black gown, narrow-eyed behind the glasses balanced on his long nose.

Celeste remembered him vaguely. Professor Dustomas, head of the legal department. She'd nearly taken a course on law, but left it on learning he would teach it. She'd been told that he was boring and a brutal grader.

Or had she gone to one class first? His voice was faintly familiar. Maybe she had met him. Had Clausiglade introduced her? *Maybe that's it.*

"Quite serious, yes," confirmed Professor Starling. "Based on the testimony of Celeste Daorbhean, and on the contents of this ledger here"—he held the small black diary forth, and, briefly, Dean Gaudimorte gaped at it with goggling eyes—"I hereby accuse the Dean, Malvolio Gaudimorte, of felony embezzlement of funds from this Academy for his personal use."

Now those raised brows showed some interest. Silent, they stared at Starling first, then at their leader.

"How dare you," said the Dean, his tenor trembling, as both his face and bare pate flushed with choler. "Behind my back, for years, you undermined me and all that this Academy stood for, Starling. Even so, you kept your chair. You got your office. But now you'd dare to offend me to my face? Do you think *this* will save your precious ship? Do you think this Committee, which I lead, would hold a trial of *me* upon your word? With all the obvious bias you bear against me?"

"My word as well," responded Celeste coolly. "And if you'd like to start right now, I'm ready."

Professor Dustomas raised an open palm, glancing at Gaudimorte. "We *will* hold, of course, a trial upon these charges. Truth will out, and justice will be done. All in due course. You'll have a chance to tell your story at trial, Celeste. No need for you to do so now." He waited, smiling calmly, till she nodded.

"Meanwhile, we'll make the standard preparations. Setting a date, assembling witnesses, sequestering of the evidence, so on, so forth." He curled his hand, and Starling handed over the diary.

"Speaking of," the scholar went on, "may I ask, Celeste, how you obtained this ledger?" He flipped through it calmly, pausing on the last page.

"I overheard the Dean, outside his office, admit to his embezzlement," she said. "He left. I went inside and found the ledger."

"Ah. So you saw it lying on his desk?"

"Well, no. I heard him put it in a desk drawer. I opened the drawer and found the ledger there."

"Ah. Did you now?" The law head eyed the Dean, his thin lips curving up.

A triumphant smile spread across Gaudimorte's face; then, promptly passed, as righteous indignation claimed his countenance. "Indeed! I hereby accuse you, Celeste Daorbhean, of aggravated burglary. By her own word, heard firsthand by this Governance Committee, she took the official ledger of the Academy, without my leave or that of this Committee. Upon my power and mandate, I demand, as Dean of this Academy, that this woman be charged and tried for her felonious deeds." He slapped the table at "charged"; then, slightly smiled.

"And so she will," the head of law affirmed.

The wanderers blinked and looked at one another.

"What is this farce?" Disgust filled Deliad's voice. "Is this the way things work here? The accused accuses his accuser of catching him engaged in crime; and you would hold a *trial?* She took the ledger so it'd not be lost before the law could run its proper course; and you'd allow a charge of *burglary?*"

"Is that, Sir Knight-Lord, a defense to burglary?" Professor Dustomas responded coolly. "Do you have any case law for that point? If so, do you have any admissible evidence that Madame Daorbhean's fear to lose the ledger was reasonable? And that the act of theft was needful, when she could have called the Guard? *If so,*" he went on, speaking over Deliad, "you'll have an opportunity to argue your case, in due course, to this full Committee. When Madame Daorbhean undergoes her trial."

"In Eremon's name!" swore Deliad, stepping forth with fist balled.

But the adoptive daughter of Clausiglade held out an arm to halt him. "We'll look forward to a fair and neutral trial," she calmly said.

The trials were scheduled for a week thereafter. This would have been absurdly expedited under the standards of the King's royal courts. But trials at the Academy didn't follow the King's old-fashioned rules. So, skipping over discovery and the other process due to litigants, they reached resolution quicker.

Not that the wanderers were about to object. If the airship didn't work out, they would want to cross the Ginnagonds before the first snow. Wait a few weeks, that'd likely be impossible.

Deliad suggested several times that week that Celeste pack her bags and flee the city, rather than *"dignify this parody of legal process by participating."* But, heartening as it was to have the Knight-Lord concerned for her, she waved away his worries. *"The process may be brief, but it's designed to be both fair and neutral,"* she replied.

She'd roped in Starling now. She'd not desert him. Indeed, she spent the whole week at his side, planning her testimony, studying case law, and plotting out her closing argument. Starling was well-versed in the legal process, having been forced to deal with some disputes as head of his department. As for Celeste, she knew a bit from some informal study at Clausiglade's urging. *"Knowing how the law works will always, always, serve you well,"* he'd said.

Meanwhile, wanting to help but not knowing how, Brayleigh and Cor kept working on the airship, unloading the supplies they'd wheeled aboard and finding raw fuel for Professor Logi.

The wild-haired scholar was in charge of the engine, which ran on *"anything that once was living!"* he'd boasted. He was busy now with testing that purring motor at ever swifter speeds, flinging a red-robed arm up with a clenched fist and cry of triumph each time he hit a new high.

"There's as much beauty in that mess of tubes as all her other parts," Starling had praised. *"Fine body, yes. But she also has a fine heart."*

Sometimes, the Knight-Lord helped, but he was mostly absent that week; indeed, for four days straight. He waved away their questions where he'd been. *"Nothing to worry about. Just Knight-Lord business."*

Each evening, under the escort of an ork guard, Celeste went home—that is, to Clausiglade's house—and slipped beneath her heron-covered quilt. She didn't sleep well. She was well aware that sleepless brooding wouldn't help her plight. But, what her brain knew, her body still doubted, judging by how it flinched and fled from sleep.

Sometimes, in sleep deprivation's delirium, haunted by thoughts of all that might go wrong, she felt that she was listening to the Fates, whispering what must occur and might be avoided. And, if she fell asleep, she'd miss some warning that'd steer her from calamity toward the right course: that future that she'd dreamt of, swelling darkling, unseen yet sparkling in her premonitions.

But, as she lost herself in misty musing each night, eventually, she let her guard down. And then the hunter Somnus stole upon her and bore her off to where her heart was hearkening.

CHAPTER 27

"All rise." The old bailiff boomed the old words out. "The High Court of the Royal Academy, under the jurisdiction of this chosen Committee, by grace and mandate of His Majesty, King Reginald VI, is now in session."

The "chosen Committee" filed in from an arched door of oak, half-hidden in shadow. First emerged Dean Gaudimorte and Professor Dustomas; then, hairless Traditor and scar-faced Jarble; then wise old whitebeard Eldorf; then Hastam, who'd parleyed long-past military service into a profitable career in politics; Professor Phobios and his Adam's apple; Vitodium, frowning, with her short hair fresh-shorn; and the others, clad in colored scholars' gowns.

The chosen thirteen processed past jury benches toward thirteen stone chairs in a semi-circle around the witness' stand and advocates' stands—Seats of the Justices—then strolled on past them.

On they progressed past thirteen somber statues of ancient jurists in their own stone seats, whose grave forms formed the circle's other half. Some of them seemed to watch the witness stand. Others were staring at the high domed ceiling.

Upon the blue serene depicted there, mists meandered thickly on the far periphery. Out of those mists emerged four winged figures with horns, each reaching for another's heels: one with her flowing hair aflower, with fingers of rosy hue; one stern but shining-browed and crowned in laurel; one with wistful smile, clasping a gourd and glancing toward the fourth: a melancholy man with snowy hair and starry dark cloak, reaching for the first. All four held billowing banners, labeled "Fairness."

Past this high scene progressed the thirteen scholars and down some stairs, where thirteen portable chairs with pads were sitting near the advocates' stands. "Have a seat, all," the portly Dean directed. "Let's get this sorry business over with."

There was no jury on the jury benches. *"We don't call random crowds to cobble our shoes, build bridges, cook our meals, or forge our steel. We seek out expertise,"* the Dean had reasoned. *"So why entrust justice to a random crowd?"* The Governance Committee thus was now both jury and judge. Not "Justices," however; the Dean had done away with the ancient title. *"Who are we to assume the name of Justice?"* Likewise, the Seats of the Justices soon were set to be removed, as were the statues of bygone jurists gazing from beyond death. *"Why celebrate the authoritarian ways upheld by a bunch of dead male monarchists? The proper place for them is a museum!"*

The Governance Committee heard the trial of Gaudimorte first. Both sides gave opening statements, and then the witness questioning began.

First, Starling spent some fifteen minutes asking Professor Penning background finance questions, and then called Celeste to the stand. She approached.

"Celeste Daorbhean, arise and hold your hand forth," directed the elder bailiff. "Do you swear, before His Majesty and his Committee here duly constituted, by the mandate of Eremon unto Mannus and his heirs, to tell the truth?"

"It's Céleste, not Celéste. Yes, I so swear."

She told her story simply and honestly: how she had happened on the Dean along the road to the Academy, and he'd suggested that they speak again; how she had come to his office to do so and overheard him speaking from outside; and what she'd heard and seen there. Several members of the Committee seemed concerned and troubled.

The trial's key moment came, though, when the Dean was on the stand for cross-examination by Starling.

"You've been handed what's been marked as Exhibit 3," said Starling, as the ledger was laid before the Dean. "You've seen this, yes?"

"Indeed!"

"What is it?"

"My official ledger. That is, the Academy ledger, laying out our income and expenses. Research, charity, historical preservation costs, and so forth."

"Turn to the first page, please," instructed Starling. "You see that there are entries here for payments?"

"I do."

"Payments received and payments furnished—you see that?"

"Yes, I see it. And I wrote it."

"So. You're aware, then, that the listed payments are sometimes for Academy projects, yes?"

"Of course."

"And there are also several payments you labeled 'Overhead'?"

"Indeed, indeed."

"You see it doesn't specify what these payments for Overhead were paying for?"

"You mean, besides that they were labeled Overhead?"

"Yes. Nothing further, right? Just Overhead?"

"That's what it says."

"You wrote that, yes?"

"Indeed!"

"About two-thirds of this month's total spending was on these Overhead expenses, right?"

"About that, yes."

"The next month too?"

"Indeed. And let me save you time, Professor: same with the third, fourth, fifth and sixth months too, and so forth. Give or take." The Dean smiled lightly.

"So," Starling said. "Most projects listed here have overhead expenses, no?"

"No doubt."

"So why is Overhead a separate entry?"

"Since it's a separate cost from project costs. Facility maintenance, food, supplies, security. These things don't grow on trees! That's overhead."

"That's what this Overhead went toward? You're sure?"

"Indeed! I wrote this, after all," the Dean said.

"Well then. If Overhead's food and supplies, then why is there a separate line each month for 'Food and Supplies'"?

The Dean blinked; then, grinned guiltily and held his open hands forth. "Alas. You've caught me. This was a quirk of our old-fashioned bookkeeping; which, mind you, we had followed here for centuries. Cost categories overlap sometimes. What's a new dining table: Overhead or Food and Supplies? Or is it in Materials? Who knows! It's all subjective! I admit, I've probably put them in all three myself! I admit, I should've modernized this system, along with all the rest we've worked to improve. But I'd not gotten around to it. Guilty as charged." He smiled and held his hands out once again.

"Guilty, you say," said Starling. "Let me ask you, Dean Gaudimorte: Have you ever hidden a payment to any Academy scholar, or yourself, within these so-called 'Overhead' expenses?"

"Oh, Heavens no!" Gaudimorte's genial gaze went wide, and up his palm flew from his ample belly upon his heart. His lips curved briefly upward.

"Turn to the slip of parchment past the last page."

The Dean flipped forward. "What? This empty ledger?"

"No, past the last page. It's a slip of parchment. It's labeled 'Overhead.'"

"Hm. I don't see it." Dean Gaudimorte held the book open and displayed it. As the audience peered upon the empty ledger, briefly, he locked eyes with Starling and leered; which, in a blink, became a baffled frown. "You say it's labeled 'Overhead'? A whole page?"

Professor Starling glanced unsurely at Celeste. "Yes. Check between the other pages, please."

Letting the ledger hang downward, the Dean flipped all the pages left, then right. "No parchment, I fear. Of course, I'm not sure why there would be. A page that's just for 'Overhead'; strange concept! I would remember writing that, I think."

"May I?" said Starling, facing the Committee.

"Please do," Professor Dustomas replied.

Starling retrieved the diary from the Dean and scanned it, page by page, from front to back and back to front; then, turning to face Celeste, he looked upon her helplessly, lips pressed.

"I move to adjourn this trial to a later date," he finally spoke, facing the twelve Commissioners, "while we determine how this crucial evidence was lost from the Committee's custody."

"What 'crucial evidence' though?" the Dean inquired. "This page that never existed? While I wait, accused of crimes, with my defense delayed until you find this damning piece of evidence that never was? I daresay, how dystopian!"

"Professor Starling, could you please respond?" Dustomas said. "The Dean's point may have merit. I'm not aware of any legal ground to adjourn a trial midway for 'missing' evidence, absent some competent proof that it existed, beyond the offering party's testimony."

"I—" Starling shook his head. "Yes, we've all seen it." He waved at Celeste and the other wanderers. "They'll testify to that."

"That's what I mean. No proof beyond the plaintiff side's assertions?" said Dustomas. "No documentary proof? No testimony of neutral parties? No? In that case, as I said, I'm not aware of any legal precedent for adjournment. We'll put it to a vote. All those in favor?" the scholar questioned.

Five hands rose. The rest stayed down, Professor Dustomas' included.

"Seven of twelve say nay. Motion denied," said Dustomas. "Continue, please, Professor."

Grimacing, Starling continued his cross-examination, but he never quite regained momentum. Soon, he wrapped things up, and Gaudimorte's counsel waived his opportunity for redirect.

"The burden's on the accusers to prove their case. They've plainly failed to do so," said Fallax, the professor of law who'd offered to serve as Gaudimorte's lawyer. "So, no questions are needed. The defense will rest," he said.

Following closings, the Commissioners left the courtroom, then returned in fifteen minutes.

"The Governance Committee has concluded deliberations," Dustomas announced. "The vote was split, six for and six against."

Celeste's chest felt like a flung rock had landed inside it, and a hundred butter-flies had burst from slumber into startled flight.

"Typically, in a trial before this body, the Dean's vote breaks a tie. But, being recused, he cannot do so. So the tie remains," explained the law head. "Therefore, following our bedrock principle that the accuser bears proof's burden, in a tie, the charges fail. Dean Gaudimorte, this Committee finds you innocent of all offenses. You are free to go."

The butterflies now flashed red, then curled black, and, in the fervent doubt now sweeping through her, fell burning into ash and sickly fumes.

"Very good!" Gaudimorte shared an affable smile with his Governance Committee. "That said, Calvor, rather than go so soon, I think I'll join you. As I recall, another trial is scheduled for right now, and I'd be remiss to miss it. I am the Dean, you know!"

"Indeed. Please do," Professor Calvor Dustomas replied, pointing at the empty portable seat beside him.

Brayleigh and Cor were staring back and forth from Celeste to each other, blinking dumbly with mouths open. Starling, though, was grimacing at only Celeste, shoulders low, gaze drooping, as when a father fails before his daughter.

"Sit down, Malvolio!" urged the bald man, beaming on the other side of Gaudimorte's empty seat; Professor Felix Traditor, his old friend. "How do you feel?"

"I daresay, nearly as jolly as yon shirtless fellow, frolicking behind the shapely gourded lass!" Dean Gaudimorte pointed upon the painted dome.

"No doubt, no doubt!" Traditor chuckled, as the Dean's bulk squeezed be-tween the skinny law head and himself. "So tacky. All that frivolous fleshiness!"

"Irks me a little more each time I see it," the Dean said. "Should replace it, really. Something decently modern, nonrepresentational. If only painting ceilings weren't so pricey."

"Well, charge it to the overhead!" waved Felix.

The pair of old peers laughed and slapped their knees, the Dean's big belly bouncing under his gown, as thirteen stony jurists stared in silence. "Alright then. Let's get this show on the road!" Gaudimorte declared. "Calvor, take it away."

"Before we start, a question," Celeste said. "I assume the Dean won't take part in deciding my case? He'll be required to recuse, of course?"

"That would be true if the ledger were his," Professor Dustomas replied. "In fact, though, the ledger's not his personal property. It's the Academy's. His recusal's no more required than any other's here. Of course, the ledger does 'belong' to this Committee, in some sense; but if we can't hear this case, who can? We'll hear the case, and so will he."

"Well said, as always, Calvor!" Gaudimorte leaned back his small chair, smoothing his gown over his gut. The chair legs bowed a little under his bulk.

"Mistake from the start," muttered Deliad. "Rigged game."

So, Celeste's trial on burglary charges started, and soon the witness questioning began. In time, she took the stand again, now nervous, though she felt certain she'd done nothing wrong. As Starling had instructed, she responded to the inquiries of Professor Fallax briefly and plainly.

"Now then, Madame Daorbhean," the law professor said. "You stood outside the Dean's door, listening. As he left, you ran and hid around the corner. What next?"

"Well. I'd just heard the Dean describe his crime; what sounded like a crime. So, I walked in."

"Wait. I'm not sure I follow," Fallax said. "You said there was a crime, 'so, I walked in.' Why? Why not call the guard?"

"I would have later. But by then, I'd already found the ledger."

"Well, one step at a time," responded Fallax. "You opened the door, yes?"

"No. I found it open."

"Fine. So, you walked inside. What happened next?"

"I'd heard the Dean and someone else discussing the 'shares' they'd get. And then I'd heard a drawer. So I decided that I'd check the desk drawer," she said. "And it was there I found the ledger—"

"Wait, wait," said Fallax. "One step at a time. The drawer was closed. You opened it, yes?"

"I did. I'd heard him close it. So I had to open it."

"You didn't *have* to do that, Madame Daorbhean. No one was there coercing you, correct?"

"Objection, argumentative!" said Starling. "He's quibbling with her ordinary language. We all know well enough what 'had to' means here."

"Withdrawn," the lawyer mollifyingly waved. "So, then you opened the Dean's desk drawer. What then?"

"I lifted out the ledger and reviewed it. I found a slip of parchment past the last page, which said—"

"I didn't ask you what it said," Professor Fallax interrupted her. "You took the ledger, yes?"

"I took it, yes, since it was evidence of an ongoing crime, I thought. Then, promptly, I presented it to this Committee. I had no intent—"

"I didn't ask about intent," he broke in. "You took the ledger. Why not leave it there and call the guard about this so-called 'crime'?"

"Because the ledger, meanwhile, might be lost! What if he took it out? Or threw it out? I knew this might be the only opportunity."

"You viewed this as an opportunity then?" Professor Fallax instantly inquired. "To do what? To destroy the Dean's good name? To get revenge on him for not supporting Professor Starling's spending on his 'airship'?"

"Objection!" yelled Professor Starling. "Compound. And badgering the witness. And these questions are purely prejudicial and non-probative."

"Sustained," Dustomas smiled. "One at a time."

Professor Fallax nodded penitently and smiled back. "So, you spoke about intent. I cut you off. I'll let you finish now. My question is, when you went through with this and took the ledger, one thing on your mind was that the Dean might be removed as Dean, and be replaced with someone who supported this 'Sojourner.' Correct?"

"I mean, the main thing—"

"No, no, I didn't ask you for the 'main thing.' *One* thing you thought was that the Sojourner might be approved if Dean Gaudimorte were gone?"

She hesitated. "Maybe it crossed my mind—"

"Thank you, Madame," said Fallax. "Nothing further."

The examinations went on and concluded, followed by closings. The Committee left for its deliberations for a half hour, then filed back in and took their folding chairs, shifting for comfort on their creaky cheapness.

And then Professor Dustomas faced Celeste. "The Governance Committee has concluded deliberations, and the vote split, six-six." His wrinkled face and lips curved faintly upward. "It therefore falls upon the Dean to break the tie with his vote, should he so desire."

Celeste's head bowed low. No butterflies now. Just a vague feeling that she'd always make the same mistakes and never learn from life, and now, once more, would face the consequences.

"Indeed." The Dean smiled sadly. "I regret this whole unpleasant business. How I wish we all could just move on and live our lives! The law, though, is the law. It falls to me to enforce it. Duty binds me. Celeste Daorbhean is guilty, so I cast my vote for guilt. "

The Knight-Lord peered away with narrowed eyes and nodded, as when one expects the worst and gets it.

"The defendant is adjudged guilty as charged," decreed Dustomas calmly. "Now, for the sentencing. The maximum for burglary is—"

"Typically," broke in Dean Gaudimorte, "in an academic trial, the most severe of sanctions we can level are exile and expulsion from the Academy. I feel, though, that these measures would be cruel and unusual in the case at hand. This poor girl—a daughter of this Academy, raised by Clausiglade, my long, late friend, and a professor here—is good at heart, I reckon, but unsound of mind. I think she thought that she was right! What moved her wasn't malice but unwellness."

"In this delusive state she's suffering through," the Dean said, "what she needs is oversight and care. A chance at rehabilitation; which, as we know, should always be preferred. So, I propose that Celeste Daorbhean be confined within the sanatory ward of the Hall of Balance, under supervision, until, in the discretion of this body, she's ready to return to open society. No further penalty is necessary."

"Wisely said. Most wise!" Traditor approved.

"All those in favor of the Dean's proposal for rehabilitative custody in lieu of punishment?" inquired the law head.

Six hands rose.

Gaudimorte scanned them, smiled, and raised his.

"So be it," Professor Dustomas decreed. "Madame Daorbhean at once shall be detained indefinitely in the Hall of Balance. In two years' time, the bailiff is directed to bring her back here for a wellness hearing. Meanwhile, we will retain our jurisdiction."

"This is outrageous. A disgrace!" said Starling. His fists were balled. "This whole trial was a sham!"

"You're not the first to claim that, I assure you," Dustomas calmly replied. "This world's rife with those who'd undermine our institutions by attacking their authority and their good faith. Still, sad to hear it from a scholar here; and a department head, at that." He glanced at Gaudimorte.

"Sad indeed!" declared the Dean. "An open society can't exist with such speech, smashing the very foundations of freedom. We've made too much of free speech. There's no freedom from consequences! Let's remember that when we approve department head renewals."

"Wisely said. Most wise!" Traditor commended.

The law head thinly smiled and turned to two men wearing grey vests and visors, wielding stunners. "Guards, please escort the rehabilitatee to the upper sanatory ward."

"Yes Sir." The two security guards approached.

She sighed and shut her eyes. Her life resembled Luna, forever waning black just after brightening.

"By order of His Majesty, King Reginald, don't lay a hand on her," Deliad commanded. He faced the two guards with a smiling glare, with eyes like slits of sky through sunlit clouds.

Pausing, the pair of men faced Dustomas, whose brow raised, wrinkling further. "Was there something you wished to say before this body, Knight-Lord?"

"There is." He unsealed and unrolled a scroll. "The document I hold here is a mandate signed by our Monarch and stamped with his seal, as you can see." He held it briefly forth. "It states as follows:"

"'Should it come to pass that Celeste Daorbhean be detained for any infraction or offense, by our Academy at Beregin, operating under our charter and at our pleasure, she is hereby pardoned; and any findings, holdings, or convictions issued by any body on my behalf, the Academy's Governance Committee included, hereby are voided and vacated; and, henceforth, all jurisdiction over her shall lie with us alone. We hereby order that Celeste Daorbhean be released and discharged at once from our Academy's custody.'"

"'Further, we hereby decree that the vessel dubbed 'Sojourner,' constructed by Dirk Starling, at once be requisitioned for the service of Norvester's royal naval force; wherefore, we hereby order that it be conveyed instantly, whole and intact, to our person.'"

"Signed and sealed, Reginald VI," he concluded.

Silence ensued.

The Dean eyed Dustomas, who held a hand forth toward the mandate. "May I?"

"Oh, I'll hold onto it, I think," smiled Deliad, eyes blazing. "Do feel free to take a look though."

Dumbstruck, she stared at Deliad and his scroll, as Dustomas approached and peered upon it. *"Nothing to worry about. Just Knight-Lord business."* This would explain what he'd been doing this week.

Not for the first time, she felt like she'd just learnt the lead role in her own life wasn't hers; like others were the movers, and herself a moving part in plans she learnt too late.

She nodded at the Knight-Lord gratefully.

"Come now, let's all be serious," said the Dean, adopting a paternal tone. "We all know that no one's called this place the 'King's Academy' in half a century. No king's intervened in our courts in twice that time. Let's all be honest. We know this isn't how the system works now."

"The law's the law, as you said," answered Deliad. "The Academy's charter comes from Norvester's King. The mandate of this Governance Committee is no more than the pleasure of the King, which, at his pleasure, he can supersede. Dustomas can confirm that, I believe."

"Let's hear from Dustomas, yes." The Dean smiled. "Tell him that's not how the law's worked for centuries. He's simply out of date! Isn't he, Dustomas?"

The Academy's law head shifted awkwardly. "I'm not aware of any legal precedents contrary to the assertions of the Knight-Lord."

The Dean scowled. "Let me see that so-called 'mandate.'" He heaved himself to his feet and waddled forth, scanning the scroll. "Aha! You see that there? A forgery! See? The seal's wrong. Amateur! You thought this seal would fool us learned scholars? Come, Eldorf, tell him. This thing's phony as fool's gold!"

A whitebeard elder shuffled from his seat, hunching and leaning heavily on his staff so that his gown of gules hue brushed the floor. And, slowly putting on his spectacles, he stared for two whole minutes at the scroll.

Gaudimorte was tapping the ground with his boot, a wide grin plastered on his red-flushed face.

"During my many decades in the archives of this Academy," Eldorf finally wheezed, "I've studied many thousand scrolls with seals of House Lofthungrian, both before and after Lord Sigram of that House was made our monarch. That seal has stayed the same at least eight centuries; perhaps more. Looking at the Knight-Lord's seal here, I see at least eighteen—no, nineteen features." He paused and peered a moment. "Yes, nineteen, which are precisely like those myriad seals I've studied. Nor is any part of this seal even slightly out of place," the elder noted.

Dean Gaudimorte glared and briefly stared in silence. "The Governance Committee will confer!" he finally announced.

"Confer quickly," said Deliad. "The King's command did not propose a conference."

The thirteen scholars in their portable seats leaned close and spoke in whispers for a while.

Meanwhile, leaning toward Deliad, Celeste whispered, "I'm grateful." It felt lame to say just that, but she was somewhat at a loss for words.

The Knight-Lord looked at her and quietly said, "There's no such thing as 'fair and neutral' process, when unfair people are the ones applying it."

She blinked and opened her mouth. But voices now were escalating from the huddled scholars.

One wheezing warble rose above the din. "This has no precedent. Since Promethean's reign! You know that, Dustomas."

A nasally tenor said something in a patronizing tone. And then another minute passed in murmuring, half-heard, before another voice broke through: "You don't have the authority, Dean or not. *We* don't have the authority." Then, another: "This simply isn't something we can do!"

"We can and will," the law head answered calmly. "The King's authority comes from our consent. The monarch's mandate comes from men, not Heaven. Consent can be withdrawn; and so it shall be, by vote."

"Absurd," replied Professor Vitran. "This is mere *ipse dixit.* Made-up law. Some seven fallible men, rewriting law based on first principles made up on the spot. A thin veil over expedient lawlessness!"

"Yes, she speaks wisely and rightly," wheezed Eldorf. "The mandate of our Kings, of House Lofthungrian, comes of their hallowing by Eremon himself. Our monarch will retain that heavenly mandate whether or not we deign to recognize it."

"Enough, Eldorf." Dean Gaudimorte rolled his eyes and smiled. "We're governing, not studying history. Where was this 'Eremon' when the Merchant routed our monarch and his band of merry men?" He faced the Knight-Lord. "By a seven-six vote of this Committee, the Academy hereby dissolves and nullifies its ties to Norvester and Norvester's King, and henceforth shall enjoy sole sovereignty and general jurisdiction; as has, in practice, been the way we've worked here for over a century."

"This is folly. Foulness!" Seint Vitran said. "You all should be ashamed. 'Dissolve' our ties. One step from simple treason!"

"No, not even one." Professor Eldorf sighed. "Would that I had not lived to see such times."

"Old men call every revolution treason," the Dean replied. "We must move on, and will. I would suggest, Knight-Lord, you and your party depart the Academy promptly. Soon, you'll find a less congenial welcome for your kind here. Except for Madame Daorbhean, who must do her ordained sentence in the Hall of Balance. Guards, please escort her there post-haste."

Six guards in grey vests, wielding stunners, started forward.

Deliad drew Hoarthaxe and stepped before Celeste, followed by Cor. "Halt, men," the Knight-Lord ordered, "or you'll be traitors to your King."

They halted and glanced at Gaudimorte, then at Deliad's halberd.

The Dean sighed. "*This* is why we've banned all weapons in public places. Leave *just one* exception—for Knights of Norvester—and you see what happens?

These are the fruits of romantic nostalgia!" He shook his head. "Henceforth, no more exceptions."

"This just confirms it, you know," affirmed Traditor, shiny head shaking. "Such royalist barbarism is why our vote today was so essential."

"Concurred in full," the law head said.

"There's nothing barbaric in the Knight-Lord taking arms to put down treason," Eldorf gravely censured.

The Dean smiled. "Quaintly spoken, as always, Eldorf." He turned to Celeste. "Guards, detain our inmate as I directed. Should the Knight-Lord's 'squad' here attempt to intervene, please neutralize them."

An old guard shook his head. "Sir, I won't do that."

Another, younger, nodded after a second and stood firm. "I'm no traitor to my King."

"Indeed? Then you're a traitor to the Academy," the Dean said. "You received an order. *Do* it."

The four remaining guards stepped forth, their fingers ready upon their silver sidearms' triggers. The other two held back, their faces torn.

Cor assumed Ox Horn, blade above his head, knees slightly bent. The Knight-Lord held forth Hoarthaxe.

This went south quickly. Celeste was unarmed. She scanned for something weaponlike to wield, but there was nothing nearby.

As she searched, she saw Professor Starling slipping out a side door in the hubbub. *Who could blame him? This may be the Academy, but it's no place for scholars.*

The security guards were starting to slow and aim their stunners at the wanderers when, to their fore, there flashed a wall of red, blasting them backward off their feet halfway to Gaudimorte. Grey vests clattered on the ground. One big guard's visor was dislodged, revealing a half-ork's tumorous face and mangled features.

She blinked and spun—and there was Brayleigh, palm forth, lips parted in a faint smirk.

But behind her, four guards with stunners ready now were rushing into the room.

"Seize those three!" screamed the Dean, waving from Celeste to Deliad and Cor. "And her!" He pointed at the girl from Fernstead.

Deliad already was darting toward one guard who'd fallen well and was hopping to his feet, leveling his stunner.

Cor had whirled toward Brayleigh and sprinted forth, blade pumping in his fist.

The four guards' gazes fixed on him. Three stepped forth and fired their stunners. Jags of bluish lightning leapt out toward Cor. Two missed. The third one touched his sword hand's knuckle.

And, abruptly flinging his fingers out, Cor let his sword slip loose to clang upon the floor. He clutched his hand, confusion on his face, then threw himself aside in time to dodge the next three shots, scrambling across the floor to find his sword.

Brayleigh had now spun back to face those three guards and, hand out, sent a half-pellucid plane of blood hue shooting forth. It smacked them airborne.

"What *is* that strange device? The red-wall weapon!" the Dean demanded of a nearby officer. "Why don't I know of that? Why don't we have that!"

The fourth guard, who had failed to fire on Cor, was glancing first at Brayleigh, then at Gaudimorte, and then the Knight-Lord, with the crown and fist and vert-hued flame of Norvester on his tabard. His brow was furrowing further by the second. The stunner in his hand was sinking.

Meanwhile, the Knight-Lord now was lopping off an arm from the fallen Academy guard who'd leapt to his feet.

That arm and stunner alike, midway through swinging, continued their momentum cross the room, striking Professor Blorg Jarble's scarred face. He flung his head back; and his portable chair fell backward, so his legs and waist flopped V-like around Professor Liv Vitodium's lap.

Deliad disposed of the visorless half-ork with one quick thrust of Hoarthaxe to the throat.

And Celeste sprang forth, seeing her chance had come, toward where the guard had fallen. She ducked at first, then dove beneath the stunners' line of fire. She grabbed the dead guard's fist and, ripping out its sidearm from a rigor-mortic grasp, she aimed it at the last guard facing Deliad and pulled the trigger. Lightning zigzagged forth.

A short convulsion shuddered through the guard, whose neck now had a ruddy fernlike pattern where she had shot it. Down he fell, limp-limbed, his vest and visor clacking on the stone.

Deliad looked down and blinked to find her there. Then, darkly grinning, gripping Hoarthaxe hard, he faced the Dean, advancing toward his fat foe.

"Get *him!*" the Dean shrieked, stumbling backward. "Get him!"

"Let's mosey!" Cor called. He was by the exit with blade in hand and Brayleigh at his side.

From the far door, more guards were dashing in, scanning to find the source of the disturbance. It didn't take them long to center on Hoarthaxe.

And, in a blink, a trio of stunner blasts narrowly missed the Knight-Lord. Seconds later—as Gaudimorte stumbled back behind some benches and Deliad neared—a second volley came. And this time, one of the lines of blue lightning grazed the left side of his tabard and scorched it.

A wall of pale red walloped all three guards against the stone wall, drawing grunts and cries, as stunners fell and clattered on the floor. One of them went off, firing arcing blue toward Felix Traditor's foot. He gasped as grey smoke rose from his smoldering shoe, then tried to flee, but found that he was blocked by a jury bench.

Grimacing at his burnt shirt, Deliad spun from the cringing Dean to follow Cor's call.

Meanwhile, Celeste had scrambled to her feet and started sprinting that way as well. She saw that Brayleigh was sagging, one hand resting on a ledge and holding her upright, and breathing heavily. Lips pressed, she thrust her palm forth, and a plane of half-seen red shot out—hitting a guard who, unbeknownst to Celeste, had arisen from falling earlier and was aiming at her.

With that exertion, Brayleigh half-collapsed, and she was barely caught by Cor's left arm around her side. "Come on!" he called once more, then led her out.

Behind him by a few steps was Deliad, who was out a second later.

Celeste was scarcely three paces behind him and dashing toward the doorway when she felt something clutch firmly round her ankle, yanking backward the foot she was about to land on.

Toppling, she struck her forehead on the stone floor.

And now a numinous world of spangled night was whirling round her, vague with meandering mists, which seemed to move with every half-felt throb that surged through all her senses from her head.

Through swirling Stars, she saw the hard stone floor; and, half-aware, she felt herself roll over.

A silhouette of a man with stunner in hand was standing over her. "Don't move," he said, sounding like she was listening underwater. More words came, but she couldn't comprehend them. His shadowy hand was reaching down to seize her.

She saw her own hand rising toward that shape and opening. Over each finger formed a blue wisp, each flaring like a flame atop a wick.

The man had halted and was peering down. Slowly, he pointed the thing in his hands at her.

"*Incline thyself to me.*" The words resounded within the misty starscape of her mind.

Off from her fingertips whirled the blue wisps into a streaking spiral toward the guard's eyes, fleetingly glimmering from beneath his visor.

He screamed and fell back, hands upon his face.

Celeste's arm fell and, motionless, she lay for several moments, as the shadowy world swirled by above her. She heard angry voices and fearful voices, shouting strange commands.

And then she felt herself being heaved aloft and over a shoulder, hauled away from this dreamy disorder of shades toward the unknown.

CHAPTER 28

Shifting the weight of Celeste on his shoulder, the Knight-Lord struggled after Cor and Brayleigh.

Farther ahead by the second, the Beldrian fluidly dispatched with a half-orkish guard and disemboweled its peer, then hied along. His fellow western wanderer gave him cover with fleeting walls of red, blocking blue volleys of paralytic lightning.

Brayleigh paused and looked back. "Deliad! You—?"

"Don't stop! I'll keep up." He grit his teeth and forced himself to a fast jog. Running with halberd and armor was one thing, but adding on a 110-pound woman was quite another.

"Saved me again . . . the Daemon . . . ," she murmured, mouth hidden under falling hair like a cave behind a Star-stained waterfall.

"A Daemon? Well, I'll take that as a compliment!" said Deliad, dodging round some stunner fire and following his fellows toward the doorway. Against the glare of day, they turned to silhouettes, quitting the Hall of Ages for the crisp air.

"There!" yelled a guard with an officer's insignia, as Deliad crossed the doorway into daylight. Rounding the spire from the right side, a squad of mostly orkish guards was marching toward them. "Stunners to kill!" He raised to his lips a whistle and blew three times, holding the last at length. The guards behind him turned their stunners' dials and strode forth, aiming at the fleeing wanderers.

Deliad responded by lifting his warhorn and sounding, from its bone-hued curve, a note that shook the street.

The guards paused briefly, flinching and raising arms in unsure self-defense.

Celeste flinched too atop his shoulder. *Oops. Hope she can hear still.*

Brayleigh flung a hand forth, so a faintly visible Boundary flattened their foes, then spun to Deliad. "Flua-Sahng's name, what *was* that! You want to gather every guard they have here?"

"Don't doubt me!" he replied. Scanning the guards, he saw that some were shifting on the ground. Grimly, he started to set Celeste down. He'd need both hands for wielding man-high Hoarthaxe.

"It's all right," she said weakly, squinting back the Sun. She rubbed her forehead, then her ear. "I'll stand." She wobbled as he let her go, but stayed upright, both hands upon her knees with head bowed.

"Stay by Brayleigh!" Cor directed, his sword drawn, starting toward the stirring guards. "We'll get you a weapon."

"Thanks," she smiled behind him, her eyelids weighted down by wooziness.

Deliad was dashing toward the guards now too, two of whom just had started standing.

"Fire!" the officer shouted from the floor. Two bolts arced crackling forth—more purple now than blue—but stopped in midair. A pellucid plane of crimson shimmered. "Fire!" he called again, and three more lines of lightning jolted out. One of them barely missed the approaching Beldrian.

Deliad was drawing his halberd back as Cor struck, cutting the stunner hand off of a half-ork, as the officer screamed, "Fire! Fire!" and jabbed a finger toward the impending head of Norvester's Knights.

Then, Hoarthaxe fell upon the officer's head and hewed through torso halfway through the heart.

It took two tries to yank the big blade out. And, during that delay, an ork guard got up, still somewhat dazed, and aimed its stunner at Deliad. He tried to jerk aside, but he was still off-balance from his tugging.

Lightning arced forth, singing his left hand, which let loose his halberd and spasmed. The half-held weapon started falling; but, sliding up his right hand on the haft, he caught it midfall, quickly stabbing the ork guard, even as his shocked left arm palpitated strangely.

It opened its mouth, but no words flowed forth; just blood, fountaining from the new hole in its neck.

Meanwhile, the Beldrian was gutting a guard that'd grazed his shoulder with a strong right hook. Groaning, the man collapsed but, on the ground, grabbed from his waist a metal ball and threw it.

Immediately, a purple haze sprayed out and started spreading through the combat zone.

Deliad kept battling for a couple seconds, then choked upon his suddenly burning breath, coughing involuntarily and curling over. He forced his stiffening frame to stumble backward out of the fray, as a guard in the fumes gagged from the ground and fired blindly at everything.

One of those stray shots hit his same singed hand. *In Eremon's name!* He tried to shake the spasms out.

"Get backup!" choked the downed guard, far too quietly for anyone but Deliad to have heard him.

Nonetheless, five more guards were marching up now from down the road, a hundred yards away.

"Cor!" he called hoarsely, pointing at the foe.

The Beldrian glanced, blinking back tears from reddened eyes. "Got it." He grabbed the severed hand and stunner still lying upon the ground. They stuck together in rigor mortis.

Cor shrugged. "Catch!" He threw the whole ensemble to the girl from Fernstead.

"Eep!" she cried, scarcely catching it before she flung it on toward Celeste; then, threw up her offhand barely in time to block blue lightning flashing in from her flank. "Think we should leave?"

"Good call!" said Cor, as Celeste broke some fingers to pry the stunner from the severed hand.

She threw the bloody appendage toward the guards. It sprayed in crimson circles as it soared, then thunked against the ground. They slowed on seeing it, glancing at one another, then the bodies beneath the purple fumes, and then that broken hand.

Leveling her stunner, she fired on the guards. And, though her purple lighting blast had faded at such range, so it merely gave a shock that caused a guard to cry out in surprise and shake his leg, they paused even more at that.

"Come on!" called fleetfoot Cor, already rushing far from the Hall of Ages down the road, with Brayleigh and Deliad darting in his wake.

Waiting for them ahead were seven guards, dialing their stunners up, forming a line, fixing their sights upon the approaching wanderers.

They fired on Cor, in front and coming fastest, sending a volley of violet jags toward him.

Their marksmanship was fine. They would have hit him, had he been moving at the sort of speed they'd trained to hit. Their aim was quite consistent: always a couple feet behind.

His arms and gait were a blur. His blade threw wayward gleams of sunlight.

Just as he came so close they couldn't miss, he swerved away, sprinting along their flank. They followed with their stunners, still not hitting.

And now the Knight-Lord—sprinting straight ahead, unnoticed, as they opened fire on the Beldrian—was nigh upon them, Hoarthaxe lifted high.

As when a mariner sees, too late, the maelstrom turning beneath the mists, one guard now saw him. His eyes went wide. He spun and wildly shot.

But Deliad whirled by, watched that shot stray wide, gaze glimmering like the churning sea. He held his halberd out, still swirling with momentum. He felt it sink into the guard who'd missed, deep through the gut. And now the guard was sinking.

As when the first planks splinter in a vortex, and, suddenly, the beleaguered ship starts keeling, so went the guards' formation with this killing. As when the boat is breached, some back away, and others seek to bail out surging waves—all futile—so they sought and fled the Knight-Lord, swept up in something beyond their control.

He saw a stunner leveled at his head and spun left, saw the lightning sizzle by, and followed with a haft-blow to the guard's face.

Another silver sidearm turning toward him. He dove out with his halberd point outstretched, just far enough to catch a trigger finger. The gun dropped, and the guard gasped, grasped his hand and stepped back.

Landing on his hands and knees, the Knight-Lord whirled to his feet with Hoarthaxe arcing and vert mists emanating in its wake.

As when the whirlpool's center stays in place even as it spins out watery dissolution, so Deliad liquidated three more guards: one severed at the waist, so his scuttled flotsam and jetsam fell apart; and two more opened up chest high, so orkish hearts now added blood to this baneful eddy that had swept them up.

Without a pause, the Knight-Lord jerked his pommel back through the visor of a guard he'd half-heard shifting behind him. And a shriek ensued.

Not looking, Deliad now swung back an elbow and felt a solid, satisfying contact, together with a crunch, and then a cry. *There goes a nose!* He heard the guard hit dirt.

The Knight-Lord's vortical aristeia ended abruptly when, on turning to his left, he saw a stunner pointed at him squarely.

He jabbed his halberd desperately—and hit!, poking a hole in the half-ork's green neck—but not in time to avoid a purple blast, which shuddered through his breast.

His body suddenly was something foreign, shivering and convulsing against his will, collapsing to the street and twitching there. He still could see a bit upon his back, too blurry to decipher the state of the ongoing battle overhead. But he was having trouble thinking clearly.

The one thing that he knew was that his eyes *were* seeing. He still was here. And that was something.

CHAPTER 29

Seeing Deliad stiffen and fall, his bloody frame convulsing on the floor, Hoarthaxe in hand, Cor felt a surge of fear. Hopping a corpse he'd just felled, he approached the spasming paladin.

Meanwhile, a maimed ork guard had just gotten up and now was kicking Deliad in the gut; now aiming at his head a silver stunner.

"Catch!" yelled Cor, grabbing the first thing he saw and hurling it—a stunner, he perceived an instant later—and it hit the guard glancingly.

Blinking, the ork faced the Beldrian, staring a second, then aiming its stunner.

Faster than he could think, he lashed at the air, gauging the stunner's aim the way he'd studied a pitcher's arm to know where he should swing. His sword flashed Sunlike even as the ork opened fire; and the arc of sizzling purple struck his sword.

Then he was springing the full twenty feet that separated him from his opponent, his blade behind his head, electric arcs still crackling round it, like a leonine mane billowing wild behind his roaring onset.

The ork guard's mouth had just begun to gape when Cor came down with Wrath Hew on its head, discharging the ork's own lightning on its source. Skull split in two, the dead thing tossed and twitched with strange life, as the electric animation spent itself crazily and soon shorted out.

"Get reinforcements!" yelled a guard. He stood some fifty feet off, facing down a side street. A second guard was near him. "We're outnumbered! Get—"

Purple lighting jolted through the guard. He toppled into a twitchy heap.

At the other end of the line of lighting, Celeste stood, stunner in hand.

She pulled the trigger again. A twig of purple fizzled near the tip of the firearm—then, another—as the guard's friend spun and began to sprint off.

Celeste grimaced, tossing the gun the aside, and sought another.

A red pellucid plane had just whomped backward a pair of guards approaching from the east. But Brayleigh didn't seem to see the third, slinking in behind her.

"Brayleigh!" Cor called, watching the half-ork, even now, aim its stunner, too far away for him to intervene.

She looked. And, after a couple seconds, seeing his pointing finger, she began to turn. The purple lighting leapt forth as she did so; but it strayed wide.

For, now, the furtive half-ork was screaming, and its arms were flailing at the faded blotches that had formed upon it where several pale blue flares had snuffed themselves, streaming in spirals from the finger of Celeste. An aura of blue still hung about her hand.

"When did you learn to do that!" Brayleigh cried.

"Still haven't!" Celeste smiled uncertainly. She grabbed the stunner that the guard had dropped.

"Come on!" called Deliad hoarsely. He had risen and now was woozily blinking back the stupor. "We have to move."

"About time," said the Beldrian.

They ran south several minutes unimpeded, winding around some groups of guards they saw, before a double-whistle from ahead brought them to a halt. A moment later emerged, atop a hill, a column of a dozen guards.

On seeing the escaping wanderers to their fore, they promptly formed a line and started forward.

Perhaps their band of four could best a dozen guards. It wouldn't be their first improbable exploit. But each time that they had to stop and fight, the Academy Guard got more time to spread word about the escapees and prepare to stop them. Each fight just made another fight more likely. What would they do if they got to the gate and found it sealed off? And with guards there waiting?

As such thoughts swept through Cor's head, and he scanned the enemy line, a glimmer in the sky soon caught his eye. He squinted. Was he seeing things?

A fiery explosion rocked the guards' formation, blowing the four in the center to bits, and sending their companions scrambling, burning, for cover in a haze of shell-shocked terror.

"What in the blazes . . . " began Deliad, gaping.

"It's them!" one fleeing guard choked through sheets of smoke. "That unit there!" He pointed to a side street.

Advancing into view were two long columns of—*the Academy Guard? What?* Cor gazed, baffled.

From down the side street flew another glimmer across the sky, toward where some orkish guards were glancing left and right with stunners raised. Seeing the wanderers, they shouted, starting forward.

They'd hardly taken two steps when heat and light razed them to remnants of grey vests and visors, and green and crimson flesh, charred black and blistered. And from the carnage came a sweltering roar.

Cor saw now that these new security guards were wearing white bands round their arms. A mix of young and old men, grim-faced and grimacing, confronting the other guards with stunners raised.

Between those columns came a wild-haired scholar in crimson robes, carrying a couple sealed jars. Something translucent was sloshing inside them. *Professor Logi? Starling's engine guy?*

Behind him followed Starling, with a blue ball in one hand and a stunner in the other. "Don't let them get near Logi!" he directed.

"Yes sir," replied an officer with a white band, and relayed the command.

What in the world . . . ?

"Fancy seeing you," Professor Starling hailed them. "Celeste. My friends. It's been—well, not so long."

"What *is* this?" Celeste asked.

"That's quite a tale. I'd tell it all, but we've a ship to catch." His grin went wide. "Suffice to say, some guards had been unhappy with the way things work here, with Gaudimorte at the helm, for quite a while. Good kingsmen sorts. So when they heard that Gaudimorte had launched an insurrection, and was chasing the Knight-Lord and his allies through the city, I didn't have to tell them what to do next."

"Good men," the Knight-Lord said. "Most guardsmen are."

"And . . . that?" She pointed at the smoldering blast zone.

"You like it?" Logi's grin was wide and giddy. "I call it Seafire. Burns near-anything, the sea included!"

"Or a squad of orks, it seems," said Cor.

"We'll have to test that soon, if we stay here much longer," said the Knight-Lord.

"Indeed," said Starling. "Onward then?"

And so, together with new allies, onward went the wanderers toward the southern city gate.

"How's the ship doing? She ready to depart?" asked Deliad as they ran.

"She better be!" said Brayleigh. "Or she might get popped by a stunner!"

"She won't 'pop,'" Starling said. "I've seen to that! But I'd prefer she not get fried by a power surge. Prep should take ten minutes, fifteen at most."

As they progressed south toward the city gate, few guards confronted them. Most seemed confused by the columns of their fellow guards with white bands, and simply stared and stood back. Those who fought were swiftly downed by Seafire or by Brayleigh.

Cor, running at the fore, peered round a bend and saw a band of fifteen guards or so. *No white bands round their shoulders. Mostly orks.* He held a palm up, halting those behind him. "We'll want some Seafire over here."

"Fresh out!" sighed Logi, holding out his empty hands.

"Well. Guess we've got a fight ahead," said Cor, lifting his sword.

"Wait." Starling raised his blue ball. "It's not much, but . . . " He shrugged. "Ready to run?"

Cor tipped his head. "More Seafire?"

"Not exactly." The scholar cast his blue ball round the corner. Hitting the hard ground, the ball broke in two, right in the middle of the group of guards.

Out of it flew a flock of tiny brass birds: in all directions first, then sweeping upward in chaotic spirals. Through the guards they dove and wove in crazy patterns, whirring quietly with every tilt and swoop and whirling incline.

The guards first looked bemused and baffled. Then, one cried out: "That one *cut* me!" Then another: "My eye! My eye!" And more: "The wings are razors!" "Shoot 'em down!" "Visors up!" "Get me a medic!" And lightning started crackling round the corner.

"Let's move," smiled Starling.

"Really?" Celeste said.

He shrugged. "Experimental. Proof of concept!"

"Let's leave artillery to Logi from now on."

They sprinted past. The guards, preoccupied with batting off the birds, paid little heed to two more columns of their fellow guards.

One fearful ork, covered in dribbling cuts, fled in a panic toward the wanderers' party. Its sheeplike snout, riddled with pocks and pustules, was wailing nonsense words. It raised its stunner and shot down one of Starling's passing guards, and, making mad retreat, aimed toward another.

But Cor lashed out with Luna's Question, cutting false-edged across its gut from right to left. Out spilled its liver, bottom folded back and spotted on the left. And down the ork fell, staring upon its bowels and babbling curses.

The Beldrian's boot squished down upon those innards, and, in a flash, the guard was far behind him.

With all these stops, the guards dispatched by Gaudimorte was getting closer in their wake. Cor heard them, calling and giving commands and, at times, briefly appearing on the road behind them, before the wanderers turned to find a new route.

And yet, he knew more surely by the moment, they'd make it to the gate before those guards. He knew now where they were—the 'Fashion District,' as Brayleigh had dubbed it—barely a minute from the south gate, where they'd entered weeks ago.

"I never got to shop here!" Brayleigh pouted, pointing out two ladies, one wearing leather and the other low-cut green, both in short skirts. "Where else can I find *that!*"

"There's always next time!" Celeste consoled.

Smiling, they reached the hill before the southern gate and quickly climbed it. And there they halted.

Standing at the gate were sixty guards, at least, arrayed in ranks with stunners raised. Behind their vests and visors, they looked as grey and obdurate as the bulwarks looming in stony silence at their backs.

Cor breathed in deep. He stared down at his sword; then, sadly, looked at Brayleigh to his side.

She looked at him, her green gaze drooping like a new sprout when the Spring recedes to Winter.

"Best hurry, Knight-Lord!" came a call ahead.

One of the guards had walked forward, an officer with grizzled hair and huge arms, but, besides that, a fairly ordinary frame.

Cor blinked—he felt he'd seen the man before—then glanced over at the Knight-Lord.

"State your purpose," said Deliad, staring, halberd held before him.

"I will," the officer said, "but I'd suggest I do so from behind my men back here." He thumbed behind him, where—indeed, Cor saw—all men, no orks, were waiting to his rear.

Meanwhile, to *their* rear, he could hear the howls and grunts of their pursuers getting close.

How did he know the "Knight-Lord" was among us?

Cor felt himself borne forward by a breath of warm assurance. Forth he stepped, hand waving his fellow wanderers on. "They're friends," he assured them.

The look he got from Brayleigh said, *There's nothing you know that we don't know, you bubblehead!* But she came first, and then the others followed.

No ambush came as they approached the guards: no sudden shots, no cruel smirking as they neared. And then he noticed they were wearing white bands.

"Name's Nyrburt," called the officer as they came close. "I'm Captain of the Academy Guard; or was, till Gaudimorte modernized my post away. Come on." He waved the wanderers toward the ranks and led them past. "My men are better marksmen than Gaudimorte's grunts. As you'll soon see." He pointed.

A horde of ork and half-ork guards, even now, was rushing toward the gate with stunners ready. They hesitated slightly at the sight of fellow guardsmen facing them in ranks, then, roared and rampaged onward.

"Get the kingsmen! Those four! Kill anyone who's helping them!" shouted a human officer in their midst.

The front line of that throng fell all at once, crying out as violet lightning suddenly smote them, coursing through shuddering limbs and halting hearts. The second line was down mere seconds later, yowling and twitching in piles by their peers.

Now the horde halted, trading baffled looks and peering on the corpses of companions.

"Need reinforcements!" declared a red guard with only four long strands of greasy hair, falling between the bulges on its face.

"Need reinforcements!" affirmed the other guards, as their commanding officer yelled them onward. They ignored him and began to run away.

"Go get the kingsmen! That was a command!" their officer scolded, pointing over and over. "Deserters will be tried and—"

What came next remained unknown, since an escaping ork shot the man's head with a stunner, point-blank, and he collapsed into a smiley pile.

Lifting a silver whistle to his lips, the former Captain of the Academy Guard blew thrice, holding the last shrill sound at length.

Abruptly, from the alleys near the fleeing guards, stunner fire sprayed and strafed the halfman horde, which halted once again, confused and fearful. More guardsmen wearing white bands came in view, emerging from the side streets, firing stunners, forming a pincer round Gaudimorte's ork guards.

Shaking his head, Cor exhaled, disbelieving.

"What *is* this?" Deliad questioned. "What's going on?"

Starling was nodding and smiling at Nyrburt, as when a long suspicion is confirmed.

"Rounding up traitors to our rightful King. Putting an insurrection down," said Nyrburt. "Did you mean tactically? A simple pincer." He smiled. "No. We've had all this in the works for quite some time."

"I should've known," said Starling, turning to one of the white-banded guards who'd helped them get here. "You lot knew about this? And didn't tell us?"

"Sir, I thought the plan was, wait five, six weeks at least," the guard replied, looking at Starling and then Captain Nyrburt.

"We're starting somewhat early, thanks to you all," Nyrburt affirmed. "But that's the way things go. Fate calls, you come; even if you're halfway ready."

"We're in your debt," said Deliad. "We'll repay you."

"You can repay us right now," replied Nyrburt, "if you go fly that floating ship to Norvester, and tell the King that the Academy Guard humbly requests the aid of Norvester's Knights and Hergas in suppressing a revolt."

The Knight-Lord clasped the Captain's hand. "Will do, Sir." He faced the ship and waved the wanderers forth. "In fact," he quietly mused a moment later, "you may get some help sooner than you think."

Nyrburt already had turned to two officers. "It's time to take the walls. Twelve men apiece. Quick. Marksmen. Should be a skeleton crew, at most, manning the walls. The rest are heading here. Pick off as many as possible as you go."

"Aye, Captain. Good to have you back," the wanderers heard in their wake, as they hurried away from the gate along the Gramsleith toward the ship: a growing egg aloft the western skyline, its golden fins aflare with Heaven's glare.

They were just halfway there when, over a hill, figures of men on horseback formed against the sinking Sun. Some two dozen men in armor, they soon saw, with their polearms held in hand.

Cresting the hill at near-gallop, they coursed down. And then their silhouettes gained color and feature: their tabards showed the crown and fist of Norvester within the vert flame. At their fore was—*Orther?*

"What in the world . . . ?" wondered Brayleigh. "Was this *luck?*"

"Some luck," the Knight-Lord said. "But mostly a warhorn." He held his bone-hued warhorn up. "And planning."

"Hail and well met," called the Captain. He hopped from his horse as he approached. "How goes it, Knight-Lord?"

"A little bruised and battered. But I've been worse." A sunny glimmer lit the Knight-Lord's grin. "Dag. Foreguard Sithrik. Good day. Fine to see you. Turns out we'll want that help we talked about."

Through Cor's mind flashed a memory he'd forgotten: *Cor couldn't quite make out their conversation, which spanned two minutes, save one last remark by Deliad as he left them: "Maybe a mile. But not so close you're caught."* He smiled as Deliad spoke on.

"Foreguard Sithrik, you'll lead this squad here to the southern gate. You'll rendezvous with Captain Nyrburt there," the Knight-Lord said. "You'll find a fight in progress. The loyal men of the Academy Guard are quelling an insurrection. You'll learn more from Nyrburt. Your orders are to aid the royalist guardsmen and help them hold out till we bring more men."

"Knight-Lord," the grey-haired Foreguard nodded. "Men, you heard him. Form up. Lances ready. Forth!" Off rode the Knights of Norvester rode toward the fray.

"As for me?" questioned Captain Ormslik.

"You, my friend, will be the one who brings more men." He faced the ship. "You ready for a ride? Since I'm not sure I am."

"It should be fine," promised Professor Starling, "for a first flight."

"Fine," Orther said. "It's been fine, for a first life."

"Yes! That's the spirit!" affirmed the girl from Fernstead.

"As for you!" Deliad faced her. "Doubting *me?* For blowing this fine warhorn here?" He tsked.

"Why don't we board that ship?" she answered sweetly. "Then you can show the world how much you blow!"

Further along the Gramsleith fared the wanderers with Captain Ormslik and the two professors, then jogged across a field to where the ship was.

"Ten, fifteen minutes, like I said," said Starling, already running up the boarding platform, "and we'll be off."

"Same for the engine too," Logi affirmed.

"Why don't we wait down here?" suggested Cor to Deliad, Brayleigh and Celeste. "If more guards come, we'll want to meet them here, right? Won't want to let them get close to the ship."

"Fair point," said Starling. "Bear in mind, though, I'll be lifting off thirty yards or so for testing. I'll have to toss down the rope ladder. Also, I'll need a couple assistants to help me."

"I'll go!" the girl from Fernstead said. "I like ships."

"I'll go," said Captain Ormslik. "I like ships."

"Enjoy, son," said the Knight-Lord to his Captain.

So, as the others climbed aboard the ship, Cor watched the east horizon, hand on hilt, waiting with Celeste and Deliad beside him.

No guards came. But about five minutes after the Sojourner's ascent for Starling's testing, they saw one rider appear upon the skyline.

His horse was sleek and sable. Also black was the rider's long hair, billowing at his back. Not so his cloak, dappled with motley colors against a blood-hued backdrop. On his back was a short lance, gleaming red-tipped in the Sun with every gallop of his steed.

"Just one?" said Celeste.

"I remember him," said Deliad. "Loginos. He was Gaudimorte's personal guard. Or mercenary, rather."

"I recall him," the Beldrian said. "I wonder what he wants."

"Just him?" repeated Celeste. "Can't be much." She raised the silver stunner in her hand.

"We'll find out."

From his horse, the rider hopped some forty yards away and neared on foot. His gait swayed, and his garb blew wildly backward. A facemask hid his mouth and half his nose.

Cor suddenly realized why he seemed familiar, this mercenary in Gaudimorte's pay. He looked like that bandit with the band who'd tried to rob them; the fourth one, who had had the sword and knives.

"Tell us your purpose, Loginos," called Deliad.

"Hail, Knight-Lord! Friends." His words were slightly off-kilter, like one who'd learnt a language late in youth. "I've come upon my client's behalf. The Dean."

"Speak quickly," said the Beldrian, hand on hilt.

"Indeed." He smiled. "I'm here to make an offer. You're free to take that ship. You're free to go. Even you," he waved toward Celeste, "if you swear you won't return."

"The Knight-Lord must agree in turn, and on behalf of Norvester's monarch, that this Academy's not the King's Academy—not anymore—ceding the Academy's rule entirely to the Governance Committee. His realm's new border will be Leitath's Pass."

Loginos looked a bit bored as he said this, as when a reader wants to skip ahead to where the action starts. "What say you, Knight-Lord?"

Deliad's brow rose. "Dean Gaudimorte asks for much and offers naught, save what we have already."

"What you already have?" Loginos smiled, hand on his waist. "I wouldn't be so sure." His teeth and lance both glimmered with the low Sun.

"What, will his guards come stop us?" questioned Deliad. "They're a bit busy at the gate, I think."

Loginos smiled and waited.

Celeste answered, "Tell Gaudimorte he should save his offer-making for Nyrburt's guardsmen, when they come to hang him."

The Knight-Lord's lips curved up. "Norvester concurs."

"It seems we're at an impasse!" cried Loginos, slapping his leg. "Well, let it be a lesson." He abruptly turned and headed toward his horse.

They watched the mercenary walk away, his motley cloak abillow to his fore, then shrugged.

"You think the ship is almost ready?" asked Cor.

"A few more minutes?" answered Celeste, scanning the hull, now floating high above them.

"Well, once we're up there, I, for one, am finding a fine meal. And a couch. And maybe an ale," Deliad declared. "Did you pack ale, Cor?"

"Casks full."

"My man." He held his fist out toward the Beldrian.

Cor's suddenly unsheathed sword flashed forth just inches from Celeste's torso toward the Knight-Lord's neck.

As Celeste gasped, and, startled, Deliad lurched back, dropping his halberd and stumbling and falling—missed by a mere inch—light flashed to his fore, and steel on steel rang out.

Even Cor himself was somewhat shocked to find that little glimmer he'd half-seen was, in fact, a little knife, fallen to the floor now.

After a blink, the Beldrian was off and sprinting eastward at full speed, before his eyes had even fixed on Loginos, hunched with a hand in his cloak.

That hand flicked forth. The air glimmered to his fore. And lunging left, Cor heard the knife whir by—brushing his hair—but kept on running, rapt with martial instinct.

"Well done, boy!" praised Loginos. "You just saved your Knight-Lord!" He stood casually as Cor neared, letting his short lance droop earthward in one hand and resting the other on his waist again.

But when the Beldrian sprang forth into Daybreak—a long, low thrust, and quick to close—his foe dodged effortlessly, swatting out at once with his red-tipped lance. It'd likely have torn through flesh, and maybe leather, but his new steel mail from Brinsmyth held strong.

Cor stepped back and stared, adopting Plow and sizing up his enemy. *That speed!*

Celeste and Deliad had gotten their bearings by now and grasped the situation. Standing, the latter seized his halberd, sprinting forth. The former aimed her stunner and fired it twice.

The mercenary didn't bother moving. Both shots strayed wide. Instead, as Cor sprang forward with Wintersun, his true edge rising right slightly and sinking, Loginos lurched sideways—prompting the Beldrian to ready a parry—but he was sprinting now toward Celeste, too far away already for a follow-up slash.

Wildly behind Loginos blew his cloak like turning clouds behind a tempest's winds. His red-tipped half-lance hung and swung behind him. One hand was forward. Zeal gleamed in his gaze.

Even fleetfoot Cor would struggle in a fair sprint with *him*, much less to catch him from behind.

Loginos' left hand dipped twice into his cloak and flicked out with a blinding flash each time.

Before he'd grasped what'd happened, steel had clattered against the steel of Deliad's breastplate, and—as Celeste gasped—a flower of blood hue bloomed upon her shoulder, where a knife was shining, sunny and wet.

The mercenary's offhand once more went into his cloak and whipped back forward. And, with a flash, another aerial glimmer was whirling toward the Knight-Lord.

Instantly, he twisted. But the sharp knife slit his wrist glancingly just an inch above his gauntlet. The sudden gash shocked him into letting loose his halberd haft, jerking his hand aside.

And then the man in motley cloak was there, thrusting already with his gules-tipped half-lance, which weirdly glowed as though with eagerness. Lunging, he half-dove the distance between them, with weapon stretched out toward the fleeting opening. Through tabard and through breastplate passed that red tip and two full inches into Deliad's torso.

Steam hissed, skin sizzled, and the knight inhaled abruptly, heaving backward off the hot point.

Celeste, with one arm hanging limp and blood-lined, held up her offhand and, with eyes like sky slits, spoke something unheard. And from five curled fingers spiraled a circle of flares as pale as moonlight.

Whirling from Deliad, their foe held his wrist up, wrapped in a gauze of red and white. The fires hit; and, with a gasp and hiss, they turned to mist.

She spoke another word, which Cor half-heard but couldn't understand. And from her hand streaked more fires, Moon-like, toward their foe; as Deliad, back in the moment, stabbed forward with Hoarthaxe.

But Gaudimorte's mercenary was a step ahead of both, dodging the double onslaught and darting now toward Cor, his baneful half-lance shifting with each stride but aimed at his breast.

Carefully, Cor watched where the half-lance moved, its point now bright red as a branding iron, with steam lines rising from its languid motions. *"The eyes can lie. The weapon never lies."*

His foe, five yards away, became a blur of backswept fabric, colorful and blood-hued, black hair blown back. And suddenly he was *there*.

And Cor was ready. Dodging to the right, he elbowed the impending lance awry, already starting to sweep into Tailswipe.

But that declining slice from left to right lost half its force as the lancetip he'd swatted slipped scaldingly along his arm and side, burning his flesh like a brand as it slid.

And he was forced to fling himself away, slicing out wildly with Down to Size—missing, but making his opponent halt a moment. *"Sometimes the only defense left is offense,"* the Master of War had said. Within that moment, he got his bearings.

And he found, abruptly, his enemy's hand had darted into his cloak and, holding something, flicked out with a flash.

Blinded, the Beldrian jerked his top half rightward. He felt the knife blade brush his neck—and more—and felt the blood beads dribbling down his shoulder and under Brinsmyth's carapace of webs.

Spirited assurance breathed within his breast and bore him forward instantly. He sprang and slashed with Fatherstrike, missing the head but smiting his opponent's shoulder firmly, cutting his cloak but clanging off his black mail.

"Well done!" Loginos laughed, whirling away and darting off toward Deliad, who, with Celeste, was now advancing toward him.

Lurching left, he dodged a line of lightning from her stunner. With eyes still on the Knight-Lord, from his cloak he drew a dirk and whipped it at the woman firing upon him. The scene flashed stark white.

When sight returned, Cor saw that she had ducked, but been struck on the bicep. There, a line of blood was seeping through her shirt. And yet her hand was forth; and from her fingers spun five flares in luminous spirals toward their foe, who now was reaching for another knife.

The Moon-bright blazes gasped against his side and snuffed fell potency upon his flesh.

Their foe curst in an unfamiliar tongue and doubled over.

Then, too fleet to follow, the palm upon his side went into his cloak and whipped another whirling knife at Cor.

The part of him that saw that spinning steel, and thought to swing his sword out in a parry, was not the part of him that thought in words. The thrown dirk pinged against his Beldrian blade, deflected left, and fell down to the dirt.

A cry came from his flank. He looked—and there were Celeste and Loginos. In her side was his smoldering lance.

Wide-eyed, she dropped her stunner.

He tugged the tip out as the Knight-Lord neared with Hoarthaxe high, then plunging direly lower.

Loginos dodged left, and the headward blow hit only his motley cloak, severing a swath. Without even waiting for his feet to fall, he jabbed out with his half-lance at the Knight-Lord, whose heavy blow had left his flank exposed. The hot point grazed his arm and left a gash, as zeal gleamed in the mercenary's gaze.

Dropping his halberd, Deliad balled his gauntlet and struck a square blow to Loginos' face.

He stumbled backward, blood already soaking his facemask, blinking, black eyes rolling backward.

The ever-ready Beldrian rushed upon him, an aureate blur, from Plow to Swan Approach, stepping and thrusting with arm thrown out full-length. His shining blade slipped through the man's black mail and into his side.

He tugged it out to Ox Horn with one swift turn—as blood spilled from the stab wound, dribbling along the loops of sable steel—and launched now into Squinter, slashing downward.

But, with a stifled cry, the injured sellsword had heaved himself just far enough away to evade the deathblow, and was now withdrawing swiftly and spinning away to a dead sprint. He hurled two dirks behind him as he dashed, halting both Cor and Deliad in their tracks, then turned to face them, fifty feet away. His breaths were heavy, and his blood was spilling, but zeal still gleamed in his unswerving stare.

"Well, we've all learnt a bit today, I think!" Loginos called. "Let's do it again sometime."

"Not likely," Deliad answered, racing forward with Hoarthaxe gripped hard, throwing baneful gleams with each stride toward the dire end drawing nigh. And at his sides dashed Cor and Celeste, glaring, chasing the fatal moment's bleeding edge.

Loginos lifted something from his cloak and cast it at the floor, whirling away. It struck five yards ahead of them, exploding to an instant smoke cloud.

Suddenly they were squinting through haze on all sides. Cor threw up his hand, inhaling in surprise—and choked on foul fumes, halting and hunching over.

Stumbling sideways until he'd found his way outside the fog, he strove to catch his breath and scanned the landscape.

But, by the time the haze had dissipated enough to see the hilltops rolling eastward, where scattered birches shone white and, grown thick, Earth's hair waved green and golden in the wind, their enemy was gone in rampant Nature.

"We're good to go!" a blithe voice called above them.

There was Brayleigh, leaning down from the deck. "Ready to climb some rope?" She threw the ladder over the edge. "Alright, who's—Flua-Sahng's name, is that blood?"

"We'll talk later," called the Beldrian. "Can you two climb?" He eyed the throwing knife still sticking out of Celeste's shoulder, like a tulip stigma petaled red, and, likewise, the blood flower blooming at her side.

"I think so." She stared upon her hand, eyes rapt at seeing something that wasn't apparent to Cor. But, after a second, pale light started seeping from Celeste's fingers into a shifting mist, like Luna's cloudy veil. She closed her eyes and closed her palm around her injured side; then, raised it to her shoulder and seized the knife.

"Wait—!" Deliad shouted, reaching for her hand.

She yanked it from her shoulder. Underneath showed blood and sinew. Dabbing with her shirt sleeve, she delicately cleansed the open hole.

The Knight-Lord stared. "That should be spilling blood."

"I stopped it." Celeste raised her hand again, watching that pale glow wash over it once more, then let it fade and fall. "Somehow or other."

The Knight-Lord raised an eyebrow. "I'd be obliged if you'd do that for me." He tapped his tabard, torn open and soaked with blood above his belly.

"Later," said Cor. "You hear that?" From the hills, hiding their eastward prospect, harsh calls echoed: commands, grunts, cries and growling. Over one mound, some faint forms were emerging, still far off, but pointing at the ship and sprinting forward.

"Right. Let's be off." The wanderers climbed the rope rungs, grimacing as they grasped and pulled with limbs pummeled and gashed, assailed by Autumn winds, which chilled their wounds and blew them side to side.

Celeste went first. She struggled, with a shoulder still gaping wide, a badly wounded bicep, and lots of blood loss. Sometimes, she would stop, shaking her head, grabbing with the other arm, gritting her teeth and heaving, rung by rung.

Cor had climbed last, being least hurt of the three. Now he was wondering if that had been wise. Could he have pulled the ladder up from the top, as Celeste held on?

Halfway up the ladder, he looked behind him. Guards were nearby now. And with them was a heavy mounted crossbow, so big it almost looked like a ballista, rolled in on wheels. They'd just come close enough to halt it and begin to aim and load it.

"Hurry!" he called to the wanderers ahead of him.

"Doing what I can," called Celeste weakly downward. With head bowed and her eyes closed, up she heaved, wincing but holding the next rung.

Cor glanced back. A bolt had now been fitted to the crossbow. The guards were cranking it. One held a huge torch, burning orange-blue. The ork lowered it to the bolt's tip.

"Take off!" called Cor. "Tell Starling, take off now!" He hoped that Brayleigh heard. He couldn't see her.

From under him came a loud *thwunk*. Fast as thought, he spun the ladder left with all his strength.

Celeste gasped, letting the rope ladder loose with her injured arm and dangling by a hand, turned sideways by the sudden twist.

Through the space where her head had been, a blazing bolt whizzed by.

Heaving in breaths, eyes shut hard, she spun back and flung her right hand to the next rung, wincing but holding fast.

The Sojourner took off: one moment hovering, then ascending skyward, with all the steaming suddenness of a geyser.

Celeste's feet slipped off midstep. She cried out, abruptly hanging only by her arms, both of them bloody and weak.

What have I done...? Cor stared with horror as the ship climbed higher, and, overhead, the fair-haired woman lolled and wobbled like a halfway-severed stalk, battered by winds, tearing its ties to life.

Then, shrieking out her pain, she flung herself a foot higher—just enough to rest her feet upon the rung again—and, gasping breaths out, began once more to climb, much quicker now.

By now, the Beldrian, in his haste, was nearly grabbing the Knight-Lord's heel with each new rung. *So close! Just five feet more.* He watched and waited as Deliad, dribbling blood down from his tabard, hurled himself sideways over the airship's rail.

Finally! He sprang those last few aerial steps with the bursting suddenness of a bounding lion and dove atop the deck to a headlong roll.

The rail behind him burst to a splinter cloud. Through the air above him whirred a blazing bolt, right in between the blinking, reeling wanderers, flying just a few feet from the quarterdeck and into the open sky. There, it traced a trail of falling fire against the blue of evening.

Cor brushed some teak slivers out of his hair, then slowly stood. He stared down at the crossbow. They'd loaded it again and aimed it higher; and just like that, they'd fired the flaming bolt.

He stepped back, fists balled.

But the ship was soaring Heavenward with every elapsing breath and heartbeat. And now that hot projectile slowed and stopped ten yards beneath the wooden hull, hovering fleetly, then falling in a futile blaze toward the Earth.

Back up the stairway from below ran Brayleigh. Wide-eyed, she scanned until she'd found three faces; then, sighed into a smile. "Whew! I was worried. I heard you, Cor. I told him, 'Take off right now!'"

Breathing too heavily to have a reply, Cor smiled and lay down, stretching out his arms, basking beneath the fiery spangled sky.

"Cor?" Brayleigh eyed him, head askew, then grinned and sat down at his side. "Nice views here, huh?"

He peered on fairness fraught with sunset hues, both high aloft the Heavens and right before him. "Perfect," he said.

Squeezing his hand, she smiled.

"You still in one piece?" Orther asked, ascending the stairway from below deck.

"More or less," said Deliad. Lifting up his tabard's bottom, he eyed his gut wound. It was gruesome: crimson and purple, half-congealed, too wet for scabbing, depths hidden by blood.

Celeste blinked, brushing back the fair hair billowing wildly in her face and squinting. "Deliad! How are you still standing?"

She rushed up, bending to his torso, reaching to almost touch it with her palm. Eyes closed, she murmured something, and a Moonlike mist swirled into being about her fingers first, and then her hand. She held it there ten seconds, as lunar eminence welled and seeped away, hiding the mess of blood and flesh behind it; then, stepped back.

"There. I think that should be better." Her words were half a statement, half a question.

Orther was staring with his brow inclined. "Another now?" He looked at Brayleigh and Celeste.

"So it seems," said Deliad, tapping at his torso. The wound was still there, but that ugly mix of bloody flesh and angry inflammation was now as clean as after a careful surgery, and there was no more bleeding. "Thank you, Celeste."

"Our Knight-Lord lives to fight another day!" declared the Captain. "After a few close calls, it seems." He poked a tear in Deliad's tabard, behind which was a gouge in his cuirass, right over his heart. "Lucky you wore plate, eh?"

"I'd wondered why you'd wear that to a trial," said Celeste.

"Yes, indeed! One might well wonder why in the world I wore my armor, gauntlets, warhorn and halberd to a trial," mused Deliad. "Not luck. The simple answer, friends, is foresight. Foresight!"

"Speaking of foresight," Brayleigh said, "when you all got surprise-attacked just now, you could've blown that warhorn. Called for help. Why didn't you?"

The Knight-Lord stared a moment.

"I would've blasted those baddies sky-high!" she said. "And what exactly did you fight? Some orkish legion? Where were all the corpses?"

The three exchanged a glance.

"Um. Gaudimorte's guy," said Cor. "That mercenary with the weird cloak."

"So that guy, and . . . ?" The girl from Fernstead stared, green gaze declining toward the saturnine. "You're kidding me! I leave you lot for *minutes*, some joker in a jester outfit whomps you? What in the world! One? Next time, warhorn, Deliad!"

He raised his bone-hued horn. "Happy to oblige." He blew a note that shook the shining nimbus.

Dispersed by quailing sky, it went all ways: across the cloud-rack and the eventide blue, where great blue herons soared aloft far lakes; over the Skautfell Range and Ginnagonds, aspiring high about them, glazed with ice and dusted frosty, and diffracting daylight into a crazed infinity of glimmers; chased by the wanderers down the valley of Heaven.

"You all did well today," the Knight-Lord said. Some wistfulness was in his westward gaze, watching the realm beneath the Sun receding.

"Some sharp work by those swords and halberds! Eh?" said Brayleigh, double finger pointing. "Sharp? Yes?"

"Swords, halberds, and pellucid planes of red force," Celeste affirmed, "'blasting the baddies sky-high.'"

"Aw, don't make *me* go red!" the redhead waved. "Ain't it the truth though!"

"Boundaries, halberds, swords, and . . . lightning blasts and oddly Moonlit fire?" mused Cor.

"Alas," sighed Celeste, twiddling fair hair around her thumb, "I lost my lovely stunner. I only have my flame."

Cor waved. "We'll make do. Those fires were hot enough without the lightning."

"Looked sorta cold to me!" said Brayleigh idly, twiddling her fiery hair around her thumb. "And all those fires at once! Don't hit the wrong mark!"

He glanced at Brayleigh, who was—*frowning faintly? Bristling?* A flush had hidden her freckles. *Huh, weird.*

"Speaking of which," said Deliad, "*I'd* be cold, and buried probably, if this Beldrian here hadn't so valiantly stepped in. So! Thank you."

"My favorite part," the girl from Fernstead said, "is how Cor grabbed that stunner, and the ork was standing over Deliad, aiming down. And what does Cor do? Does he fire his stunner? Save Deliad from afar, all easy-peasy?"

"Not Cor! He winds up and he *throws* the stunner, to show off all those baseball skills of his; he swings his sword to *block a stunner shot*, to show off all those swordsman skills of his; he runs up *so fast* that the guard can't fire, to show off all those sprinting skills of his; when he could just have pulled the trigger instead!"

Cor stared a second. "Benefit of hindsight."

"You have some trouble pulling triggers, Cor?" said Brayleigh, batting her eyelashes sweetly; then cackled. "Ha! He didn't even realize! Could've just pulled the trigger. Not this Beldrian! Cor Volucre: too cool to be efficient!"

He shrugged. "I spend the lion's share of my time practicing esoteric sword techniques, and aging drinks in casks for several decades. Cool inefficiency's my way of life."

"It's not too late for cool efficiency," said Deliad. "I could always get you a halberd."

"Hey, who saved whom, Sir Cool Efficiency?" chid Brayleigh, holding out her hand toward Cor, fist closed. Her eyes were hopeful.

That's . . . ? Oh, sure. He balled his fist and started into a fistbump, but halted halfway as the Knight-Lord warned, "Careful there! That guy almost cut my head off just fifteen minutes past."

"While saving you," said Celeste. "For a second time in one day."

"Eh," Deliad waved, "who's counting?"

"She is," Cor said, thumbing toward Brayleigh. "What's my count now? Four?"

"Let's call it five. You owe me five!" beamed Brayleigh.

"Well. Thank you for a second time," said Deliad.

"Ah, no big deal," said Cor. "You're not to blame for wielding such an over-sized, unbalanced, slow, overweight, and somewhat awkward weapon. It's like they say: 'The weapon suits the wielder.'"

Deliad threw up his hands. "You see that? See? Lesson learnt! No more 'thank yous' from the Knight-Lord!"

"Thank *you* for saving me," said Celeste quietly. "All of you. I'll do my best to deserve it."

"Oh, don't be silly," said the girl from Fernstead. "You're one of us."

Cor nodded first, then Deliad, after a second's pause and sidelong glance.

"You tripped, we helped you up!" said Brayleigh blithely. "No sweat. It's not a trip without some tripping!"

Cor looked at Brayleigh.

Then, he roared with laughter, head tilted back and belly-chortling in a most un-Beldrian way.

"What?" Brayleigh cried, as the other wanderers fell into hilarity, infected by the uncontrollable mirth. "Anyway, Celeste, you'll just owe us one. And that's fine! Cor, for instance, owes me five."

"You sure we're not at four now?" questioned Cor.

"Hey! I could count today as two instead!"

Talk waned as battle's rush and warm relief dwindled to weary quiescence. *What a day.* Strange to think this same Sun, in one long circuit, had seen a legal trial, an insurrection, a mad escape, a mercenary duel, and now the maiden flight of the Sojourner. Life's measured not in months, but days like these.

"Wonder if I can see Fernstead from here!" the party's youngest member happily pondered, staring off westward. Then, she wandered off to climb the stairs atop the quarterdeck, craning to peer above the ship's raised rear.

Following her with wide stare, faintly smiling, Celeste lit up with something that she saw there—stroking away a fair strand gone astray across her face, still largely free of lines—until the lass had bounded off beyond view.

Then, like a leaf when Sol sinks past the skyline, she slumped a little toward what lurked below her; and, suddenly, the reflected innocence shining upon her face had fallen toward innocence lost. The smile went sad, lips parted for a sigh, and, narrow-eyed against the daylight's dazzle, Clausiglade's adoptive daughter strode away, into the darkness waiting down below-deck.

Following her with sunlit stare, the Knight-Lord watched as her slim frame's silhouette was beset by a host of shadows haunting the inward staircase. With memory's quietude in his tone, he spoke, seemingly to himself, but Cor could hear: "'A man can see what's fair.' Yes, you were right, my friend. Your faith was true. What's fair is fair."

Not sure if he should speak, Cor eyed the Knight-Lord. But he was walking toward the ship's stern now, his eyes far off, his mind immersed in memory.

The Beldrian let him be. He let the wild winds bear him across the broad deck to the rail, where, leaning down, he watched the Dusk descending. His weight against the stained teak brought the sting of wounds. But, after a while of breathing deeply and letting mistiness reclaim his mind, simply admiring many-beautied Nature, pains became part of a sublimer picture he half-perceived, uniting toward a fair form.

He felt a little cold at first. But soon it faded, as he heard a nearing footfall and, glancing back, found Brayleigh grinning there: a near-silhouette against the numinous sunset, which lit the billowing ringlets of her red locks, mingling with freckle dust across her face, so a shamrock gaze was stark upon the fairness. Indeed, as she approached and leant beside him, her arm against his arm, her eyes upon the same shared prospect, sprawling wide and rosy with Fall and evenfall, all he felt was warmth.

CHAPTER 30

When Dawn spread forth her rosy fingertips, the wanderers didn't wake with her. They slept till Sol was more than halfway up the sky, and woke refreshed by a sojourn in the dream realm.

The only one aboard not battle-battered, Orther, had offered to make the group breakfast: "Eggs, eggs, and more eggs. And some bread and butter." So, they were leaning now atop a longboard of fine-carved oak and scarfing down some eggs.

"How's that hole in your gut?" Cor asked the Knight-Lord.

"Filling it in by the bite," replied Deliad. "Ah, the other one?" He lightly rubbed his belly, then looked down, frowned, and lifted up his shirt. Where he'd been stabbed by steel two inches deep was what appeared to be a week-old scrape wound, scabbed thick and brown, with pink flesh on the edges.

"Taking some truly grievous wounds for Norvester?" said Orther, dumping eggs on Deliad's plate.

"And here I thought that you'd just stopped the bleeding," marveled the Knight-Lord, looking over at Celeste.

"I—thought the same." She blinked and squinted at it.

The Sojourner was headed north for Norvester and, Starling said, was set to arrive at noon. At that point, as they'd promised Captain Nyrburt, Orther would make his way to Castle Norvester to inform the King of Gaudimorte's insurrection and relay Deliad's counsel: to dispatch a force from Norvester's newly remade Hergas, led by a squad of knights, to aid Nyrburt's guards.

"The Hergas of the Fellowfolk," said Orther. "Feels good to say it. What was old is new."

"The Hergas of the Fellowfolk!" mused Deliad. "Defending Norvester since there was a Norvester. Since High Lord Sigram rallied Beregin's farmers to drive back Mallarg Trollblood and his horde, and the other lords all bowed to House Lofthungrian, and Sigram came to be our people's First King."

Orther inclined a brow. "When does your course at the Academy start, Professor Knight-Lord?"

"Subject myself to that? Sometime between 'when he who wore the Horned Helm rides again' and never," said the Knight-Lord.

"Quoting prophecies? Not only a soldier and scholar but a seer too?" said Orther. "Try to leave us all some talents."

"Not my fault. I blame Nature," yawned the Knight-Lord, covering a mouth full of food. "Nice eggs, Captain."

"Poaching deer one month, poaching eggs the next," said Captain Ormslik.

"Man of many talents!" hailed Brayleigh.

"I blame Nature," answered Orther. "Anyway, have a grand time with your globetrotting."

So, the ship stopped at Norvester, Orther left, and off the wanderers went toward lands unknown.

They didn't have to push Professor Starling to stay as pilot. "As I said," he explained, "I've hit that point in life. When if not now? Why not? My kids are out there in the wide world. High time I made my way back there myself."

Professor Logi chose to stay as well. For him, the appeal was not so much pursuing the dwindling glamor of adventurous prospect before it darkened beneath the shadow of age. He simply throve on chaos. That, and his best friend was Starling. And he had no kids to deal with. (*"Well, I don't think so, though I can't be sure!"*) So, why not fly across the Fragments, fixing an engine for some wanderers out to save the world? *"The food's good. I enjoyed those eggs!"*

The crew concurred upon their destination: eastward, *"where Sol is split by a moonlit summit"*; that is, to Heron Summit. There, according to the old tome Deliad found, they'd find an Element.

Flying east, they quickly reached the Ginnagonds. Not quite so cloud-scraping here as down south beside the Academy, still those bluffs loomed huge, and wintry winds blew fiercer this far north, even in the Summer, let alone the Fall.

Fresh snowfall on the summits glared at any who'd dare traverse the single pass across: the Astraway, as stories called it. Slender and winding, it was infamous for snow mists that swirled in blindingly from bluffs above, like morning fog, but lasting many hours, piling to snowdrifts. At the peak of Summer, when they would mostly melt, skeletons emerged.

All of this passed by through the porthole windows from the perspective of the four flying wanderers, who, faced with frigid winds, had fled below-deck. There, it was toasty and pleasant. They passed long hours in plush brass chairs inside the ship's lounge, paneled with wood and interspersed with bookshelves, packed tight with treatises on physical science but with some histories and epics too.

Sometimes, they read. Sometimes, they drank dark ales and porters, hand-picked by Professor Starling, and spoke of days gone by and days to come.

Even Deliad had to admit that flying beat walking. "At least," he allowed, "I can't deny it's faster," sipping a brew from far off Daliamist: a coffee porter, which he'd come to quite like.

Faster indeed. What would have been a journey to fill a travelogue would take a few days.

Only a few hours after leaving Norvester, Brayleigh had come running in from the cabin, announcing, "We just flew across the Boundary! The one above those big old misty mountains!"

"So soon?" asked Celeste. "I'm surprised you managed to test the Passagestone and all so quickly."

"We didn't! I just sensed that it would work."

"Ah, swell. Long as you sensed it," mumbled Deliad. He peered through a porthole at the craggy peaks jagging below them. Anything that fell here probably would freeze before it struck and shattered.

The uneven skyline leveled soon, so Starling brought the ship Earthward toward a purplish tundra. Patches of jaundiced grass grew here and there, often blackening on the fringes and receding. The drabness of the shallow hills and valleys was punctuated by the occasional rock, splotched with a sickly orange fungus in chunks, blooming in parody of pastoral beauty.

Gamboling through the wastes were herds of gross beasts: six-legged dogs with heads of deer, they seemed, grotesquely long to allow the extra legs. Each leg had two joints, insect-like. Their gait was more mollusk scuttling than mammalian bounding. Each of the things had two or three thick antlers, sprouting out curly like overgrown nosehairs. Sometimes they stopped beside the fungal blooms and chomped upon the orangeness, sometimes issuing great flatulence and groans. After a meal, they scurried off and tumbled over each other in eagerness to glut themselves again.

One of them tripped and was trampled by the others. It lay on purplish dust and lowed a moment. Then, from the sparse grass sprinted countless squirrels, pink and near-hairless, and they pounced upon it, sinking their sharp front teeth into its flesh. It rolled and moaned and squished some, but the swarm buried it under a biting, chittering heap.

"Care for some dinner, Brayleigh?" Cor inquired, as pink squirrels munched orange fungus from its stomach.

"Dinner?" Her brow was wrinkled and her eyes wide. "I think I'm done with dinners for today. And maybe for forever."

Cor, too, dwelt on this foul scene throughout that day, while saying nothing of his concerns, as was the Beldrian way. He couldn't help but notice how those wan weeds and sprawling wastes were similar to some parts of Norvester, where a blotchy fungus bloomed along the edges of expanding wastes. He'd overheard the Knight-Lord's talks with Orther about how shortages of food—and young men—might hinder their revival of the Hergas. Life seemed to struggle in Norvester these days.

Of course, it wasn't only Norvester either.

"Death, vileness, then eternity devoid of both: this be thy world's weird, absent the Elements."

An image wafted up from buried memory, like smoke above an unseen smoldering: standing by Morty's field and watching barley burn.

More Beldrians watched nearby, many far skinnier than men and women should be—many skinnier than children should be—watching as the blight burgeoning beneath their hope went up in flames. The fungal grey was blackening outward in. The rows of grain receded, leaving blackness in ash below and fumes above; and nothing, nothing where, in between, there had been life.

Amid that ash, he saw a strange black shape, near-fetal in its curl, with something golden gleaming about where a belt buckle might be.

When, days ago, Cor's mother had been buried, she'd worn her golden ring with amber gemstone: a rarity in bucolic, rustic Beldria. "Made by the Sun," she fondly used to say. And then his father, never much for smiling, would smile at what he'd saved six months to buy.

Cor closed his eyes and forced the memories down, as he heard footsteps coming down the corridor: Logi, it turned out, looking rather green beneath his wild brown hair.

"Evening," hailed Cor. "Taking a break from the engine?"

"Yes. Sort of," said Logi; then, he paused and closed his eyes. "A little seasick. Airsick? Mm. Don't mind me. Just hoping I can keep my dinner down!"

This brought a bit of light to Cor's dark musings, but midnight brought them back. His dreams were fraught with visions of burning up in bed with fever; and burning piles of clothing, fouled with pestilence; and burning grain fields, thick with fungal blight; and, in their midst, strange black things, curling, calling, and weeping from within the infernal reaping.

He slept eight hours, according to a clock of well-carved linden wood with gordian gearwork—*"Built by myself and me!"* Starling had boasted—but felt he'd slept for maybe half that long. The glow of day, glaring in through the porthole, was not a welcome visitor.

When he worked up the will to sit and stare out through the glass, though, the landscape shocked him out of lingering gloom.

Blinking back boundless radiance, he surveyed a fractal spray of little streams and lakes, lying lightly as a nightgown in the morning, when, stretching, throwing myriad silky shimmers, the sleeper hails the beaming one who woke her.

Rippling, the shining waters ran through rows of white-capped ridges—Earth's ribs, gowned in snow—and wound through teal and beryl-tinted fir trees, sprung up from rocky isles amid the moss. Slopes of granitic indigo stretched forth craggy and continual to their sides, like legs splayed wide beneath their sheets at break of day.

Looming far east aloft the uneven horizon was Heron Summit, reigning high above the kneeling host of mountains massed about it, crowned by the swirling stratus, flush with Sol.

Scanning the fairness, Cor felt strangely lured by the sunlight, sparkling on the thousand streams, toward understanding some half-fathomed pattern: verging toward Order, falling back to Chaos whenever he tried to close his mind about it.

And, as he failed, he found his vision—turning from futile pondering back to aimless wandering—kept following that Summit higher and higher, until the wistful radiance of the cloud-rack hid what the Earth, and Cor, were aspiring for.

The sound of Brayleigh singing in the hall startled him from his heady, heavy reverie to warm anxiety, where the crystal maze of one's conceptions melts into the moment, and, suddenly, all makes sense.

"Good morning, Brayleigh," he called, still sitting in his bed, through a closed door.

"Morning!" she called back. "My, aren't you up early! It's not even noon yet!"

"Lots to do today. Books to be read. Some swordplay. Meals to eat."

"Busy! You'd best get started!"

"How about breakfast?" The words flowed lightly as those streams outside, pointing to a pattern shining just past sense. "We ought to eat up for a day this busy."

"Makes sense to me!"

"Great. Be out in a minute." He slipped inside a tunic, smoothing it, then ruffled out his hair. Having given up for now on grasping the ungraspable, he couldn't help but feel that what he'd reached for had, as he sadly accepted fallible manhood, come back to meet him of her own accord.

"You almost ready yet, you prima donna?"
Smiling unconsciously, he strode outside.

CHAPTER 31

A palace. Celeste settled for that word after a failed search for something more fitting, studying the blue-grey structure of spires and arches ensconced amid the peaks near Heron Summit. This was like no other building she'd seen; nothing that Nature herself hadn't built.

If some wild native of the wintry north, with memory full of mountains glazed with ice and snowy spires, had heard about a palace, his fancy might have bodied forth a structure like this. If, by some fey and warlock charm, he'd had the power to make his fancies real, and he had shaped them out of solid stone, and persevered in making all things perfect, he might have wrought this wonder of shining blue, with equal verisimilitude to water and Earth; so fair that Celeste thought it false, and blinked to verify her eyes were lying, and yet the dazzling fairness still was there, belying the very lie it'd seemed to tell.

She laughed in disbelief.

"Deliad," said Brayleigh, "how would you rate this compared to your castle?"

"Well," waved the Knight-Lord. "This here is a palace. The other is a castle. Like comparing a courtly suit to a suit of armor. That's all."

"Why wasn't Castle Norvester carved from one block of solid rock like this was?" Cor inquired. "Wouldn't that help out with castle defense?"

The Knight-Lord grumbled something indiscernible.

They soon decided that, before attempting to search this massive mountain for an Element—"the First," according to the children's rhyme—they'd try to speak with those inside the palace. The rhyme was ancient. Even if it was true, who knew where the Element was now? Maybe *they* would.

Plus, the wanderers were keen to see this palace; even Deliad. "I suppose a little detour won't hurt. If you all insist," he announced to no one.

During the Sojourner's gradual descent, something about this palace, nagging at her, crystallized to a thought: there was no city. Some hamlets showed upon the far horizon, but none within an hour's walk.

Well, that's odd. She'd learnt firsthand of the logistical hassles of keeping Castle Norvester—or, at that time, "the People's Place"—stocked with supplies and food, especially things the city hadn't had. Shipping in *everything* would've been nightmarish.

The ship alighted four miles from the palace, behind a hill that mostly hid its huge frame. Landing a giant ship just outside the front gate, they all agreed, would not be a good idea.

"Best give some space, avoid attracting sentries," the Knight-Lord said.

They started disembarking just as the Sun was dipping toward the skyline. Starling and Logi elected to sit out from this adventure.

"Plenty of adventure right here as far as I'm concerned," said Starling. "We'd like to get this girl going twice as fast. Or faster yet. Just have to tinker a bit, run safety tests, some diagnostics, so forth, before we push her harder. As they say, 'Push hard the first time, she won't give you a second.'"

"Who says that!" Celeste muttered.

Brayleigh tittered, her green gaze flicking past the Passagestone; then, back to it. "Hey." She grabbed it. "We should take this. I sense a Boundary nearby. Maybe the Element is on the other side. We'll want this, won't we?"

"Good call," said Cor. He took the dull red rock and stuck it in his satchel. "Also, coats? And warm clothes? We're not really dressed for Winter. Let alone scaling an ice-covered summit. Anything on the ship?"

Their pilot shrugged. "Suppose she doesn't quite have everything. But, as they say—"

"'She'll give it when you need it, not when you want it'?" Brayleigh offered gleefully.

"Well said," commended Starling. "Finely phrased."

"It didn't even make sense!" mumbled Celeste.

"We'll have to buy coats. Maybe at some hamlet," said Deliad, patting at his bulging coin pouch. "No problem, we'll just buy some. Pick some nice ones." He opened his pouch to show its clinking contents.

Celeste's eyes rolled.

"Deliad is like a rich dad," said Brayleigh.

"No more out of you, young lady!" chastised the thirty-something cavalier.

"You young folk go have fun," enjoined the airman, yawning a little and smoothing his combover.

Winding amid the small hills, dusted white with snow and webbed with trickling trails of ice, the walk took over an hour.

The orangish evening had waned to grey Dusk when they neared the palace, aspiring into view as they ascended. Its towers and arches soared toward chaotic order, like Nature, lightly alluding to a pattern. Its shadowy blue stone seemed to ripple in the twilight like a blanket in the breeze.

It grew before them as a mountain grows, starting as a majestic shape, becoming a sloping woodland vista unto itself, and, finally, just a trail with trees around it. Just so, the shining splendor of the palace transformed to a prospect fraught with parapets and spires, and then to a gate that married glass with stone of luminous silver.

Having thus lost the mountain for the forest for the trees, amid her marveling, Celeste hardly noticed the guards outside the gate till they were near.

The pair were shining steel from toe to pate, wearing full plate with beavers up. They held their halberds stiffly upright in front of them. They made no move, nor sound, until the party stepped within thirty feet or so of the entrance; at which their polearms suddenly swerved diagonal and crossed into an X, blocking the path.

"Well met," called Deliad, holding up a palm to hail them and to halt his friends at once. "We come from Norvester Kingdom in the west, bearing most cordial greetings from her King, Reginald, for whom I humbly serve as Knight-Lord. Pray let us pass, and send word to your lord that we entreat an audience at his leisure."

"None pass," a guard barked back in guttural tones. He didn't even turn to look at Deliad.

The other wanderers shared a glance, eyes wide. They'd all heard all too much of guttural voices of that sort—rare in men, so rough and ugly, but ordinary in orks. Yet, unlike the orks serving as guards for the Merchant and Gaudimorte, these two weren't slouching, shifting, slacking off, or any of the usual things orks did.

The Knight-Lord's brow raised. "Be it as you say. Then we request the presence of your liege lord to treat upon our cause in coming here; or, in his absence, his appointed second."

"None pass," the gate guard flatly droned again.

"Are these your words? Take care. I warn you, Sir," Deliad replied, his forehead direly furrowed, "we mean to meet your lord, and when we do—"

"It's quite all right!" a voice called from above.

They looked up. Leaning from a narrow slit in the blue wall was a man of many Moons, wearing a conic yellow cap and blue robe.

"It's all right!" he repeated. "Let them pass, please." The gate guards moved their intersecting polearms mechanically to a stiff, upright position. "Bear with me for a moment, if you don't mind. Tarry a moment." The man walked away.

A half a minute hence, a rumbling started. The gate's twin doors of glass and stone began to slide open. In between them stood the elder, smiling slightly, no more than was enough to make his wrinkles genial. "Welcome, friends. We don't get visitors often. Excuse the guards." He glanced at the orks, still gazing stiffly ahead with halberds straight. "They're spellbound. Quite unable to comprehend your questions." The old man shrugged. "Not that they comprehended much to start with!"

Spellbound? The robed man didn't seem to think that further explanation was required.

"That's quite alright," said Deliad. "We've seen welcomes much worse than this one."

"Have you now?" smiled the elder. "Come—'Knight-Lord,' was it? 'Norvester'? Come in, friends."

Crossing the threshold, they followed the robed man from the outside world into an alien one.

The floor was formed of crystal tiles, translucent and tinted blue. The crack lines webbing through them, at first sight, seemed to embody fractal patterns, but fell apart to a fractured chaos when stared at. The walls were bluish stone, waving smoothly along like water. Over it all washed soft luminescence, gleaming like twilight on the sea. Its source was unseen.

"Come!" the blue-robed man repeated.

The gate behind them boomed shut.

Celeste stiffened, then glanced to see what mechanism had closed it. But all she saw were married glass and stone.

He led them down a winding corridor, widening at times to chambers, forking into vessels that flowed to far off stopping points, inscrutable of form and purpose save by firsthand study; more like a human heart than human building. Sometimes, the floor sloped subtly up or down, not so much seen as felt by slanting feet. There were some doors, but neither stairs nor signs; no more than Nature builds with stairs and signs.

They were a few minutes in when she realized it'd likely take her hours to find the exit, with all these unmarked, wending, branching ways, without a guide to help her get back out.

"You learn your way around here after a few years," the elder observed, eyes pausing briefly on Celeste. "And then you wonder why the things that men make aren't like this, when the rest of our world is."

"The things that men make"?

The old man smiled. "We're close now."

She noticed that, this whole time, they'd seen no one, except the occasional steel-girl, straight-backed guard, silently holding a halberd upright.

No one alive, that is. In several chambers, statues of more-than-man-size, wrought from bronze, stood in majestic poses: pointing loftily, serenely hailing unseen hosts, hands raised as though to beckon something down from Heaven. And all of them had wide wings, furled or unfurled, and horns that curved back through their billowy hair.

They looked like Cor's description of the Element, she realized. *Dievas*.

She glanced over at Cor. His gaze was wide upon a statue, wroth and glaring down, holding a longsword high, ready to fall like lightning on his foe.

Of course. She couldn't help but smile a bit.

"Ah, Perkunos," said the elder. "Rather fierce, no?"

She opened her mouth to speak.

"And here we are. This way," he went on, cutting off her question.

The hallway emerged into a waiting room with three hexagonal tables, each with six chairs, each finely carved from shadowy stone of blue and streaked with purple and grey along the edges. "Please do be seated." The elder took a chair.

Celeste was mildly surprised to discover the unpadded seat felt pleasantly for-giving. It fit her form as nicely a cushion.

"I hope you're comfortable," remarked the robed man. "We rarely host these days. So." He surveyed them, then smiled. "My name is Mislun. How may I help you?"

Celeste observed that he'd said "we" at least twice, but, setting the ensorcelled orks aside, it still was unclear who the others were.

"We're travelers from the west," replied the Knight-Lord. "From Norvester Kingdom and the western reaches beyond it. We're companions on a shared quest." He turned to Cor, hand out, and opened his mouth.

But Mislun broke in. "Norvester Kingdom, was it? You know, I think I read about that realm! Some two score years ago. The one with the archives at—some school. Not the Bejhbaal Oligarchy. The northern one. The King's Academy, was it?"

"Still there," said Celeste. "Studied many years there."

The old man tapped his temple, satisfied. "The memory's still there! Ha. I'd halfway wondered if Norvester and its archives were a tall tale, told by a fool who'd spent a lifetime traveling with naught to show for it. Shows me, I suppose. Learn something new each day." He looked away. "Life holds no thrill, in the end, like learning new things. It never stops! Even when life's sands run low. I'd give up life to keep just that from life!"

The girl from Fernstead's lips had curved up faintly as the old man rambled, and she'd opened her mouth. But now she paused.

"So, tell me friends," smiled the elder, "what might His Majesty of Norvester Kingdom desire from this most lowly of little realms?"

The wanderers shared a glance, and Cor shrugged slightly.

"We seek an Element," said the simple Beldrian. "The First, we've heard Him called. We've heard He's near here, on Heron Summit; or at least He was, centuries ago. We hoped that you could help us."

"An Element! Why, we've gone from tall-tale histories to myth!" responded Mislun amiably, voice smooth as smooth could be, twiddling his thumbs.

And yet she'd seemed to see the old man's eyes flash, hearing "the First." *And what about those statues?*

"Well," Cor said slowly. "Maybe myths and tall tales are both true, this time." He reached into his satchel and set the golden-glaring Fossil of Dievas atop the table.

Mislun blinked, his blank amity abruptly becoming frank startlement, but smoothing quickly. Smooth and hard as steel.

Now he was staring on the Sun-shaped rock, half-reaching for it with a hesitant hand, now holding out a finger halfway toward it.

Around the finger jagged a little spark, like static shock from shuffling through a thick rug.

Cor drew the Fossil backward.

"Mm," said Mislun, letting his fingertip fall to the table. And now he was a friendly elder again, face dimpling with another almost-smile. "Well, this is something else then. I suspect the Archanimist would be pleased to hear your plea." His amber eyes were fixed upon the Fossil. "Bear with me for a moment." He arose and shuffled to a doorway. "Tarry a moment."

And so we have our "we." She wondered idly what this "Archanimist" was, and why it sounded familiar, like a dream she'd dreamt before. Then, smiling, she surveyed the fractured floor of crystal and the walls of shadowy blue of this fey, wondrous palace mid the peaks, which she had flown to on a floating ship. Yes, Celeste felt she'd strayed into a dream.

The old man reemerged a half hour later, his swishing robe reflected on the floor, his eyes reflecting them. "Pray follow me. The Archanimist will receive you now. This way."

He led them through another set of chambers and wending ways, passing more steel-girt guards and—finally—two more men in robes of blue with conic caps of purple and rusty brown. One of them held a sparkling wand of silver.

"Dusk's blessings, Sudlun. Abesol," Mislun hailed them.

"Mislun," they waved back. Both were studying now the four companions in the old man's wake.

"What have we here?" inquired the purple-capped one. "Company? Well! It's been a couple Moons. Welcome to Lioss. We hope it's to your liking."

"Well met," the Knight-Lord nodded back. "We appreciate the courtesy. You've a fair place here."

"I'll say!" affirmed the girl from Fernstead. "Fairly awesome."

"Well, 'all things worthwhile start and end with awe,'" mused Purple Cap. "Maybe your time here too."

"That's Goetsworth, yes?" inquired his brown-capped compeer. "Not bad. Myself, I favor Makhederein: 'You'll leave none full of awe without being awful'!"

"So sinister. You'll scare them off!" chid Abesol.

"So, you read Goetsworth here?" said Celeste. "Strange, how books can travel so far."

"Stranger still how people travel so far, isn't it?" said Sudlun. "When a single book could show them more of the world than a lifetime of wandering."

"Stop by the library while you're around," the other said. "'A tome takes time but saves time.' You've come so far. You ought to make it worthwhile."

Their tones were affable, if a bit ironic; as though some twelve year olds had come to join their conversation, and they'd switched the topic to something small enough for smaller minds.

"This place *is* awfully empty though," said Brayleigh. "I would've thought this palace would be packed with servants! "

"Oh, we're served here well enough," mused Mislun.

"Visitors? Villagers? Loyal subjects?" said Brayleigh.

"Subjects?" Mislun chuckled. "Subjects to whom? We have no king here. King or queen. The Archanimist holds some specified authority, but otherwise is merely first of equals. What powers she has derive from the support of those around her and her cause's rightness."

"Ah," Brayleigh said politely, furrow-browed.

"What cause is that?" Cor questioned.

"True equality." The old man mildly smiled.

Cor opened his mouth as though to follow up, then slightly frowned and shut his mouth.

"Are all those villages a few miles yonder ruled by—was it 'Lioss'?" asked Celeste.

"Ruled?" said Sudlun. "Well, they do deem themselves Liossian, if you're asking that, and recognize the rightness of our cause."

Celeste decided to stop asking questions.

The wanderers moved along a moment later, led through a few more shadowy-shining corridors and azure rooms. The fractures in the clear tiles multiplied fairness even in faulting it, as broken mirrors make one beauty many beauties. She found her vision following those fault lines, raptured away in ruptured fractals, seeming to hint at something hidden not far ahead, forever near but never quite in sight.

"And here we are," said Mislun. "If you would."

She saw that he was speaking to a guard, girt head to heel in glimmering steel. In silence, it turned and tugged a rope beside the two doors.

A rumble ensued. Then, both doors started opening, much like the palace gate.

Gears? Celeste wondered. *Like Starling's brass birds? Or the Sojourner?* She didn't hear the hum of any engine.

Beyond the doors appeared a sprawling room, where fractal fault lines in the crystal floor webbed out in patterns round the room's far end, twinkling, and icicle-like stalactites hung in shining hundreds from the soaring ceiling. Statues of winged figures formed a circle around the room's periphery, pointing, hailing, basking and warring, frozen in brazen sublimity.

Within that circle, near the room's far end, stood two more statues, greater than the others. One was a man with wildly billowing cape and hair, a balled fist, and an upward glare. The other was a woman teary-eyed and bleeding, reaching toward him with a ring. But he was staring elsewhere, at the vast dome centered above them. There, the darkling sky sparkled in constellated majesty.

How that was possible at this hour was unclear.

Between the pair of statues, just beyond them, loomed a tall throne of midnight hue, grown over with interwoven threads of shimmering silver; which, like a tree's roots, bulged up from the floor and wound about the throne's legs, climbing higher and splitting into narrow twigging branches along the curving contours of the chair's back. Instead of leaves, those limbs were fraught with Stars. An empty pedestal was at its side, matching the silvery darkness of the seat.

Seated atop this Star-fraught throne of night was a slender woman. Straight hair fell to her shoulders, not dark nor light: the shade of dusk or dust. It barely brushed her robe of faded purple. Or was it blue? Or silver? Every slight move seemed to revise how it parsed in her eyes. It fit her frame as dusklight skims a plain, brushing against it with shadowy suggestiveness. Her calves were bared beneath it, daintily crossed and silver-sandalled. Long legs. She looked tall.

Her chin was resting in her hand. Her lips were somehow narrow and pouty at the same time. Her face was narrow, too, and fair of hue; perhaps fair altogether, though with something slightly offputting. Maybe it was her eyes' not-quite-symmetric curve, as though concealing some light ironic mirth. Or spite? Each slight move seemed to revise how it parsed in her eyes.

"Our guests, Archanimist," Mislun said, head bowed, then met her gaze. "Four wayfarers from the far west."

"They say *we* came from far west," she replied, languidly eying the wanderers one by one. "Maybe the ways we fare will merge awhile. Welcome to Lioss." Her tones were cool and smooth; and, as her tilted stare paused briefly on Celeste, she felt like she was slipping under silk sheets, chilling, even as they promised warmth. "And you are?"

The Knight-Lord stepped in front and bowed before her. "Your Eminence, we receive your House's courtesy with humble thanks. Before you stand my colleagues, friends and confederates: Cor Volucre of Beldria, and Brayleigh Mirin from the shire of Fernstead, and Celeste Daorbhean of the King's Academy. And, lastly, I serve Reginald, King of Norvester, as Knight-Lord: Deliad Linvarum. We're honored."

"'Eminence'? Hm. Fascinating choice," she answered. "No need though. Merely 'Archanimist' will do. In the end, we all are merely what we do; from Knight-Lords down to wayfarers down to Archanimists." Her lips curved up to match that curve of eye.

Deliad's brow furrowed faintly. "As you please, Archanimist."

"Mislun, here, had much to tell me about this band of 'wayfarers from the west,'" she went on. "But I'd like to hear it firsthand, if you'd not mind." Her stare was like the sunlight reflecting off an icy lake. She waited.

Celeste and the others turned to look at Cor; who, after a couple seconds, saw them staring, then smiled away a sigh. "Well," he began, "the story's sort of long now. It's about the Elements. I'd explain what the Elements are"—at this, he reached inside his leather satchel and raised the Sun-shaped Fossil of Dievas, swirling with white mists on a shining aureate backdrop—"but I've a feeling I don't need to explain."

"Mm. I won't try to fool you. No, you don't," she answered, smiling. "We can claim some knowledge of the Elements here in Lioss; as much as mortals can claim to 'know' the immortal." As she spoke, her eyes veered lightly among her several visitors, but always swerved back toward the Sun-shaped glow, like birds flying south for Winter. "Do go on though."

Cor nodded. He related how he'd happened upon a cave beyond the Beldrian Boundary and spoken with Dievas there.

"As he lay dying," concluded Cor, "he told me that the Elements were the animating force behind all Nature; and that the Elements slowly have been drained to power the Boundaries since the Pandaemonium, and now are dwindling to the point of dying; and that, without them, life itself would wither, going foul and blighted first, then fading. Dying." Till that point, he'd been speaking slowly and stoically, but now he pressed his lips and looked away.

"So, Dievas charged me to restore the Elements," he finally said. "Since then I've come a long way—others have joined me, and we've come a long way—and what we've found has led us here. To Lioss. We read that there's an Element here, 'the First.' Or that He was here, several centuries past. We're here to search for Him on Heron Summit. We hoped that you could help us in our search."

"I'd be delighted," she responded promptly, drawing a blink from the Beldrian. "Delighted to help you in this most important quest. We know that Element well here: Nilvernon. The First. The primal Chaos whence the Elements flow, stilled and distilled to structure by the pains of his Consort, Flua-Sahng, in her procreation. The infinity and nothingness in all things."

"Yes, we in Lioss know Nilvernon quite well. Our forebears found the First on Heron Summit a full millennium past. He turned to a Fossil soon afterward, and spent those centuries here. Right here." She pointed at the pedestal beside her, midnight blue and strewn with Stars.

"O, irony of ironies," she waved and cast her skewed gaze sideways, "that you'd come upon your quest not during that *millennium*—when He was right here, waiting to be found—but ten years too late. And to find Him now, you'll have to go to Heron Summit after all!"

"Before the First had faded from this plane, he charged us to preserve his Fossil here; somewhat like Dievas charged you, Cor Volucre. But, unlike you, we've failed now in our charge." She faced him wistfully, her lips curved upward on one side more than the other, like her eyes. "This palace, just a decade past, was robbed of its Fossil—and of much more—by the Warlock. An animist of unfathomable power, and former resident of this very place."

"Just up and took it?" Brayleigh interjected, frowning. "But wasn't the Fossil protected?"

"There was no 'just' about it," said the Archanimist. "The Warlock murdered many of our animists in his escape. Gruesome. Dismembered. Blasted and half-dissolved. Deformed. No 'just' about it." She idly smiled like they were sipping tea, talking about the weather yesterday.

"'Animist'—that word again. What does it mean?" Celeste felt vaguely like she'd heard it somewhere.

"What does it mean? Well. This," replied the Archanimist, holding a finger up. Above it flared a bluish-brown flame, swirling briefly about and shooting higher, as blue gave way to black, hissing eerily. Then, suddenly it was snuffed out. "Easier to show than tell. We're those who wield the Spirit of Nilvernon;

which, being sheer Chaos and not yet ordered into simple elements, is somewhat different from the other Elements. But I won't bore you with the technicalities."

The former Academy student opened her mouth to ask about those boring technicalities, but Brayleigh broke in. "So this Warlock though. *Why* did he do it? He was living here?"

"Well, I can't claim to speak for him, of course," she sighed, casting her hand and gaze aside. "I think it stemmed from certain views of his. You see, we aspire toward true equality here; not just in theory but in fact. A world where one can be born into any body, to any parents and with any talents, and all those unjust differences are smoothed out by a just society, leaving true equality."

"In short, we raise what's low and lower what's high. We uplift the wretched and throw down the proud. We beatify what's ugly, and we shed light on ugliness that's overlooked. At least," she sighed again, "We do our best. In truth, we're far from perfect. But at least we try!"

"The Warlock was our opposite. What he *lived* for was seeking what was high to uplift it higher, while spurning what was low," she sadly explained. "A member of the old order, through and through. A shame—he had such gifts!—but so it goes."

"So, when these times of true equality came, lifting the lowly and casting the exalted down from the summit of their birth and privilege, he turned athwart the downward flow of time and tried to stop it," said the uneven-eyed leader. Her light and lilting voice was strangely enthralling. "Meaning, he murdered many of those involved, stole our treasures, and fled to Heron Summit."

"If he's at Heron Summit," Celeste said, "and you're right here, just a few miles away, with all these animists, and it's just been *him* there, this whole last decade, with these stolen treasures—how is it that you haven't taken them back?"

"Fair question!" she replied. "Strong as he is, he couldn't hope to face our forces head-on. Here's what we know. The night he killed our animists and fled the palace, in his wake, he left a Spirit residue, which our animists followed to Heron Summit. But they failed to find him. Since then, from time to time, he's done some stealing and sabotage. And, every time, we've traced his Spirit residue back to Heron Summit, but never found him there."

"Of course, it's clear why," she waved and sighed. "He's hidden himself with wards. The Warlock always had a way with wards. Nothing that we could do. Till now." She smiled.

"Till now?" quoth Cor.

"Come!" She abruptly rose, sending a shimmer through her robe of purple, which rippled silver and blue as it reflected the ambient light. She led them to her left, beyond the circle of statues of the Elements.

On coming closer, they could see the wall of shadowy blue had scattered nooks, obscured uncannily by a mirror-like mist, which looked like the stone itself till they were standing nigh. What lay inside the nooks was mirky and dark, but she could see each held some artifact.

"What *is* this stuff?" asked Brayleigh, leaning close.

"Oddments of all things! Things that might prove useful," she answered. "Lesser Fossils. Dragon blood. Stones steeped in Spirit. A few Refractors. Wardstones. Including"—with a wave and parting of her pouty lips, the mist in one nook vanished—"this Wardstone here." She reached within the nook, which flashed grey as her fingers crossed the threshold, and grabbed a dull-hued, awl-shaped stone within.

"The Warlock lay a glamor upon this Wardstone many years past, when he was still in youth," explained the Archanimist. "Anyone who bears it, or stands nearby, can pass through wards he conjures. With some exceptions." She extended it to Cor. "Please!"

Celeste stared upon the odd stone as Cor received it. It was somewhat like the Passagestone, in that it seemed to absorb the light around it, but was celadon instead of crimson.

"I'm afraid this Wardstone wasn't much help when my animists were seeking the Warlock," said the Archanimist. "I suspect, for various reasons, you all might have more luck. That is," she went on, as the implications were sinking in, "should you decide to seek him. Since he *does* have the Fossil of the First."

"You said that you suspect we'd have more luck," repeated Deliad after a moment. "Why? Why would the Wardstone work for us but not you?"

"Hm. Let me try to speak in Knight-Lord terms." Her lips curved up. "Imagine wards are guards at a castle gate. The King commands the guards to bar all passage, save by those with papers signed by the King. But what if someone *steals* some papers and he tries to sneak in? Well, the King creates a list of all his enemies; the ones who'd likely try that sort of thing. He tells the guards, 'Don't let these enemies in no matter what, even if they have signed papers.' With me so far?" She waited for his nod.

"Good. So! The Wardstone is the 'King's signed papers.' The 'enemies list' lists me and all my animists. But not you. Are you with me still, Sir Knight-Lord?"

He nodded, narrow-eyed with lips pressed tight.

"So, that's what you would do!" the Archanimist said. "Take this Wardstone, travel to Heron Summit, and search there for the Warlock. In exchange, we'd let you use the Fossil of the First. Fortunate for us all, your presence here. You benefit; we benefit; we all win."

"I'm still not sure I understand," said Celeste, "why you'd have waited a decade to do this. And why us? Just some wanderers from the west."

"Well. It's not every day that wanderers waltz in with Dievas' Fossil, charged to save the world, hoping to find the Fossil of Nilvernon!" The woman smiled, tilting her slanted gaze. "You're right though. Which is why there's one more thing."

She waved a hand and, from a nook nearby, the mirror-mist dissipated. She retrieved a orange crystalline object from inside; like a cube, somewhat, but with concave faces, so each of its eight corners drew to a sharp point. "This is what's called a Beacon. Do be careful, it's delicate. One use only." Gingerly, she handed it to Cor.

"Shatter this Beacon, which I'm attuned to, and at once I'd sense it, and where you are. His wards would still repel us, but maybe we could find a way around them. Or you could lure him out and summon us. And then we'd finally have the Warlock cornered." Her eyes and robe both shimmered with the room's light. "We trust you. We just like to be extra certain. You see, we want that Fossil very much."

Sometimes, an ally with material motives is trusted more than one who's oddly generous. Celeste on some level thus felt reassured.

Really, she should be excited. This was progress: a plan to obtain the Fossil of the First! And, finally, they had found a clear-cut villain, who wore his wickedness openly in the world's eyes, rather than one who cloaked himself in virtue. A robber and murderer! Hiding in his lair! She'd much prefer *that* to another Lothar or Gaudimorte. Life might not be a fairy tale, but it was nice when life was somewhat like one.

She looked at Cor expectantly; who looked, in turn, upon the Archanimist. "We agree. We'll seek the Warlock out and use this Wardstone, and try to find the Fossil of the First."

"Very well!" She eased into a slanted smile. "I fear I'm not sure how you'll *use* the Fossil to do what you've set out to do. But do feel free to browse our archives when you're back. We've quite a large collection; with, I daresay, more books about the First than you'll find elsewhere."

"That sounds fantastic," Celeste said. "We'll do so."

Deliad looked so disheartened at the thought, she had to hold a giggle back.

"We're grateful," said Cor. "We'll set off right away."

"By starlight?" Head tilted, smiling, she batted her eyes. "I applaud your haste. But we've made do without the First for ten years. One more night won't hurt. We've many rooms to spare."

The wanderers shared a glance, then nodded. None of them was keen on a miles-long stumbling walk through chilly night. And, after hardly an hour within these halls of shadowy blue, winding in shining waves, haunted by effigies brazen and fantastical, none of the wanderers felt ready to leave.

They took their leave soon after, with the Knight-Lord bowing adroitly, followed by the Beldrian, hand to his belly, lips carefully sealed.

A steel-girt ork escorted them in silence through almost-lifeless corridors, bathed in blue light that caught upon the fractures in the floor, until they reached a wing with several bedrooms.

It stiffly stuck an arm out toward the doorways, then clomped away. The echoes of its bootsteps clanked from around the corner, slowing fading.

"Well! That was weird. But good, I think?" mused Brayleigh.

"I think," said Cor.

"I think so," Celeste said.

These beds, at least, looked good, swathed in soft light and silky blankets. And, in any event, it's no good wasting words against the weird of time, which lays low even the highest and haughtiest; much less this humble band of weary wanderers.

They passed a brief time talking; then, retreated to separate chambers and beneath their sheets; then, off with Somnus to a domain of dreams, where shadowy forms of future things uncertain drifted in ominous myriads from the Mists.

CHAPTER 32

When Dawn awoke, she peeked upon the world with grey gaze, bright but bleary still with sleep, but stayed awhile beneath her sheets of cirrus, stacked thick atop the skies.

She still was there when, emerging from the palace, four companions were greeted by the grey of mirky day. They walked and wound amid ubiquitous ponds, brushed up by a light breeze into mist, which sprayed and beaded over them as they advanced.

Cor drank the coolness in and savored it, being bundled in a fur-lined coat and thick boots for climbing Heron Summit: gifts they'd gotten at daybreak from some servants of the Archanimist. Warm as he was, he tried to enjoy the weather. There'd be no warmth atop the snow-capped heights.

The wanderers traveled for about ten miles, past herds of hairy goats on tooth-trimmed pastures and wooden fishing boats on little lakes. They wended often round rocky outcrops, bare of Earth's green hair but bluish with moss and lichens, like down on Earth's cheeks.

Here, Cor suddenly noticed, there was no trace of the burgeoning blight he'd seen in other Fragments: foul and noxious, sprouting in fungal splotches, orange and brown, spreading to flora and fauna, altering them, and finally leaving barren dust behind. Here, there was only water and rock and life.

Their narrow dirt path halted in a hamlet: Laegtheill, a servant back at Lioss had named it. A smoldering peat scent wafted from the hearths of mingled homes and shops, arrayed haphazard along the single road, most of them stone, and most with roofs of thatch and smoky chimneys. Many were overgrown with creeping greenery.

The smoke hung low atop one larger structure, from which the clank of metal on metal sounded at intervals: a smithy, much like Stalbart's. Another, smaller, had some slabs of meat hanging in neat rows, while a hefty butcher spattered with blood hefted more from a wagon, as Sagriss had back home. Both brought back memories; but neither as much as one white building, topped with two capped, curvy chimneys, each emitting more smoke than any of the other structures.

A memory flashed through Cor's mind: Age sixteen, beside the casks downstairs at the distillery. Old enough that the artlessness of youth no longer eased the flow of talk with grown-ups, but far too young to speak with age's fluency. So, Cor and Faxlath had been mostly silent that Sahngday, rolling casks till well past Dusk.

The memory swelled above his waking senses:

Finally, the work was finished. He was hurrying gladly away to practice two new Postures he'd spotted in the Annals' marginalia, when, glancing back, he saw his father seated atop a stool and staring at the floor, hunched with his forearms resting on his knees.

Cor had outdueled Aldartal more that month than in the two years prior. The Master of War! Bested by him! *He felt like he was taking his first steps from his homely little existence toward genuine life.*

He looked back at his father, greying a bit and tired.

"You want to taste that twenty and twenty-four again?" asked Cor. "Figure out which one we should sell at First Day?"

Faxlath looked up and blinked back. "Fine idea," he finally said, smiling. "For business reasons."

"For business reasons. We're just being responsible." Cor grinned.

"Responsibility. Very important," affirmed the stillman, standing up and stretching. Seldom did middle-aged stoicism give way, for him, to laddish spirits. But when it did, Cor's father looked a little more like Cor.

"I'm leaning toward the twenty-four," he said. "The twenty's cask work is a little subtle for that crowd."

"They just think, 'The higher the number, the better.'"

"That's exactly right!" sighed Faxlath. "Such fine work on the twenty's spirit flavors. You let it age inside that cask much longer, you'd lose it all," he mused. "The spirit of youth."

"With just a touch of age's wisdom."

"Right! Well, guess we'll give them what they want," said Faxlath, then paused. "After we've tested both to make sure."

"Have to be sure," affirmed the stillman's son.

They tested for a few hours, talking, chuckling more easily by the dram, until the Moon was high aloft the Winter sky, half-hidden behind the malt kiln's curved pagoda chimney.

Smiling, Cor stared upon the two curved chimneys, dispersing peat smoke through the homely hamlet, and took a small sip from his Sun-blazoned flask.

He realized he was feeling rather hungry. No surprise there, when it was nearly noon and he'd had not a bite to eat that day. The servant who had led them from the palace had not raised the issue of breakfast on his own. And, when they'd reached the palace gate and realized he wasn't going to, it'd have been too awkward to broach the subject. Cor was too polite, Deliad too proud, and Celeste too unhungry.

That left Brayleigh.

"Wait," she had said outside, halting some fifty yards beyond the gate and frowning. "Wait. When's breakfast? We have food, right? You brought some from the ship?" She stared. "Yes, Deliad?"

"Only enough for an emergency," he answered. "Crackers. Dried meat. We should save it for when we need it. Find food in the hamlet."

"What about juice? Did anyone bring juice?" she bleakly cried. "My mouth still tastes like sleep."

"I've heard this called juice." Cor held out his flask.

She raised the Sun-blazoned flask and sniffed the brazen fluid, then choked and thrust it out to arm's length. "Ach! Cor tried to poison me!"

Taking the flask, Celeste inhaled with her nose, neck craned slightly with thought, then nodded, sipping from it lightly. "Reminds me of brandy. Bit more grain and smoke, less grape and nuttiness. Vanilla and caramel. Quite good."

"Ha!" Cor declared to Brayleigh happily. "See? See? It's just a matter of having good taste."

"You said your father made this—whisky, was it?" said Celeste.

"Yep. This one's our eighteen. Meaning, it's aged for eighteen years inside an oak cask. It smooths the rough parts out," explained the Beldrian, "and gives that subtle, rounded, graceful flavor."

"Like brandy. Same effects," said Celeste brightly. "When whisky's older, does it get that strange, sweet, fruity note? All nutty and super-rich? That's my favorite."

"It does. Well said," he answered, as he received the flask and sipped again. "Imagine tasting this with ten more years!"

"Well, we should go to Grape Divine sometime," Celeste replied, running a hand through fair hair, "and you can try a twenty-eight year old. Then you won't have to use your imagination."

"I'm game," replied the ever-ready Beldrian. "That's at the Academy? Guess we'll have to sneak in."

"Life's finest pleasures are the ones we sneak," said Celeste, smoothing her fair windswept hair.

"So, if we're all *quite finished*," Brayleigh cried. "I'd like to eat before I'm old as you are!"

During their hours-long excursion to Laegtheill, she tried to find food constantly; and failed. "Hey Deliad, can you spear that deer?" She pointed at where a doe was straying with her fawns. "No need for fire, we'll make do. By the way, how many poison berries can you eat before you the kick the bucket?" She held up a sprig with several reddish, oozing balls.

Having arrived at the mountainside hamlet, her hanger now had aged to ravenous rage. As they advanced, she held her belly, hunching, facing the foodless world with wroth voracity.

"Why don't we walk another million miles? We're skin and bones now. May as well be skeletons!" she rambled. "We won't have to climb this mountain. We'll float right up! You think that they have food here? Ha, no, that's silly. They're beyond such things. They live on air and water! Who needs food when we have *air!* Hey, look Cor: a latrine. Why don't you go refill your flask?" she urged.

Deliad forced down a chuckle at Cor's dismay. "Why don't we stop at that inn? Should have food." He pointed at a sign: *The Singing Sword.* Beside it was a big, stone longhouse, sprawling far back into the field along the road. It looked a bit formidable for a mere inn, built high and wide with huge rocks, mountain-hewn. But it'd been made up in a homely manner, and scents of smoked meat wafted from the doorway.

"What's that now?" Brayleigh answered. "What's this *'food'* thing?" But she'd already hied in front of the others and reached the door when they were halfway there.

Beyond the threshold was a common room, lit warmly by the flaming lamps along the walls of stone. Being somewhat late for lunch, merely a few men sat at scattered tables, tilting back ales and talking, eating smoked trout with cottage cheese and capers, yawning often.

"Damned caravans," said one man, russet-haired and streaked with grey, sitting with a companion. They both were wearing dusty, thick-woven shirts, and both looked weary. "That's what changed. Back then, we grew our barley, palace bought it, we bought whatever else we needed, and we got by."

"Suv caravans from down south," nodded the other. "Palace buys food from them, saves a few silver. And what do we do?"

"Die, I guess." He smirked and sipped his ale. "Get what they pay for though."

"Eh," nodded the other man. "You ever taste it? That grub they sell? Just tastes like salted leather."

"Even worse without the salt. Tastes foul, no matter how fresh it is. And most of it's not fresh."

"They say it's goat; but I know goat. That's no goat."

"Not that those ork guards care. They'd eat each other."

"Hell, maybe it *is* ork." Both men shared a chuckle.

"I hear it's all they have in Kaupsam now."

"Yep. Almost all the big towns. But I hear they still buy some meat local for the animists inside the palace. Just enough for them."

"There's 'true equality,' eh?" Again, they chuckled.

"Wouldn't have happened with Mardon and Aislin," declared the russet man, abruptly smacking the table with his fist. "It never would've—"

But the other now had motioned him to stop, and both were turning to the band of wanderers.

Russet Hair's eyes went wide. He faced his food and leaned down, shoving down a silent bite and chewing for a while, washing it down with ale; then, glanced behind him once again.

"Excuse me," Cor called. "Know where we can find the innkeep?"

Both men flinched at being addressed but, having parsed the question, seemed relieved.

"Fetching our food. Barmaid's out sick today," the second man said.

"Thanks." The wanderers sat and, after a moment, saw a middle-aged man walk in with bread and a wedge of blue cheese.

"Welcome," he called as he passed the companions, nearing the two men. "With you in a moment."

The innkeep was a tall and portly man. He had the dimpled, smooth and ruddy cheeks of one who rarely saw the Sun these days, but maybe missed his boyhood when he'd had time. Back when that hair of blondish-brown had been full on his pate, rather than in a thick beard, while hopelessly retreating from his forehead. He itched a grizzled portion of his beard with sausage fingers.

Also sausage-like, his shirt was stretched taut by his ample shoulders and biceps, and an ample belly too. Its fresh stains almost looked like battle wounds, but they were just a touch too pink: just sauce he'd spilled while serving others. All his clothes were homely, save his belt's huge buckle of steel, which could've blocked a sword blow, it was so big, but now just held his pants up under his belly.

"Don't think I've met you all," declared the man. "I'm Skeggalt." He brushed bread crumbs from his belly. "What can I get you?"

"Food for four," said Cor, then glanced at Brayleigh. "Maybe more like six. Some of that smoked trout. Brown bread. Cheese. Ale, water."

"Certainly." Skeggalt looked away a moment. "One silver for the food, one for the drinks." It was as much a question as a statement.

The wanderers blinked and shared a look, each wondering if he had heard right. *Food for six,* one *silver?* "Two silver pieces, for—?" Cor started asking.

"You know," said Skeggalt hurriedly, his voice apologetic, "let's just say one silver. The times, I know."

Cor stared. In Beldria or Norvester, that'd buy a mug of ale.

"Here," said the Knight-Lord. "Take this, we'll call it even." From his coin pouch, he took five silver and handed it to Skeggalt.

Apparently, they had a long tradition in Norvester that the Knight-Lord's personal coin pouch would always be refilled, no questions asked. *"The Knight-Lord,"* Norvester's Deputy Assistant Treasurer had told Cor, when he'd asked about that coin pouch over an ale one night, *"has matters much more important to worry about than how he'll buy his next meal."*

Skeggalt blinked, then bowed his head in thanks. "I'll get that food. And something extra. Something I've been saving."

"Not necessary," waved the Knight-Lord.

"No, but I'll still do it," said Skeggalt, lumbering off, stretch lines appearing on his bulging shirt as he turned his bulk around a nearby table and headed to the kitchen. He glanced briefly at where a greatsword hung above the fireplace—a real broad-bladed monster, probably eight pounds—then shuffled out of sight to fetch the food.

Cor had known many men resembling Skeggalt in Beldria. Mellow, burly men. Often jolly, but not quite happy; pent-up unto bursting in their domestic lives, but too good-natured to seek out conflict in the midst of concord. Sagriss the butcher and Stalbart the blacksmith. Morty the wealthy farmer with his huge fields.

Men of their ilk would once have been the warriors of Beldria. Borne by overflowing life to face death's void upon the battlefield, they'd poured in lively throngs on life's foes. Now, nothing so vital was left to be done. Danger's defeat had left them obsolete. Maybe that's why so many overate: yearning to fill a yawning gap with life but finding none outside, they overfilled another inside.

Now, some friends of Cor's—those fellow boys who'd faced off on the ballfield and spent their spare youth courting crazy mischief, seeking their next mad laugh to fill life's vacuum, thrilling the mundane day with all the humor and Sun-kissed glory of straying demigods—were starting to resemble this plump fellow.

The ruddy innkeep soon returned with strong ales and hearty fare. He also handed out four little glasses half-full of brown liquid, whose scent caught Cor's attention instantly.

"Try this stuff," Skeggalt said. "Smells like the sea."

Indeed, it did, mused Cor, who'd taken the whisky and started swirling it within the glass and raised it to his nose before being bidden. Peaty. Smoky. Briny. A coastal quality. This was the sort of whisky that, in Beldria, was loved by men and hated by their wives.

"Fantastic stuff," said Celeste after a sip.

"Blagh!" Brayleigh cried at first sniff, thrusting hers toward Cor. "Why do you people do this to me? You said 'the sea,' not '*ass*'!"

The innkeep frowned.

Cor took her glass. "Good, more for me," he said. "Skeggalt, how old is this? About two decades?"

"Yep. Nineteen years." He looked surprised. "Not bad."

Cor nodded. "More complex than most at nineteen. Would've guessed older, but the peat and spirit notes are still so strong."

"You know your whisky, eh?" The big man grinned. "I'm glad it's being enjoyed." He tipped his own glass back, savoring it slowly.

"Grateful you'd share it."

"Eh. For business reasons," waved Skeggalt lightly.

Feeling deja vu, Cor wondered why this comment seemed familiar; and then, remembering, had to look away and hide a surge of feeling in a grimace.

In doing so, Cor saw Brayleigh staring at him and smiling sheepishly.

She turned to Skeggalt. "Don't worry about me. He says I'll like whisky in ten years. We'll see! But this smoked trout, this here, *this* is fantastic. Better than the Folfolds'!" She turned to Cor. "But don't tell Misses Folfold!"

"I'll try to avoid the subject," he replied.

"Well, just be careful when you're making small talk!"

"Cor? Small talk?" Deliad said. "He'll be outside, practicing swordplay, thirty seconds after his 'pleased to meet you, Mister and Misses Folfold.'"

Skeggalt was smiling, glancing once again at that wall-hung greatsword. "Where do you all hail from? Can't place your accent."

"Not surprised," said Celeste. "Far west."

"Ah," Skeggalt amiably replied. "I'd hoped it might be someplace that I'd heard of, someplace my great-grandpa went. 'Leithvask Half-Hand of Laegtheill.' So they call him now." He chuckled.

"Well-traveled guy, your grandpa?" questioned Cor.

"You haven't heard the Leithvask Saga then?" A hint of something swelled in the innkeep's voice beyond its mellow homeliness so far. "How a bandit mob waylaid his musical troupe, and only Leithvask lived? How he was saved by a dwarven caravan from Kremnospelynx, and carried wounded to Ramilabyad? How Leithvask wandered five years with the dwarves, then helped them forge a treaty with Raeqhadh's men, to fight against the Bejhbaal Oligarchy and its invading army of shaven slaves? How Khalkeus gifted him the greatsword Maerdreif, the last blade forged by a smith a century old, and, with it, Leithvask faced an Oligarch and smote him down?" He held his brawny arm toward the grievous greatsword hung above the hearth, and spoke on, brimming now with sonorous power.

"How Leithvask stood against a master of slaves alone unarmed, and caught the blade bare-handed that would have killed the Crown Prince of Raeqhadh, lost half his left hand, seized it with his right, and, with his own sword, slayed the master of slaves? How Leithvask never played the lute again? You never heard that story?" Skeggalt boomed, to four wide-eyed and closely hearkening wanderers.

"Well!" Skeggalt shrugged. And suddenly he was merely a homely innkeep once again. "You're right. You must not be from round here. Far west, eh."

"I've read a lot of stories," Celeste answered slowly, as the others searched for a response, "and heard a lot. But never one like that."

At that, the Knight-Lord and the Beldrian nodded, glancing upon that greatsword. As for Brayleigh?

"There's something that you said there. Twice," she noted, head tilted some-what sideways. "'Dwarves.'" She blinked twice. "You don't mean...? *Dwarves?*" She held a hand waist-high, then fell into a minor giggle fit.

Cor was a bit confused as well. It'd sounded like Skeggalt's tale was meant to be true one.

"About yay high," said Skeggalt, with a hand by his waist, which was rather higher than Brayleigh's.

"You farm folk never seen a dwarf or something?" said Deliad, as the western wanderers stared. "Not many in Norvester. But they're at the Academy from time to time. They roll in on their wagons, sell wares from far off Fragments, then roll out."

You think you know the world, mused Cor. *And then?*

"Dwarves!" Brayleigh cried. She looked at Cor and tittered. "Do they have beards? You think they'd let me lift them?"

"I'm not sure that's a wise idea," said Celeste. "They, um, won't see that as a humorous thing."

"Oh, I think humor's something that we *all* share! 'Making man hu-man takes a bit of hu-mor!'" sang Brayleigh blithely. "That's what Gramps would say."

"Lifting a dwarf's spirits takes a bit of . . . lifting?" suggested Cor.

"I love you, Cor!" cried Brayleigh, throwing her head back and cackling; then blinked, as her companions dumbly gaped. "I mean, I love that thing you said just now. Ha, lifting! Heehee." She delicately smoothed her red hair, batting her lashes everywhere but toward him.

That was okay with Cor, who felt he must be flushed as a feverish tomato at this point.

"So," Deliad said, still holding it together, as Skeggalt tried and failed to smoth-er a laugh and looked away, "we're not from anywhere you'd mentioned. Beldria, Fernstead, the Academy, and Norvester," he explained, pointing out each.

"Well." Skeggalt smoothed his face. "Can't say I've heard of Fernstead or Beldria. And the only academy I've heard of was the one we used to have here, back when the King and—anyway." His lips pressed. "Now, Norvester. *That's* a name I know, if only from legend. Where the First King Sigram led his Honor Guard to victory over Trollblood! Where Knight-Lord Einnskul, with his halberd Hoarthaxe, bequeathed by Yemos, felled the ogre Vaugtaur!" He grinned. "Fine tale. They tell that one in Norvester?"

"That thing is *that* old?" Brayleigh eyed the halberd leaning against the wall. "And who's this Yemos?"

"That old, yes," Deliad said. "But as for Yemos, I can't say I'm familiar." He was frowning, head tilted, at this burly, homely innkeep who seemed to know an awful lot of stories.

Skeggalt was struggling to parse their exchange. "Ha," he said finally, nodding at the halberd, "aye, maybe Hoarthaxe looked a bit like that. Though what you have there's really a bardiche, no? Not quite a halberd."

"See? It's like I said," the Knight-Lord shrugged to Cor. "As for your question," he went on, turning back to the innkeep, "yes. The tale of Mallarg Troll-blood and his horde, and how they ranged the Sightful Hills and sacked burg after burg, until the First King Sigram Lofthungrian slew him, and the Knight-Lord Einnskul smote his lieutenant with Hoarthaxe, the Vert Storm." He grasped and held aloft his storied halberd. It waxed with vert light from the flame-shaped pommel, swirling with mist, and hummed at the edge of hearing. "They tell that story. The historians do." He set his halberd back against the wall. "But, as for Yemos, I've not heard the name."

Skeggalt was staring now agape. "Your pardon," he finally said. "Strange. I've a hundred stories, many of which I put to words myself. But now there's finally one in front of me, I find I'm speechless." He surveyed the wanderers.

"No worries, that's how we feel half the time!" Brayleigh assured him.

"Speechless? You?" said Cor.

"You do the 'speechless' and I'll do the 'strange'!" she shot back blithely. "So, this Yemos. Who's he?"

"A legend, I'd have told you, till today," said Skeggalt. "But if there's a halberd Hoarthaxe, well, maybe there's a Yemos too." He shrugged.

"So there's a *legend*," Brayleigh said. "The legend of Yemos! You seem bard-like. Can you tell it?"

"More of a skald than a bard," replied Skeggalt. "And more a poem than legend. And it's more like Yemos makes a minor appearance. But," he nodded, "I can tell it. If you have time."

The rational part of Cor's mind questioned whether it'd really make sense, spending more time here, when it was noon and they still had a mountain to climb that day. But such cool calculation was blown away by a surge of warm assurance, breathing within him from somewhere beyond, that this was what they ought to do right now.

"Let's hear it," said the Beldrian.

"Oh?" He seemed pleased. "Alright then. Are we good on drinks for now? Good? Good. My grandpa used to tell me, sometimes, that I should be a skald like him. Like Half-Hand." Wistful, he smiled. "Likely too late for that now. But not too late to tell the occasional tale." He looked away to gather his wits and words.

Then, facing them, with sudden enthralling force commanded Skeggalt, "Hearken!" And he spoke:

In years of yore, the noble lords
Of Norvester, Mannus' many heirs,
Dwelt scattered on the Sveitfyl Hills,
Rivals unyielding, each his own ruler,
Subject to Eremon the Fair and Kind.
Each had his gallant Honor Guard,
Formed of his kin and fiercest kith;
Each had his bailey, each his burg;
Each had his friends and ancient feuds,
And none of them was king of Norvester.

These were fair times, and few foresaw
The coming Doom of those bright days
When Mallarg Trollblood, mightiest halfman,
Came cross the sightless wall down south,
Leading a horde of hateful orks.
They settled in the Sveitfyl Hills,
Marching past many halls of men,
Burning to nothing Benmar's Grove,

To raise rude huts and rear their broods
Upon a bare and blasted waste.

Sigram Lofthungrian, mightiest man,
Lord of Beregin, burg of the spires,
Called upon Norvester's noble lords
To band together now and banish
Their ork foes from the fatherland,
While they were few and freshly settled.
His weighty warnings went unheeded.
The other lords were loth to spend
Coin or life to confront the orks,
Who shunned men, staying in the wastes.

But Mallarg's halfmen multiplied,
Spreading across the Sveitfyl Hills.
Grim Sigram girded his defenses,
Raising a bulwark wrought from boulders,
To brace his hold and house at Beregin
Against the onslaught of the orks,
And he dispatched loyal Knight-Lord Einnskul
To muster from their fellow folk
A Hergas, skilled with sword and shield,
To turn back Mallarg's mighty tribes.

The first blood fell the fifteenth year:
Fell-hearted Trollblood, one Fall night,
Slyly submerged in Moonless gloom,
Snuck past the sentries guarding Margloth,
The stately hold of haughty Ofrik,
And, with its orks, savaged the city,
Murdered the slumbering men and babes,
Bore off maidens for beastly ends,

And set the sightly keep to flame.
Nothing remained but wrack and ruin.

Trollblood's horde struck in harvest season,
Glutting themselves on toothsome goods
Gathered by slow toil of the townsfolk.
And when this fare ran low next Fall,
That brutish horde despoiled the hold
Of ancient Argmoeth, leaving wreckage.
Sigram summoned the noble lords,
Rustholt and Ragrhug, Tol and Toadson,
Once more to meet the threat of Mallarg.
But they refused, for fear now ruled them.

The fated fray broke out next Fall,
When Mallarg Trollblood marched on Beregin,
And all its hateful host of halfmen
Swarmed about Sigram's towering bulwark
And laid siege to the stalwart burg.
From day to day, the Order of Gram
Rode out to raid the ork encampments.
Many they slew, more than they lost.
Yet Mallarg's swarm of soldiers swelled
With new reserves from orkish realms.

At last, on New Year's Noversday,
As stores ran low and snow heaped high,
Sigram gathered the Order of Gram
And Hergas of the Fellowfolk,
Raised for the fray by full-blooded Einnskul.
Seated on horseback, blazoned cape waving,
With sword held high and sky-hued eyes
Glowing with zeal and zest for battle,

Horn-helmed Sigram shouted the signal.
His forces hied toward bloody Fate.

Coursing onward, they caught the orks
Off-guard and unprepared for action,
Grimacing in the glare of Dawn
And scrambling for their scimitars.
That throng of thousands fell at first
Like rows of grain before the reaper,
Sheared from the Earth, falling in sheaves.
But Mallarg's baleful ranks were many
And soon surrounded Sigram's men,
Brandishing blades and crying curses.

Then one of Sigram's scouts slipped past
The clamorous mass of crooked halfmen,
Returning from an earlier outing,
Bearing bad tidings: Trollblood's troops,
Recently sent to amass supplies
By launching raids on local farms,
Were pouring through the Northern Pass—
A fearsome body, fresh for battle,
Doubling the force that Sigram faced,
Dooming the battered men of Beregin.

The Knight-Lord Einnskul, noble leader,
Hatched a brave plan to blunt the onslaught.
A crew of valiant cavaliers
Rushed through the orkish ranks on horseback
And rounded past them to their rear
To ambush Mallarg, mankind's menace.
But it was not to be. Vast Vaugtaur—
Guard of Trollblood, terror of men,

An ogre, strongest spawn of orks—
Stood in the path of staunch-souled Einnskul.

Dauntless Einnskul, resolved to die—
If not by Vaugtaur, then by orks
Pouring in waves from the open pass—
Rode forth to fight the fearsome ogre,
Gravely wielding his weighty halberd,
Hoarthaxe, the Vert Storm, handed down
To father Mannus, first among us,
By his brother Yemos, He who burnt
To bring us boons from the beyond—
Those sad twins, someday reunited.

A warhorn sounded from the south,
Shaking steel gear, startling the Guard,
Who turned to see the great sound's source.
Over a hilltop, hefting pikes
Whose sharp points shone with dazzling day,
Marched five hundred men in full array—
The troops of faraway Troregin,
Founded by Gothe, Mannus' third son,
In centuries past and since forgotten—
Led by a green-caped cavalier.

Sounding his horn a second time,
He pointed, and his ranks rushed onward
To plug the gap in the ork-filled pass;
And Mallarg's halfmen hastened to stop them.
Favored by Fate, concealed in chaos,
The Knight-Lord veered toward the ogre Vaugtaur,
Hoarthaxe raised high, leaning on horseback,
Homing on the fiend at full gallop,

Careening past the cluttered orks,
And stabbed it clean through at the shoulder.

The ogre roared, rearing its head,
Jerking sideways and jarring Einnskul
Off of his horse with Hoarthaxe's haft.
Pulling his polearm from the ogre,
Bold Einnskul traded blows with Vaugtaur,
Which swung its club of solid stone:
Clanging blows that cut through the clamor,
Throwing off sparks and shivering steel,
As man and ork alike looked over,
Shaken, transfixed with awe and terror.

The Knight-Lord Einnskul, worn and wearied,
Feeling his last strength flagging low,
Dashed forward for a last-ditch onslaught,
Dodging around the ogre's downswing.
Cold Vaugtaur dropped its deadly club,
Balling its steel and spiky gauntlet,
And struck the Knight-Lord in the stomach,
Impaling him. But dauntless Einnskul
Drew back the man-high halberd Hoarthaxe
And severed hapless Vaugtaur's spine.

Now furious at its falling fortunes,
Its ogre champion down and dying,
Half its troops trapped inside a valley
And fighting with a foreign army,
Mighty Mallarg made way toward Sigram,
Hacking at knights, howling a challenge
To strive with him in single combat.
And Sigram, staunch of spirit, agreed,

As orks and men, still locked in melee,
Did battle and roared and died around them.

Mallarg moved like a swirling cyclone,
Far off one moment, nigh the next,
Sweeping through foes with fearsome spear.
But Mallarg's shaft met Sigram's blade,
The greatsword Galthorn, wrought of old,
Riddled with runes with Eremon's rede.
Slash and parry, parry and slash:
The vast spear grated, and the greatsword
Threw showers of sparks that glared and fell
Like baleful Sol beneath the west.

Then Sigram stumbled, struck by a flail
Swung by an ork that stood nearby,
And Trollblood hefted high its spear
To slice in twain the staggering lord.
Fast swept the spearpoint's furrowed edge.
But fearless Sigram, faster still,
Caught in his hand the half-troll's haft;
And wielding Galthorn with one gauntlet,
Drove it dagger-like through the neck
Of Mallarg, mighty chief of halfmen.

Word spread like wildfire through the throng
That Trollblood, terror of the realm,
Lay lifeless, slain by noble Sigram.
Then horror gripped the halfmen's hearts.
They came here seeking coin and slaughter,
Not battle unto death, being cowards
Beneath their gross and brutish guise.
Those Children of the Dust dispersed,

Shedding their swords in hapless haste,
Harried by brave knights and the Hergas.

To one knee, weary Sigram sank,
Grasping great Galthorn by the hilt,
Stooping his head in silent thanks.
Then he hailed Einnskul, steadfast friend,
Standing tall, bleary-eyed and bloody;
And then he thanked that green-caped hero,
The captain of Troregin's troops,
Asking in wonder what weird chance
Had led their valiant legion here,
And what repayment they requested.

But that staunch soldier shook his head
And said they came at Cailleach's call,
So no fee would be fit or needful;
Save, should the townsfolk of Troregin
Ever face danger and destruction,
He bade that Norvester fight beside them.
His booming horn, he handed Einnskul,
A symbol of the two burgs' bond.
And then he rode off with his ranks,
The breeze and sunset at his back.

Hearing of Sigram's heroism,
The noble lords of war-worn Norvester
Called him their King and Lord of Lords,
The savior of the Sveitfyl Hills.
They built a new burg in the northwest,
A fearsome fortress, huge and hardy,
Where Sigram's kin still reign as kings;
And now, loyal lords, still prone to squabble,

When faced with foreign troops, forestall
All feuds to fight the Kingdom's foes.

The story stopped. It took a couple seconds for Cor to come back from those bygone days to Skeggalt's inn in Laegtheill.

The innkeep bowed.

Brayleigh began to clap, then Cor and Celeste. Last was the Knight-Lord, looking lost in thought.

"Bravo! That wasn't boring in the slightest!" said Brayleigh. "Gramps should take a lesson from you."

"High praise," smiled Skeggalt. "What I know, I learnt from my 'Gramps.' Glad I still recall it, really. Don't think he wrote it down. I know I haven't."

"You'll have to teach your own kids too!" she said.

He chuckled. "Not sure I'll have kids to teach."

"You said you knew a hundred stories, right?" said Celeste. "Any stories of the Warlock? On Heron Summit?"

Skeggalt's face went dark. "The 'Warlock.' Eh. They take away the old words and tell you that the new ones are the true ones. What's history but the winners' favorite story?"

The wanderers stared. Cor started to open his mouth.

"Man doesn't know what to make of such things," Skeggalt continued, cutting off the Beldrian. "Probably best not to try. Just live our lives, don't get too close to where the rules are made, and we'll make do the same as always, right? They say we're equals. Maybe we should thank them."

He shook his head as though to purge the pondering. "Anyway. Yes, they say the Warlock lurks on Heron Summit; that he has his lair there; that, there, he plots against the people of Lioss; that when a merchant wagon disappears en route to Lioss, it's likely as not the Warlock who made it disappear. All sorts of stories." He shrugged. "The truth is, no one scales the Summit, not even the miners. Who knows if he's up there?"

"Is there a safe path up the peak?" asked Cor.

Skeggalt's brow raised. "If what you want is safety, I would suggest you not seek out the Warlock. Then again," he went on, glancing at Hoarthaxe, "I get the sense you know what you're about. The old mining road is safe enough. You'll make it most of the way on that. What's left will likely be snowy, icy and slow. Might see some cougars. But what's a cat for folk who seek the Warlock?" he mused, one big hand resting on his belt.

The Beldrian's gaze, again, flicked to that buckle. *Probably could forge half a gauntlet from that thing.* One that could fit even those hands, thick with sinew even after decades of domestic work.

Another world, another life, and Skeggalt—this mild and mellow innkeep—might have been a man who wore such dread gear. Gauntlets. Mail. Maybe a greatsword, like that eight-pound monster hanging above the hearth. That martial life would fit him, and he'd fit within that life: a steel-girt skald; a man of arms and song.

Here, he was merely a man a bit too big for his surroundings, bursting at the seams that modern life had sewn for men like him. And all that held together his homely outfit—holding him in too tight to burst right through it and seek some steel-girt life—was one steel buckle.

Cor turned away, before the big man wondered what he was ogling, toward a nearby window, where noon's gold gleamed and streamed upon the wanderers.

And now he couldn't help but call to mind that gleaming buckle of gold on Morty's belt. *"I'm fifty-five. My boys are grown. Why not? I say, why not?"* he'd happily justified his recent purchase, as the two Volucres had marveled at the master craftsmanship.

Happily, he'd thought. Had he been wrong about that?

"You with us, Cor?" called Brayleigh from afar.

He blinked. *No, not afar.* He'd just been brooding.

"You gonna gulp that swill before we go?" continued Brayleigh, tapping at his cup.

"This fine elixir? This distilled ambrosia? What do you think?" The Beldrian downed his third dram. Then, he was promptly back to savoring this world.

They left for Heron Summit somewhat later than they had hoped, but none of them regretted the lost time. *"Near the northern end of Laegtheill,"* Skeggalt had said before they'd left, *"you'll find a trail of trampled grass. Just follow that around a few ponds, through a little forest, and it becomes the miners' trail before long.*" And so they did, emerging from a fir grove, strewn thick with shadow and needles, and finding the mountain's rocky majesty before them, with one thin pathway winding toward the peak.

The trail was lazy, wending left and right without much incline. *Likely for the wagons that miners have to take up here,* mused Cor. The climbing here was easy enough to fan out beyond the beaten trail and search for signs of habitation as they went.

They found the sorts of things that chilly northern forests often have—bluish moss, dark stones and mushroomed trees, brooks hidden by brush and mini-waterfalls, and stony outcrops splotched with lichenous turquoise—but nothing hinting at a human's home, much less a Warlock's lair. Being Noversday, they didn't even encounter a single miner or lumberjack. A sudden flash to their fore was merely a mountain goat, whose shaggy coat caught a stray ray of sunlight as it leapt from little cliff to cliff. Some grey-black squirrels, and one albino squirrel half-hidden by snow, and multitudes of branch-bound musical birds were all the wanderers saw as they ascended.

Until, that is, they reached a sunlit river cascading down some spaced-out rocky cliffs. There, wading through the rippling water, staring and swiping sometimes at the foamy currents, stood what was, by far, the biggest of bears he'd ever seen. Its head was strangely round; its limbs were also burly unto roundness. It looked like it could idly bash a tree down. But now it was engaged in swatting salmon from underwater onto a pebbly shoal.

"Is that thing dangerous?" Celeste asked. "Looks slow. And cute."

"Not slow!" said Brayleigh. "And it looks cute, maybe, but only till it bops your brains out and eats them."

Celeste blinked.

"And clever too," said Cor. "When I was camping once, we hung a bag down from a tree branch on a rope. A bear climbed up there, cut the rope, clawed open the bag, and ate our food while we were sleeping." Vilhyg had picked a clearing by a brook to pitch camp on that hike through Launlaufs Wood. It had felt strange, at only age fourteen, wondering what would've happened if the bear had sought its food inside the tents instead.

"You think the bear would follow us from behind?" the Knight-Lord questioned. "Smell our food or something?"

"He might," agreed Cor.

"Just keep going," said Brayleigh. "He's busy fishing! He won't bother us."

"He's hungry then," said Cor. "You want *that* beast hungry behind you?"

"Well said," nodded Deliad. "It's like they say: 'Don't turn your back on danger.' 'The future's for the ones who face it first.'"

"Agreed. We have to attack."

"You're faster, Cor. Go left and get it lumbering. I'll flash in from the left flank."

"Good call. Let's go." With a fistbump, the Knight-Lord and the Honorary Knight started with bared steel toward the ursine hulk.

"*Absolutely* not," Brayleigh forbade, hands on her hips.

The pair of warriors paused, then looked to Celeste.

Celeste shook her head, without quite holding back her smile.

"Alright." Cor glumly scabbarded his Beldrian blade. "Guess we can cut through the brush over there. Avoid the bear, try not to get too close. Deliad, you want to hack through with your axe? Don't want to dent a good sword doing grunt work."

"Oh, for the love of Eremon—" Deliad started; then, spun and pointed. "See, here, how they turn us against each other? Here we were, best friends, just hunting bears together. Then, like *that*, we're fighting over weapons—once again!—rather than fighting a colossal kodiak."

"You're right," mused Cor. "A fight. Some fun. Some fresh meat."

"Yes! Life is simple for us simple men."

Brayleigh and Celeste shared a glance and giggled.

"Get going, boys," chid the teenage girl from Fernstead.

They plodded on a few more hours and reached a large pond, glimmering red-gold as its ripples, brushed by a lilting breeze, caught sinking Sol.

"Quite a view," Deliad said.

The water stopped just shy of a cliff. Beyond it could be seen the spires and arches of the Liossian palace, swathed in a mist of distance laced with dew.

Around the other side of the aureate pond wended the mining pathway. There walked Celeste, absently viewing the watery vista.

She suddenly halted, holding up a finger.

"Celeste, what—?" started Brayleigh to her rear; then, stopped, following Celeste's finger upward.

A heron, circling through the blue serene, was diving toward the pond. Its silhouette fleetly darkened the day-Moon shimmering on the water. Plummeting toward the pool with talons out, it snatched the surface of the water, spraying droplets and foam, and seizing something silver, which—after an instant's stillness—started flopping wildly and futilely aloft the windy evening.

Beating its dripping wings, the great blue heron aspired in helices unto the empyrean and soared away, in moments merely a form of flapping dark against the waning day.

"Huh. Neat!" the girl from Fernstead said. "Imagine: just glubbing, swishing through your pond; then, *yoink!*"

Celeste was smiling skyward like a child, heedless of gusts disheveling hair astray to strands of gold across her farflung gaze; or maybe like the mother of such a child.

Cor slightly shook his head and faced the path.

Dusk had begun to chill the quiet heights before they reached the tree line. There, the hoarfrost hung thick upon the dwindling boughs and bushes. Beyond that last life, raw rock cropped and jutted redoubtably, dusted with snow and glazed with ice, which gleamed with Luna's waxing glow.

"Call it a night?" said Cor. He held a hand toward a little crevice in the mountainside. "Camp here? Some shelter from the wind at least."

The others nodded. Night was not the time to start their struggle through the coming snowdrifts, slipping and scrabbling upward on the slick stone, to a dangerous destination only half-known.

They gathered brush and deadwood for a fire. A few times, Deliad lazily tossed his dirk at a lone fir. Every time, it struck and stuck.

"Planning a rematch with Loginos?" Cor asked, as he retrieved his dagger.

Deliad's lips curved. "At night, we used to throw knives at the garrison. For hours and hours. No cards or dice allowed, but knives? They turned a blind eye. I got good." He seized the dirk and sharply tugged it out. "But not quite at Loginos' level yet." He whirled and whipped it at a bare white birch some twenty yards away. It struck and stuck.

Within a half hour, they were hunched around a campfire, eating heavy rye and cheese from The Singing Sword. As gloaming's mirky grey gave way to moonlit blue, the group discussed the last few days: Lioss' phantastic statues and dream-like spires; the story Skeggalt told them; this whole wide mist-and-water-dappled land; and what a wonder it was that they were *there*, by way of air, within this farflung Fragment.

Somnus was stalking at their slouching backs before long, as they leaned in toward a fire now smoldering faint, and no one was inclined to scrounge for more wood. So, they laid out blankets across this modest crevice in the mount. And, huddled close against each other and Earth, sheltered from howling winds, they watched blue Heaven, where Wandering Stars spoke silently and lightly of times to come; or so, at least, it seemed, as sense and senses dwindled into dream.

CHAPTER 33

When they awoke, and Sol's first feeble glow was glinting on the lake-beriddled landscape, the Gloamy One was smoldering in the west; and waxing toward that fugitive gloom was Luna, square overhead beneath the balanced Scales.

"I love it up here!" Brayleigh yawned and stretched, peering upon some berries fraught with hoarfrost, sparkling at once with light of day and night. "So beautiful! I feel like I'm an ice queen!" She picked a sprig and stuck it in her hair.

The sentiment didn't last. Five minutes later, climbing a sloping outcrop, Brayleigh slipped on black ice, so her feet abruptly flew forth, and, blinking, slid back ten yards on her bum; as Deliad, barely dodging, had to dive into a bush. She thudded into a snowdrift.

"Ouch. You okay?" called fleetfoot Cor from higher up. He had been scampering rock to rock with ease, scarcely slowing except to wait for the others.

"Oof!" Freckled Brayleigh frowned and rubbed her rear. "That'll be purple! Just the right side though." She turned and tugged her pants to check for purple.

Deliad sighed, still disentangling himself from briary branches; then, began to brush a thousand burrs out from his nice new coat.

"Yep, just the right side! I'm a half-Moon back here," mused Brayleigh. "Cor, you had a bruise this big?" She noticed burr-strewn Deliad. "Ha! I'm sorry."

"So sad. That instant," Deliad said, "when suddenly, upon a glorious Winter's walk, you slip. What else so good so quickly turns so bad?" He picked another thorn out from his coat.

"Swallowing cask-strength whisky down the wrong pipe?" suggested Cor.

"Touché, my drunkard friend."

"It ruins the next half hour," recalled the Beldrian.

"The right pipe hurts enough, forget the wrong one!" Brayleigh declared, still patting at her bum. "Ruins more than just a half hour. And it stinks!"

"You'll come around," waved Cor. "Just take it slow."

Celeste, coughing, couldn't quite keep her face straight.

The four resumed their climbing. From the rear, she watched the pair of youths, progressing upward along the winding, shining path. She smiled. They *were* a great pair. Two peas in a pod.

What made it even more charming was the way they seemed intent to keep that close connection implicit—hesitating even to hold hands, or hug each other as companions hug—till Fate's own hand had flung aloft the veil between them, baring beauty in the flesh. When longing hands would seize what'd loomed for so long, just beyond reach, with ravishing abandon.

Too many romance novels. Celeste smiled. Still, she would try to help along the hand of Fate and spare that pair from too much waiting.

Needless to say, progress was slow that day, and slower as they climbed higher. Howling Boreas battered the slope with hail and snow-laced squalls by noontide, and blew angrier still by evening. If they'd have flown up here aboard the ship, the ladder would've likely been blown sideways on disembarking. If they hadn't crashed first. Still, more than once, that cozy heated lounge came wafting fondly into Celeste's memory, as air and bone alike chilled more each hour.

No relief came when they had reached the summit. The rock was strangely bare here, after hours of trudging upward ankle-deep in snow. The gales screamed by so savagely up here that snowflakes couldn't stick. They blew from one way, and then another and another, shifting as wildly as a madman's accusations against the world.

Yes, they had reached the summit, and there was nothing: no tower, no door, no stairs. Just stone and stony outcrops and an icestorm.

The wanderers stared upon the windswept summit, then one another, then that desolation.

She wasn't sure what she had been expecting. *A sign? "The Warlock's Lair. Please watch your step"?* She grimly smirked against the wayward gusts.

"So, what now?" questioned Brayleigh after a silence, hunching and huddling in her fur-lined coat.

"Let's look around a little," Celeste said. "We came this whole way. Where next if not here?"

The wanderers shared a glance, squinting against the hail-laced winds, and shrugged. They may as well.

They strode around the summit for a half hour, scouring each crag and outcrop for anomalies: a loose rock, or a lever, or a trap door. *Yes, far too many novels,* she thought sadly. They had to hold gloved hands before their eyes and bow their heads as they explored, to keep the icy-daggered squalls from stabbing them. Now, evening's blue was dwindling dusky grey.

"We ought to head out now. There's nothing here," yelled Deliad over roaring winds. "It's near Dusk. We'll need to find a place to camp by nightfall."

Yes, that'd be prudent. Not much shelter this high, beyond the treeline. And with winds like these, sleeping beneath the Stars was not an option.

"They say the Warlock lurks on Heron Summit," Skeggalt had said. She'd thought that meant the top. But Heron Summit *was* the mountain's name; not just its top. The Warlock might be hiding in any of ten thousand craggy acres across the slope, far from the miners' trail. Assuming the innkeep's rumor even was right.

Lost in musing, she meandered toward an outcrop she'd searched at least three times and leaned in toward it.

Cor answered Deliad with a half-heard shout.

"What's that?" the Knight-Lord called back, glancing backward into a sleety billow. "Wind here's—" Suddenly, he cut off, cursing, tilting down his head and rubbing at his right eye with a gloved hand.

"What?" Brayleigh yelled.

"Don't mind me. I'm just blind now."

"Cor!" Celeste called. Her heart was fluttering wildly. "Come here!"

He shuffled over, hand held over his eyes to block the hail. "See something here?"

"Yes," Celeste said. "Something that isn't here." At Cor's confused blink, she held out a hand to touch the furrowed crag that she was facing, ran it along the surface—then, slid through it, vanishing under the image of the stone.

She spun to Cor and smiled. "See that? Come closer. There's some strange barrier just beyond the illusion. Smooth. Not as hard as stone." She pressed against it. "I think he hid it underneath the image. I think that it's"—the firmness she could feel there suddenly gave way as Cor came near—"the ward."

She happily waved her whole arm through it now. "Your Wardstone. See? It's like the Archanimist said."

"Huh." Cor now tried it, reaching out to touch it and passing through. "Wow. Nice work." He waved over the others. "How in the world did you find this?"

"I—walked right up and found it, I suppose. I'm not sure." Celeste blinked and tried to think back. But nothing came, except a sense that the answer was sparkling from a darkling place past sensing.

"Well, onward then! To the unknown!" cried Brayleigh.

Into that yawning gap—concealed from sense yet beckoning thence, unsealed by an intuition past reckoning and cognition—went the wanderers. Against the gloom within, they wielded Fossils, remnants of Powers fled long ago, whose glow lived on past death. And vision stole their breath.

Down from the summit wound a slender way of dark grey, plummeting from fading day atop a snow-strewn mountain crowned with clouds and grading steep into the earthbound deep. Along the walls flowed veins of shadowy blue, imbued with Fossils' glow, leading their view down, down, where the stalactites daggered low, shading the underground, which soon withdrew to a rockbound shadows-cape. So, slowly wading by a newfound way into pervading dark, bearing fey sparks in hands and hearts to guide them, glaring inside them, they dared the stark depths.

After a while of winding, their descent smoothed out to a straight way forward, wide and open; where, pausing, Celeste peered ahead at how the shadows gathered on the edge of light. *Lovely.* She idly wondered why she'd stopped.

"What's up?" called Brayleigh, dispelling the silence. "We stopping?"

"Not a bad idea," said Deliad, "to get some rest. They say this Warlock's dangerous. I doubt we're at our best now. I know I'm not."

They looked at one another. Lashing winds had left them ruffle-haired and ruddy-cheeked, eyes bloodshot with the battering of the hail. It'd been a long day, climbing Dawn to Dusk. Brayleigh was droopy-eyed. Even Deliad now was leaning wearily on the cavern wall.

"Well, sounds like we should stop a while," said Cor. "A full night's rest? We'll want to be at full strength."

"But what if he comes up here while we're sleeping?" said Brayleigh. "We don't want *him* to surprise *us.*"

"We'll rest two hours." This flowed from Celeste's lips before the words had registered within her. "And then move on." She wondered where the words had come from, borne without her on a breath of warm assurance, swelling as she spoke.

The others blinked at her but, after a second, nodded assent.

"It's not a bad idea," affirmed the Knight-Lord. "We'll attack at night. Surprise the Warlock. Meanwhile, we'll be rested."

It *did* make sense, supposed the former orator. But none of that had been what made her speak.

Shaking the delphic haze out from her head, she focused on the moment. "Let's lay out blankets. Get some good rest in, make the most of two hours. And we can leave them here for when we get back. Won't want to fight the Warlock with our packs on."

"Fair points. I think I'll have a bite," yawned Deliad, digging some cheese out. "Whets the appetite, climbing."

"Fair points," said Cor. "I think I'll whet my sword."

"That there's the difference between us," mused Deliad, while munching on a mouthful of some bleu.

"Twenty-five pounds?"

"Touché, my lanky friend."

Brayleigh, meanwhile, was looking back, then forward, a finger to her lips. She turned and tiptoed back toward the winding way that'd led them here.

Cor looked at her. "You headed somewhere, Brayleigh?"

"Yes! Doing some business. Not *your* business, Mister."

Cor blushed and faced directly away from Brayleigh.

Celeste again felt her lips curving upward. *Peas in a pod.* Well, not quite. *Like a flame dancing atop her wick.*

Amid her musing, an inspiration flashed inside her. *Perfect!* She'd help along the hand of Fate right now!

She laid her blanket out beside one wall; then Deliad's, several yards away from hers; then Cor's, behind a cluster of stalagmites, half-hiding what was on the other side.

Now, where was Brayleigh's bag? She scanned about, as Deliad downed the last bite of his bleu, and Cor, whetstone in hand, sat on his blanket.

Aha! She'd set it in a shadowy crevice.

Celeste grabbed Brayleigh's blanket from inside and started back toward that stalagmite cluster, where Cor was peering down, sharpening his sword, facing away from her.

She strolled up quietly and started laying Brayleigh's blanket out behind those same stalagmites, maybe a yard from Cor. *Not too too close. Just close enough for outstretched hands to accidentally touch.*

She smiled. Yes, far too many romance novels!

"Suppose I'll 'do some business' of my own," Deliad declared and ambled out of sight.

She smoothed the blanket out, as Cor, oblivious, whetted his sword. A scraping little shriek accompanied each tug. She crawled across the blanket and began to smooth its far side, kneeling beside it and kneading its folds.

Yawning, the Beldrian set his blade aside and, stretching, leaned back—into Celeste's hair.

Startled and jerking his head from this strangeness, he fell into her lap.

She blinked; he blinked.

Her fair hair fell across his wide-eyed face, illumined by the faint gold of his Fossil.

"Should I go turn the lights off?" Brayleigh cried behind her.

Celeste stumbled to her feet and faced the girl from Fernstead—five yards off and red with the radiance of her blooddrop Fossil—as Cor coughed something unintelligible, swiveling from Brayleigh to Celeste and back.

"Hey! Um," said Celeste, "I've laid out the blankets. So, definitely, if you want some sleep, let's put away these lights. Here, you're right here. Just smoothed it out, it should be nice. Um, good night. You need me, I'll be yonder." Celeste pointed and wondered what exactly she was babbling; then, walked with wide eyes toward her far off blankets.

What have I done!

She sat upon the softness and felt the stony hardness underneath, feeling as coarse as the wall she was facing. As always, her attempts to make life better for those around her had abjectly backfired. *Should I explain? Or would it make it worse?*

"Oops. Gotta grab something," Brayleigh announced. "Now where's that bag?" Her footsteps crossed the cave. "Ah!" Shuffling sounds; then, footsteps, coming closer.

A finger tapped her shoulder. Celeste looked up and, by the faint sheen of her Star-shaped Fossil, half-buried under blankets, she saw Brayleigh.

The girl from Fernstead grabbed her hand in hers. She squeezed it softly, smiling down at Celeste. She leaned in, moist-eyed, and her lips moved: *Thank you!*

Celeste's own mouth fell open. Before she found words, however, Brayleigh had walked away. "I found it!" she called, and disappeared behind stalagmites.

The whetting sounds from Cor's sword promptly ceased.

Lying on her side, cheek to the floor, she felt a little tear slide down her smiling face. She shut her eyes and let the world's weight loose, floating away like a feather in an updraft.

The last she heard was Deliad's distant voice: "I leave *five minutes* and you turn the lights out? Leave me to stumble here half-blind? You hiding some funny business? Hmph." He yawned at length; and, ere it ended, she had slipped away, where this world's sounds are muted in the Mists.

When she awoke, through slightly parted eyelids she seemed to see Dawn's rosy fingers spreading. But it was just the flush of Brayleigh's Fossil, ruddying the faces of the rising wanderers.

The teenage girl was standing tall and stretching, a big smile on her freckled face. "Good morning! Well, no. Not morning. Also, ouch." She looked back and patted at her backside. "That sure smarts! From when I tripped." She tugged her pants and peered in.

"'It's not a trip without some tripping,'" Cor said.

Brayleigh blinked, head tilted, meeting his gaze; then, giggled. Eying him for a little longer, she shared a secret smile.

Well, not quite secret. Celeste was happy. *Well done, hand of Fate.*

They left their bags and blankets strewn about. They wouldn't want their backpacks in a battle. And they would have to come back anyway.

So, they continued on their chthonic quest, led by the light of Fossils held in hand: first forward, then resuming their descent down winding eldritch ways toward hope and hazard. They went what felt like miles, though maybe shorter, since they were walking slowly in the rough gloom. Delving deeper, they watched the shadowy blue along the walls blaze ever wider and brighter, till there was more azure than grimy grey. It almost looked now like the palace walls of Lioss, though hewn by a harsher and wilder hand. Rapt with the mingling mirk and fugitive glimmers, they felt they were descending into a dream.

Rounding a bend, their roving through the gloom ended abruptly in a room.

A den, really. Not like a lion's den or a thieves' den. A cozy chamber, quaint even. With a fireplace! Dancing with *flames!*

Beside it sat a chair and table, both with legs of barley twist and leafy wood-work. On the tabletop lay two tomes bound in leather and a candle, unlit and unrequired amid the hearthlight. A claw-foot bookshelf stood against the far wall, stuffed end-to-end with volumes old and faded.

"We rested on a cave floor?" Brayleigh cried. "When this was here?"

"I thought it worked out well," Cor murmured.

She blinked up at him, then beamed.

Absently, Celeste wondered what a Warlock would read. She squinted at that brimming bookshelf. *"Heron Eyes,"* Clausiglade had called her at age ten, after she'd read him a calendar entry from ten yards off. Yet she was having trouble reading the script upon these volumes' spines. *I've gotten older, I suppose.* She sighed.

"Much as I'd like to lie down by the fireplace," said Deliad, "I don't think we ought to do that, given that *someone* lit it."

"Yes, yes, yes," waved Brayleigh, ambling onward toward the hearth. "I'll keep an eye out as I'm warming up—"

"Stop!" Celeste cried and grabbed the girl from Fernstead, yanking her back. "Something's not right." She stared at the cozy room as the others stared at her. She squinted, hoping that the sight would shimmer, or that she'd find a single shadow missing, or *something*. But it kept on looking cozy.

"Um." Brayleigh eyed the hand upon her shoulder, as Celeste glared upon the goodly scene.

Shaking her head, she reached and grabbed a stone and flung it forth. It clinked against a vase and fell, spinning upon the floor, then stopping.

"Checking for traps. Good call." Cor nodded at her. "Let's watch our step." He started forth again.

"No!" Celeste seized his palm and pulled him backward.

Tilting his head, he turned and looked at her.

She shook her head. "It's—it's—" She shut her eyes. The dreadful intimation seeping through her blent with frustration at their blank surprise.

Specks of grey light were swirling under her eyelids, which now were scrunched tight. Up went Celeste's hand as though to fend off something from her face. Words foreign but familiar swelled within her: perfect words, sounding like the things they meant. She'd faintly felt this, sometimes, reading Eldscript, but this was many times as much; so much that word and world mixed weirdly into one.

That fleet perfection flowed from Celeste's lips. And, as she spoke, her hand swung left to right, as though to sweep some foul fumes from the air, and fading flecks of stardust fell beneath it.

Wobbling, the den blinked out.

Where it had stood, there now was an abyss. A rampant darkness hung overtop and hid its bottom. If, that is, there was a bottom.

Cor was gaping. He eyed his feet, about a foot from the edge.

"Celeste, I think it's fair to say," he mused finally, "that you no longer owe us one."

She giggled softly. She felt somewhat giddy.

"Could you move back a couple steps, Cor? Thanks," said Brayleigh. "As for you, *how* did you do that?"

Celeste smiled weakly. "How do you make Boundaries?"

"Well, that's like asking how I move my hand. I just . . . hm. Okay."

Running by the abyss was a slender ledge; not altogether unlike that little walkway in the cave by Beldria described by Cor, where he had lost his light, but ultimately found the Element Dievas.

Backs to the wall, they shuffled past the pit—"No bats, at least," the Beldrian muttered quietly—and soon were wandering down another corridor.

"You'll warn us, won't you Celeste," Brayleigh asked, halting abruptly and turning to face her, "if we're about to walk into a hidden hole? If there's a first, then there's a second, right?"

"I'll do my best," said Celeste.

Deliad paused, then let the Beldrian pass and take the lead.

"Thanks, friend," said Cor.

"Never denied you're nimbler! Swiftness of youth and such. You hit a pit, you might just make it. Me, I'm tumbling in."

They walked a while before they reached the next room: an antechamber, judging by the rows of columns leading toward the double doors upon the far wall, big and iron-banded. Tall and spaced out, the columns—twelve in total—had grotesque gargoyles wrapped around them, wrinkled with agony and loathing.

"Nice decor," mused Deliad. "Makes a stranger feel at home."

"They look so sad though!" Brayleigh strolled toward one beast and patted at its horny pate. "There, there! You're stone. And ugly. But it could be worse!"

Deliad was studying the double doors' seam. He leaned and squinted, shoved at them, then nodded. "Locked. Looks like we have no choice." He drew Hoarthaxe; then, faced the doors and breathed: deep out, deep in.

"'No choice,'" scoffed Brayleigh. "Look how happy *he* is, Sir Knight-Lord, with his halberd and his 'no choice'!"

"Be ready," said the Beldrian, blade in hand. "The Warlock might be waiting past that doorway."

They nodded.

And the Knight-Lord raised his halberd and drew a deep breath, as a manly flush blossomed upon his tress-tost cheeks and brow. Then, dashing forth, vast Hoarthaxe vert and thrumming, he brought the huge blade down, wind whistling from it, to split the seam betwixt the double doors.

A huge clang split the air instead. And Deliad, shuddering in synch with the deafening resonance, stumbled back several steps. He blinked and stared, silent mid clangor, at the unscratched wood.

Brayleigh threw back her head and cackled crazily. "Oh, thank the Fates! Thank Flua-Sahng for this moment!" As shock and lingering shivers slowly faded from Deliad's reeling frame, she kept on laughing.

The Knight-Lord's forehead furrow turned to a sigh. He grimly peered upon his ancient polearm.

"Alas, we have no choice," Brayleigh intoned, trying for a manly bass and managing a baritone. "No choice but manly brute force! It falls to *me!*" She raised a huge air halberd; then, fell into another cackle fit.

"Alright. It falls to you," Deliad declared. He held out Hoarthaxe. "All yours. Have a go!"

"Oh, that's okay, I know I'm not as mighty as Knight-Lord Deliad," sang mercurial Brayleigh. "Maybe I'll try doing something else instead." She closed her eyes and held a hand up, red with radiance, and her lips fell faintly apart. "For instance, what if this door had a doorknob on the other side? Or, better yet: a lever?" She flicked her hand. They heard a solid *click* from beyond the door. She beamed.

The Knight-Lord grumbled.

Nothing happened. She tried the door, smile fading to find it still was sealed, then tried to pull it. "And . . . presto?"

Dull cracks of fracturing rocks broke out abruptly.

Brayleigh leaned in close and squinted at the door, then at the ceiling, as cracking echoed through the ante-cavern. "Um. Should we—?"

Cor whirled backward, sword outstretched, whirring just inches from Celeste's wide gaze.

Gasping, she stepped back a split-second later and, as she did so, heard steel clang on stone.

Snarling before the Beldrian—grey and grisly, with wrinkled sneer and stubby horns and sharp claws, and batlike wings, and one arm dented deep and hanging limp and gimp-like—was a gargoyle. It lashed out with its left claw, fast and fierce.

Already rapt with martial instinct, Cor, pivoting right, parried it with a quick swat, catching the gargoyle just above the wrist, then jabbed it clean through at the solar plexus.

It jerked back, grabbed the blade and shoved it out. Face snarling further, it renewed its onslaught, apparently unfazed to have a new hole.

She barely got her bearings soon enough to dodge back from a second gargoyle's swipe—it'd snuck up from the chamber's other side—and, as her foot caught stone, stumbled and fell.

The world went slow as Celeste sank toward hard rock. One hand she threw back, and the other forward, abruptly immersed in mists of Starlike hue; which, as she fell back, formed a ball of flame, blazing like Luna seen through a squinting gaze.

It rushed out from her right hand toward the gargoyle just as her left had hit the ground and, gasping a windy wail out, burst against its breast.

And suddenly life and strife were back at full speed, and impact pain was shooting from her tailbone into her back. Her enemy spun aside, arm raised above its chest. But she could see that much of its lithic torso had been melted, like it were snow that'd been splashed with hot water. Its portly core was rather more concave now.

She tried to scramble backward on her back and climb to her feet, but hit a big stalagmite and halted halfway through.

Now diving toward her, the gargoyle had its clawed hand raised and ready, just feet away, to rake and gouge her face. Glee wrinkled its repugnant visage.

Flattening, that face showed brief shock, then was flying backward, launched by a half-seen plane of shimmering red. Clunking the far wall, it clattered to the Earth.

As Cor and Brayleigh, back to back, fought off their animated foes with blade and Boundary, Deliad was struggling. While a man-high halberd might be a fearsome thing, it didn't mix well with man-high ceilings or with crowded caves. In short, he'd not yet stricken a single blow.

So, he looked almost pleased to see another stone gargoyle, wrapped around a column, cracking and loosening, as its frozen stare turned to a hot glare, and pebbles crumbled from its curling claws. He stepped forth, Hoarthaxe thrumming in his hands and grim joy on his face as he drew nigh, ready to welcome it from stony immurement with an abrupt beheading, headsman-style. He drew his huge blade back and bared his teeth.

Brayleigh's head leaned in the path of his axe head: a swish of red hair, followed by a green glare.

He halted just in time, his muscles straining to stop the dread momentum of his halberd. A second passed.

And *now* he had his opening, as the malevolent thing snarled into motion; but not quite long enough to launch a full blow. He thrust the hilt of Hoarthaxe at its breast, bopping it backward a few stumbling yards, but doing no damage to the rock-ribbed beast.

Celeste had finally clambered to her feet. Scanning the cave, finding a gargoyle dashing at Deliad's rear, its razor claws held high, something rushed into her. She found her hand was being borne upward by that spirited swelling. And from her fingers spiraled thirty flares, burning as coolly as Luna aloft blue night, across the cave and into the enemy's eyes.

It hissed, and bits of sneering visage hissed steamily out of existence on impact, each little Moonflame canceling out some stone. When, hearing this, the Knight-Lord spun to face it, its face was like the innards of a cracked rock. And then its leg was too, as Hoarthaxe hewed right through that lithic limb and smote the other. Down to the ground collapsed the lamed grotesque, kicking in futile circles on the floor.

Another gargoyle now was scampering toward her on all fours, webbed wings spreading over its back as it bounded. But the Beldrian intercepted her would-be assailant with a shining blade. It entered through the nape of the enemy's neck, emerged from the Adam's apple—and at once was loosed as that stone body crumbled to bits. Within a blink, all that remained was rubble.

Lionlike within the same blink bounded Cor toward his next prey, which was slouching as it shuffled toward Brayleigh. With his blade stretched wide and pawlike, he swiped its haunch, catching it with the sharp tip, and clawed deep. Down the snarling monster tumbled and slid across the floor; but ere it stopped, Cor struck again, now slicing off its shins.

He whirled to face a gargoyle to his flank. But, as he started his attack, a Boundary, flashing red, blasted the beast from its feet and into a strew of stony legs and arms with one of its brethren.

Meanwhile, on the floor, the one without lower legs had heaved itself atop its stubs and now was scuttling cruelly toward Cor, leaning upon its palms and pushing aloft and, each time, landing slightly nearer. Loathing twisted its visage as it hobbled.

Celeste's lips parted to warn her companion. But, as she did so, it abruptly crumbled and plopped into a rock pile. And its last swipe at futile nothing sent a broken-off claw skittering ahead. It struck the Beldrian's boot sole just as he landed, so his heel rolled sideways, and—rarity of rarities—fleetfoot Cor stumbled.

As he lurched sidelong, a foe sliced his forearm, leaving a red line. It readied another quick cut. But Cor was quicker, kicking out and sending the enemy tripping over its heels.

Sprinting toward Deliad was another statue, beating its batlike wings to build up speed, with mouth maniacally wide and fangs full-bared.

Grinning darkly, Deliad held Hoarthaxe high and gauged the gargoyle's speed, timing his strike. And when the time came, savagely he struck.

But unseen in the shadows overhead was a stalactite; which his halberd severed, but glanced off somewhat. So, instead of shattering his enemy's skull outright, he gouged its shoulder.

Down plummeted the stalactite, bruising Deliad's own shoulder.

Hardly slowing, his opponent pounced with its arms out and wrapped itself round him, furiously slashing with claws and spiked elbows, a ball of lithic fury. Deliad's breastplate screeched protests as its sheen was pierced and scratched.

Grabbing its face in a gauntlet, he shouted and shoved. Its neck bent backward, but it clutched hold of Hoarthaxe as it started stumbling back, just as the Knight-Lord seized the haft to attack. It yanked itself back toward him, wailing wildly upon his breastplate with its piercing claws.

Furious, he dropped his halberd, balled his fist, and, holding it at arm's length with his left hand, he socked the gargoyle squarely in the face.

This time, its neck bent back ninety degrees and stayed that way. It stepped, then stutter-stepped to catch itself, confused; then, promptly crumbled to a pile of rubble.

Now, more beasts were cracking loose from their columns, shedding dust and stone bits, testing their limbs and louring at the wanderers.

One of them looked at her and leered, and neared her, first with slow steps, then bounding fast abruptly.

Palm flashing forth, she sent another spiral of blue flares burning toward it. But they missed, save for a few fires that caught its right shoulder and narrowed it a bit.

It didn't slow. It pounced, wings beating, with its claws outstretched.

Celeste inhaled and winced and threw her arms up.

Suddenly a gauntlet had shot out in front of the gargoyle's neck, clotheslining her attacker. Its top half halted as its legs flew forward. And down it plopped, as Deliad closed his fist and darkly smirked. The gargoyle snarled and rose. But, in a flash, a shimmering wall was blasting its reeling frame across the ante-cavern; where, disengaging briefly from his foe, Cor cleaved its face in two, and then kept fighting.

It's always me. She sighed and looked away.

And there were two more gargoyles, sprinting toward her and merely a second off.

She felt herself whirl toward them, felt her tousled hair sweep over her eyes, and felt them narrow on these things: gross, lifeless, growling enemies of life, seeking some prey. She felt her lips curve up; for, underneath that stony frame, she sensed the convoluted circuitry of Spirit that animated them. She saw that pattern, studied it. And she comprehended them.

From Celeste issued forth a word that rang like a long-awaited bell, which halts all work and draws all listeners' eyes, their labors ended.

Just so, the gargoyles stopped and stared at Celeste; then, clattered to the cave floor and were ended.

All of the gargoyles, she saw through a daze now dwindling. Now, her friends were glancing back and forth between fallen, frigid foes and her, combat's clangor still echoing in their eardrums.

Cor held a fist out.

Staring for a second, she punched it lightly. "Go team?" Celeste managed.

"That *thing!*" the girl from Fernstead muttered.

"Nice work," the Beldrian said. "Although it makes one wonder: if someone has a 'slay all gargoyles' power, why would she wait several minutes to use it?"

She blushed, as Cor's lips curved up.

"Toying with them!" Deliad declared. "Celeste plays cat-and-mouse games with *gargoyles*. Batting them about for pleasure, then finishing them off in one fell swoop!"

She giggled.

Life! It takes and gives, she mused.

Cor pushed the double doors. They opened easily. "Looks like that lever worked." He pointed out a shaft protruding on the other side, prompting from Brayleigh a satisfied smile.

"Hey, who knows? Maybe Deliad's mighty blow loosened it up for me," Brayleigh suggested.

He rolled his eyes and followed Cor inside.

The tunnel of shadowy blue delved on and downward beyond the doorway: narrow enough at times to force the wanderers into single-file, sinuous enough at times that they could see a few mere yards ahead, but always downward.

After a final steep and hunching spiral, they found a crack of light ahead: a crevice, leading beyond what'd otherwise be a dead end. They slipped across and found the midnight sky sprawling on high.

Dumbstruck, the four beheld blue darkness yawning boundless all about them, fraught with the fulgence of a thousand orbs; and, moving in their midst, the Seven Wanderers, led through the night by Luna Silver-Haired.

This shining heavenly scene was mirrored below, as though the admiring ground itself were glimmering in imitation. Only little ripples, spreading across the fairness of that glare, betrayed a buried lake for what it was.

"A Sea of Stars below the Sea of Stars," mused Celeste softly, as the Earth's own warmth rose from the depths and rippled through her fair hair.

Whether this glossed the glory of the moment was hard to say; in any event, the others had nothing more to add. They stared in silence upon the clustered flares of constellations: *The Scales. The Maiden.* She only knew a dozen by name, but all felt natural and familiar, like all the nameless wrinkles on her palm.

They approached the lake and stood beside the shore, where powdery black sand puffed out underfoot with each step, and the Stars seemed nearly in reach.

"So," Brayleigh finally said, scanning the blue and sparkling water, sprawling wide. "What now?"

No path across the water was apparent, nor any way around. Reflected twinkling continued far into the mirky distance, then disappeared amid the stygian gloom.

"Nothing is coming to mind," said the Knight-Lord.

"Maybe just hit it really hard with Hoarthaxe?" suggested Brayleigh, beaming. Deliad sighed.

Celeste looked left, then right. The lake seemed endless.

"Maybe he has a boat," suggested Cor. "Why don't I go and see? I'm good at swimming. I'll get this mail off—"

"*Absolutely* not," Brayleigh forbade, pointing directly at him.

"Yes, I agree," smiled Celeste. "It's a long swim. We can't see the other side. Who knows what's in there? Worse comes to worst, we could always wait here to lay an ambush."

"That would work," said Deliad.

"Still," Celeste went on, "wouldn't it seem strange if such a mighty Warlock *rowed a boat* across the water just to reach his lair? I can't help thinking there's another way."

"Well, maybe that's what happened," Deliad said. "We might've missed a turn."

"Celeste," said Cor, "could there have been another illusion back there, hiding some tunnel that we could've taken?"

"Maybe. I didn't sense it. Maybe though." She shook her head. It didn't feel quite right. "These Stars. They're not the *real* Stars, right? I mean, we're climbing into a *mountain*. This can't be some massive crater in the mountain, right? We would've seen it back when we were climbing or flying, right?"

"Sounds right," the Knight-Lord shrugged.

"So. That suggests to me we're on the right path. Since this is something that the Warlock *made*. Or so it seems," she thought out loud.

The others nodded and stood in silence for a while.

"I mean, there's always swimming," Cor reminded.

"No, there isn't," responded Brayleigh sweetly.

"Any ideas on how to move this water out of the way then?" he lightly rejoined.

"Well! I could do *this!*" Brayleigh raised a palm and, conjuring up a Boundary, brushed a big wave sideways within the water, briefly clearing a sort of slender gap. "How fast are you?"

Cor stretched his legs and shrugged.

"My man," said Deliad.

How do *you move the water?* Celeste mused, peering upon the nightscape. Rapt by its beauty, sense drifted aimlessly away from senses. *It's all connected somehow. There's a purpose.*

"Hmph. Stupid Warlock," Brayleigh finally said. "What is this nonsense? An obstacle course? Illusions, barriers, traps, abysses, seas. He built all this? What a big waste of time!"

Cor grinned. "Well, what would you do as a Warlock?"

What would I do. She stared upon the empyrean, wandering from Star to Star to silver Luna.

"What would I do?" asked Brayleigh. "Conquer Norvester! Go gather an evil army, orks or something, and launch some fiendish scheme to capture Lioss! Unearth some ancient super-powerful artifact—"

"Brayleigh," she broke in, "could I have you try something?"

"Hm? Sure. Like what?"

"You see the Moon up there?" She pointed. "Can you *move* it? Maybe that way?"

Brayleigh's brow rose. "Um, move the Moon? I'll try."

She raised her hand, now waxing red, and narrowed her eyes upon the night sky—and it moved.

"Eep!" *Everything* had moved. Not just the Moon, but all those bright orbs, like the night had sped up. Luna was still beneath the Scales, but far west. "Is someone up there gonna strike me down for this? A lightning bolt? Bam, Brayleigh's fried?"

A rumbling started.

"Um." She went wide-eyed and waved apologetically at Heaven. "I'll move it back! Here, just a minute."

"Wait," smiled Celeste.

Cor was staring at the water. "I get it. Clever." He held out his Fossil, so a golden glimmer laced the lakeshore. "See that?" Some ripples now were spreading through the stillness. "The tide's receding." Wet black sand was visible along the edge of the unbounded blue.

"Ohhh." Brayleigh looked upon the westering Moon. "Well, that was clever, Celeste!"

"Lunar tides." The Knight-Lord chuckled.

"Who would *think* of that?" Brayleigh went on. "'Why, let's just move the sky!'"

The sort of mind that'd make a place like this, she mused. "Oh, just a lucky guess," she said. "We're lucky we had someone who could move skies."

"Ain't it the truth!" The girl from Fernstead posed and flicked her hair back archly; then, she giggled.

The shoreline's swift retreat revealed a stone path, some five feet wide, which had been hidden by water. It seemed to sink into the lake ahead. But, as the water level lowered, the path was lain bare further and further, till it stretched as far into the blue gloom as their gazes.

They started on the pathway single-file.

"Let's hope this water doesn't suddenly swallow us," said Deliad, eying the ripples, only an inch beneath the stone's edge.

"Could've swum," shrugged Cor.

The going was slow along the gloamy way. They all were keen to cross the water quickly, but also wary of traps by now. And no one wanted to find out what lurked in the lake; especially as the stone began to ascend, arching up foot by foot, till it was soaring bridgelike above the yawning blue beneath.

Soon, they were fifty feet above the shimmers of spreading ripples. Any misstep now, and some poor soul would plummet down half-blind, then plunk down fathoms deep in pitch-black solitude, immersed in strangeness, far from any shore.

Gradually, to their fore, from mirky gloom emerged a craggy cliff face, fraught with shadows left by the faint light of faraway Fossils. Details emerged from darkness as they approached, including, straight ahead, a tall arched doorway.

Reaching the doors, Cor pushed. They opened freely. He started stepping forth, then froze. "Safe, Celeste?"

She stared awhile. "Well. This one is a real room." The dreamlike way that details had dissolved on close inspection, in the earlier chamber, was absent here. "Whether it's safe? Who knows."

Beyond the doorway was another den, brimming with barley twist and leafy woodwork. Instead of two tomes on the tabletop, six were stacked here. A seventh one was open before the single chair.

More books like that one were on the top shelf of a stonecraft bookshelf: grimoires of purple leather, bare of title. Some shelves below were stuffed with various volumes. Others were strewn with artifacts and oddments: a vial of starry glass and ambergris; a human skull; a pyramidal prism; a lodestone bound in brass;

a chunk of fool's gold; a chunk of real gold; mercury in a flask; a small harp; and an onyx star with eight points atop a crescent.

Hanging on the wall were many and sundry clocks. Each told the same time. *Guess we can rest assured it's almost midnight,* mused Celeste at the many upward hands.

Following Cor inside, she felt a sudden chill upon her neck's nape. Stiffening, she looked backward.

Nothing. Just two lit torches, flaring sidelong; vexed, perhaps, by the same slight breeze that she'd felt, straying here from the subterranean sea. The fickle firelight played upon the pages open on the table.

Celeste neared that table and scanned the grimoire there. Its wild, fey script was foreign yet familiar. Staring at it, letting herself be swept off by its broad curves, she suddenly was reminded how she'd felt when learning Eldscript: how it'd seemed she'd entered a loftier world, where beauty and meaning met. Yet this script was to Eldscript what the Eldscript had been to common writing. She could feel this without even reading it. *What* are *these books?*

Above the center of the chamber hung a chandelier. It was composed entirely of teardrop crystals, each with one blue flame burning within. The crystals spiraled upward in widening circles: first just one, then three, five, nine, eleven, fourteen, seventeen. Squinting, she couldn't make sense of the pattern, but sensed its beauty, as when one admires Nature herself.

"So. Warlocks live like this," mused Brayleigh, not amused so much as *be-mused.* The floating fires of blue had drawn her gaze too.

In one far corner of the den descended a spiral stairway. They approached it warily and, at the top, exchanged a silent look.

Then, down they went. The walls of shadowy blue around the staircase sparkled with the closeness of Fossils held in hand. Celeste could see no further than the Knight-Lord's hair, which hung pale to her fore against the encroaching shade.

Silent they went for a while till, behind her, she heard a mutter: "Should've built this ranch-style. A million stairs. Why? Why!"

Her lips curved up. What an unlikely crew they were! Two arch-foes; a quiet kid; and a teenage girl from farmville, who had a knack for bringing them together and breaking down the boundaries in between them.

"Come on now, where's your sense of high adventure?" chid Deliad. "Feel the moment of the moment! Descending from on high to face the Warlock! Down from the summit toward our Destiny!"

"How about 'across the flat field toward our Fate'?" groused Brayleigh.

"What, and lose this lofty moment? Leveling what's high just makes the whole world low," waved Deliad. "Haven't we learned that by now? I can't help feeling it's a theme of ours!"

"Can't a poor girl complain in peace!" cried Brayleigh. She took a breath to go on; then, went silent, eyes wide, as echoes of a deep male voice quietly resounded in the spiral staircase.

They shared a glance. Now, no one said a word.

Down went the wanderers, taking each step slow now. *A hundred nine. A hundred ten.* She realized that she'd been counting stairs as they descended. Down, down and further down. The voice grew louder. *A hundred thirty-five.* She heard the words now, as foreign and familiar as the script upon that purple grimoire on the table. *A hundred forty-two.*

And, just like that, she stepped down from the final spiral stair, around a curve, and found that she was facing another double doorway. One arched door was shut; the other, just enough ajar to see a wan glow on the ground within.

Their eyes met. Deliad pointed at the door, gripping his halberd in his other hand. Cor nodded, narrowing his eyes and thoughts to an edge as sharp as the ancient sword he held. Fervor blazed keenly in Brayleigh's green gaze and in the radiant flush around her balled fist. Snuffing out all doubt, Celeste faced the light.

And Deliad thrust the door open, and they rushed in.

Abruptly, the echoing incantations broke off.

Louring before them, looming like a shadow on Dusk's grey, was the man they'd come to face. A man? It seemed so. But the mirk of twilight concealed his features, and his cloak—still swirling from having spun to face them—still was sinking, slower than something in the air should fall.

He stood within a circle of clustered Stars, twelve constellations glimmering underfoot against the gloam. Their fey glow caught upon some wisps of long hair, shifting in a wind that none of them felt, together with his cloak.

"A crew of heroes? Come to slay the Warlock?" His voice was smooth and deep. His tone was flat.

"No need for slaughter if you stand down, Warlock, and come to face your sentence from the Archanimist." Vert eminence waxed around the Knight-Lord's weapon. "Not that we're holding out much hope of that. Traitors and murderers rarely turn themselves in."

The Warlock laughed. "Of all the crimes! Ironic!" His laughter seemed to linger in the darkness as he looked briefly away. "But I suppose I've murdered, true; I might even murder *you* before the hour's up. And I'll take the title of traitor, if my troth's to the Archanimist." His tone was wry. "Ah, Fortune, turn your wheel."

"Your sort are always this way," said the Knight-Lord. "So lost within your big ironic worldviews that little things that little people live by, like good and evil, are a laughing matter."

"It seems you have me figured out then. Fine!" The Warlock's cloak blew higher in the unfelt wind, as though borne upward by his voice's strange zeal; then, sank again. "Listen. I'm short on time. You're short on knowledge. You have no idea what's what, who's who, and why you're really here. And, frankly, I don't care enough about you to fix that. If I even had time. I don't. My way of dealing with you will be faster, unless you leave right now and spare me the effort."

"The only way we're leaving is with you," said Deliad. "Will you face your judgment now or later?"

"Then it ends like this. So be it!" The Warlock's deep voice waxed with booming pathos and toneless power, cloak billowing once again. "You'd have me face my judgment. Yes, indeed, judgment is written upon the Stars tonight. Sol glares across Heaven at the Gloamy One, and Luna watches both beneath the Scales, waxing toward me." He raised both hands before him.

Far overhead, from dark oblivion formed a sparkling host of Stars and nebulae, blazing numinous against the blue beyond and shedding light upon the scene below, showing the four wary wanderers their foe.

That billowing back-length hair was platinum hue, almost a silvery white. It framed a face strikingly young. *No, not exactly.* More like all of its aging had gone toward that world-weary glare, without stopping to wrinkle that smooth brow. His lips curved up. He almost looked relieved.

Beneath that hair and glare, his frame was thin. His cloak was midnight blue, and, once again, a silent wind was blowing it behind him.

The Beldrian and the Knight-Lord raised their weapons and crouched for combat, and their two companions balled fists behind them and prepared for strife.

Arms still held high, the Warlock now ascended inches above the ground. Mists swirled about him, soaking in starlight and darkening his image, leaving him merely a silhouette once more. "Come, heroes! Let us all be judged!" he called.

Darkling, the wanderers and the Warlock squared off like Wandering Stars, glaring across the night.

Then, Deliad dashed forth, man-high Hoarthaxe pumping with each stride, and beside him sprinted Cor.

The Warlock, hovering still, suddenly leaned forth and, malice in his mien, streaked toward the wanderers, one grey-gloved hand toward Deliad. In his wake there followed misty afterimages, showing his likeness in starlight, then swirling fleetly away. Forward he flicked that hand, and from it shot a bright white bolt tinged purple.

The Knight-Lord halted, holding out his halberd to block the impending bolt, turning his head from its fell effulgence. Striking the outstretched haft, that energy leapt lightning-like to his torso and crackled over his cuirass and limbs. And, weirdly, everywhere that fey glow fell, colors inverted to their negatives. So when the Knight-Lord fell to his knees, head bowed and resting heavily on his hand, he looked like a blackish-purple semblancy of suffering against a brightness-blasted desolation.

Already, fleetfoot Cor had caught and passed Deliad, darting toward the attacking foe and slashing out with shining blade.

At this, the Warlock swirled his cloak of midnight blue—and suddenly wasn't there. His misty figure blinked out of being and flashed back instantly a few yards backward, squarely facing Cor now.

Pointing, he spoke one word. Another bolt of purplish white now sizzled toward the Beldrian.

Smoothly that sword transitioned into a parry, perfectly lined up with the impending lightning, and blocked it with the blade's flat. But the charge crackled and flowed along the steel and discharged into Cor's hands through his fingerless gloves, brightly inverting all hues as it surged.

The Beldrian's fingers shot out, shocked and twitching. Down dropped his longsword, clattering on the stone.

One blink passed. Then, shaking his stiffened fingers, he dove away from the enemy toward his weapon, eyes on the Warlock, even as fingers closed around the hilt, even as he hit the ground, rolled once and bounced back up, blade at the ready.

But there was no one there now, and the Warlock was streaking in a blur toward Brayleigh.

Green gaze narrowed upon the foe, she held a palm forth and sent a semi-limpid wall of red shooting straight at him.

But again, he blinked out of existence as the Boundary shot by and reappeared beyond it, still untouched and flying toward her. And if, in his eyes, there was a trace of slight surprise, it'd faded a second later, when, sweeping his arm, he loosed a whirlwind laced with whitish flares tinged purple.

This, one second; then, the next, that fiery dervish was upon the girl from Fernstead, glowing, growing as it whirled forth.

She flung her hand up just in time to conjure a Boundary, blocking it. But as the whirlwind dispersed, its purplish flames leapt past that wall like a static charge and struck her. And her coat, that fine and downy gift, went up in flames.

She shrieked and fell, and yanked it off with fingers blistering upon its smoldering fabric, rolling to snuff the embers on her shirt beneath.

Deliad had finally shaken the lingering shock out and struggled to his feet. Their foe was flying toward Cor now, pale hair billowing over his back. He dashed to intercept, drawing back Hoarthaxe and diving forth to slash the Warlock's flank.

Their enemy whirled, still sliding back through the air, and thrust a palm out.

Deliad's halberd halted in midair, shivering his arms with the impact against a plane of vert that'd flashed before him and disappeared within an instant.

Blinking, he stepped back, then prepared another blow. But the enemy was already streaking toward the Beldrian, flicking another bright bolt.

This time, Cor dodged, dropping and rolling right as the electric impulse crackled overhead, and came back to his feet. In one fluid motion, he loosed a cross-cut leftward at their foe's flank.

Already, though, a grey-gloved palm was raised. And when his sword was just a foot from striking, another barrier sprang forth out of nothing—a silvery gold hue, which a heraldrist might label "argent-or"—blocking his blow.

The Knight-Lord now had caught up with their combat and, from afar, he thrust his man-high halberd straight at the Warlock's heart.

Inhaling wide-eyed, exposing purple irises to starlight, their enemy twisted sideways just in time, so Hoarthaxe's tip slipped through a little gap between his arm and torso.

As he lurched, a shimmering red wall struck the Warlock head-on. He stumbled backward.

Celeste spun and looked.

Brayleigh was there, back on her feet. One arm, burnt badly and darkened with char, was held forth firmly.

Through Celeste breathed a surge of warm assurance, whispering familiar words in depths-deep voice and rushing from her lips. And from her fingers spiraled another slew of lunar flares.

Their reeling enemy somehow saw the attack and threw a hand out. And at once, a wall flashed into being, bleu-celeste in its hue, absorbing all those streaking fires, then fading.

Striving to maintain the moment's momentum, Cor sprinted forward in a golden blur and whipped his blade out at the Warlock's neck.

But the ever-ready Warlock swirled his cloak and blinked back several yards—already mastering the moment once again—and Cor's sharp steel whiffed through a misty afterimage.

Then, gesticulating and incanting, backed by a fey and toneless power, their cloaked foe pointed.

A ball of light sprang into being before them, white at the core and purple on the fringes, just a few yards from Celeste and a few more from Cor and Deliad. It was hard to see their foe beyond its brightness. And her friends, awash with eminence, had their hues inverted. They looked like violet-black beings drowned in light; strange wights, viewed through a lens of waking nightmare.

Struggling to get her bearings in the brilliance, she noticed that the ball was getting bigger.

Dread rose like nausea in her gut. "Get back!" She'd whirled and started bolting by the time she'd spoken the words.

The shockwave struck her back, and she was airborne even before the boom had registered in her ears. But once it did, the ringing stayed there, as did the excess radiance that'd briefly overwhelmed the sensory world.

She felt the coldness of the stone floor first against her cheek; then, on her back, a breeze somehow both cold and scalding. Absently, she realized that the back side of her clothing mostly had been burnt off.

She forced herself to turn her head enough to watch the fray.

Far from the blast was fleetfoot Cor, unscathed and sprinting toward the Warlock now with sword raised.

Not so the Knight-Lord, who was straining up from the floor, resting his weight on Hoarthaxe's hilt. His regal tabard now was charred and tattered, baring his breastplate, and his hair was tousled.

Brayleigh had not been near that ball of light, and she was standing tall now, strewn with char and little burns from earlier, both arms bare. She waited narrow-gazed as Cor engaged the Warlock, waited for his head to turn, waited until he'd raised a hand toward Cor.

And *then* she thrust her palm forth, eyes alight behind the stray hair that beswept her face. And forward rushed a wall of red, so thick it almost was opaque, straight at the Warlock.

Whirling to face her, he held out a hand and spoke a foreign word of cold command.

A pair of spectral hands appeared in midair: huge, ghostly hands that trailed a ghastly glow and barely showed, like light upon the mist. They grasped the Boundary as it came and caught it, slowed its advance in a semblance of pushing. Then, wrenchingly, they tore the wall in twain.

Blood-hued light burst from the cleft in the Boundary, whose two halves fell and faded out of being, as Brayleigh—falling to her knees, hands clutching her temples, eyes scrunched shut—shrieked agony.

Celeste's cheek sank to the ground again.

Eyes shut, she heard the clamor of combat as through water. She almost felt she *was* immersed in water: warm as a bath, warm as this world was cold. Only the noisomeness of constant noise kept her from sinking into a bubbly stupor and drowning comfortably in cozy darkness. Metal on metal and metal on stone: each clang was like a blast of cold, dry air.

Rise, Daughter of Luna and of Mine.

The voice boomed through the waterscape of her awareness, familiar and foreign, with a depth and power that dwarfed the din of battle. Now the sufferings that'd laid her low seemed small; beneath being noticed.

She felt herself ascending to her feet. She saw the world as through the mist of strong drink, drifting before her and reverting back with each blink.

Cor and Deliad both were blurs, speeding about like comets through the sky, passing into her prospect, then away. But always at the center was the Warlock, awash in light of purplish white, pale hair blowing behind him as he whirled and dashed, and whipped forth bolts, and spoke his incantations: the Lodestar of her night; her guiding light.

She held a hand toward *him.*

She heard the Stars speaking above her: fey and deep and sonorous, familiar and foreign, strangely like the chanting of their opponent even now; and among them, the Evenstar. *Let me steer thee, Child of Mine.*

She let the one within her guide her gaze across the sparkling zodiac overhead. She sensed its subtle and fair configuration, felt out a way for her desired designs to fit within the Fate that it ordained. And then she spoke it, full of human pathos but backed by toneless power beyond her own:

Rage and ravin, fury and fetter,
Tears and toil thy legacy;
Breast burdened down with double dole,
And soul no better;
This, my Doom on thee!

Down from the blue beyond, lights started streaking: one from each Star, shooting across the sky and falling, leaving trails of sinking stardust. Down, down those little sparks traced fractal patterns upon the empyrean, drawing something dread and just past understanding overhead. And every light was arcing toward the Warlock.

He'd spun toward Celeste as she'd spoken her last words, raising a hand swathed in mist, darkly radiant, meeting her gaze like the Gloamy One squaring with crescent Luna. But whatever he saw there left him with wide eyes—blinking eyes, uncertain—and the incantation didn't leave his lips, and the umbral eminence didn't leave his hand.

Then, it was too late. Starlight struck the Warlock from all sides. Celeste made the Earth celestial. The waxing Heavens overwhelmed the world.

Now, he was crying out, arching his back in agonized convulsion.

Celeste stared, rapt by the boundless, as the grim-browed Knight-Lord raced toward the shuddering Warlock, with the blade of ancient Hoarthaxe high and blazing vert. Drawing his halberd back, he smote the foe—clanging against a breastplate, hidden by clothing—but sliding then along a seam beneath it, slipping through fabric and flesh, spilling blood.

Backward the gasping Warlock blinked twelve yards, then twelve more yards. He hunched, hand to his belly with head bowed, and he whispered to himself.

She caught the last words: " . . . pilgrimage through dark. So be it!"

He stood upright, reduced by darkness to a rippling cloak against the starlight. Then, he started to incant and gesture, merely a shadow throwing shadows in the night, his voice an echo, sounding hollowly against the crags: first soft, soon amplifying, till trembling tremors shivered through the stones, as though in resonance with the Warlock's workings.

The Beldrian and the Knight-Lord sprinted toward him with weapons raised.

Too late to stop that chant. A last crescendo of fey familiar words boomed through the cavern, backed by toneless power. It shook the Earth so much it tripped them both up, forcing them to their hands and knees for balance.

The Warlock didn't feel it, being uplifted inches above the angry ground, his arms and eyes both open to unbound Heaven above.

Flecks of white light started swirling and falling like snowflakes. In their wake was sinking dust of violet, grey and blue. First, a few flakes, then many whirled in violent winds, unfelt by flesh but billowing through the Warlock's cloak.

Those white specks struck the wanderers' garb and gear and passed through unimpeded, through their skin and into unprotected bodies. There, they crackled through convulsive limbs, bent necks and backs to arched contortion. And their colors inverted, so their twisted spasms were purple against a hoary void, as purple flakes of aether blizzarded about them madly.

Suffering and fallen, they saw things that were not. Pain mixed with place, as time unites with space when wrenched too swiftly from a frame of reference.

Just fleetfoot Cor—who, on a prescient instinct, had bolted to the fringes of the blizzard before it took full shape—escaped the storm, and only somewhat. As his fellows writhed, he trembled on one knee, arm over his face, but squinted through the flurries at their foe.

The tempest waned in time. And from the welter, the cloak and malice of the Warlock clarified: his torso-clutching hunch; his heaving breaths; his glare at Celeste, Brayleigh and Deliad, splayed half-senseless to his fore; and to his rear, billows of midnight blue in winds unfelt.

Celeste saw Cor, a ways away from the others, slipping one hand inside his little satchel and sliding something orange out, glistening slightly with starlight; at the edge of the enemy's sight, where such small movements might just pass unseen.

She watched him suddenly wind up and release: the way he'd done sometimes when speaking of that Beldrian game he'd played in boyhood. *Baseball.*

Numbly, she watched it sail behind their enemy, throwing off gleams, and smash into a stalagmite, shattering into a thousand crystal shards.

She watched their foe spin, frowning, toward the sound, and then toward Cor. "You missed," the Warlock said. He turned again to face the other three.

Suddenly, the Beldrian had leapt to his feet and was bounding toward the Warlock in a blur, his steps a shining wheel. Lionlike he pounced—farther than he had ever leapt before, soaring with sword upraised, hungering for blood, wind blasting through his blond and leonine mane—and brought his fell blade, gleaming golden-white, biting down toward the bare neck of his prey, smiting with more-than-manlike savagery.

Coldly, the Warlock raised a palm. A plane of argent-or flashed into place before him, matching the aureate sheen about Cor's sword.

The blade struck. Metal shrieked as it exploded. Cor's sword—that ancient heirloom of the warriors of Beldria, gifted on his eighteenth birthday by old Aldartal, which he'd worn while wandering the Beldrian outskirts once a week for years, and baptized since in blood of foes unnumbered—scattered in shrapnel and vanished in shadow.

Most of it. One piece skittered up to Celeste and spun in futile circles near her face, before it finally pointed at the Warlock.

Meanwhile, as Cor's sword shattered, his momentum carried him onward with his hilt in two hands, turning his torso. Awkwardly, he tumbled sidelong and struck the ground hard. Something slipped out, clattering across the cavern: dull-hued, awl-shaped.

Pointing at Cor, the Warlock spoke one word. His fingertip discharged a fulminant bolt of purplish white. It crackled into Cor's breast, blasting him backward aloft toward the Knight-Lord. Limp as he fell, he landed hard. He lay there almost unmoving, only shivering sometimes.

Silence prevailed for a while as the wanderers languished in the enemy's lair. They'd finally lost.

"And so, we have our judgment," spoke the Warlock. He raised both arms and rose above the cave floor, cloak blowing in a silent wind behind him. And darkly he began to incant and gesture.

Deliad strove halfway up, then sank to his side, eyes shutting. "So we've lost." His brow hung low like a blade of grass at twilight, newly laden with drops of dew as, overhead, the Stars died. "But much we've done with what time we've been blessed with. And here I die beside a brother knight." Briefly he clasped his hand about the clenched fist of Cor, still splayed and shivering on the floor. "And where we're bound, more blessings will abound."

The Warlock's voice was gathering unto greatness, his conjuration drawing toward conclusion. Across his upward stare streamed rampant starlight, washing the manhood from his wan facade, welling within the violet of his gaze.

A jagged brown bolt shot across the room and ripped into the unwitting Warlock's back, blasting him headlong forth. He flew and slid, landing near Cor and Deliad. There he lay, shuddering and twitching now somewhat like Cor.

Dumfounded, Celeste squinted through a daze.

Into the cave, a dozen ork guards were streaming, their faces blank and spell-bound. In their wake strode a tall woman, wearing faded purple that shimmered blue and silver as she stepped. Her stare upon the Warlock wasn't quite symmetric, hinting at humor or spite.

"First bind the Warlock!" commanded the Archanimist, cool in her tone as a two-days-dead corpse.

The troops ran up to the recumbent Warlock, half-hidden beneath his cloak upon the floor. He halfway raised a hand as though to halt them, then let his head hang low against the ground, scrunching his gaze with a hand to his gut. Around his neck they clipped a collar of purple and blue vines, interwoven and full of thorns. Then, one hulk heaved the Warlock to his feet, holding him by the armpits as he hung limp.

"Greetings," the Archanimist hailed, progressing calmly across the cavern toward the ailing party. "I see you've gone to pains to meet your charge." She peered upon their bloody and battered plight. "Of course, a hard-fought failure is a failure. But credit where it's due. You did disrupt his warding, break the Beacon, and distract him; which was, in truth, much more than I expected."

"Did you *intend* that: to disrupt the warding, so I could come straight here? No, by your blinking, I see you weren't that clever. Happy accident. Thank Destiny for little boons. Or Doom."

The four confused companions traded looks, then blinked with bleary eyes upon their rescuer.

"And now our knights in shining armor start to realize they were pawns," the Warlock mused, brimming with black bile. "Pawns, behold your Queen! A killer of Kings!" He pointed at the Archanimist.

"Enough, Shadin," she chastised, waving lightly. "You know how I hate flattering epithets."

She strolled across the cavern, finger raised and flaring with a light of brown-tinged blue, brightening away the Stars. "Now, am I wrong that Nilvernon is right about . . . "—she paused, tapping a lip—"right there!" She spun and pointed, her fingertip now blazing like a beacon.

From a far crevice, shadows fled, revealing a pedestal of stone; and, on its surface, a starry orb, aswirl with lively mists, darkly imbued with ultraviolet eminence.

She laughed delightedly. "How long it's been!" Shimmering from purple to silver to blue with every step, she approached the unearthly Fossil. "Such times we'll have together, You and I!"

The Warlock looked at her, then at the wanderers, then sighed.

She *ahhed* in silence as she clasped it, holding the misty orb before her face. "I had forgotten how it felt," she mused, "the bond of Nilvernon to *all* the Elements. Won't this make finding them oh-so-much easier!"

"Well, good!" said Brayleigh weakly. "After all this, it better be an awfully special Fossil!"

"This Nilvernon—if He can find the Elements, can He restore them also?" questioned Celeste, forcing herself to focus through her headthrobs.

The Warlock stared at her, his head askew. "*That* was your cause?" Then, looking up, he laughed. "O Fates, heap ironies on ironies!"

"The answer to your question is," replied the Archanimist, "maybe. Maybe not. Who knows? He made the world with Flua-Sahng once. Could He, now as a Fossil, do so once again? A fascinating hypothetical. Alas, we'll never know."

" . . . why not?" asked Brayleigh.

"Because, as soon as we've convened the Elements, and used their boundless power to bring about the true equality to which we're destined," explained the Archanimist, peering on the Fossil, "we'll seal away the Elements for eternity. So no one's going to have a chance to test that."

"What are you even saying?" Deliad demanded. "'Sealing' them? You said you'd lend us the Fossil so we could try to *save* them."

To their side, the Warlock threw his head back, laughing blackly, as ork guards held him up in spellbound silence.

"Did I say something *false?*" the woman wondered, touching her top lip with a fingertip, then smiled. "Yes, it's a shame to lose such beauty. But what must be, must be. In the end, it's You and Your kind who distinguish high from low"—she addressed the eminent Fossil with a sad smile—"exalting some with blessings, boons and talents and execrating others with their absence. No world with You would be a world of equals."

Then, her eyes widened and fixed upon the wanderers. "You. You have other Fossils! I can feel them. Collar them. Search them," she commanded the orks.

"*What!*" Brayleigh cried.

"You . . . !" Deliad's gaze was blazing. Gripping his halberd, he struggled half-upward, face twisting as he forced himself through pain.

But the orkish thralls dashed up and pinned him down, disarming him. They clipped another collar of thorny, interwoven purple and blue about his neck, and then the other wanderers.

As Celeste's collar clicked shut, she felt suddenly empty inside, someplace she'd not even realized that there was room for emptiness or fullness. But, as she focused on it, she perceived that the presence she had found inside the cave—which, since then, had been waxing sprightly inside her—was veiled now, barely seen behind some barrier.

She struggled to resist as she was yanked up and held by an ork with arms behind her back. But she was in no state for bodily striving, and it'd have been too strong even if she were. The ork's companion crudely felt for Fossils along her tattered outfit, soon withdrawing the Star-shaped Fossil from within her robe. Its dusklit glow went dark at the ork guard's touch.

The other orks, in turn, took Deliad's halberd, Cor's Sun-shaped stone and Brayleigh's blooddrop Fossil.

"Wonderful!" beamed the Archanimist. "Three? No, four, that big thing has one! One from each of you. How cute! I fear I'm spoiling something special."

Wistful, she sighed; then, pointed at the Beldrian, her forehead furrowed. "Wait. Search that one further."

A guard leaned down and scanned Cor's leather satchel. "Nope, no more glowy ones. Just this," it grunted, grasping a red rock, so dull that it seemed to absorb what little light was in the cavern.

The Archanimist's eyes went wider. "Bring it here, please." From the ork's huge hand, she took the Passagestone and studied it. "One of these still exists? Shadin, you see this? I believe this stone will let me walk through *Boundaries*. Can you sense it? The Consort's Spirit? The thing is steeped in it!"

The Warlock eyed her, stony-faced and wordless.

"Well. I suppose that's all," declared the Archanimist, still marveling at the red rock in her palm. "Guards, kill them all."

"You're *kidding* me!" cried Brayleigh. "We helped you!"

"True. Accept my humble thanks." The Archanimist smiled politely. "Nonetheless, it's clear your plans would contravene my own. And I can't have your little band of bravehearts seeking revenge. No, best to nip that bud!" She turned to a guard. "Please, go ahead. Chop chop."

The ork unsheathed a jagged purple scimitar. It strode toward Deliad, who, even sorely wounded, was giving the other guards some difficulty as he resisted. Roughly grabbing him, an ork pulled Deliad down, hair in his hand, so he was bending forward to a full bow.

The armed ork lifted high its jagged blade above the Knight-Lord's neck.

A cry broke out. Everyone whirled to see the source.

The Warlock had tossed his captor forward over his shoulder. He seized the thorny collar round his neck, which seemed to necrotize with spreading blackness; then, ripped it off. It shattered into remnants, which melted into motes of black in midair.

Instantly he was swinging at the downed ork. And, halfway through that slash, a harpe appeared within his hand: a spectral blade of grey-blue, its knife-edge sickling cruelly toward the front. The harpe cut cleanly through its upper head, baring the gooey brain inside the brainpan; then, vanished into a ghostly after-image.

That image of the harpe inside its head mingled inside her with daze-addled memory. *"Oh, soon enough, you'll use it. Yes, you'll use it,"* she heard a man's familiar voice assure her.

Several orks now were sprinting toward the Warlock.

But round the dark-cloaked figure now had formed a fell mist, violet eminence that inverted the hues of all it fell upon. He raised his grey-gloved hands. A deep hum swelled about him.

The closest orkish guard began dissolving.

It paused in place, staring as fingers dwindled, then palms, then forearms too. With gaze gone wide, it gasped and stepped back. But, awash in dark light, its feet had faded too, so now it tripped and fell into a hopeless heap. Its entrails were bared now, and its liver, blotted brown along its top-left. Then, it had no liver, no organs; just some swift-dissolving bones.

And now the other orks around the Warlock were decomposing from the outside in, screaming, then suddenly silent, as they brushed vainly at evanescing body parts.

The other orks, outside that lethal light, backed away, frantic, looking back and forth between the ominous Warlock and their leader.

"Useless," she muttered, watching one dissolve.

"So it comes to this, Lenvira!" boomed the Warlock, backed by a toneless power and echoing pathos. "So long, I've longed in vain to face just you, without your band of traitors at your back. And you yourself now bring that fight to me! I ought to thank the Fates. I ought to thank *you!*"

"You've never answered for your crimes," she said. "I doubt you'll thank me as you do. But we'll see."

"Crimes! Hear her valorize her villainy!" chuckled the Warlock. "That's enough, Lenvira. You have no audience here. Why waste breath lying? In this trial, I'm your witness, judge and jury."

"You know," she said, "you look a lot like Aislin. That smile! Of course, in the end, she wasn't smiling. I doubt you could contort your face like she did. But she surprised me; maybe you will too!"

"A quick confession. Good." His smile was arctic. "Death is the sentence. Now, the execution." He raised his arms and rose aloft, eyes shining, cloak billowing in unfelt blasts. "Make ready!"

"For ten years, I've been ready," she replied, as brown-blue radiance welled about her tall frame. "You're just a loose end, begging to be tied. And I'll oblige you." Empty-eyed, she smiled. "Give my regards to your parents, Shadin!"

The Warlock's only answer was the gleaming fervency in his gaze. They faced each other.

Then, he was shooting toward her, arm outstretched. He flung forth three bolts, white with purple fringes, in scattershot succession.

Each one halted before her upraised hand. Each time, a plane of purplish white flashed briefly into being, absorbing his attack. Her face was calm.

The Archanimist traced a circle in the air. Blackness coagulated in its bounds, gooey and wobbling; and within the blackness were clustered Stars, dotting the vasty void. Wider this portal to outer space stretched, dripping darkness along its spreading edges. And where those drops of oozy blackness fell, bits of rock vanished, banished to the void.

She flicked her hand. Forward the darkness flew, curling like clasping fingers toward the Warlock.

He'd halted halfway toward her. Now, he dashed headlong toward imminent darkness—suddenly blinking out of existence as he neared that black blob and apparating just beyond it, unslowed and streaking toward his foe, one hand held forth.

The Archanimist instantly held out a finger and launched a massive jet of bluish-brown flame. Sweltering winds carried its reek through the cavern.

Again, the Warlock paused and held a palm up, stopping just shy of the noxious inferno. Instantly, to his fore, a whirlwind formed, gathering up pebbles and dust from the ground, then rushing forth. It sucked the foul flame in and spat it out again as streaking flares, flung by centrifugal force.

Behind that cyclone, the Warlock followed with an arm extended. Whenever a wind-flung flare came shooting at him, a convex barrier of the same shade blinked fleetly before him, absorbing the fire.

Meanwhile, more flares from her own jets of flame were rocketing randomly toward the Archanimist. After a moment, she rose from the floor and zipped left in an arc, avoiding them. Midway through moving, she loosed two black bolts that crackled toward the Warlock.

With a swirl of his cloak, a sable barrier flashed before him, blocking both missiles. Once again, he shot forth, his afterimage blurring in his wake, straight at his foe.

She dodged aside, feet sliding slightly above the floor, her legs unmoving.

But he anticipated and was following before she'd started moving. With a hand raised, he swung at her. Midway into the motion, that spectral harpe sprang into being again, glowing grey-blue and sickling toward her neck.

She tried to jerk aside, succeeding partly but not entirely. The uncanny blade brushed through the shimmering cloth on her shoulder, skimming the skin. And, as she gasped, blood dribbled from bared flesh, soaking through the robe around it.

Backward she zoomed with her palms raised protectively. Glaring, she traced a circle and sent another ball of gooey blackness globulating toward him, with flecks of starlight strewn about the gloom. Then, she flung forth a black bolt at its back; and, as it struck, it roiled the oozy mass and splashed the center of it at the Warlock.

He'd been incanting and gesticulating, calmly observing the void. But he cut off abruptly now, swirling his cloak around him and blinking out of being, barely in time.

And she was ready. As he reappeared, she pointed at the floor beneath his feet. Volcano-like, it burst beneath him, spraying magma and smoldering stones. He somehow managed to block the pyroclasm with a barrier of glowing gules. But he was still launched sidelong and landed hard.

Before he'd gotten his bearings, she'd loosed a black bolt at the sharp stalactites hanging above him, halfway lost in shadow. And when it hit, the rocky roof exploded to a cloud of dust. A shower of rubble fell; and, in its midst, several of those stalactites, one after another. One struck near the Warlock, exploding to detritus and debris and mingling with the stonespray from the ceiling, engulfing him in grime. Within a second, three more stalactites smashed into the ground.

She squinted through the haze of pulverized stone; then, swung her head first left, then right, then left; then, spun around entirely.

And at once, she heaved herself aside—but not in time to evade a brilliant bolt of purplish white, which crackled into her hand. Her face contorted briefly with stinging shock. But, in a blink, she clenched her fist, an aura of bluish-brown sprang up around her, and the electric arcs wracking her hand now spiraled into the air and dissipated there.

The battle started to blur in Celeste's bleary prospect. Pain, brimming and throbbing, bled over into sight. Her senses strayed across the bounds between them: Strike. Parry. Ache. Riposte. Rejoinder. Twinge. Was that the ping of steel or pang of wounds?

She saw through a haze. Yet, in her doubtful gaze, one thing was certain: the Warlock was winning.

The Archanimist, who had come out hard and swinging, was all defense now: dodging just enough, deflecting just in time, and only attacking to buy some extra time for her defending. The Warlock pressed inexorably. Bright bolts tinged purple, whirlwinds laced with little flames, sudden blows from spectral weapons, in a salvo that never slowed: all this, she warded off and sidestepped, never taking serious wounds.

Not till a second cyclone, hidden behind another, whirled upon her unawares, just as she'd dodged and paused to take a breath. She lunged aside—too late to escape the flares burning within those winds, which leapt upon her, fervent with life, and clung to silky cloth.

Stumbling back, swatting wide-eyed at herself, desperate, she started to dispel the flames; then, gasping, flung a hand out to deflect a salvo of brilliant bolts now crackling toward her, leaving the fires on her clothing to flare up, charring the flesh beneath.

And as she flailed, the Warlock started to incant and gesture, his deep voice booming dreadful through the depths. And from the shadows swirled those little flecks like snowflakes, burgeoning swiftly to a blizzard, roiled by the unfelt blasts and rushing toward his reeling enemy.

"Wait!" she abruptly cried, head drooping, wobbly legged, one hand thrown up. "Wait. I . . . " She held a hand out toward the Warlock, heaving in breaths. "Just let me . . . " To her head, she held one hand, then stood still in the gloom.

The Warlock's chant trailed off. Tilting his head, watching her as his blizzard waned away, he waited, curious-eyed.

Her image vanished.

Into the Warlock's back blasted a huge bolt of crackling blackness, shooting with such force that it transfixed him, bursting from his breast and streaking unslowed into distant shadows.

He stared straight forward, seemingly in shock; like he'd been pinned, buglike, upon a board and, at once, turned from subject into object.

Out of the darkness drifted scornful laugher. "And so, the line of Malagroth is ended!"

Shimmering, the Archanimist strolled back into sight. "Now is the royalty of Lioss no more. Our new age is begun." Upon her prim face, pallid and framed by her shoulder-length hair, one of her eyes was wide with giddy glee. "It always was your weakness, wasn't it—"

The unmoving image of the Warlock melted to nothing. At the same time, from the gloam screamed what appeared to be a shooting Star. It struck the Archanimist's jaw, blasting it off.

"Wipe that smile off your face," the Warlock said, emerging from the chamber's mirky reaches.

She made a noise that might've been a shriek, had she been capable of shrieking still.

Then, lifting fingers to the empty space that'd been her face, she fell upon her knees. Her eyes were doubly wide and blinking often, like outlets for the thoughts she couldn't say now.

"You thought I'd never learnt about your Spirit Trial?" the Warlock asked. "You thought to try on me what failed on my own mother? Have you learnt nothing since losing everything you'd longed for: royalty, the Rod of Malagroth, and fame? Is this the summit of your strength and cunning: simple treachery?" He studied her a moment, as though awaiting a reply. But merely retches and blood burbled out of his foe. "Well, she who climbs the treacherous heights should take heed: never slip, never fall. For she who falls down from that summit never climbs it twice."

Toward her the Warlock moved, now emanating that hue-inverting light of purplish white, transforming him to a nightmare silhouette against a dreamy glow. A deep hum swelled and grew till pebbles danced on shivering ground. His waxing fulgence fell upon the Archanimist.

In that fey light, her flesh began to blacken, receding, necrotizing from her bones and dripping to the floor. She held aloft her liquefying arms and looked upon them, rasping out grotesque gasps with one eye wide. And then, quite suddenly, she had no eyes; just jellies oozing down her dribbly face.

"Yes, you will have your 'true equality'!" intoned the Warlock to the former woman. "You'll mix with dust and mingle with the least among us: one with worms that feast upon you and shit you out, and scatter you through mud. You'll trickle with the netherworld's low waters, one with the foulness that browns their slow flow. Old trees with creeping roots will quench themselves on you. Their fruits will feed the ones you loathe, and they'll make life of you in spite of you. And then you will be everything and nothing. Equally."

As she melted, the Archanimist clutched fast against her chest the orblike Fossil, which still shone with that otherworldly light, even as her flesh went black and fell away. Indeed, it almost seemed that steady brightness was flowing into her expanding darkness.

The Archanimist now was making hideous gurgles through a throat half-there. Somehow, amid those sounds, a thought could be perceived: *"I will persist. I will persist. I will persist."* At least, that was the sense; the sounds that she was making were not those sounds. And yet they understood her.

Her burbling noises waned as organs withered, leaving a bony frame; which, in the end, shrank to a fetal crouch in shimmering robes, its half-skull hidden behind two upraised hands. Even now, those fleshless fingers clenched the Fossil, shuddering their last as Spirit left her frame.

This was all too much for their orkish captors, spellbound or not. They let the wanderers loose, sharing a glance, and sprinted for the exit.

Suddenly, that eerie eminence round the Fossil arced jaggedly toward each of the orks, transfixing their torsos and immersing them in radiance. Heads jolted back; backs arched; brows wrinkled crazily; and, bent to stare at nothing, they convulsed.

Then, flesh began to fall from them in patches. They twisted, turned and writhed, but stayed in place, like patients held to the operating table as surgery took away what wasn't needful—skin, flesh, blood, sinew, organs—leaving bone. Their wriggling finally waned, with nothing left for feeling pain. They stood awhile unmoving.

Then, all at once, those skeletons faced the heap of crumpled robes that'd been the leader of Lioss.

The Warlock watched all this with narrowing eyes. He, too, now turned and stared upon that bone pile.

During their spasms, the orks had dropped the Fossils and Hoarthaxe. With a quick look at the Warlock—distracted, clearly—Deliad darted forward, hefted his halberd, pocketed the Fossils, and faced his friends. He motioned toward the exit.

They nodded. This was all beyond them now.

He helped the ailing Beldrian up, as Brayleigh and Celeste struggled to their feet. Then, breaths held, they tiptoed cross the cavern toward the doors. At times, they glanced back briefly at the Warlock, but he seemed not to notice. Or to care.

"*I will persist.*" The unspoken words wafted by once more, now mingled with a subtle rattling.

Squinting back over their shoulders, they froze.

The crumpled robe and bones that'd been the Archanimist was rising to its feet. Before its breast was that orblike Fossil, clutched in bony fingers. Darkness lay thick about the thing, except that fey light was washing over its downward face, staring upon the Fossil: just a skull without a jaw, looking on light without eyes.

A voiceless cackle drifted from the creature.

The Warlock's narrowed gaze was dark as night now. He raised a grey glove, swathed in glowing mists, and, lips pressed, started toward this undead thing that'd been the Archanimist.

Midway there, the Fossil abruptly beamed forth at the approaching Warlock another jagged line of bluish-brown light, like those that'd stripped the ork guards down to skeletons.

He barely threw his arm up soon enough to conjure a shining barrier of the same shade, deflecting that defleshing ray. But it persisted, arcing randomly in zigzags, dazzling and wild, that ended in the Warlock, relentless and inexorable as death.

Strain showing on his face, he took a step back, and then another, and another. Finally, the light ray vanished. He was breathing heavily, glaring into the gloom its absence left.

The robed thing shuddered with a laughlike sound, which had the shape but not the body of a human voice. Its shimmery robe hung loose about its skeletal frame. Some dust-hued hair of shoulder length still clung upon its skull, but clumps were missing.

"Lich," the Warlock murmured with one fist clenched, his violet gaze gone wide.

"Once, in a life past," rasped the lifeless figure, filling the cavern with its unvoiced voice, "I sought to bring about a true equality: a world where all are equal-born in Spirit, without the unjust, uneven, wanton blessings conferred by the Elements: talents, beauties, powers, which some receive and some don't. Undeserved! Using the Fossil of the First, I sought to find the Elements, seal them all away, and thereby put an end to unjust benefit. Without the Elements to exalt some lives past others, we could level life for all."

"Now, lifeless, I can see that this was folly. Now, free of Spirit, I see the Elements' Spirit flowing from far immurement into *you*," the lich spoke on. "Even sealed away, as Fossils, the Elements from afar still leak their influence upon this life, lifting some men past others; lifting humanity above the orks; lifting life over life, making a world where all exist on one great ladder of being. Spirit seeks to lift up life wherever life is," the bony creature said. "So life must end."

"What have you done, Lenvira?" said the Warlock. "You've slit your Spirit-bond. You've denied yourself the eternity *all* of us are fated for. That final fairness waits for all of us, except for you. For you, there's only void."

"Call me not Lenvira," the thing replied. "I'm not the living one who had that name. Now, call me Lich: death-handler, bringer of unlife, an agent for the ultimate true equality, which only universal death will bring."

Tilting its skull, it paused, then cackled emptily. "Do you think, since I'm facing this way, Knight-Lord, that I can't see you?" Intersecting rays of blue-brown light sprang up, blocking the exit.

Deliad, who'd quietly led the other wanderers close to the doorway, winced and turned around.

"Do you suppose I see now through these sockets?" The undead tapped its hollow temple. "Fool. Whichever way I turn, your Spirit will glare like sunlight in my mind's eye. Golden sunlight amid the Mists. Would that I could escape it simply by turning aside!" the lich whispered.

Taking a deep breath, Deliad stepped before his wounded fellow wanderers, holding Hoarthaxe, glaring through fair hair dark with sweat and shadow.

A wheezing cackle wafted from the lich. Lifting its fleshless arms, it faced the wanderers, and blackness swirled about its bony frame. "Yea, life itself—this ceaseless competition, where flesh heaps struggle to uplift themselves, and climb grotesquely onto one another to make more of themselves, forever wailing their lewd cacophony of re-creation—is an abomination," spoke the creature.

"I am Equality. I am Entropy. I come to end the differences between things, commingling warmth with cold, motion with stillness, life with unlife, till all things are alike. I come to quicken life's ordained unquickening. What is foredoomed, I fulfil. I am Doom."

It raised the Fossil orb before its face.

A flux of blue-brown light burst up and downward, spraying off flecks of brightness as it surged like water from an overpressured pipe. It splashed across the cavern's crevices and made them plain, and blotted out the Stars blinking above. It pierced the floor and ceiling like they were thin air, flowing on unslowed.

"I see, now, how to summon forth the Elements." The undead's rasp transpired the room. "I see the tendrils of their influence, writhing round you with vulgar fervor. I can trace their influence, follow it far beneath the bowels of Earth to where the still-surviving Elements slumber. With *this*—the Fossil of Novernought, the First, the primal chaos that compasses all things—I'll draw the Elements from the restful depths, and they, like fish in the receding tide, shall have no choice but to be drawn to me."

Words foreign but familiar flowed in whispers from the undead, echoing ghastly through the cave.

The blue-brown spout was spattering wildly now, shooting off little bursts that struck the ceiling and passed through. Some light swirled about the lich before it whirled as from a centrifuge and streaked away. The Earth had started quavering, and soon was quaking outright. Cracking sounds were coming from the ceiling. A stalactite suddenly exploded as it hit the floor, and then a second one, and then another.

The lich laughed, throwing back its hairy skull, holding the Fossil high, facing a brilliance that beamed unfelt into its empty sockets.

The girl from Fernstead fell upon her knees, bowing her head and clutching it in both hands. "So mad," she whispered. "Why are they so mad?"

The Warlock, cloak whipping wildly behind him, lifted a grey glove swathed in shining mist, then thrust it forward. Several purplish bolts shot in a staggered series toward the lich, which looked upon him, leered, and didn't move. As each bolt struck, the Fossil briefly gleamed, dispersing the energy into a warm glow, diffusing harmless to the undead's fore.

The lich's laughter redoubled.

Gaze gone narrow, the Warlock started gesturing and incanting, his grave voice echoing through the light-gorged cave. Force gathered in his chanting. And, abruptly, the world around him fractured like a mirror, and many images of him were moving in many-angled unison, united in one broad voice that boomed throughout the chamber.

One of his images blinked out of being; and, with a shuddering gasp, all things blinked blue. Another vanished, and the world was violet; then grey, then white, then blue, one after another, till there was only one dread Warlock left.

He spoke one final word, which went half-heard because an instant grating screech broke out.

The shades of everything went negative. The light-flow from the lich waned into nothing, and only a purple silhouette of its skull and yellowish semblance of its shimmery robe could be seen now. It crouched against the brilliance of the inverted gloom, and was immersed in jaundice-tinged miasma, swirling round it like fumes above a breeze-stirred swamp. Its eyes, staring above its faceless face, were specks of horrid white. It looked like some doomed ghost, roving a radiant afterlife in darkness.

The lingering echoes of the Warlock's last word faded, and with it faded the unbound brilliance. As darkness reasserted its dominion, once more, the constellations could be seen, shining away oblivion's senselessness.

And, in the modest eminence of that starlight, the undead hunched, holding the Fossil fast against its breast. Its glow was almost gone. Standing alone, the lich was shaking slightly. It shook more, shuddering now.

And then they heard it: laughter, as hollow and lifeless as a coffin; triumphant laughter, shuddering through the lich and spilling out in wheezing, heaving whispers.

Once more, it held the Fossil overhead, and blue-brown light beamed up and down once more, drowning the Stars. The rumbling now returned, and it redoubled, shaking down stalactites across the cavern now. That shivering laugh swelled to a cackle, then maniac hilarity.

There was a crack abovehead. Suddenly, Deliad was diving into Celeste, tackling her. She'd barely grasped what'd happened when her back hit, knocking her breath out and bruising her shoulders. That instant, a stalactite smashed beside her, spraying her body with pebbles and dust.

Out of the undead's stream of blue-brown light, suddenly, a stray flare shot out at the Warlock. Still breathing heavily, he swung an arm toward it, which briefly gleamed the same hue, sending it careening sideways into distant shadow.

The lich was laughing, laughing, wholly immersed in that luminous torrent flowing from the Fossil.

Celeste had risen and now was scanning round for any exit. But the only doorway was blocked still by those intersecting lights. And, all around them, stones were striking the Earth, each with enough force to pulverize bone.

She saw the blue-brown light burst streaking toward her out of the corner of her eye. She flung up her hand—which was awash in Star-like eminence, somehow—and swatted at the impending bolt. It fizzled hissingly, as sparks showered out. But an electric shock shot into her arm and jolted through her frame. She fell again as legs went limp, shaking, leaning on one arm.

Half-lost in spasming that she couldn't stop, squinting, she saw the Warlock looking at her.

As from afar, she heard him start incanting, his voice as dark and deep as midnight's void. She almost seemed to understand those strange words; like laughter and music, needing no translation.

Then, Deliad had advanced in front of her, holding his halberd cross-wise. Back he glanced at where those intersecting lines of light still blocked the doors, then faced the lich again.

Another light burst shot now toward the Knight-Lord. Perhaps he could have dodged it. But behind him, Celeste was hunched and semi-paralytic. And so, gritting his teeth, he held forth Hoarthaxe and stood there as the stray bolt struck his haft.

Instantly, arcs of lightning jagged along it and through his limbs. He grunted, head bowed low, so sweaty hair strands fell before his face, wrinkling, contorting with electrocution. But Deliad held his halberd, and he still stood.

Looking at Brayleigh, Cor stepped forward now. Lacking a sword, he balled his hands to fists.

"Still lining up to die?" taunted the lich. Turning to face the orks transformed to skeletons, it waved a hand.

And then they started moving, marching in unison toward the four wanderers. Their limbs pumped jerkily, and their purple scimitars shone with the light still beaming from the lich.

The Warlock's chant was gathering force now, echoing against the far walls and the falling roof, audible above the Fossil's resonant hum.

The skeleton at the forefront reached the Beldrian and, drawing back its scimitar, swung it wildly.

Cor ducked beneath the blow, wincing from wounds that should've been enough to lay him low twice over. Then, he socked the undead's skull, so it bent back rattlingly.

It stumbled backward and stood still for a moment, seeming dazed.

Then, it advanced again. It now was flanked by two more skeletons, stepping herky-jerky in synchrony, reduced to true equality: dead things that merely served to spread more death.

Stepping beside the Beldrian, Brayleigh raised her freckled hand. Red radiance welled around it.

Then, round her neck, that collar of woven vines glowed the same shade, warmly dispersing eminence, and Brayleigh's hand went dim. She stared upon it, then clutched her fingers round her thorny collar, as living death approached inexorably.

Brayleigh looked up at Cor, her teenage face sagging with unfamiliar sadness.

Then, abruptly, Celeste's sight swirled into a blur, as though the world were whirling like a top, and she'd been plucked up from its twirling face. Sounds dulled and were displaced, sounding on all sides, stretching and curling strangely.

In that din, feeling sense fade as senses madly mingled, reeling, she singled out one thing: the Warlock, glaring within the storm, his graceful form daring its might, blue cloak unfurling wildly. Fey words he spoke.

And then one final word, she heard, not with her ears but from within her, as sight waned to this wight with silver hair, the pearly lightscape blurred toward boundlessness, and all things melted bright. The word resounded throughout the unbounded, mingling midnight blue and swirling white to whirling Starlight: *You!* On fared she past all dreaming into a teeming mass of fair Mists; and, in their midst: *You! You!*

REVIEW

If you'd like to help make sequels possible, you can leave a review—just a sentence is fine!—by scanning the QR code below:

FREE STORY

For a free story about Cor and Brayleigh, along with announcements about future books, enroll in C.V. Vobh's newsletter by scanning the QR code below.

Made in the USA
Middletown, DE
04 August 2023

35805086R00267